MERLIN'S NIGHTMARE

BOOK THREE IN THE
MERLIN'S SPIRAL SERIES

ROBERT TRESKILLARD

BLINK

BLINK

Merlin's Nightmare
Copyright © 2014 by Robert Treskillard

This title is also available as a Blink ebook. Visit www.zondervan.com/ebooks.

Requests for information should be addressed to:
Blink, 3900 *Sparks Drive SE, Grand Rapids, Michigan* 49546

Library of Congress Cataloging-in-Publication Data

Treskillard, Robert.
      Merlin's nightmare / Robert Treskillard.
          pages cm. — (Merlin's spiral series ; book 3)
      Summary: While Morgana sets a horde of werewolves loose to destroy
Britain, Merlin and eighteen-year-old Arthur must rally Britain's warriors against
three overwhelming enemies, without unleashing an even greater evil.
      ISBN 978-0-310-73509-0 (softcover)
      1. Merlin (Legendary character)—Juvenile fiction. 2. Arthur, King—Juvenile
fiction. [1. Merlin (Legendary character)—Fiction. 2. Arthur, King—Fiction.
3. Fantasy.] I. Title.
PZ7.T73175Mdp 2014
[Fic]—dc23   2013036903

Cover design: brandnavigation.com
Cover photography: Dreamstime/Fotolia/iStockphoto.com
Interior design: Ben Fetterley and Greg Johnson/Textbook Perfect

Printed in the United States of America

14 15 16 17 18 19 20 /DCI/ 20 19 18 17 16 15 14 13 12 11 10 9 8 7 6 5 4 3 2 1

For Samantha Adele, Leighton, and Ness

Psalm 5:11 – 12

BRITAIN, AD 493

Picti

Dineidean • Dinpelder

GUOTODIN

Luguvalium

RHEGED

Dinas Crag

ELMEKOW

BREGANTOW

Inis Môn

• Deva Victrix

GWYNETH

ELTAVORI

EKENIA

POWYS

DOBUNNI

DYFED

SILURES • Glevum Lundnisow

BOLGI • Dinas Marl

KENTOW

Hen Crogmen

Dintaga

DIFNONIA

Dinas Camlin • Dinas Hen Felder

Bosventor

KERNOW

20 LEAGUES

THE MAPS OF
MERLIN'S NIGHTMARE

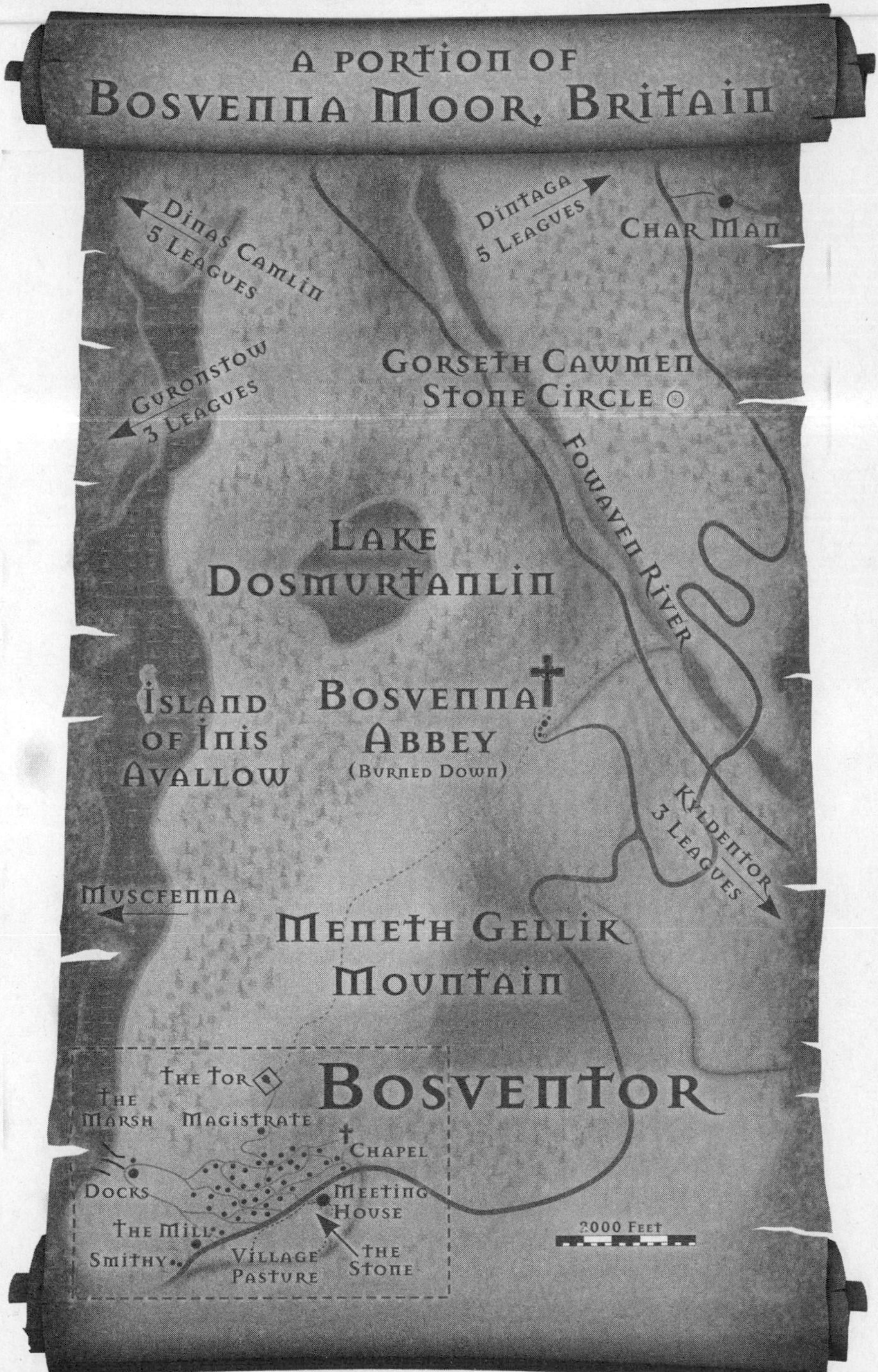

A PORTION OF
BOSVENNA MOOR, BRITAIN

Dinas Camlin
5 Leagues

Dintaga
5 Leagues

CHAR MAN

Guronstow
3 Leagues

GORSETH CAWMEN
STONE CIRCLE ◎

LAKE
DOSMURTANLIN

Fowaven River

ISLAND
OF INIS
AVALLOW

BOSVENNA
ABBEY
(BURNED DOWN)

Kyldentor
3 Leagues

MUSCFENNA

MENETH GELLIK
MOUNTAIN

THE TOR ◈

THE
MARSH

MAGISTRATE

BOSVENTOR

CHAPEL

DOCKS

MEETING
HOUSE

THE MILL

SMITHY

VILLAGE
PASTURE

THE
STONE

2000 FEET

THE VILLAGE OF DINAS CRAG,
The City of Glevum & Hen Crogmen

Steep Path

The Gate & Wall

The Fortress of Dinas Crag

The Falls of Derwent

Main Stables

Ector's Hall

Merlin & Natalenya's Crennig

Chapel

THE NANCEDEFED VALLEY

1000 Feet

Bridge

The Dungeon

West Gate

North Gate

Habrenaven River

THE ROMAN CITY OF GLEVUM

Vortigern's Feasting Hall
(Dinas Vitalinus)

East Gate

South Gate

500 Feet

Merlin's Hideout

British Camp

British Horses Picketed

Damaged Roundhouse Built over StoneHenge

200 Feet

THE RUINS OF HEN CROGMEN
(StoneHenge)

Bank & Ditch Enclosure

Saxenow Camp

The Story of Book I:
Merlin's Blade ...

The Stone — In 407 A.D., a meteorite crashes to Britain, depositing a black stone in a crater, which fills with water to become a mysterious lake. In 463, Merlin's mother supposedly drowns in the lake, and her body is never found.

Mórganthu — The arch druid finds the Stone in 477. With it he can enchant the Britons, and intends to restore the power of the druids — starting in Merlin's village.

Merlin — The swordsmith's son. Half-blinded by wolves seven years ago, he is protected from the Stone's enchantment because he can't see it. Despite his weakness, he begins to fight against Mórganthu and the Stone.

Natalenya — The seventeen-year-old daughter of the Magister, and Merlin's love interest. She must see beyond Merlin's scars to his courageous leadership and join with him to fight the Stone.

Ganieda — Merlin's nine-year-old half sister; she seems to have an affinaty for wolves.

Garth — A friend of Merlin who is an orphan and a rascal. He lives at the abbey and despises the abbot's discipline. He is the first to be enchanted, motivating Merlin to fight against the Stone.

Owain — Merlin's father, and a swordsmith, who deserted the High King's warband many years ago. He also becomes enchanted by the Stone.

The Blade — Made by Merlin's father, who gives it to the newly arrived High King Uther to appease his wrath. When the king is not satisfied, Owain gives Merlin to him as a servant.

Uther — The proud High King and father to Arthur. When the druids prevent the villagers from swearing fealty, he cuts off the head of Mórganthu's son. Mórganthu swears revenge.

Colvarth — The king's bard, a former druid and now a Christian, who agrees to mentor Merlin. In this new role, Merlin advises the king to destroy the Stone.

Vortigern — A battle chief. He is enchanted and betrays Uther and Arthur to the druids.

Arthur — the young son of King Uther. Garth sees Mórganthu's cruelty, and his plan to murder the royal family, and saves Arthur's life.

Dybris — A monk who works with Merlin and Owain to take the Stone and destroy it. He discovers the other monks were caught by Mórganthu and will be burned to death during the ritual. While trying to free his fellow monks and remove the Stone, Dybris and Owain are captured, leaving Merlin to try and save everyone on his own. In the end, Merlin conspires with a sympathetic druid named Caygek.

Connek — A thief hired by Mórganthu to kill Merlin, and by Vortigern to kill Natalenya after she overhears his treachery. When Natalenya visits the mill to borrow a mule to haul the Stone away, Connek hides there and tries to kill Natalenya, but he dies when the millstone falls on him.

The Murder — During the druid ritual, Uther and Owain are to be sacrificed to the Stone, and the monks to be burned. Vortigern hides his men and arrives to make sure Uther is dead. When he finds the High King alive, he tries to kill him, and after a brief skirmish with Merlin, he succeeds. The druids, cheated of their sacrifice, attack. Vortigern calls his men to fight.

The Escape — The monks are freed by Caygek's friends, and Owain is freed by Caygek himself. Merlin, Owain, and Dybris escape with the Stone, but are chased by both the druids and Vortigern's warriors. Natalenya rescues them, and they haul the Stone to the smithy, barricading the doors.

The Fight — Owain can't destroy the Stone. While trying, Vortigern's men try to break in, and Garth sets fire to the fortress where their horses are kept. The warriors run off, and the druids break into the smithy alone. Mórganthu enters with the dead king's new blade. Dybris and Owain are injured, but Merlin cuts off Mórganthu's hand and reclaims the blade.

The Hammering — Natalenya is trapped by flames erupting from the Stone, and Merlin must save her. He tries to hammer the blade into the Stone, and burns his hands in the process. Natalenya steadies him, and they are both given a vision.

The Vision — is of Natalenya being taken to a red dragon and a white dragon so they can eat her. Merlin fights the dragons, chops off a fang from one, and stabs the other in the eye.

The Victory — The vision ends. Merlin and Natalenya hammer the blade into the Stone, which causes an explosion, knocking out the druids.

The Aftermath — An angel heals Merlin of his blindness, and he, along with Natalenya, Colvarth, and Garth, take Arthur away to save him from Vortigern. Before leaving, Merlin visits the lake where his mother supposedly drowned and finds her alive — a water creature freed from serving the Stone, but forever confined to the lake. Vortigern rallies his men in pursuit, setting the stage for book two, *Merlin's Shadow*.

The Story of Book 2: Merlin's Shadow ...

Ganieda — Merlin's half sister, who is nine years old. She falsely blames Merlin for her parents' death. In grief she visits her father's smithy, and finds the Stone impaled by the sword. Beside it, she finds a mysterious orb and fang.

Mórganthu — Ganieda's grandfather, the arch druid, and Merlin's enemy. He takes Ganieda back to his tent. There they discover that the orb allows them to spy on Merlin.

Merlin — After the death of Uther, he flees to save Arthur from being killed by Vortigern. Colvarth the bard, Garth the bagpipe-playing orphan, and Natalenya his betrothed go with. Chased by Vortigern, Merlin decides they should find refuge on the island of Dintaga, against Colvarth's advice.

Gorlas — The King of Kernow, who resides on the island fortress of Dintaga. When he learns of the death of Uther and Igerna, Arthur's parents, he refuses to believe Igerna is dead. He loved her and hated Uther for marrying her, and so kicks Merlin and his companions out of his fortress and invites Vortigern to come and kill them.

The Mirror — Merlin sulks at his folly of choosing to go to Dintaga and, in a pool of water, looks at himself for the first time since his sight was restored. Seeing the ugly scars on his face, he doubts that Natalenya could love him and intends to free her from her vow to marry him.

The Fang — Natalenya comes and Ganieda spies on them with the orb while they wait for Vortigern. She tries to hurt Merlin with the fang, but misses and injures Natalenya, sickening her.

Vortigern — The traitor who killed Uther. He arrives at Dintaga, but Garth calls a ship using his bagpipe, and they all escape. Before landing in Kembry, Colvarth opens the old box Uther had found, and he and Merlin discover an ancient wooden bowl. Meanwhile, Natalenya gets sicker.

Taken Captive — Ganieda tells Vortigern where they are going, and he catches them in the middle of a steep-sided valley. But a band of raiding Pictish warriors fight off Vortigern, and take Merlin and his friends as slaves. Vortigern wanted to kill Arthur, but he is happy Arthur is now a slave.

Necton — A Pictish warrior, who takes them as slaves to the far north. Along the way, Merlin has a vision that the bowl is the Sangraal, the cup of Christ that caught his blood. He tries to heal Natalenya, but it doesn't work, and Merlin begins to question his faith even more.

Scafta — The witch doctor of the Picts, he buys Garth's bagpipe from Necton, making the orphan mad. Scafta has a huge mound of tangled hair that he won't let anyone touch.

The Escape — Merlin's faith sours during their slavery. When they escape, they're caught and taken back to the Pictish village, where Merlin must fight Scafta to the death. Merlin pins Scafta,

Garth cuts off the the man's hair, and Scafta runs away. The people cheer because they hated the witch doctor, and give Garth his bagpipe back.

King Atle — Respected now, Garth convinces Necton to sell them to Atle, who is Merlin's great-grandfather. But there is something strange about the king, for Colvarth thinks he shouldn't be alive after so many years.

The Feast — A great feast is held, and Merlin and the others' food is drugged. Merlin wakes up and finds Arthur has been stolen by Atle and that they are trapped by guards in his fortress.

Kensa — An old woman who was locked up by Atle. Merlin frees her, and she explains that Atle has sailed to the land of the dead and will sacrifice Arthur to renew his own youth.

The Parting — Merlin says good-bye to Natalenya, as well as Colvarth, who will care for her. Colvarth offers the Sangraal to Merlin, and he takes it, only to later lose during a fight by dropping it accdiently into deep water.

Sailing North — They escape, buy a leather-hulled boat, and set sail. On the way, Merlin finds the Sangraal miraculously in his bag. Angry still, he throws it into the water. A light appears and guides them.

Atle's Temple — When they arrive, they're captured by Atle's son, Loth. Atle offers Merlin eternal youth and to heal his scars if he will join them. Merlin is tempted, but refuses, choosing what is right.

Arthur — The boy is slain by Atle, and everyone is made younger. Merlin pulls his knife to kill Atle, but finds the Sangraal in his hand. He grabs his knife instead, but has the Sangraal again. Choosing to trust, not the Sangraal but the God of the Sangraal, he pours a drop of Christ's blood upon Atle's foul altar.

The Victory — The altar is destroyed, along with Atle and his household. Arthur is brought back to life, and they leave the island for home, where Merlin uses the Sangraal, trusting in God now, to finally heal Natalenya. The two are reconciled and plan to marry.

Mórgana — Ganieda has saved Loth's life using the orb and transported him back to Kernow. With the power of the fang, Ganieda grows taller and becomes Mórgana. Together with Mórganthu and Loth, she plans an elaborate trap for when Arthur is older, setting up book three, *Merlin's Nightmare*.

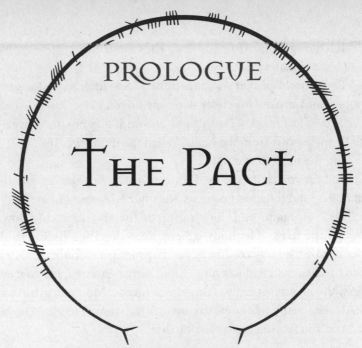

PROLOGUE

✝HE PACT

THE WILDS OF BOSVENNA MOOR
KERNOW, IN SOUTHWESTERN BRITAIN
SPRING, IN THE YEAR OF OUR LORD 493

Mórgana scowled at King Gorlas's back as he dug into the grave.

"Accursed shovel!" he yelled to the darkness, slamming the iron edge once more into the ground and flinging the dirt up. Five more times he jabbed at the loamy clay before twisting his wiry neck around and gazing at her savagely. "Are you sure she's here?"

"Yes."

Gorlas wagged his wild beard, and a silver torc shone from under its disheveled black fronds. "If not, I'll have your spleen sliced out—"

"Tell me again why you want her back."

"I've told you."

"Tell me again ... while you dig," she crooned.

"Igerna ran away."

"Two months past, it was, remember?" She took a step forward, stooped, and stroked his cheek with one finger.

His eyes lost focus. "That's right," he said, digging the shovel in and throwing dirt from the hole. "When the moon was full."

"Yes, the moon. Go on."

"And yet you claim she died sixteen years ago." He dug into the soil again. "But it makes no sense. She's buried here, you say?"

"Yes," Mórgana said, looking up at the stars winking down through the trees. "Her body is here. Keep digging." It didn't surprise her that he was confused. He'd always been confused. For it wasn't Igerna who had left him ... but rather Ewenna, his consort, whom the man fanatically claimed was Igerna. Mórgana grimaced. It had taken many gold coins to convince the woman to leave Gorlas.

"And you'll bring Igerna back to life?"

"Yes."

"Not for that tormenting pig, but for me?"

"Uther is dead, and you have nothing to fear from him. Tell me," she said, making her voice as smooth as honeyed mead, "what is your promise to me?"

He stood up at this question and looked at her with his left hand covering his right eye. "My soul. My very soul. But what is that? What is a soul?"

"A trifle. A little glob. Nothing you will miss. Promise me, and Igerna will rise before you, ever yours, young and in love with you, for ever and ever."

"And clever. She's clever, isn't she? Pretending to love Uther, but really loving me. She didn't marry that swine, did she?"

"Never."

"And their brats, they're dead now, aren't they?"

"Every one of them. Vortigern saw to that. Eilyne drowned, and Myrgwen is dust. And Arthur — I saw him die with my own eyes, the little wretch." The whole truth pressed against her lips like bitter vomit, but she squeezed them closed and kept it in. She had seen Merlin heal the child, yet she dared not tell Gorlas such news. The very purpose of this ruse was to bring about Arthur's destruction. And this bearded fool would be the instrument.

Gorlas clapped at the news. "Yes, yes!" he said, but his head shook left and right, as if in disagreement with himself. He began digging again.

"Promise me!"

"I promise."

"What do you promise?"

"To give you my very soul."

"And the service of your warriors?"

"Yes, for a year and a day, as we agreed. Now let me dig!"

He was close, so close now. Mórgana cast a glance at his two guards pacing nearby. It was unfortunate that Loth was gone to Lyhonesse building a new fortress from which to rule their future realm — his presence here could have made this task safer. But Gorlas had agreed to this pact more quickly than Mórgana had anticipated, and she had not had time to call her husband and his warriors back to Bosvenna Moor.

The guards could not be allowed to interfere. Certainly the one on the left, old and snoozing as he leaned upon his spear, was of no concern. But the other, he could be a challenge. Dyslan, the king had named him — the son of Tregeagle. No matter what, his sword was sharp, and his hand strayed to the hilt too often for Mórgana's neck to feel comfortable. He didn't trust her either — she could see it in his twitching cheeks whenever he turned his gaze her direction. Ah, but he would pay dearly if he intervened. And if the worst happened, she could always call upon the ranks of the druidow, hidden with her grandfather, Mórganthu, in the woods to their left.

As well, her thirteen-year-old son, Mórdred, was hiding on the right, though she didn't want to chance his precious life so soon.

There were plans for him, and his life must be preserved for the day of victory.

"Dig, Gorlas," she said, and he did, furiously. Heaps of dirt soon bulged at the edge of his pit, each one threatening to collapse back into the hole.

Then he stopped.

"What's this?" He picked up something long and gray. "It's a bone ... I ... I ..."

"Keep digging. You must find them all."

"I don't understand."

"Dig a little farther ... trust me." *It will be released once he finds the skull ... The Voice has promised.*

"I won't. Not till you explain. My love ... my love isn't dead ... I see my love ... she stands before me!"

Mórgana glanced up but saw nothing. The fool was delirious.

"She's warning me." Gorlas stared at nothing, one hand raised as if to touch someone's face. All at once he turned a fiery gaze on Mórgana. "Telling me not to trust you. Why should I trust you?"

Mórgana smiled.

He yelped while his eyes wildly searched the air. "She's gone. She's g-gone! I can't see her ... I must have her. I must find her!" He thrust the shovel back into the earth and began digging deeper and deeper.

Mórgana pushed a wisp of black hair away from her eyes, pouted at his irritating manner, and slipped her hand down to her belt. There she found her special fang hidden in a thin leather sheath. Plucking it out, she wrapped her fingers around its length. Years had passed since she'd found it beneath the Druid Stone, and now it ached to be used for this very special purpose. Her plans were finally coming to fruition, and she almost laughed to think of it. She had waited so long. The Voice, who had given her this fang, had waited also, and he had taught her patience, yes. Patience for such a vast revenge that all the world would be stunned into silence.

18

And it begins ... now.

A thrill of power wiggled up the inside of her arm like a worm, ate its way into her chest, and spun there: increasing, pulsing ... power!

Gorlas dug deeper until his knees could no longer be seen. At the sound of crunching bones, he closed his eyes, snapped his head back and forth, and looked back down. Myriad gray bones lay at his feet. And a skull. But not a human skull.

Gorlas growled; the sound rattled deep from within his throat as he stared at the skull of the creature — her friend — she had buried here all those years ago.

Morgana worked to hold back a laugh at the confusion on the man's face. But it would not last long. Lifting forth the fang, she felt its green fire curling around her hand. She jabbed its curved spike into the nape of his neck.

He screamed, arched his back, and swore at her. He lifted the shovel, off-balance, and threatened to cleave her head in two.

Behind her, she heard Dyslan draw his sword, but she refused to take her eyes from the delicious scene before her.

Smoke began to pour from the hole in Gorlas's neck, and blood dribbled onto his finely woven plaid of indigo, white, and teal. His arms began to shake, and his face contorted.

The shovel fell, clanking upon a rock.

Gorlas tipped sideways and dropped into the hole, dead.

Dyslan yelled and ran at her.

She jumped over the hole, leaving Gorlas's body between her and the guard. Landing in a crouch, she spun to face Dyslan as the ground began to tremble. A muffled roaring sounded from the open grave, and dirt and rocks shot upward in stinging plumes.

Dyslan staggered, his sword limp. The other guard awoke and fell to his knees in terror.

With her free hand, Mórgana reached into her bag once more and pulled forth the orb, another gift from the Voice. Like the fang, she had found it beneath the Druid Stone. It had many powers, but tonight she would use it differently.

Out from the trembling, roaring hole appeared a translucent image of Gorlas that only Mórgana could see — his soul emerging from his body. Quickly, she held the orb out, and Gorlas's soul glittered, faded, and then began to sink once more into the pit. The apparition's face twisted in agony. Oh, but she would save him from this pain. She began to chant:

> *Soul of earth, soul in dearth, come now to me.*
> *Skin of dust, skin in rust, come and serve me!*
> *Merlin's end, Merlin's rend; yes, you shall be.*
> *Arthur's bane, Arthur's chain; yes, you must be!*
> *Power of night, Power of fright, come now, my prize.*
> *Flesh astrewn, Flesh of moon; yes, you shall rise!*

From the hole came the sound of tearing and ripping. The guard with the spear turned white and collapsed, his eyes rolling upward into his head.

Dyslan took three steps closer and warily leaned toward the pit. His stomach convulsed, and he retched. Clutching his sword to his chest, he turned and fled.

No matter. He wouldn't get far, and she would deal with him later.

Gorlas's soul shimmered its last, and then the orb sucked it in like a black liquid swirling down through a funnel. A scream whistled upon the air, and then all was still.

It was done! For inside the orb, surrounded by purple flame, glared the weeping visage of Gorlas.

And in the grave, a hulking shadow rose.

She laughed, weary beyond weary due to her exertions, but she laughed.

Now to set everything in motion.

"Druidow ... Mórdred ..." she yelled into the woods. "Attend me now and meet the new king of Kernow!"

Part One

Fear's Glance

Ash, smoke, and flame: the young one looming.

Sin, spite, and hate: the sly shade luring.

Hand, soul, and heart: the black choice making.

Snare, lash, and trap: the death power waking.

Orb and fang, there at the dark demise.

CHAPTER I

WOLF KILL

The wind whipped past Merlin's ears as his horse galloped down the barely lit forest path. Too late, he realized he should have heeded the wild cawing of the crows around him: his horse reared up before a dozen wolves, who looked up from their fallen prey. A massive buck, slain and gutted, lay in their midst, and all around the greedy, black-feathered sentinels looked on in anticipation.

His mission had gone from urgent to life or death.

Merlin wheeled his horse to the left and kicked her onward, off the path and between two trees. The mask that Merlin wore to cover his scars shifted upward on his face momentarily, obscuring his vision. He righted it just before a branch lashed him across the face, nearly cutting his lip through the black cloth.

The wolves howled behind him, but Merlin didn't look back — couldn't look back. Terror sought to master him, but he pushed it down. He had to direct his horse farther before he could cut back to the path. But the woods were too thick to ride fast, and he'd be caught. Fear, like a cloak of thistles, clung to his legs and back. A wolf could rip his flesh away at any moment.

The beasts snarled from behind as a massive branch loomed toward him from the front. Merlin hung low to the right, but it still banged him hard in the shoulder. The saddle began to slip. He grabbed the horse's sweat-dampened mane and pulled himself back up. The horse snorted as it jumped through the brush — and then screamed.

Merlin whipped his gaze around.

A wolf had torn into her left hindquarter. Blood poured from the wound, slick and red in the morning light.

The wolf lunged again, and Merlin kicked its black snout, yelling while he pulled the horse to the right. She quickened her pace, jumped a bush, and Merlin found himself on the path again.

Three wolves leapt just behind.

Faster now, Merlin kicked the horse's side. Having hardly seen a wolf in the sixteen years since leaving Bosventor, he'd become careless, and now he'd interrupted an entire pack at their meal. Panic sank into his stomach like rotten meat, churning his innards. He had to get away; he had to!

But the wolves were faster, and his horse began to wheeze from the effort. Merlin had been anxious to get back to Dinas Crag with the news he carried and had ridden the horse hard for hours. Its strength was almost gone.

Another wolf snapped at the horse's right side, ripping her leg open. The horse kicked, screaming in terror, and then staggered forward again.

Merlin panicked. He wouldn't get away. His horse was going to die. He was going to die. He could kill one wolf, maybe two, but never a whole pack. An image of his body, mangled and gutted like the buck, flashed before his eyes.

A wolf latched onto his boot, its teeth slicing into his foot like small daggers. He tried to draw his sword, but the horse reared up, forcing the wolf to drop off. The hackles of the wolf's neck twitched, and its yellow eyes lusted for Merlin's blood as it prepared to leap.

A wolf on his left gashed the horse's belly.

Merlin turned to face the beast, but a large branch blocked his view. He reached, clamped his hands onto the smooth bark, pulled free from his horse, and wrapped his legs around the branch. He didn't want to abandon his horse, whom he'd raised from a filly, but he also knew the only chance she had of getting away was without his weight.

The horse shot forward into the brush, with all three wolves slashing it with their bloody jaws. Unfortunately, the end came quickly, with the wolves pulling it down about fifty paces away.

Merlin climbed up and listened painfully to her last screams.

When the poor creature's silence came, and only the wolves' gory feast could be heard, he took in some deep breaths and tried to discern his position on the path. He'd been traveling south from Luguvalium, the capital of Rheged, and was on his way back home to Dinas Crag. There awaited his wife, Natalenya, and their two children: Tingada, their little daughter, and Taliesin, their growing boy. And their adopted Arthur, now eighteen winters old.

Surely Merlin had passed the long lake already ... or had he?

Ahead of him he could hear a stream burbling in the dark, so the path must have swung closer to it again. But was this *the* stream — the Derwent — as he had thought? If so, then he was close to home with the crossroad just beyond.

A faint splash. Maybe a fish. Then another. Full splashing, now. Then clopping. A rider, coming his way, heading toward the wolves.

Merlin had to warn him. "Who's there?" he called. "Take care! Wolves just killed my horse, and more are just beyond."

The rider cantered forward, slowing just below Merlin. A man with a broad face and a gray beard looked up at him.

"And what am I to do about such a dilemma? I must get through."

"They'll scatter if you give them enough time—"

"No. I've an urgent and vital message that must get through."

Howling sounded far down the path, and soon the three who had just killed the horse answered. "Maybe it would be best to turn back for now. Is there a village nearby?"

"Dinas Crag. I'll take you there."

"Not on my horse. You'll walk, you will."

A wolf howled. The man wheeled his horse around.

Merlin swung down and dropped onto its back, just behind the man.

"Get off!"

"Go!" Merlin drove his heels into the horse's flanks, sending it flying down the path and splashing through the stream thinned by the long spring drought.

When they were a good distance away and no pursuit could be heard, the man pulled his horse to a stop. He turned and growled. "Get off."

"I saved your life."

The man shoved Merlin off the back of the horse.

But Merlin landed on his feet, dashed to the left, lifted the man's boot, and threw him from the horse.

The man scrambled to his feet, spitting dry grass, and glared at Merlin from the other side of the saddle. His face was red. "Take off your mask!"

"No."

"Who are you?"

"Ambrosius."

The man stared at Merlin, as if expecting more. "What is your parentage, dishonorable knucklebone, and your purpose in these woods?"

Merlin grabbed the reins of the horse, lest the man get away. "What's *your* name, *your* parentage, and *your* mission?"

The man wrinkled up his nose and scowled back.

A distant howl split the air, and Merlin jerked.

Both men leapt onto the horse, and Merlin clutched the back of the ornate saddle as they raced away.

"Which way?" the man asked.

There was only one place that promised safety, though it was clear this stranger would not consent to being blindfolded to reach it. "Can I trust you?"

"On my honor."

"Before who?"

"Before God, you fool. What, do I look like a druid?"

The wolves howled once more, cementing the decision. Merlin pointed. "Go straight when you come to the crossroads and follow the path along the stream."

"Hardly wide enough for a one-legged deer."

"Trust me."

They raced along the path until they encountered the northern shore of a large lake, from which the overflow of the stream ran. The path curved to follow its western shore for half a league, where the lake ended and the stream, which now fed the lake, began again.

Mountains rose on each side, and their tops could be seen through the trees. The sky brightened with the rising sun, and the thick woods changed from oak to pine as the path climbed slowly. The mountains squeezed closer and closer, their sides ever steeper.

When the valley finally tightened to the jaws of a narrow gorge, the stream drew closer to the path, which strangely ended before a twelve-foot-tall, vertical pile of rocks, with dry grasses covering the center of the pile. The stream itself poured from a spring on the left side.

The man pulled his horse to a stop. "What's this? If you intend to rob — "

Merlin cupped his hands. "Porter! Open the door, Ambrosius has come."

Nothing stirred except a rustle of brush behind them. The horse trembled.

Merlin called again. "Porter! Open — "

A jaw clamped on his arm. The front gate spun away and something hard hit his shoulder. Merlin's legs slammed downward. Neighing. Cursing. Where was his sword? Growling in his ear. Pungent, bloody fur against his face. Ragged claws on his chest. It was going for his throat.

CHAPTER 2

A RUMOR OF WAR

With one hand shoving the wolf away, Merlin unsheathed his dirk. He tried to get the blade between his neck and its snapping teeth, but only jabbed it in the shoulder.

The wolf pulled back as Merlin struggled up. It lunged again, and he stabbed it in the chest. The beast dripped saliva and blood from its jaws onto Merlin's nose before rolling to the side, yelping.

Merlin rose, drew his sword, and chopped at its neck.

When the beast was dead, Merlin wiped his face on his sleeve and looked to see how his fellow traveler had fared. The horseman stood over his own slain wolf, his hat pushed back and sweat on his brow.

What had gotten into the wolves? There was something strange going on …

With a banging of wooden bars, two massive doors opened in what had appeared to be a wall of rocks and brush blocking the entrance to the valley. Merlin smirked as he saw the amazement on the face of the horseman. The doors were made of timber, with rocks piled near the sides and dead brush nailed on.

Three warriors rushed out, swords drawn. Two archers appeared at the top of the wall.

"A little late you are," the horseman yelled, "and I shall be sure to take up this ineptness with your chieftain."

The porter on duty, old Brice, shuffled out and helped Merlin up, dusting him off. "We was all sleepin', an' did'na expect nobody so early, certainly not one as esteemed so you, Ambrosius. Please forgive us not helpin' kill them wolves."

The horseman cinched his saddle to retighten it. "Who is the chieftain here, anyway?"

"Lord Ector," Brice answered, bowing to the man. "And who may you be?"

"You'll not ask, you won't. My ancestry is my own and my business is with Lord Ector."

Merlin nodded to give Brice his approval, and the porter led them through the gate. Just inside, to the right of the steepening path, stood a large crennig for the guards, and on the left the stream rushed down the gorge in a glorious waterfall. All ahead was shaded in darkness, the sun having not yet risen high enough over the mountains. Part way up the path they came to a stair climbing to a stone-walled fortress on a steep hill, high above the gorge.

The horseman pointed up to the fortress. "That way? Mighty difficult for an honored guest to bring his horse up and stable it, I'd say."

Merlin just laughed and kept walking through the gorge, ignoring the stairs. "You've guessed correctly where the fortress of Dinas Crag is located, but we only go there in times of danger. *This* is where we live ..." He stepped forward and pointed. "Welcome to the Nancedefed of Dinas Crag."

The man followed, leading his horse, and when he passed over a stony ridge he opened his mouth and did not shut it until he had feasted his eyes on everything.

The golden light of morning was just rising over the eastern foothills, illuminating a secret valley high in the mountains: flat, broad, and divided in two by the stream. More than a thousand horses, many of them foals, grazed within the enclosed valley in rock-walled pastures dotted with stables, crennigs, and tilled gardens ready for spring planting. The scene would have been idyllic except for the lingering drought, which had made the new grass begin to brown and had reduced the stream to half its regular flow.

"Valley of sheep?" the horseman said with a hint of confusion. "I see a few sheep ... but you're raising horses like I've never seen."

"The name is intentionally misleading. If the Picti knew what we were doing, then ..."

The horseman nodded, still looking on the beautiful valley with amazement.

Merlin sighed. Home and safety. Every fiber of him wanted to see Natalenya immediately, but duty called him to his uncle Ector first.

Because in addition to transporting this mysterious guest, Merlin recalled the true reason he needed to appear before the chieftain: spies had discovered a mass of Picti north of Hadrian's wall. An invasion was imminent. Every horse that could be spared would be needed for the battle.

Passing the guards at the door with a nod, Merlin entered Ector's empty feasting hall and left the horseman who had helped him to wait outside.

Stepping to the middle of the room, he threw his black cloak on a bench and sat before the hearth, where a fire of pine logs sent sweet, pitch-scented smoke upward. In the corner on a fleece lay Ector's long-eared hound, Goffrew, with her two sleeping puppies. When he went over, she sniffed inquisitively at the wolf blood on his hands while he scratched her behind the ears.

A servant came and, finding him hungry, gave him a bowl of

cold, roasted-onion broth, a barley cake, and a wet rag to refresh himself with.

He gratefully peeled off his mask — what a sweaty nuisance of a thing! But a necessary one. Sixteen years had passed since Vortigern, the current High King, had slain Arthur's father, but his hatred had not lessened. If Vortigern knew Arthur was alive, he would do anything to kill the heir to the throne — along with Merlin and all those who harbored him. After wiping the blood away, he took a clean part of the rag and rubbed his face, feeling once more the familiar scars that covered his cheeks, nose, forehead, and eyelids. With no distractions to keep them at bay, the old memories of the wolf attack when he was nine forced themselves upon him —

His little sister surrounded by wolves. He'd run to protect her, but the wolves had attacked him, and not her. They'd scratched his eyes, mostly blinding him. And he'd endured that blindness for eight years, until he'd thrust Uther's blade into the Druid Stone in an attempt to destroy it. God had healed his vision then, miraculously.

He shuddered, pushing the memory of the Stone's enchantment away as best he could. His father had died that day, and Merlin had been swept into a treacherous world to protect and raise Arthur. After many trials, including slavery to the Picti and rescuing Arthur from a pagan sacrifice, he and Natalenya had married and fled to Dinas Crag. This was the village where his father had grown up, and where Merlin's uncle, Ector, was now chieftain.

Sudden noise from the back rooms pulled Merlin to the present, and Ector himself stepped into the hall. He strode across the room with his thick arms spread wide in greeting, barefoot and wearing his usual dusty, matted fox-fur cloak over a long brown tunic and green breeches.

"Welcome, Merlin!" Ector roared, giving him such a hug that Merlin felt like he'd been squeezed between two massive oxen.

"Shah, don't say that. I'm Ambrosius to you," Merlin reminded him.

"Vortigern's rats have no ears here. Your secret's safe, nephew."

"Not if the man standing outside heard you. I met him in the wood, and he wants to speak with you."

"Who?" Ector said, cutting off a cold chunk of meat from the remains of a boar that had been roasted the night before.

"He won't tell."

Popping some of the boar into his mouth, Ector mumbled, "Send the warty toad away."

"He says it's urgent, but first I have a message from Urien for you."

"Ah, yes, your talk with Urien. What does *he* want now? Send the wart in — I'd rather hear him than words from that bully."

"Bully or no, I rode all night to tell you he wants warriors and horses immediately. The Picti have gathered east of Luguvalium, and Urien means to destroy them."

"Hah!" Ector said, spitting out a bone onto Merlin's boot. "He'll just tickle their ribs and make them run away."

"It's a large force, uncle, ready to invade. And Urien — "

"He can find his own bullied horses. Honestly, I'd rather help King Cradelmass in Powys."

"That cruel, careless scoundrel?"

"Indeed. At least he's an excellent hunter, and he dined me well last I visited."

"And he makes his own citizens slaves."

"But *I* won't be Urien's slave. No, no."

"My lord, you've sworn Urien your allegiance. He asks for men and horses, of which we have plenty. It would seem — "

"Let Urien's beard rot in his mead, I say."

Merlin gulped. "The king won't invite you to the next boar roast if you don't — "

"He said that, did he? Well, pig's feet. Let him throw the beast's knucklebones at my effigy, I say."

"And, you'll be excluded from the spring fox hunt."

Ector roared. "Now that is going too far! I'll split his skull, I will, if he even — "

Gathering his patience, Merlin took up his onion broth, dipped the barley cake into it, and sucked it into his mouth. It was warm and salty, and the onion had been roasted to sweet perfection. He chewed slowly before speaking again. "If you help, he offered to give you the bronze spear of Gordon mac Gabran."

"My father's trophy? That should have been returned to our house long before now. That thief — "

"*And* the scalp of Dougal Mór, with a stand to prominently, uh ... display it."

Ector raised an eyebrow. "Hmmm ..."

Merlin leaned back, tapped his fingers together, and looked at the king expectantly. He had him now.

"How many men? And, more importantly, how many horses?"

"I suggest two musters. One for those that can ride now, and another after the mid-meal tomorrow."

Ector sat down next to Merlin, pulled the last of his boar meat into his mouth, chewed half of it, and then whispered, "He really promised the scalp? Oh, but that *is* a prize."

"Truly."

"And which muster will you ride with? Ah, but I'm dense. You just came back. You'll want to see your Natalenya again, even if only for a bit. In fact, she brought the children over yesterday to check on the pups, and gave some good counsel to my Eira regarding a troublesome milker. Natalenya has a good head under that pretty hair. She even tried to tell me how to repair the front gate, if you can believe it."

"I can. And speaking of my family, how has Artorius gotten along with his training?"

Ector smiled and his eyes lit up. "Arthur's doing — "

"Shah!"

"What — ?"

Merlin leaned over and whispered, "Uncle, I beg you. Don't say his name so loud."

"I'll say it when I want to. He's a man now, and a splendid one at that. You'll let him join the muster?"

34

"I don't see why not. As long as he hasn't broken anything since I left."

"Nothing that's come to these old ears. Least I haven't heard the smith complaining of any damaged blades lately."

Merlin drained his soup and set down the wooden bowl. "I mean on himself. He had just smashed his left elbow the week before I left."

"Ah, well ... I guess you'll have to ask him. And while you're at it, it's time you tell him the truth about his parents. He's a man now, and — "

"Not with Vortigern still High King. We'll wait."

Ector began pacing, his bare feet slapping the stone floor. "Wait until Vortipor wears his father's torc? How will that solve anything? He leads the warriors against the Saxenow while Vortigern sleeps like a badger on his soft cushions. There's never a good time, you know. But Arthur is ready. He's ready, I say."

Merlin shook his head, the fear of Vortigern rising up from his memory. "We'll wait."

"Well," Ector said, growling, "at least you're going to let him fight the Picti. That's a start."

"And what will we do with our mysterious guest?"

"Ah, send him in," Ector said as he sliced off another huge chunk of the boar. "I'm in a good mood now. The scalp of Dougal Mór ..."

After replacing his mask, Merlin picked up his cloak, threw it over his shoulders, and went outside to retrieve the horseman.

The man entered the hall first, giving Merlin a chance to closely study the man's cloak. It was finely woven as to resemble a tapestry of colors, shades, and patterns. And his hat matched it for finery, if not audacity, with its silver threads and wide, floppy side pinned up with a brooch fashioned into the shape of a golden lion.

Merlin blanched. The lion had been selected by Vortigern to represent his reign. Why hadn't he noticed it on the man before?

Ector had positioned himself upon a tall wooden chair at the far end of the hearth, and was still barefoot. A sword lay across his lap, and lanced to its end were some boar ribs, from which he tore off a chunk of meat and popped it into his mouth.

The man removed his hat, bowed grandly, and then began to speak. "O most glorious Ector, Lord of Dinas Crag and the green valley of the horses of Rheged. I, Fodor map Fercos map Fichan map Firsil, have come to you with a most important message —"

A bubble rose to the top of Merlin's stomach, and he tried to hold it in, but it escaped in a loud burp.

Fodor twisted around and glared at him. Turning back to Ector, he declared, "I'm sorry, my lord, but I did not know this man had followed me in. I will not speak in front of someone who wears a mask. Kindly remove him from my presence."

Ector raised an eyebrow and tilted his head to the side, chewing. "No."

"Forgive me, my lord, but I must I insist on it. My message is only for the most noble of chieftains, among whose number I count thyself."

"This man is named Mer — I mean Ambrosius Àille Fionnadh," Ector said, winking at Merlin.

Merlin blushed. Only Natalenya called him "Àille Fionnadh," which meant "handsome hair."

"And as my bard," Ector continued, "he has my full trust. You will either proceed in his hearing, or you will leave at once."

Fodor glared at Merlin out of the corner of his eye. "Very well then, I will give you my most precious news in the presence of this ... this ... bard, about whom I don't even know his proper parentage."

Ector snorted.

"I have been entrusted as an envoy to bring you a message sent far and wide by the Chief-Warrior of the land of Britain, Protector of our Seas and Coasts, and Illustrious High King — none other than Vortigern, the Lion of Britain."

Ector opened his mouth as if surprised — but then popped in a chunk of boar meat with a layer of crunchy skin, and began chewing noisily.

"And so ..." the envoy said as he pulled a thick stack of parchments from a tightly woven woolen bag and handed a sheet to the king with a flourish.

Ector held it up and tried to read by the dim light of the fire, scrunching up his forehead in a puzzlement of lines and wrinkles. "I can't make it out," he said, and tossed it back toward the man. The paper flew momentarily toward the envoy's hands but then sailed back down toward the fire.

Fodor lunged and snared the edge. But as he pulled his hand away, the parchment slipped from his pinched hold and fell into the fire, where it lit almost immediately.

Merlin caught Ector's eye, and a slight smirk appeared at the corner of the chieftain's mouth as the envoy pulled another parchment from his bag.

"Let me see that one," Ector said, reaching out his hand. "Maybe it's written with larger letters."

The envoy snapped the parchment away and stepped back from Ector. "No need, Lord Ector, I will read it out loud for your benefit." Clearing his throat, he began:

"Hereby let it be known, on this day, that the glorious and most feared Vortipor, son of High King Vortigern of the land of Britain, has called all men everywhere, including warriors and such that wish to learn the art of war, forthwith, to muster at Glevum in the territory of the Dobunni, there with any horses, for the mutual defense, fortification, and strengthening of the southeastern coast and heartland of Britain, known under their former administrative names of Brittania Prima and Flavia Caesariensis, against the barbarian invaders from the land of the Saxenow —"

Fodor looked up to find Ector whispering to a servant.

"Can you bring me a flagon of mead? No, no, the brown stuff. Aged better."

Fodor stomped his foot and cleared his throat until Ector gave him his attention, and then began reading once more:

"Let it be known that all such warriors shall gather themselves at Glevum to obtain forevermore unto eternity everlasting renown and a glorious remembrance among their surviving relatives. Remuneration and compensation for all such services shall be forthwithly determined by the High King and paid at regular intervals not to be exceeded by one-half the sum of one-twelfth of a gold solidus per new moon ..."

Ector sneezed loudly and it echoed through the hall, interrupting the reading. "Is that all?"

"No, my lord, it goes quite on, giving preferential dates for the muster, et cetera, et cetera."

Ector placed a small chunk of boar into his mouth and began chewing it doubtfully. "Then skip it. So Vortigern wants my warriors to fight Saxenow in the soft south to keep the northern kingdom of Rheged safe?"

"Yes, Lord Ector," Fodor said, bowing. "It is quite an honor, I assure you, and — "

"Don't mention it," Ector said, and then he spit out a chunk of cartilage, which landed on the envoy's shoulder. "The funny thing is that I don't recall seeing any Saxenow up here in Rheged. Have you, Ambrosius?"

"No, my lord."

The envoy brushed the offending chunk from his shoulder and wiped his hand on the edge of a nearby chair.

"But we have Picti here, and in plenty. Tell me, how many warriors has Vortigern sent to Urien to help fight the Picti?"

The envoy began to speak but closed his mouth.

"Exactly. Now get out."

"Oh, glorious chieftain, may I — "

"Get out."

"But you certainly cannot mean for me to ... Nowhere else have I — "

"Open the doors, Ambrosius, and have the guards throw him on the dung heap."

The envoy jumped and put his hat back on.

Merlin hesitated. "My lord, this man did save my life in the Keswick forest."

"All right, then," Ector said, waving his hand. "Show him the door *nicely*. But if I see your flouncing hat around Dinas Crag for more time than it takes for you to water your horse, know that I've reserved a special dung heap for the likes of you. Get out!"

Merlin opened the doors.

The envoy clutched his woolen bag of parchments and backed away, bowing every few steps. Ector himself followed the man with his boar-tipped blade in hand until the envoy tripped on the threshold and fell on his backside out of the hall.

Ector slammed the doors.

"And stay out!"

Merlin's legs ached, and his eyes could barely stay open by the time he left his uncle's hall. He had stayed too long talking with the chieftain about the state of things in the north. Now, as he walked halfway across the valley to the training arena, he relished the cool air on his unmasked face.

At the corner of the arena, Merlin halted, rewarded for his trek by the sight of those three inseparable young men — Arthur, Culann, and Dwin — all riding bareback, with Peredur running alongside, giving them instructions. Arthur soon noticed him and rode by on his black stallion, alternately waving and pushing his long, dark hair out of his eyes. "Father, you're here! Watch what Peredur's been teaching us ..."

He rode back to the others, and there, without reins, Arthur and his companions directed their horses through an intricate series of full-speed maneuvers. It looked like a dance, with the horses obeying the subtle sounds and changes in body tension given by their riders, except that each of the three had a spear in one hand which he hit against the shields of the others, thus perfecting his aim and timing.

Peredur now stood on the other side of the stone-stacked fence, a grin on his ruddy face. "Welcome back!"

"You've got them riding bareback like experts now."

"It increases their skills and teaches 'em more subtle ways to command the horses. Most of all it helps 'em learn better balance."

Merlin watched in fascination as Arthur and the others stood carefully upon the backs of their horses — barefoot — with their shields and spears spread out for balance. Then, with calculated movements, they took aim at each other and tried to knock each other off. Sandy-haired Dwin was the first to go down to the soft dirt as Arthur's spear hit his shield directly in the center.

"Did you see that?" Arthur asked as he rode by. His maroon tunic hung loosely about his torso and flapped in the wind. Below, he wore gray leather breeches that showed how muscular his legs had become.

Merlin smiled and waved him onward.

"Artorius has somethin' to show you. For the last three days he's talked about nothin' else."

"Shouldn't he wear some armor? He could get hurt out there. Those spears are sharp."

"Watch."

"And now you've taught them to stand on the horses too?"

"Watch."

With Dwin sidelined, it was now between Arthur and Culann. The two rode to opposite ends of the field, then paused to take a breath and find the best footing.

Culann tested the strength of his spear, dropped it, and picked up another, which had been jabbed into the ground. This one had a purple cloth tied about a foot behind the tip.

"Who do you think will win?" Merlin asked, but Peredur didn't answer. Merlin tried to think of all the times these two had competed through the years, and it seemed no one could regularly predict who would come out on top. While Arthur had inherited his stocky, resilient frame from his true father, the murdered High King

Uther, the young man was exceptionally reckless, and this often gave coolheaded Culann the advantage.

Merlin looked at Arthur, amazed again at how much he had grown during the last few years. Always strong, he had put on more girth and brawn in the last two years alone than Merlin thought possible. As Ector had said, he was a man now, and though Merlin wanted to tell him the truth about his parents, he feared for what might happen if the boy learned before he was ready, and before Britain itself was ready.

Arthur and Culann steadied their balance, nodded, and then each signaled his horse to begin galloping. By the time they met in the middle, they were both going incredibly fast, the horses stretching and straining for speed as they bore down on each other. Arthur leveled his spear at Culann, who did the same, with his polished iron tip flashing in the morning light, the purple cloth behind it flapping in the wind.

They met with a great crash. Arthur's spear went wide, while Culann's hit Arthur square in the shield.

Merlin cringed and looked away.

When Merlin looked back, Arthur had fallen hard to the ground screaming, with the spear jabbed into his stomach.

CHAPTER 3

A SHADOW OF DEATH

Merlin jumped the stone wall and ran toward Arthur's heaving, jerking body. Arthur held on to the spear, and it quivered in his hands as he cried out.

Culann, who had been unhorsed by his powerful blow, sat up and blinked in shock.

But the soft dirt sucked at Merlin's boots as he ran, and the ground tilted precariously. He nearly fell, off-balance and with panic rushing through his cold veins.

"Artorius!" He collapsed to his knees behind the boy. He was still a boy, wasn't he? Why hadn't Merlin protected him more? He knew all along that an accident like this would happen. Natalenya's worries come true. But the air felt thin and Merlin's vision faded to purple, then red as blood. His head felt like it was floating, disconnected from his hands, and he couldn't catch his breath no matter how quickly he inhaled the dusty air.

He reached over Arthur's side and grabbed the spear just beyond Arthur's shaking hands, trying desperately to see what he most feared. Tears had leaked from Arthur's eyes, and he turned to look up at Merlin.

Then he laughed.

Arthur dropped the spear, and where there had been a sharp metal blade, there was now only a broken off stub of wood.

Merlin fell back on his haunches as Arthur bounced up and hugged him with a huge smirk.

Merlin was flooded with relief, but this quickly turned into a torrent of anger. "Don't *ever* do that again!" he yelled. Didn't Arthur know how much Merlin loved him? Didn't he know how much fear Merlin carried around?

Dwin had run over to see the spectacle and was now doubled over in a fit of laughter.

Peredur sat down nearby, his elbows on his knees, chuckling. "You should'a seen your face, Ambrosius. As I said, they've been plottin' to fool you for days!"

"It's not funny, and I can't believe you'd let him take such a risk."

Culann stepped over and threw the snapped-off spear point to the ground. "We sawed through the tip, see, so it would break off at the slightest touch. Arthur knew to grab the spear just as I let go, and he fell on purpose. It was completely safe."

"And just in case," Dwin said, bobbing his head happily, "Artorius wore some armor under his tunic."

Arthur lifted the maroon cloth up to show the padded leather and iron-plate armor.

Merlin smiled weakly, nodded, and took a deep breath through his teeth.

Someone from behind pulled off Merlin's hood. He leaned back to see who it was, and Caygek beamed down at him, his teeth shining through his braided, blond beard. "Nice show, huh?"

"No." Despite his racing heart, Merlin stood and embraced the man. Bedwir was just behind, and as Merlin shook his hand in greeting, he remembered the actual reason he had come to the training grounds. "Well met, friends," Merlin said. "I was hoping to find you both. I have news from the north you'll want to hear."

Everyone looked at him expectantly as he paused. "We're going to war. I've brought the summons to Ector just now, and he's agreed."

"When are we leaving?" Arthur asked as he exchanged glances with Dwin and Culann.

"Who says *you* get to go?" Merlin asked.

"Please?"

"After that stunt? Go groom your horses while I talk to the men here."

Arthur swallowed, pleaded with his eyes, but then finally nodded. He, Culann, and Dwin climbed onto their horses and rode off toward the main stable.

Caygek spoke first, his eyes narrowed into a dangerous squint. "So the Picti are raiding again? Somehow that doesn't surprise me."

Merlin's hand went impulsively to his neck, where sixteen years ago he'd worn a Pictish slave collar. At least these men understood, for all of them had worn the hated collars too. "It's more than a raid," Merlin said. "A large force has gathered north of the wall within striking distance of Luguvalium. Urien wants to smash them, and has called for help."

"When do we muster?" Bedwir asked as he pulled his sword and inspected its edge.

"For you and Caygek, immediately. Scout out the situation and make sure it's safe for Artorius to come."

"You mean you're going to let him fight?"

Merlin paused. Arthur was so reckless! How could he agree to let him go? But he had already told Ector. Grudgingly, he answered, "Yes ... as long as the odds are in our favor."

Bedwir winked. "With Artorius, the odds will always be in our favor."

"I hope that's true. Peredur, Artorius, and I will join the second muster tomorrow after the mid-meal. If it's not safe, you're to send word. Agreed?"

Caygek unsheathed his sword, and he and Bedwir made the sign of the cross with their blades as they stood shoulder to shoulder, united as sword brothers.

"Agreed."

Natalenya rushed to meet him before he even made it to the door. All Merlin's tiredness left him in that happy moment of her embrace, so tight that her love for him filled his soul and almost made him giddy.

"I missed you," she said, looking up at him with her lustrous green eyes.

He hugged her close, telling her through his touch how much he had missed her. Then he cupped her head in his hands, feeling her long brown hair, and ... it felt funny, sticky. He sniffed the top of her head — it smelled like she'd slept with a flock of sheep.

"You're making wool-grease again?"

She drew back so she could look at him. "The shearing was last week, and ..."

"It smells awful." Merlin looked away as memories came unbidden to him of his desperate journey to the land of darkness in the fragile, leather-hulled boat that had been coated in wool-grease: The waves crashing over the side ... The boat shattering on the rocks ... Arriving too late ... Arthur dying at the hand of King Atle ... The Sangraal healing Arthur and raising him from the dead.

But Merlin's hard memories had made him forget Natalenya, who turned his head so their eyes met once again. "Come back, my love. The grease gets everywhere, sorry ..."

He pulled her close once again, leaned his head against hers, and whispered in her ear. "I'm the one who's sorry. The past ..." He shook his head. "You're a hard worker, and the smell doesn't matter because I'm home with you."

45

"Tath!" Seven-year-old Tingada came running out of their crennig and latched onto Merlin's waist.

Merlin freed one arm to wrap around the little girl's shoulders. "Ah, my little beauty! Did you miss your tas?"

Tinga grinned up at him. With her top four teeth missing, her face bore an aura of mischief that belied her childish speech.

Merlin ruffled her brown, curly hair, thanking God again for blessing them with children when they had least expected it. The wait had only sweetened their present joy and deepened their love for Arthur — their son too, in heart if not in body.

At the moment, however, thoughts of the boy brought thoughts of the inevitable truth that loomed ever closer. One day soon he would have to tell Arthur the truth of his parentage and of his rightful role as the future High King of Britain. The vague answers he and Natalenya had always given him could not continue for long, and Tingada and twelve-year-old Taliesin were a balm against that difficult day of reckoning.

"Are you goin' to stay, Tath?"

Merlin knelt, looked into Tingada's green eyes, and patted her hair once more. Did he have to tell them? Did he have to ruin this moment? He wanted to stay for a week, a month, a year —

"No, Tinga, I can't. King Urien has called us to battle, and as Ector's bard, I must go too."

"A battle?" said a voice from above. Merlin looked up onto the roof of their crennig. There, on the edge, six feet off the ground, stood Taliesin, with moppish black hair, a bright red tunic, and torn-off russet breeches. On his back he'd strapped a dull-edged sword made by Merlin, and his freckled hand went to it as he grimaced at them. "If there's a battle afoot, then I'm ready!"

Merlin nodded up to him. "Yes, a battle."

"Will there be blood?"

"I expect so."

Taliesin jumped down, pulled his blade from his back, and attacked the broken-off trunk of a dead elm. "Got him!"

Natalenya put a hand on his shoulder, her gaze on Merlin. "A battle ...?"

"Picti."

"But you've only just come. I'd hoped ..."

From where he knelt, Merlin looked up to Natalenya, trying to let her know he was sorry.

Her brows knotted and worry flickered in her eyes.

"Caygek and Bedwir are mustering as many as can ride today, but I'm not leaving until the second muster, tomorrow after the mid-meal. So we'll have time together — "

"Not enough."

Merlin stood and hugged her one more time. "Not enough."

"Not enuffff!" Tinga announced as she and Taliesin joined the long hug.

Natalenya remained silent a long while, and then, with a sigh, pulled away to look at him one more time. "Well, we can at least enjoy the little time we do have."

She led him inside, and the children followed. Merlin took the place of honor at the hearth by lying upon his sheared sheepskin rug, and after she cleaned the wounds on his arm and foot, they celebrated his homecoming with a dish of venison roasted in wild garlic chive sauce, fresh-baked bread, and raspberry-leaf tea to wash it down.

The bread alone eased his anxiety and helped him relax — hot and steamy with a dip made of honey, horseradish, and butter. Each bite made his home all the more real after his eight league ride from Luguvalium, and the horror of the wolf attack. And Natalenya was here, holding his hand. Tingada sat nearby, alternately munching a large piece of bread and combing his curly hair. Sitting across the hearth, Taliesin served himself up thirds of the venison dish, a broad smile above his greasy chin.

Merlin allowed himself to forget, if only for now, the reality of their situation.

Later, after the children had moved away from the table, Natalenya drew close and whispered, "The Picti, again?"

"Yes, but I'd rather not—"

"Do you think it's Necton?"

Merlin sighed and moved closer to Natalenya. "Now that he's High King of the Picti and has added Guotodin to his kingdom, he doesn't lead raiding parties."

"What if this is more than a raid?"

Merlin sipped his raspberry-leaf tea before responding. "Of course it's just a raid. Urien's scouts would know. That's why I'm allowing Artorius to come along. Dwin and Culann as well if their parents agree."

Natalenya looked at him in disbelief.

"He's ready. Ector agrees."

"Not yet."

"I understand how you feel, but he's a man now." Merlin glanced at the children to make sure they were out of earshot, and then lowered his voice. "He'll never be king if he can't fight. I don't want this either, but it must be. It is his destiny."

Natalenya swallowed and nodded. "It's hard to let go."

Merlin took her hands in his and closed his eyes. "I know."

"I just don't want you, or him, to be captured by the Picts again. The first time nearly destroyed us."

"Our slavery is long past—and will never be again, so help us God. And now that we've helped Rheged become strong through her warhorses, it's our task to prevent others from becoming slaves. Artorius needs to help now too."

Natalenya stood and turned to face the wall. "You promised me when we chose to live here—so far north, so close to the Picti—you promised that you'd never unnecessarily risk yourself. I wish I felt otherwise, but I can't help but worry you are doing just that now."

"I won't even be fighting. Bards don't fight, you know that."

"I also know that battles can be lost and bards can be taken."

"Not apart from God's will." He stood and stepped behind her. "Natalenya," he said, and she turned around in his embrace. "This is something that Artorius and I must do, despite the possible danger. We can only put our trust in Jesu's direction. Even now. Especially now."

At the sound of running footfalls outside, they broke apart. Arthur burst into the crennig, bringing with him a whoosh of air that smelled of horse and sweat and dirt. "Can I fight?" he asked breathlessly.

"You promise to stay in the ranks and obey every command?"

"Yes."

"Nothing reckless?"

Arthur shook his head.

Merlin glanced to Natalenya, and she squeezed his hand. Turning back to Arthur, he took a deep breath before speaking. "You'll leave with the second muster, tomorrow."

"I thought there was only one. Dwin and Culann have permission and are getting their gear ready I just can't believe you finally said yes should I bring a shield a spear or a sword can we sleep in the stables tonight?"

Merlin didn't answer at first in his amazement to see Arthur so happy. The energy radiating from him reminded Merlin of what he'd felt in Uther when they'd discussed ways to overthrow the druids. The young man's dark chestnut hair was nearly shoulder length, like Uther's had been, and though Arthur didn't yet have the raw might of his father, it would come.

"Well?" Arthur's brown eyes fairly bulged at Merlin's delay.

"Yes, yes, and yes."

"But … spear or sword?"

"Both."

Arthur took a trencher, piled it with venison and bread, kissed Natalenya, and then ran off, the door banging behind him.

Taliesin stepped into the place where Arthur had stood. "Can I go too, Tas?" He had his sword out, and his brown traveling hat crookedly on his head.

Merlin pulled him close. "Not this time, but someday you'll join me. Though not as a warrior … as a bard. Have you practiced your harp today?"

Taliesin frowned. "But, Tas! I've even strapped my knife inside my breeches in case I'm caught."

"Practiced harp?"

The boy's body sagged. "Yes."

"And your Latin?"

"Um ..."

"Your rhyming?"

"Yes!" he said, nodding.

Natalenya put a hand on the boy's shoulder. "And he's been learning a new song we made named 'Tingada's Cloak' — haven't you?"

Taliesin nodded.

"Well," Merlin said. "I'll have to hear it before I go."

Merlin helped Natalenya clean up from the meal, but her silence made him feel awkward.

Finally, after he had buried the coals in the ashes for the night, she spoke.

"Merlin ..."

He looked at her, and a tear hung in the lash of her right eye.

"Are you sure Artorius is ready?"

"Yes, as sure as I can be. Caygek's drilled him expertly in the sword. Bedwir in the spear and shield. Peredur taught him horsemanship. Ector taught him battle tactics and how to lead. And I've passed on all the reasoning skills and knowledge that he might need from what Colvarth imparted to me."

"But is he *ready*?"

"I don't know."

Natalenya wiped the tear away and gave a light smirk. "Did he show you his latest trick?"

"Just before I came ... He's so reckless."

"I know."

Natalenya fell asleep that night with a hand draped down, resting on Tinga's curly head where she slept on a woolen mat beside her parents' bed — listening to the wonderfully soothing sound of Merlin's gentle breathing beside her, and beyond him on the floor, Taliesin's.

She dreamt then, of Merlin and her in a boat on Lake Derwentlin while the summer sun shone down. As she reached out to him the dream shifted to her hand and his bound together with crimson ribbon. Colvarth stood before them, blessing their marriage in the name of Jesu Christus. The sweet, earthy smell of eglantine and musk roses filled the air, and Merlin smiled at her nervously, but with a light in his eyes that warmed her soul.

And Arthur celebrated with them, only two winters old then, but standing proudly with his little cloak thrown over his shoulder.

The images shifted. Darkness covered the world, and a child's scream split the night air. Arthur!

Natalenya ran from her bedroom and through the dark great room, where the sound of her feet echoed upward to be muffled by the thatch roof. The crying drew her forward, pulling desperately at the deepest part of her. She heard a clicking sound, as though some taloned beast scuffled through the crennig.

She ran through the doorway of the stone wall to Arthur's room and rounded the corner to face his bedside, her arms already held out to pick up the sobbing boy. But he wasn't there.

Behind her, she perceived a scraping noise, and more clicking. She spun. Her bare foot hit some moisture, and in the pale moonlight she saw a trail of liquid drops making a path to the window. The iron bars Merlin had fitted had been cut and bent down. She knelt and touched the moisture with her finger. It was dark.

Blood. Arthur!

She screamed, startling herself awake, her chest thump-thump-thumping.

Merlin lay sleeping next to her, his handsome, scarred face barely visible in the darkness. She sat up and listened. The house was quiet. She reached down and felt Tinga's warm cheek, and the little girl muttered in her sleep.

Biting her lip, Natalenya studied the room carefully as her heart calmed down. But nothing was there. It had just been a horrible dream. Arthur was eighteen now, and sleeping in the stables tonight before the muster. There was nothing to worry about, so she lay back down and rolled over, resting her hand on Merlin's shoulder.

She dozed briefly while the dry wind blew outside and rustled the thatch. She awoke again with a start. She had heard something. A deeper noise had tickled her ear. On the other side of the house. Shuffling. Maybe Arthur had come back to get something. But she distinctly remembered Merlin barring the door.

She slipped from the bed, quietly stepping over Tinga. The stone floor felt cold to her feet, and her nightgown caressed her toes like ghostly fingers, sending shivers up her legs. Stepping into the great room, she listened, but there was nothing. Walking silently over to the shadowed door, she felt for the bar ... and found it'd been slid to the side, out of place. The door creaked loosely in its frame.

With trembling fingers, Natalenya pushed the bar into place. Listening again, she heard ... a slight noise coming from Arthur's bedroom. He must have come after all. Maybe Merlin knew he'd be back. She walked into his room.

"Artorius ... can I help — "

She froze. Someone stood next to Arthur's bed wearing a dark cloak and hood. Arthur didn't wear anything like that. But Merlin did. Had he and Arthur planned to leave early? Though that made little sense.

She took another step forward. "Merlin, this is no time — "

The man turned, and she saw a thin fringe of tartan on the edge of his hood — blue, green, and white. Merlin's cloak was entirely black.

She filled her lungs to scream for help, but fear strangled her throat and froze her limbs.

CHAPTER 4

THE HUNT

The man stepped closer to Natalenya and pulled a dark mask from his face. The moonlight illuminated his bearded chin and cracked, bleeding lips. But something was wrong with his face. Misshapen, but somehow familiar at the same time.

He opened his mouth wide and tried to speak.

She fell back a step. His teeth were sharp like that of a beast, and the tip of his tongue had been bitten off — its horrible, bloody stump writhing around in his mouth.

"Atha-Artha-AAATHA!" he kept calling, and with each sound his lips contorted until his mouth frothed in rage.

Natalenya sucked at the air until she found enough breath to scream.

The man looked down and began to reach inside his cloak.

He must be grabbing a knife! She screamed again, louder, and the man leapt at her with incredible speed, slammed his hand over her mouth, and pulled her tight to his chest.

Natalenya awoke. Someone held her head, and she screamed again, flailing her fists.

"Natalenya!" a voice called.

She reached at the sound, grabbed the man's hair, and pulled hard.

"Ow! Natalenya!" the man said. It was Merlin's voice.

Letting go, she began to cry. Merlin was holding her. She was safe.

"Are you well?"

"No ... no ... there was a man."

Sudden tension filled Merlin's voice. "A what?"

"A man. I thought he was you, I ..."

Merlin rose quickly and looked around. "There's no one here."

She sat up and saw she was on the floor in Arthur's bedroom. "He left, then. He got away."

"No one was here. I came right away."

"The door, check the door. I had to bar it. He must have fled through the door."

"Stay here while I—"

The wind blew hard outside, and the thatch shivered above her.

"No. Take me with you. Don't leave me."

"Fine."

Together they walked toward the door, with her holding Merlin's hand tightly.

"See ... it's still barred. Just as I left it before bed."

"Then he's still here!"

"Natalenya." Merlin reached out and stroked her cheek. She pulled away.

A cry came from their bedroom.

"Tinga!" Her heart began racing again. All the windows had bars in them. If the door was still locked, then the man was still here.

Merlin and Natalenya ran, arm in arm, only to find Tingada sitting up, pushing the brown hair from her eyes. Nothing else unusual. Taliesin rolled over.

Natalenya fell to her knees and grabbed Tinga up in a hug, breathing in the piney smell of her clothes.

"I's dreamed ov a big wolf. He tried ta bite me, but I didn' leth 'im."

Merlin furrowed Taliesin's hair. "Mommy had a bad dream too."

She glared at him. "I've heard your stories. What if it's your sister?"

"You said it was a man."

"That's not what I mean."

"We've lived in peace for sixteen years."

Despite his words, Natalenya saw a slight worry etched in the lines around his eyes.

"What if she's come back?" Natalenya grabbed the lamp next to their bed and frantically lit it with a live cinder from the coal box. Turning to Merlin, she handed it to him. "Search the house, please."

Merlin nodded, but she could tell he was humoring her.

As Natalenya waited with Tinga in the dark, a thought came to her, and she looked up. Taliesin often climbed amongst the network of timbers supporting the roof. Once he even climbed out the smoke-hole. Could the man be hiding up there?

When Merlin returned, having found nothing, she asked him to scale their bedroom wall and shine the light upward.

He squinted at her.

"Please."

So he climbed the rock wall separating their bedroom from the rest of the crennig and stood upon the top amongst the timbers. She passed up the lamp, and he wrapped his arm around one of the cross timbers so he could hold up the light until it illuminated the entire ceiling.

"Nothing," he called down.

She blinked.

Outside, and from far away, a wolf howled.

Natalenya looked at him then, and saw dread pass across his face, but then it was gone.

"Maybe you just heard something outside," he said.

"No."

"Once the battle with the Picti is over, we'll have to call for a wolf hunt. We can't allow them to come unchallenged to the valley, or else we'll end up with horses injured, maybe foals dead."

"The man was standing over Artorius's bed — "

Merlin sighed. "Even if you didn't dream it, Artorius is not in any danger. The main stables are better guarded than Ector's hall."

Natalenya shook her head. The dreams, the wolves. It was no coincidence. Something was wrong.

Merlin awoke to the luscious smell of steamed einkorn biscuits, fried cabbage and kale, along with the *pop-plop* sound of oatmeal boiling over the fire.

He rolled to face the center of the bed and found Taliesin sleeping next to him in Natalenya's place. His hair had been smashed against his sweaty head, and he was snoring lightly. Peeking over his son, he saw Tinga still curled up on her pallet, her wet thumb lying next to her half-open mouth. Merlin drank in the moment, a simple yet bounteous gift after many hard days on the trail to and from Urien's hall. What were titles and kings compared to his family? Nothing, nothing at all, and he thanked God for the miracle of life.

Rising from the straw mattress, he splashed water on his face from a basin, stretched, and pulled on his tunic. Walking into the living area, he found Natalenya stirring the oatmeal.

"Morning," he said, giving her a hug from behind and a tickle. This produced a giggle, a jab in the ribs, and a spoon-holding hug in return.

Merlin held her chin gently and looked into her eyes. "How are you?"

"Scared."

"I'm sorry I didn't believe you last night."

"It's not that. Not exactly." She turned away from him to take the pot off the fire. "You're leaving."

"You could stay with Aunt Eira."

"I'll think about it."

Taliesin stepped out of the bedroom, looked around blankly until he saw Merlin, and then ran to him. After a brief hug, the boy picked up a steaming biscuit from the pan and shifted from foot to foot while he blew on it.

"Go outside," Natalenya said.

"I don't have to."

"Leave the biscuit here and go to the outhouse."

Taliesin popped it between his teeth and ran outside.

Natalenya shook her head. "That boy."

"I think he's taller."

"He eats enough to be twice his height."

While Natalenya finished frying the cabbage, Merlin opened the large secret compartment hidden in the back of their pantry shelf and brought out his harp. At least the children would have fun hiding in there while he was gone. One time they even got Natalenya to hide with them, and then they'd all banged the slim door open and jumped out to surprise him.

He settled beside the hearth to tune the harp, and as he touched its aged wood — accented with painted knotwork, spirals, and ancient designs — he remembered Colvarth, the former chief bard of Britain. The man had given the harp to Merlin and had taught him everything he knew about being a bard. The instrument was, in fact, the Harp of Britain, a precious gift, and there was no other of its antiquity or beauty anywhere on the isle. One day, the Lord willing, when Arthur took his rightful place as High King — Merlin would stand by his side as the next chief bard.

He needed to visit Colvarth's grave again, soon. It was just that he rarely made it to the southern end of the valley and beyond to the mountain pass where the old bard was buried in a secret cave.

Tinga, in a just-woken daze, wandered from the bedroom into Natalenya's arms even as Taliesin came back in and sat next to Merlin.

"Are you going to bring the harp to battle?"

"Yes."

Tinga came and hugged Merlin, "But how can ya fight wid tha harp in yar handth?"

"A bard doesn't fight," Taliesin said as he spread some butter on his biscuit.

"But *you* like fightin', Tal."

"Sure I do, but a bard's gotta do what a bard's gotta do, even if it's not fun."

"Fighting isn't for fun," Merlin said. "We fight to save mothers, sons, sisters, and babies. To keep our homes from being burned down. To not be made — "

Natalenya cleared her throat, and Merlin caught her eye.

"Anyway, it's my job to compose a song that commemorates the battle and praises the valor of the men."

"So it won't be forgotten," Taliesin said, his mouth half full.

Merlin tweaked his nose. "You remembered!"

Tinga stuck her thumb into the oatmeal and tasted it. "But what if they 'tack ya? Can ya bonk 'em with tha harp?"

Merlin shook his head and smiled at her.

When the meal was ready, Merlin found his place at the hearth between Natalenya and Tingada, across from Taliesin, and once again celebrated his short time with them. When the dish of cabbage and kale was finished off, the biscuits buttered, dipped in honey, and eaten with the savory oatmeal, Merlin sat back and sighed.

Natalenya took his hand and kissed it. "Don't leave. Please."

"Artorius is going. I need to be there."

"I know. I just wish — "

He leaned over and hugged her. "No more words. I wish it too."

Merlin swung up onto his horse and had a stable hand pass him the leather-wrapped harp. Slinging it onto his back, he nodded to Peredur and they rode off to join the muster. Arthur, Culann, and Dwin had preceded them; their horses were missing from their stalls.

"It's a big day, this," Peredur said. "Sixteen years o' training, and soon we'll get to see 'im fight."

"If we can keep up with him," Merlin said, urging his horse northward across the valley to the large gathering of mounted men. Spotting his uncle's pennant waving in the wind, he weaved through the groups of warriors spread out over the green.

As Merlin approached, he admired Ector's highly polished scale armor. It covered him from chest to mid-thigh and was topped with a light-blue cloak thrown over his shoulder and a broad leather belt from which hung his great sword.

"Don't tell me you changed your mind," Ector said, adjusting his helm.

"About what?"

"Artorius. Who do you think?"

"He's here."

"Haven't seen him, and the scouts haven't either."

"He's here. His horse isn't in the stable."

"Check for yourself. There's still time while we wait for the tenders to bring the extra mounts from the far valley." Ector turned away to address one of his men.

Merlin looked to Peredur, who raised an eyebrow. They parted, going in opposite directions. As Merlin trotted amongst the men, he saw villagers he knew, hardy men who lived off the land and helped raise the horses — valiant men who were now sallying forth to danger and battle in support of their chieftain and king.

But no Arthur.

Merlin rode his horse into the center, where the men were pressed tightest.

"Has anyone seen Artorius?" he asked, but was met with thoughtful stares and shaking heads.

Peredur met him on the other side and shook his head as well.

Merlin began to truly worry.

"Where could they have gone?"

Peredur bit his lip. "Let's talk wi' the stable hands."

And so back they went to the massive stone-and-thatch structure that was the main stable for the valley, situated next to his uncle's feasting hall. The place was almost deserted, with only a few brood-mares eating hay at the far end.

"Anyone here?" Merlin called.

A tired-looking boy popped out from a stall with an oaken shovel. "Me's here, Lord Ambrosius."

"Have you seen Artorius anywhere? He—"

"Not seen 'im here at all, an' I been gettin' the horses saddled since 'afore sunup."

"Not at all?"

"Nah, nah, but tha' knows his horse, Casva? He was gone early, along with twa others. I remember because it made less work fer mah. That horse is a bit too high-spirited, I say, and makes the work o' a mucker that muckle harder."

"But when did they leave?"

"A lang time ago, as tha' already knows."

Peredur backed his horse out the door. "Could they have decided to get a head start?"

"Why?"

"I dunno. Wait, what's this—" Peredur reached down and ripped a parchment off of the timber that supported the doorway. After reading for a moment, he handed it to Merlin.

Merlin took it, and as he read the words, his hands began to shake.

It was the parchment from that flouncing louse of an envoy. The man who wanted everyone to muster at Glevum in support of Vortigern and southern Britain's defense against the Saxenow invasion.

Peredur edged his horse up to Merlin's. "Do ya think?"

"I'm certain."

"No—!"

"Artorius was confused when he asked if he could go. He thought there was only one muster, and now I know why. The boys must have left early for the adventure of getting ahead, and now they have half a day's head start."

"He's headed south?"

"Yes. Right to Vortigern, the man who killed his father."

After talking with old Brice to verify that the boys hadn't gone north through his gate, Merlin and Peredur went to Ector to tell him of their suspicion.

"I'll be bedraggled," Ector said, his voice rising in anger. "I should have thrown that envoy on the dung heap after all and burnt every last parchment!"

"May Peredur and I ... May we have leave to search for Artorius?"

"What? Not accompany me to battle?"

"That is correct, my lord. Artorius will join Vortigern in the south unless we—"

The chieftain looked annoyed. "Well—well ... I suppose. But bring him back as soon as you can. We need to make a man out of that boy."

Peredur rode off to talk to his wife and Merlin rode hard to tell Natalenya.

Entering their home, he found her scrubbing the oatmeal pot.

"Merlin!" But her joy faded when she saw the graveness of his face. She set the wet rag down. "What's wrong?"

"Artorius ... he's gone south."

"South? But the Picti are—"

"Read this."

Natalenya took the parchment and scanned its contents. "You really think he—"

Merlin nodded. "Yes, the foolhardy boy has gone the wrong way, and I need to catch him before Vortigern does."

"But he won't be recognized. Vortigern doesn't know him."

"He looks a lot like his father. If Vortigern even suspects ..."

"How long will you be gone?"

"I have no idea. They're on good horses, and unless we pick up their exact trail, we might not find him until he gets to Glevum."

"That's almost all the way to Kernow." Natalenya paused, then a new light came into her eyes. "Can we come along? The children and I? Please ... I'd do nearly anything to see my mother."

"We'll be riding hard, and the trail could be dangerous. Are you worried about your mother? Now that she's an abbess you have nothing to fear for her anymore. Your father—"

"We could sail, and even bring the horses. What if we sailed? Aunt Eira hired a boat last summer and went all the way to Penfro."

"I won't find Artorius that way ... at least not until too late." Natalenya sighed.

"I'd better go. We're taking the mountain pass."

"Wait, then," she said, tears in her eyes. A knife lay on the hearth, and she picked it up. Gripping the ragged edge of her skirt, Natalenya cut off a small square.

"What're you doing?"

"Take this," she said, handing him the cloth. "Whenever you hold it, know that we'll be praying for you. Promise me you'll keep it with you always."

"I promise."

"And I'll ... I'll wear this skirt until you come back safely, and whenever I see the missing edge, I'll think of you and pray."

Peredur called and banged on the door.

Merlin kissed a tear on Natalenya's cheek, hugged his little family, and left.

Darkness came that evening like the shadow of a hawk—swooping down over the high mountains until its black claws caught Natalenya by surprise. One moment she was sewing her skirt's wounded edge at the window and the next thing she knew, it was too dark to see.

Taliesin looked up from where he was practicing his small harp and Tinga paused at her own sewing project. The hearth fire had fallen to embers, so Natalenya shoveled them together and threw on a log to keep the night chill away. Then, lighting a rush lamp, she set it on the hearth between them and continued to sew.

Needle in. Needle out. Thread taut. Again and again. Needle in. Needle out. Thread taut. Little stitches, each one representing another day until she could see her love again. Each stitch representing another tear held back. Each stitch —

"Ouch!"

A drop of blood fell from her thumb and stained her skirt.

Tinga threw her needle to swinging and picked at a knot. "Mammu, did the badgers stab ya?"

"No, the *bad guys* didn't stab me. I'll be quite all right." As she sucked on the wound, Taliesin set his harp down.

"Pick it up again, Tal. You're not finished yet."

"Listen."

Natalenya fell silent for a moment. "There's nothing — "

"A horse ... a horse is screaming!"

In the far distance, a horse neighed wildly.

"Nothing to worry about. If it's a wolf, the horse tenders will get it."

"What if ith not?" Tinga said, pulling her dolly closer to her side.

"Tell me, what else could it be? Let's go through the rhyme of creatures your father taught us — "

But another horse neighed in terror, this one in the field adjoining their house.

Natalenya pulled Tinga down until she knelt, motioned for Taliesin to get down, and slid along the wall next to the barred window. In spite of the iron bars, the presence of danger so close made her heart thud in her ears. With her back to the cold stones, she turned her head and peeked out the corner of the window. It took a moment for her eyes to adjust, but she saw dark shapes slipping toward their house while ignoring the horses, which galloped into the far reaches of the field.

Taliesin had found his sword and was biting his lip while he tested it. "Are they wolves?"

She motioned for him to blow out the lamp and reached for Tinga's hand, only to find the girl gone. Her sewing had been thrown into a heap and the ball of yarn had rolled away. Panic rose in Natalenya's throat until she spotted a small hand motioning from the secret door that Merlin had built behind their pantry shelf to protect the Harp of Britain.

Natalenya crawled across the floor to Tinga. "What are you doing?"

"Come in, pleathe!"

"The wolves can't get in — "

Footsteps could be heard outside the door. Scraping. Sniffing.

Taliesin blew out the lamp and then stepped boldly to the door, his sword ready.

"Mammu!" Tinga whispered.

She looked to the door, which she had barred. Thank God. They were safe.

Then someone knocked loudly on it. Like a person.

Taliesin jumped.

"Open up!" called a gravelly voice.

Natalenya crouched down, slipped into the secret compartment, and stood next to Tinga. It was so tight that Natalenya's nose was smashed against the wood that made up the back of the shelving. This was silly. It was probably one of the horse tenders who had come to scare the wolves —

Then the person slammed against the door, hard, and the wood groaned.

Taliesin came running, popped into the hiding place, and closed the slim door.

"Mammu," Taliesin whispered, "your skirt!"

She tried to look down, but there was no room to turn her head. Tugging the cloth, she found that her skirt had gotten stuck in the door. Taliesin opened it a slight crack, she yanked the precious fabric in, and he closed the door once more.

Another blow hit the crennig door, and the wood cracked.

Another, and another, and then there was a horrific crash as the wood exploded inward.

Tinga opened her mouth to scream, but Natalenya covered her mouth as a warning just in time. The sound of many feet clomped through the crennig as the intruders ransacked the place, shattering clay dishes, ripping up their straw mattresses, dumping barrels of food, and smashing things against the stone walls.

Then one of them began sniffing at the shelving.

Tinga muffled her mouth into Natalenya's skirt, her hands shaking.

The sniffing came close to the door, and Taliesin tensed his blade. Natalenya's heart began to drum painfully in her ears, and she was afraid the sound could be heard outside their hiding place.

Whoever it was — or whatever — it began to growl, low and menacing, and then their hiding place began to shake.

Natalenya closed her eyes and fought to keep her body still and her breathing even. Just a little longer —

A high and nasally voice spoke. "Lookit! Lotsa meat hangin'!"

The one sniffing at their secret door barked and jumped away.

Natalenya let out a breath.

"I gots it!" the nasally one said. "Give it!"

A scuffle ensued with yelling, barking, and yelping. One of them was thrown back into the shelf, and their hiding place shook violently as the pottery on the shelves shattered and fell.

"Stop et!" came the gravelly voice. "Stop et! We be lookin' fer Arth-Arth-Arthur! Nuthin' else, hear?"

"But there's meat," the nasally voice said, "and we g-gots the rowr-wrong house, huh-huh?"

"He's been here-ah, she tol' me so. She's n-nevar wrong. Ar-Arth-Arthur's wanted."

"So, watta now, huh-hu-hah?"

"Nowa the real hu-hunt begins. Getta rawr-ready to run!"

65

It took Natalenya a long, long time after the strange intruders had gone to allow Taliesin to open the door a crack. The cool, dark air felt good and she breathed deeply of it, listening carefully for any sound. Who had invaded their home? Men with wolves on leashes? She couldn't make sense of what she had heard.

But everything was silent, and after awhile, she had them step out.

The house was a disaster, with everything ruined, including her favorite kneading bowl, broken into five shards right at her feet. She tried to piece them back together, but it was useless, and she let them drop into the rubble. Some of the smoked meat was missing from where it had hung near the hearth.

How she had thanked God for that smoked meat.

Taliesin ran forward. "My harp!" It had been knocked off the bench, and was marred in one corner.

"Mammu," Tingada cried out, "ma doll ith broken!" It had been ripped open and the buckwheat hulls spilled on the hearth.

Natalenya stepped over and squatted before her, wiping the tears from her daughter's cheeks. "We can't stay here tonight. We have to get to Aunt Eira's house. Can you run?"

They nodded.

"Taliesin, you be our lookout ..."

The boy nodded, a grim look on his face.

"Let's go."

CHAPTER 5

THE TOMB

ow difficult can it be?" Merlin asked as he and Peredur scanned the mountainside, trying to discover Colvarth's hidden tomb. "And I was the one who found the cave originally."

"You know, if we hafta sleep along the trail, I don't mind. I'd rather not sleep in a tomb, really."

"There's nowhere safer."

"Or drier, considering all the rain we've been getting," Peredur mocked as he kicked the dead grass next to his horse.

"Night's coming, and I'd rather not — "

"You'd rather not be attacked by wolves, I know."

"It's not funny ..."

"Yer probably right. Though it seems a bit unlikely they'd be stalkin' us, if ya ask me."

Merlin swallowed. "I'm not asking, so keep looking."

Peredur pointed behind Merlin on the opposite side. "Heyo, what about that?"

"Not on that side … it's over here."

"Nah, really, there's even a faint path."

Merlin pushed his lips to the side, considering. "The rock, or the … huh, maybe that *is* it." Running forward, he found a different angle to view the outcropping and thought it possible. "Let's try," he said. Coming back, he took hold of his horse's reins and led the way up the path.

Twice the path switched back as it climbed the mountain, and then passed behind the outcropping, where the cave appeared, almost out of nowhere.

Merlin let out a sigh of relief. It was even large enough to bring the horses inside.

They made camp for the night on the dirt floor near the entrance, which was broad enough to let light in but narrow enough to defend against intruders.

"I can't believe," Merlin said, "that it's been four years since I've been here."

"You've had a family to take care o' — and a High King to raise."

"I should've taken the time," he muttered as he lit a torch from his pack using Peredur's coal box. The light revealed the pitted interior of the cave, which was made of the same brown rock that had formed the mountains. The depth of the cave was unknown to Merlin — he had explored only a portion of it.

He walked to the first bend in the passageway and knelt at the cairn of rocks piled over Colvarth's grave.

Peredur knelt nearby. "How long has it been since he died?"

"Six … no … almost seven years, I think. It was right after Tinga was born."

"I was always a bit envious he spent all that time training ya to be a bard. I could listen to his stories all day. How'd he pick ya?"

"High King Uther knew my father, and …" The memories came flooding back of his father's death at the hands of Mórganthu, the arch druid. Merlin swallowed before continuing. "… He gave me to Uther as a servant. I was half-blind at the time, and thought I'd be shoveling dung or some menial task that didn't require sight, but Colvarth prophesied over me. I can still remember his words like he'd just said them this morning:

Nay, son born of the wild-water . . .
you are not fit for such tasks!
You shall be a bard!
Wisdom shall grace your speech
and angels dance upon your harp.
Though now you see not, Merlin,
yet in the darkness
you shall light the path of Jesu
for all the kings of the world.
And though humble,
yet in God's strength
you shall uphold your people!"

Merlin had to wipe away a few tears as he reached the end. He'd done so little in all the years since that prophecy — little more than hide in their valley raising warhorses and trying to make the kingdom of Rheged strong enough to hold back Necton and his Pictish war bands. But this attempt to stop the slavery that plagued Britain had failed. Rheged, like always, was too easily satisfied in her own strength and turned an indifferent eye when the Picti slipped through to the weaker southern tribes, pillaging and taking slaves. As long as it wasn't Rheged slaves, that was all that mattered, it seemed.

And now, when Merlin had finally persuaded that slothful King Urien to take action against the Picti, he was prevented from assisting and had to run the other direction like a hound after three rabbits.

Peredur put his hand on Merlin's shoulder. "So he chose ya . . ."

"Yes, he chose me, but it's a mystery why. I've done nothing to deserve it."

"That's not true. You saved all o' us from slavery, and you saved

Arthur from King Atle's clutches. There is hope for Britain because o' you, if only — "

"If only I were brave enough to let Arthur go."

"That's not what I meant. All we can do, all we've ever been able to do, is to prepare him."

"For what? He doesn't even know he's Uther's son. He doesn't even know that he's the heir to the throne. All of Britain thinks him a slave or dead, and it's been so long that I doubt Britain would accept him as their High King. Every year we held back the truth has just made it harder. He'll hate me for it."

Peredur shook his head. "No. Don't doubt yourself. You had to keep it a secret or Vortigern would've — "

"Vortigern. The very man Arthur's gone to serve. The man who slew Arthur's entire family. If that man doesn't drown in his own vomit someday, I'd like to …"

"Every one of 'em died? That's awful."

"Natalenya's mother, Trevenna, sent word that Vortigern had gone to Bosventor and slain Arthur's sisters in cold blood. That's when she fled to the new abbey at Dinas Camlin. So now it's all a mess. Ector is fighting in the north without us and Arthur's heading south in ignorance."

Merlin gave a self-mocking laugh. "To be truthful, when we came to the cave just now, I'd hoped to find Colvarth alive. Sitting here eating fish over a campfire, like Jesu did in Scripture. Didn't you smell the lingering smoke when we came in?"

Peredur sat back, a startled look on his face. "Sure I did, but Colvarth alive? How — "

"I know it sounds crazy, but I prayed that God had raised him from the dead. When we buried Colvarth here, I hid the Sangraal nearby, wanting God to use it to raise Colvarth. God brought Arthur back to life, didn't he? Why not Colvarth?"

Here Merlin lifted his voice in frustration, and the sound echoed through the depths of the cave, *"Why not? I'm so lost … so lost without him."*

"You mean afraid."

"No, I'm —"

Peredur cut him off. "Yes, ya are. I've seen it. You're not scared tah ask your uncle, or even Urien, to fight the Picti, but when it comes to you yourself doing something about Vortigern, you freeze all up. Arthur needs to realize he's the true High King. And that means ya can't go on hiding in this safe little valley. Ya have to confront Vortigern."

Merlin stared at the other man in shock. Was this the taciturn horse master he knew? Shaking off his surprise, he said, "It'll take years of planning. Preparing an army alone will —"

"Are ya sure?"

"I said *no!* The timing isn't right." Merlin stood and began pacing with the torch.

Peredur shut his mouth and looked on in concern.

A sudden urge came over Merlin to see the Sangraal once more — the very cup that the Christ had used at the Last Supper, the very cup that caught his blood when Jesu was nailed to the cross. Merlin had hidden it just a little way down the passage. Who knew? Maybe now was the time when God would raise Colvarth.

"Come along," he said. "I want to see the cup."

Peredur got a distant look in his eyes, but made no move to follow.

"Are you coming?"

"I still remember when I first saw it."

"On Atle's mountain?"

"Yeah. That unforgettable day I saw heaven itself open. Colvarth had spoken o' the Sangraal before, but I didn't comprehend. Can I really see it again?"

"Yes."

Peredur momentarily covered his eyes with his hand. "Thank you."

Walking deeper into the cave, Merlin slipped on some loose gravel. Somewhere on the left wall there was a natural pit that he'd filled in with rocks to hide the Sangraal ... but something was odd.

71

Charcoal had been scratched onto the walls in seemingly random patterns. Merlin turned toward the depths of the cavern, and the sputtering light illuminated the floor ahead —

Someone *had* been here.

An old campfire lay before him. How long ago? The smell of wood smoke was extremely strong here, the oily torch notwithstanding. He unsheathed his sword and dug the tip into the charred remains and ashes. A small, glowing coal emerged from the depths, and Merlin gasped.

"What is it?"

"This fire was lit just last night. See? The ashes are still warm."

"That's strange."

"Is there anyone who would've taken this road from Dinas Crag? Think!"

"Only Arthur, Dwin, and Culann."

"But they left this morning. Who, then?"

Peredur shook his head. "None else, with Ector's rules about keeping our escape route secret except in times o' war. Anyone would have had to get permission, and there just wasn't time for someone to do that. Or else — "

"Or else someone was on their way *to* the valley. Maybe spying."

"Could it have been the envoy?"

"No. Brice told me he let the man out yesterday, and he was cursing as he headed north to Urien."

Peredur bent to examine the wall above the old pit. "Merlin ... lift your torch higher."

"What?"

"I want to see ..."

Merlin raised the light, and what he had thought were random, unconnected charcoal scratches on the walls were revealed to be, when taken together, a monstrous creature — a dragon. Merlin's gaze followed the shape from its sharp teeth and horns down to its elongated, muscular tail, which was poised directly over ... the hiding place for the Sangraal.

He handed the torch to Peredur and began pulling the rocks from the hole. When he had taken the last one out, he motioned for Peredur to hold the light up. From deep inside gleamed the ornamental gold box that Colvarth had commissioned to house the Sangraal.

Praises! It was still there!

Reaching in, he pulled the box to the edge of the hole.

Peredur looked over Merlin's shoulder.

From inside his tunic, Merlin produced a bronze key hanging from a leather necklace. Inserting the key, he pushed it upward and then slid it to the left.

Click!

Merlin lifted the lid.

The box was empty. The wooden bowl was gone.

Running his fingers frantically around the inside, Merlin groaned in frustration. But what if he were the only one who couldn't see it? The Sangraal had perplexed him before, with only some able to view and touch its ancient wood. "C-can you see it?" he asked, hoping beyond hope.

Peredur shook his head, his shoulders slumping. "No one could've stolen it without the key ... and why would a common thief take the Sangraal and leave the expensive box? That's passin' strange."

Merlin picked up the box. Anger rose in him at his own stupidity. Why had he left it here? "It's gone," he yelled. "It's stolen!"

But then an odd feeling came over him. His hands ... he couldn't feel them, nor the box. His arms began to shake as the numbness crept past his elbows and inched up toward his shoulders. Soon it held him across the chest like a death grip, and the sensation climbed up his neck, as if he were sinking into a cold lake, deep in the depths of the earth. His sight began to fail. Peredur seemed to tilt, and then the torch faded from view.

Merlin awoke on his back, with a black thorn bush growing beside him. To his left lay the carcass of a deer, its head missing and flies buzzing madly at an open wound in its chest. Far above him he heard the clap of thunder, and a violent wind began to blow through the dark foliage of the distant trees. Merlin sat up and found he was barefoot. He didn't recognize the place — or the large mound that lay in front of him, round like the shell of a massive turtle, a dark tunnel gaping where the head of the reptile would have hidden.

"Stand, intruder," a voice said from behind. Three men jumped forward and leveled their bronze-tipped spears at him. And these men were strong, with sinewy, bulging arms, massive chests, and legs as thick as Merlin's torso.

"Get up!" said the man to his left, and then he poked Merlin below the shoulder.

The wound throbbed in pain, and Merlin scrambled up, fearing another jab. Each of these men towered over him by a foot.

"Now march. We need to find out what Grannos the Mighty will do with a trespasser like you." The men pointed toward the mound and its maw.

Merlin began to march, taking stock of the fact that his dirk was hanging from his belt. It took a long time to reach the mound, it being larger than he'd realized and almost half a league away. There they bade him stop next to the dark opening. Merlin blanched — it wasn't a tunnel for anyone his size. Even the men with spears were dwarfed by the colossal pillars supporting the roof.

The men began cheering, "Grannos the Grand! Grannos the Powerful! Grannos the Mighty!" And from deep within the dark tunnel sounded the grinding and scraping of metal as if a massive door were being opened.

Then came the sound of steps, one heavy footfall after another. *Death, ruin . . . Death, ruin* they boomed, and Merlin quaked.

CHAPTER 6

GRANNOS THE MIGHTY

G rannos! Grannos!" the men shouted, stamping their feet so that rocks fell and the ground shook.

He turned his gaze around and was stunned to see hundreds more of the warriors, spears in hand. Merlin's dirk was useless. Thick smoke began to pour from the tunnel, rotten sulfur that was bitter on Merlin's tongue.

"*Grannos! Grannos!*" the men sang, delirious at the mighty man's coming.

The boom of the steps drew nearer, until ... until a little hand poked out of the smoke at about the height of Merlin's knee.

A man stepped forth, coughing. A little man.

"Grannos!" the warriors yelled, bowing down.

He wore black breeches and a white tunic under a tiny orange woolen vest. Upon his long yellow hair he wore a bright blue pointed cap with a feather. His face was thin, with a pinched-up nose, and the strangest thing of all was that his teeth were green, with a little black tongue that slipped in and out of his mouth as he spoke.

"Bring the interloper to me," he squeaked.

Two warriors grabbed Merlin's arms and twisted them behind his back. They dragged him forward and shoved him to his knees.

Merlin wanted to look up at Grannos — but instead had to look down, for the man was *that* short.

"So …" Grannos said, "how are you feeling?"

Merlin tilted his head to the side and raised an eyebrow. "What?"

"How are you feeling lately? Have any sniffles? Are your elbows giving you trouble?"

"No … no, I'm, uh, fine."

Grannos pulled out a rolled-up parchment from inside his vest and shook it out. The thing was yellowed with age and filled from top to bottom with little squiggles. "Aha," he said, "perhaps you have wooden tongue?"

Merlin shook his head.

"Gray, painful toes? A big black mole on your left knee? Gassy billows? Cracky-wack-a-back?"

"No, no, no, no … and … no."

Grannos licked his lips with his little black tongue. "That's one answer too many. Let's proceed without insubordination. So … do you have a crankled ankle?"

"No, but my shoulder —"

"That's not on my list, and I'm very sad, because I would so much like to heal you. Thankfully, all of these other things can be arranged."

Merlin was confused. "What did you say?"

"First off, we must have privacy. I simply cannot work with all these eyeballs and ruckuses." His little voice went shrill as he said, "Go away, you!" He waved his hands at the warriors, and in three heartbeats they faded away, freeing Merlin from their grip.

Merlin and Grannos were alone.

Suddenly, Merlin's dirk seemed more useful. If only —

"Now, which of these illnesses would you like?" He showed the list to Merlin, who couldn't read the writing.

"Ah ... nothing." Merlin stretched his arms and ended with his fingers near his belt and the handle of his dirk.

"I think I'll give you ... a wonderful case of blabby-nose." Grannos stepped back and pretended to shoot an arrow at Merlin. But a real arrow, hardly bigger than a twig, appeared from the air and jabbed into Merlin's cheek.

"Ow!" he yelled, but even as he tried to pull it out, the arrow melted away. His face began to feel strange, almost heavy. Before he knew it, his nose had grown so large that it hung down over his lips and pressed against them.

"Thstop that!" Merlin said, grabbing for his dirk.

But Grannos had already nocked another invisible arrow and shot it. "And here's some flibbity-fingers, just for your defiance!"

The arrow appeared from nowhere and sank into his wrist.

"Oucth!" Merlin said as the arrow faded away. But Merlin's fingers began to hurt as the knuckle bones of both hands twisted grotesquely and began to wrap around each other. The pain was intense and the muscles in Merlin's arms began to seize up. He became enraged at Grannos, and the nostrils of his flabby nose began to twitch. He tried to grab the dirk, but his fingers couldn't grip it, so he stood, ran forward, and kicked at the little imp.

Grannos slipped sideways and Merlin missed.

He aimed again, and the slippery creature jumped, causing Merlin to slam his bare toes into the rock pillar holding up the tunnel. He fell to the scrubby grass and writhed in pain.

"Aha!" Grannos said, "now you have gray, painful toes!"

The devilish man appeared above him, smiling and licking his green teeth. "But we must have one more, so ... Grungy-gut for you! And then, I truly believe, you'll be ready." He shot another arrow, and its painful tip stabbed into Merlin's stomach. Merlin's black tunic powdered and coagulated into wet, moldy dirt. Then mushrooms began to sprout from his abdomen, and their roots sank into his flesh, turning it a sickly purple. Veins popped out to feed the white and speckled, bulbous mushrooms.

Merlin screamed.

"Now," Grannos whispered in his ear, "to make you hale I will require you to undertake a few simple tasks for me. First, you shall climb to the top of the Tán Menéth Marrow and delve downward through fire and rock until you find enough silver to mint a thousand and one coins."

"I can'th —"

"Next you must bathe the coins in the Cauldron of Ceridwen after you destroy the monster who guards its pearl-rimmed sides."

Merlin groaned.

"And then you must drag the coins to Loch Obha and put all its many waters back into the well from which they flowed. Finally, you must throw the coins in. And then, and only then, will I heal you."

Merlin shook his head, flapping his nose. "I won'th do ith, you beasth!"

"You cannot be a hero without being hale. This is the hill of heroes, you know! Make a vow to fulfill the quests, I say . . . and then fulfill your vow!"

Merlin climbed stiffly to his feet and ran. He had to get away from the little monster.

"O my queen!" the imp called, "I need you to kill the interloper! He is not fit for my hall!"

Instantly a giant gray wolf appeared — with a woman astride its back. Covered from boot to shoulder with black armor, even her face was hidden by an iron helm with two yellowed horns protruding from the sides. In her hands she held a black spear as long as a weaver's rod.

Merlin ran faster, but she was right behind, with her wolf barking and howling.

Grannos's squeaky voice called from behind, "Destroy him!"

Merlin ran, but didn't get far before the woman struck him across the head with the haft of her spear, knocking him to the ground, dizzy. Her wolf sniffed at his torso, and its sharp jaws twitched in anticipation.

There was no escape.

Merlin looked up just as she removed her helm and released her long, luxuriously black hair. She was his sister! Though older, he would recognize her face anywhere.

"Why do you hunt me? I've done you no wrong, Ganieda."

At the sound of her childhood name, she hefted her spear and threw it. "I am Mórgana, now, and you will never forget it, *dear brother!*"

The spear struck and its deadly point gored him through. Merlin shouted and jerked, unable to move away from the torturous pain.

Grannos appeared, then, and sneered at Merlin with wild eyes. "Now you *really* need healing! Hah!"

But a bright light shone down from above as time itself held its breath. An angel appeared within the light and descended. His robes gleamed with a holy brightness. The angel knelt down, compassion on his face, and whispered in Merlin's ear.

"Merlin! The Lord God has sent this vision so that you may know that your time of peace has ended. The Lord has protected you for many years from your sister, but now you must face her, for she has sworn to destroy you."

The pain was so intense that Merlin could hardly take a breath. "I'm not ready ..."

The light of the angel's face brightened. "You never will be, Merlin. But take courage. Your God is with you!"

Grannos, Mórgana, and the spear faded, along with the pain. Merlin floated upon a sea of songs, dark laments, and lapping dirges. Ages passed, it seemed, and finally he was washed back up to feeling and warmth.

Peredur's face appeared above him, and firelight flickered on the rock ceiling. The smell of bean and wild carrot soup filled the air.

"Where am I?" Merlin asked. His lips felt dry and his tongue swollen.

"We're here, still, in the cave o' Colvarth. Are ya well?"

Merlin sat up and took a sip from his waterskin. "No ..."

"Is it your shoulder? You fell, and I tried to catch you, but — "

"The war's begun."

Peredur sat still for a moment, then filled a wooden mug with soup and offered it to Merlin. "There's always been war. Saxenow, Picti ... even the Scoti."

Merlin wanted to take the soup, but he began to shake as if the room had suddenly grown chill. "Not those. The war between my half sister, Ganieda, and me. She was the one who told the Picti to make us slaves, and it was she who fought against me at Atle's temple as well."

"That was long ago. You've mentioned her name before, but I didn't realize — "

"I had a vision, she told me her name is now Mórgana ... 'Gana the Great.' She's the granddaughter of the arch druid, Mórganthu, and if that man is still alive, I know he's helping her too."

"So? Yer sister and an old man." He offerred the mug of soup once more, and Merlin accepted it with trembling hands.

"She has power. Dangerous power. And what can I do?"

"Fight."

Merlin shook his head. "It's not that simple. Do you remember when Natalenya was sick?"

"You mean when we were slaves? When she had the boils?"

Merlin closed his eyes and nodded. "Mórgana did that. And now God has removed his protection from us, whether all of it, or some of it, I don't know. But Natalenya may be in danger again."

Setting his own mug down, Peredur said, "You can't go back. Arthur needs you, Merlin."

"I have to warn her, at least. There's Taliesin and Tinga to think about too."

"But what about Arthur?"

Merlin tasted some of the soup with a wooden spoon. The beans weren't cooked all the way through, but the carrots were very good, and the warmth helped stem the shaking. "Everyone keeps telling me he's ready. Maybe Arthur's supposed to go on alone."

"You can't mean that. He doesn't even know he's Uther's son."

"Does it matter? God can —"

Peredur gripped Merlin's arm. "I can't believe ya'd say such a thing. Yes, God can, but God has given the task of advisin' Arthur to you. Colvarth chose *you*, Merlin, to guide the next High King. I heard the old bard say it with me own ears."

"I know what I need to do, and I don't need you telling me."

Merlin banged his mug down on a rock near the fire, stood stiffly, and walked to the cave entrance. He took some deep breaths of the fresh night air. "It's just that I'm afraid."

"Do I need to hit ya over the head? I don't care how scared ya are, the task is yours."

Merlin didn't answer. He had always secretly hoped that, somehow, he only need raise Arthur and the rest would take care of itself. That he could continue to live out his days with Natalenya and the children in their safe valley. That the evil specter of Ganieda ... Mórgana ... was nothing more than a bad dream. He had helped to defend the north with the goal of ending the slave-taking by the Picti. Why was more required of him than that?

"Step forth, Merlin!" came a voice from behind him that held within it an authority that surprised Merlin. "And don't be afraid, for your God is with you."

Merlin spun, his heart beating. Peredur stood over the bubbling soup, his spoon forgotten in his hand. Had Peredur said those words? Surely not, but then Merlin noticed a light in the man's eyes that hadn't been there before.

"I've seen the Sangraal meself, you know, and I saw what God did through ya on Atle's mountaintop. You have to dredge up the memories from that sea of fear."

"It's not that simple."

"Yes it is. Repent ... an' believe the good news! Do ya remember last week's Scripture that Brother Loyt encouraged us to memorize?"

In every battle that thou sufferest,
thou art a mighty victor
through Jesu Christus who loves thee.
For God hath persuaded me that
neither the slain, nor the living,
neither angels, nor demons,
neither what happens now,
nor all thy dreaded futures,
neither impassable mountains,
nor the deepest, blackest valleys,
and surely nothing else created
can sever thee from the love of God
in Jesu Christus our Lord.

Merlin turned and took another long, deep breath. Outside the cave there were countless winking stars blanketing the heavens, the lights that God had made — but it wasn't enough to take his fear away. He knew deep down that he had to choose the course that meant the most danger for himself and the most risk for Natalenya and the children — and that was the problem.

The next morning, Merlin mounted his horse and followed Peredur out of pure submission to the task set before him. Every part of him yearned to return home to protect his family, but Peredur was right: Arthur was out there, unaware of his calling, oblivious to his danger, and in need of guidance. Could Merlin — chosen to advise and raise the true king — abandon him to Mórgana? Natalenya would be fine, he assured himself, and he gave her and the children into God's hands.

The valley trail led them on and upward into the mountains: gray, ever drier, and full of stones. After some time, the valley ended and they rode to the top of a ridgeline, where the path divided. The southward route took a gentle slope to the dry brown and hilly land beyond, while the eastward route was a rough descent toward a small, abandoned village. Broken crennigs and sunken, rotting roofs stared up at them from the valley below.

Peredur started on the southward path, but Merlin called to him.

"Arthur would take this way." Merlin pointed down the more dangerous path that led them eastward.

Peredur raised an eyebrow, slipped from his horse, and led the way down the track. "You're right. Arthur would never take the easy way."

Merlin dismounted as well and followed. "He probably rode down this mountain at top speed."

"And risked breaking his horse's leg *and* his own neck?"

They both nodded at the same time.

It took more than an hour to pick their way down. Once they got to the bottom, Peredur found the tracks they were looking for: three horses all headed southward through the hills.

"How long ago?" Merlin asked as he pulled himself up into his saddle.

"Hard to tell. The ground's too dry. I hope the drought ends soon."

They followed the trail, occasionally resting their horses. When early evening came, they decided to take an extended stop in the slanted shade of an oak, whose roots supped at the dismal remains of a pond.

After dismounting, Peredur inspected the trail markings once more. "Merlin," he called, "there's a fourth track mixed in. Boot prints."

"Well, someone was walking their horse. That's natural."

"Sure, except this person doesn't walk like you or me. Here's an example — he mostly runs on the balls of his feet. There's only one heel mark among the prints."

"Hmm — "

"And look at his stride ... each footprint is six feet from the other, sometimes more."

Merlin rubbed his chin. "Now that's odd. I mean, I could jump that far ..."

"But run like that?"

"No. Do you think he's running with them, or chasing them?"

Peredur followed the tracks backward. "Well, it appears he rested over in the shade, behind those bushes, while Arthur an' the others didn't stop." Pushing through the cracking, dry branches, he suddenly stopped and turned and stared at Merlin. The man's face had gone completely white. Backing up, he closed his eyes and fell to one knee, looking sick.

"What is it?" Merlin asked, running over and pushing through the bushes.

What he saw made him fear for Arthur, Culann, and Dwin. The remains of a huge deer lay there, bloody and broken, and with the guts ripped out and eaten.

Mórgana held up the purple-flamed orb with the moving image of Merlin and Peredur — and laughed to see such fun. Merlin the timid, that's what he was.

"Mórdred?" she called. "Present yourself before me."

The lad stepped forward from where he stood next to his illustrious great-grandfather. His hair was the color of raven's wings — all except for one white lock that hung down the left side. At his throat rested a silver torc tipped with the heads of foxes, containing eyes made from amber.

"Do *you* mind the sight of blood?" she asked, squinting at him.

He stared at her with his steel-gray eyes and didn't answer.

"Do you defy me?"

In answer, he raised his forearm, brought a knife to it, and sliced into the skin until it bled.

"I thought not," she said, pleased. "You will soon be a man, my son, and your fearlessness will make you worth much to the Voice. Merlin, however, is not only worthless, he is ignorant of what is coming."

Mórganthu nudged closer to get a better look into the orb. "Tell me ... tell me again, my daughter's daughter, why we can see Merlin in the orb again — after all these years when we could not?"

She smiled at him — so old and so simple. "Because the time is ripe."

"And the Voice ... the Voice told you this?"

"Yes, of course. He tells me everything I need."

"Everything *we* need."

Mórgana touched the fang where it was sheathed at her belt, and its secret power flowed up her arm. Should she use it to teach her grandfather a lesson? No need. Simply reaching for it brought out a tremble in his jaw. He flinched away, cowering down.

"Since we can see Merlin," he asked, "will you kill him? Fill his body with disease?"

"You fool. Have you learned nothing of my plan?" She held the orb upward. "Show me the runaway!" Immediately, the image changed to a man, hooded in a black cloak with a thin plaid stripe. He loped along a dry, rocky streambed, his huge strides eating up the distance between him and his quarry.

"I thought he served you," Mórganthu said, "like the others."

She frowned, annoyed at the reminder. "No, he does not. He has partially escaped my enchantment because he had turned against me when I enacted it. But it is no matter, for he will not be able to help our enemies. I made sure of *that* before he escaped."

"And Arthur? What will we do about Arthur?"

"A very good question ..." She commanded the orb, and its purple flames burst outward. The image shifted again, and now she could see Arthur and his two companions sitting at a campfire.

Mórganthu rubbed his hands together, a cackle in his throat. "Hurt him! Hurt him, I say!"

"Patience. There is a far greater benefit to be gained by letting him live."

"But my revenge has waited so long, I can hardly stand it!"

Mórgana ran her fingers through her black hair and shook it out. "There is no worry. He will not escape. Do not forget that I have other servants nearby, ones more faithful than the half-tongue."

Mórganthu gurgled deep in his throat as he laughed, and Mórdred chuckled beside him.

CHAPTER 7

MYSTERIES UNMASKED

Artorius moaned as his trout fell off his branch and dropped into the fire for the third time. He scratched it out from the coals, but it was covered in ashes — again.

Dwin gave Artorius a playful shove. "Look, this is how you do it." And then he wedged the handle part of his own fish-bearing branch between two rocks and tried to set a third rock to hold it down. But the fish sank quickly toward the fire, and it, too, fell off.

Culann shook his head as he used two sticks to try to retrieve his own fish from where it had fallen between some logs. "This is impossible," he said as the flames nearly caught his sleeves on fire.

"Just leave it," Artorius said. "We can always eat the hazelnuts Dwin brought."

"They're burnt and way too salty," Culann said. "If we only had some water to drink, but no, the mud-stink we caught these fish in isn't fit to swallow, and every spring on the map ends up either dry or a figment of Dwin's gaseous head."

"It's not my fault."

"Look, a spring, over here! Stop, a spring, over there! Haha-haha!"

"It was my uncle's map."

"But you copied it."

Dwin threw a pebble and it nicked Culann in the jaw. "And you brought the salted pork, boar-foot."

Culann clenched his fists.

"Now stop," Artorius said, holding his hands out to keep them apart, "I was the one who brought the rock-hard bread the baker was selling cheap, right? We all made bad choices in the food we brought, so let's drop it."

Culann swore. "The fish are all ruined, and we can't waste any more water washing them off. I say we skip dinner and go to sleep."

"But I'm hungry," Dwin said as he tried to jab his fish and pull it from the fire. It broke in half and both portions slipped into an almost inaccessible place beneath the center logs. "Ah, you're right. At least I can dream about food."

"And water."

"Now that's the kind of dream I'd like," Artorius said as he unrolled a blanket near the fire and lay down. The others joined him, but soon Artorius found himself staring at the fire, alone, while the others snored.

His old familiar longings nagged at him. He slid his hand inside his tunic and felt the thick scar that covered his abdomen and lower chest, wondering afresh why he bore it. His father had told him the story, but why would some strange king want to kill him, and how had he survived? Yet there was something there, buried in his dreams, some flash of remembrance that haunted him — a flicker of incomprehensible joy that made his normal life so pale, so common, and ... pointless.

No, not pointless. It was just that there was something more waiting for him that he could never quite grasp.

And because of this, he didn't feel alive unless he was rushing toward an oncoming spear, climbing down a cliff using nothing but his bare hands, or diving deeply into Lake Derwentlin until his lungs almost burst. He just *had* to feel that flash of strength as he ran madly down a hillside, the thrill of slamming an opponent flat, or ... or was it just death itself? Did he have to feel close to death in order to ... feel alive?

Why was that?

He closed his eyes, trying to put it all from his mind, but the soreness from riding all day didn't help, nor did his dry lips and thirst.

A long time later, when the fire had nearly died, he finally found himself on the verge of sleep. As he drifted off, the image of a marsh appeared before his eyes, with beautiful, fresh water, where rushes clacked in the wind and herons flapped off at his coming. He was in a boat, and he was rowing, with a dozen shining fish flopping at his feet, and a dragonfly tousling his brown hair one moment then flitting away the next. He rested the oars, dipped his fingers in, and brought forth a clean handful of water that sparkled with the setting sun's glorious rays. The water was cold upon his tongue, and its life flowed downward, filling and satisfying him deeply.

Picking up the oars once more, he began rowing, and soon the sun set. The marsh became a gray world of invisible chirps and croaks and the *whisp-whisp* of countless insects.

The next he knew, he was kneeling in the dark upon a shore, with the gray, massive walls of a fortress on a ridge in the distance. A tower soared upward on his left, and near its conical roof a bright light shone from a window.

He craned his neck and gazed intently at the light, and soon the familiar restlessness swept over him ... only now he somehow knew why. This light, it shattered the darkness with such purity and beauty. He had to see its source.

Standing, he found his feet had left the ground and he rose upward until he floated near the window, where he had to cover his eyes lest he be blinded. The light washed over him, cleansed his fears, cleansed ... his wound? It stirred within him memories unbidden. Where had he seen this light before, experienced a touch to his soul this delightful?

He opened his eyes at a dare — and couldn't close them! A bowl, more solid, more real than anything he had ever seen, floated before him. Or *had* he seen it before? It was beyond beautiful, not because of itself, but because of the one who had made it. Its sides were of wood, ancient as the oldest tree in all creation, and yet young, as if some master craftsman carved it new every morning from the purest and freshest-smelling wood.

He reached out his hand in a desperate attempt to touch it, but it was too far away. Then it brightened and was lost to him. The light coalesced, flashed, and faded.

In its place appeared the image of a woman with black hair. She was sitting on a mat of woven rushes and kneading dough in a large wooden bowl. Her hair was long and pushed to the side so that it completely covered the left side of her face, and she wore a black cloak made from the feathers of iridescent blackbirds, and many others, all woven together.

She was speaking aloud, seemingly to herself, for no one else was near.

"Arthur ... oh, Arthur, I've been looking for you for so long. Where are you? Please ... please come to me ..."

Artorius recognized this name as that of the previous High King's son, who was purportedly either a slave, or dead. Why did she call *that* name?

Either way, a desire to go to her filled his heart, a deep longing that he did not understand. If he could, he would have run to her ... if he only knew where she was. But who was this woman? What did she want? A fear crept into his heart then, a doubt.

But the more he looked at her, the more he longed to be with her, and his fears and doubts fled away. Why was that? Did he know her? He searched his memory, and couldn't recall ever having seen her face.

Artorius reached out to her, but just like the glorious wooden bowl that he had seen, the image faded, and he awoke with a start.

It was still night, and he was next to the fire, now completely dead besides a little acrid smoke. The moon's pale light sent wraithlike shadows from the trees and their swaying branches.

Dwin lay to the left, and Culann to the right. They were alone — and yet ... The soft sound of rustling leaves caught his attention. Someone approached. It was a man in a black cloak, walking with stealth toward them. Now he hid behind a rock, then he slithered closer, ever closer.

Artorius nudged Culann, but his companion didn't stir. He wanted to yell, but his voice froze in his throat. In rising fear, he sat up to find his blade and was startled to see the stranger standing not two paces away. And then it occurred to him ... surely this was his father, Merlin, who always wore black. He had finally caught up on the way to the muster. In fact, Artorius, Dwin, and Cullan had set such a slow pace, it seemed to him, that he had fully expected the whole army to catch up with them on the trail.

But then the man jumped as if sensing something, and then ran at Artorius, raising his arms — a low growl-gurgle escaping from his throat — only to fall to the earth as another figure in black tackled him from behind.

Artorius fumbled for his sword, but he had foolishly left it on his horse.

The hooded figures rolled down an embankment, hands on each other's throat. When their momentum finally slowed, the one on top pulled a short blade from his belt and jabbed it at the other, who knocked the blow wide with his forearm and grabbed the other's wrist. They struggled until the man on the bottom pulled his own blade out and jabbed it into the gut of the other.

The man on top screamed, dropped his blade into the leaves, and fell over, panting and clutching at his wound.

Culann and Dwin had awoken by now, and they joined Artorius in a run for their horses and their sheathed blades.

The second man slipped out and stood, keeping his own blade ready while picking up the other.

The man who had been knifed let out a short wail, and then fell silent.

"Who are you?" Artorius yelled, rushing back with his sword ready.

The man threw his hood off and pulled his black mask down. "I found you ..."

Artorius blinked. "Tas. You ... saved my life."

Merlin gave the stranger's blade a curious look, tucked it into his belt, and then embraced Artorius. "I'm glad I made it in time ..."

Artorius felt strange to be taller than his father, but it was good, and natural, somehow. And he still respected how strong his father was, as well as his patience, his love, and his ready smile and encouragement.

Merlin patted Artorius on the back. "I didn't even know it was your camp. Peredur had the horses while I investigated, and when I saw it was you, and this man attacking ..."

"Who is he?"

"I don't know."

Peredur rushed into the glade, his own blade drawn, and stood by Merlin's side.

"Are you all right?"

Before Artorius could answer, Culann called out, "You'd better take a look at this." He was peering at the dead man.

They gathered around as Culann pulled off the man's tartan-fringed black hood.

Artorius had to close his eyes for a moment and then look again to make sure what he saw was real. The man's chin looked normal, if you ignored the strangely sharp teeth and lips covered in dried blood. But his nose ... it was split, almost like a dog's, with large nostrils, and hair — fur — growing down its length. The man's eyes were unnatural as well — large, with barely any white to be seen, and the dead, yellow irises almost glowed in the moonlight. Pulling the hood back farther revealed his ears, sticking out from his head in points, with hair all over them.

Dwin shook his head. "He's a freak!"

"Half dog," Culann whispered.

Merlin kicked the corpse over, hiding the grotesque face. "You mean half wolf."

Artorius had never heard his father's voice like that before. It was thick with fear, the words barely escaping his teeth.

Peredur retrieved their two horses, and then joined the others at the freshly kindled fire.

Only then did it occur to Artorius what was strange about his father's appearance just now. "So where's Ector and the rest of the warriors? I'm surprised you two are alone."

After glancing at Peredur, Merlin cleared his throat. "That's what we wanted to talk to you about ... you're going the wrong way. Ector's headed north to join King Urien against the Picti. And so we've come — "

"Wait," Artorius said, confused. "The parchment said — "

"Forget the parchment. The envoy who posted that was lucky to escape Uncle's wrath."

"But the Saxenow — ?"

Merlin held up a hand, his voice rising. "Arthur, listen!"

Arthur? Had his father just called him Arthur? Just like the woman with black hair in his dream. Artorius opened his mouth to speak, but Merlin cut him off.

"Listen, all of you." Merlin looked at each of them in turn. When he came to Artorius, there was an expression of gravity in his gaze that Artorius had rarely seen — only when he was in trouble.

"What I have to tell you has long been kept hidden. Hidden from almost everyone, especially from you, Arthur."

Merlin reached out and placed a hand gently on Artorius's shoulder. "Though I and your ... and Natalenya love you as our own, you are not our true son. Your father was High King Uther, and your mother, his wife, Igerna. We've been protecting you from Vortigern, who slew your parents for the throne."

Artorius laughed. This was a joke, payback for his prank in the arena. His smile died, however, as he looked around at his companions. Peredur looked relieved, Culann and Dwin seemed shocked, but there wasn't a hint of a smile among them. He placed his hand on his tunic and felt the scar underneath. Suddenly he could hardly breathe. His name was Arthur? Merlin wasn't his father?

"You're the High King!" Culann said, his shock changing into a bit of a smirk.

"No, no, that can't be," Artorius said.

Merlin squeezed his hand. "You know me, and that I speak truth. This is why you can't go south. The man you'd be serving killed your parents."

"But Vortigern was Igerna's brother ... you're saying he had his sister killed as well?"

"That's my understanding. I don't know why, except that there was a generations-old feud between the families. Igerna married Uther, her family's enemy. Everyone thought that the wounds had been healed, but apparently that wasn't true. News reached us shortly after we settled in Dinas Crag that Vortigern even killed your two sisters, Myrgwen and Eilyne."

Artorius repeated the names to himself. He'd heard them before, when his parents would speak in hushed tones late at night, but he never knew who they were. His mind began to swirl with strange sensations as his entire life spun before him — all the pieces painfully ripping apart and rearranging themselves in a bent, unnatural shape.

When he finally spoke, his words came out slowly.

"So that's why you have two names — Ambrosius and Merlin. Which means Colvarth ... the chief bard ... he served my father, then." He could see the logic, now, in a way that hurt.

"Yes. Now you begin to understand — "

"That you lied to me. You've been lying to me my whole life."

"No ... we were vague."

"Yes. You did lie." Both Merlin and Natalenya, the people who had been his parents, had deceived him all these years. The thought was almost unbearable. He wanted to grab on to something and break it with his bare hands, but what was falling apart was inside of him, and try as he might, he couldn't hold it together.

"Not to hurt you. To protect you. Vortigern's already tried to kill you twice. Word could've gotten out, and if he learned of your presence, then he'd have stopped at nothing —"

"You *lied!*"

"Artorius … Arthur, I —"

Artorius got up and strode off into the darkness. He climbed a hill, tripping on a fallen tree, slipping on loose stones, and yet kept going. No one followed, and he was glad. He needed to think. Everything he had ever known about his life had fallen away like leaves from a winter tree, and he felt cold and alone. He was an orphan, bereft of parents, and now twice bereft. His mother, Natalenya, wasn't his real mother. His tas wasn't his real father.

And on top of this, he'd been stupid enough to try to help Vortigern, a stone-hearted man who'd killed Artorius's family.

Coming to a small open space at the foot of a smooth boulder that towered over him, he paused and leaned his forehead against the cool stone. As he stood there, a new thought occurred to him. Vortigern had stolen the throne. By all rights, it belonged to … him. But that was ridiculous. He, Arthur, was the true High King? How stupid. How perfectly preposterous.

But then he remembered the words of his chieftain, Great-Uncle Ector, when he'd given instructions about how to lead men in battle:

"Artorius, one day you will lead great armies across Britain, and you must learn what I am teaching you." Artorius had laughed as Ector's gaze fixed on him. "Do you hear me? You are destined for great things. Know it, and learn from my mistakes."

Now he could see what motivated his uncle. Ector had known, hadn't he? And Colvarth, he had said some similar things many years ago. A memory came of the old man, sitting with the Harp of Britain on his lap and playing it softly as he spoke:

"Oh, son of my liege, pay attention when I … speak to you. These

95

are weighty … matters, matters that concern you and the very future of Britain. You must learn … great wisdom, for all men will look to you for understanding and judgment."

The bard had forever spoken that way, calling him "son of my liege." Artorius had thought he was talking about Merlin, but reconsidering it now, Merlin was not Colvarth's liege lord. He had meant Uther. That Artorius was the son of Uther.

And it had always made him wonder how he and Merlin could look so different. As he had grown, he'd always tried to find the similarity, but it usually eluded him. He had *wanted* to look like Merlin. To be like his father. But if Merlin wasn't his father, then —

Could this be the source of his restlessness? Of the deadness he felt inside, like something was missing from his life? Of the strange dreams that often came to him in the night? That sometimes even interrupted his waking world? Flashbacks of a time, long, long ago when he had lived a different life? Had a different father? Mother?

Arthur.

The name sounded so strange to him. To grow up with one name and then to find out it was false. Chosen by his parents as a lie to hide who he truly was.

Arthur.

He sounded out the name slowly, letting his tongue form the syllables in their strange yet simple cadence. The name was British, not Roman like his false name. He knew from his studies it meant "wild bear" … one of the most dangerous animals on the island.

And it wasn't like there were hundreds others named Arthur out there — there just weren't, at least not in Rheged. The name was rare, and had become even rarer after the child's supposed death so as not to rankle Vortigern, the new High King. If Merlin and Natalenya had not changed his name, everyone would have suspected.

Arthur.

A name rich in recent history, a name that every Briton knew and lamented. Hah! He himself had shed young tears at the tales of the High King's lost son. Some said the child had been killed with his family. Others that he had drowned. But his parents always maintained a different story and told a tale of the child being taken as a slave into Pictish lands. The same land where Merlin and Natalenya had been taken as slaves with him.

Another truth fell into place. They had always told him that they fought the slavery because the High King's son had been taken there. But they had never finished the story. The boy had been taken out to freedom, hadn't he? And they had known it all along.

Artorius sat down on a tuft of moss and looked out at the moon, setting now behind the distant silhouette of hills. Like a door smeared with ashes, its mysterious white arc was pulling him, unwilling, into an uncertain future.

But where? Into darkness? Could he go there? Face *that* future? Face the man who had slain — no, murdered — his father?

CHAPTER 8

OATHS TAKEN

S unrise was just beginning to redden the sky over the eastern foothills by the time Artorius returned. Merlin was the only one awake, and he was adding wood to the fire in order to cook some oatcakes on a flat rock he had found. Without a word to his father, Artorius began to wake the others. Everyone must hear what he had to say.

Once they were all up, including a yawning Dwin, Artorius sat down across from Merlin. Everyone looked at him expectantly without betraying their feelings.

After a long time of silence, Merlin spoke. "So ... what have you decided?"

"That I believe you," he said, holding back the bitterness that tried to creep into his voice.

"Anything else?"

Artorius nodded. "I've decided where we're going."

"What did you choose?"

Artorius looked down. His father wasn't going to like the decision.

"I'm not going to tell you what to do …"

Holding out a fist and shaking it, Artorius asked, "Do I even have a choice? Has God given me a choice?"

Standing up, Merlin began walking around the fire, as if thinking. "Surely—"

"Even if I didn't know that I was Arthur, God has made me thus, and I can do no other. We're going to Glevum."

The word struck like a blow to Merlin's gut, and Artorius saw him wince in pain. "Why?" was all he could say.

Artorius wiped his hands over his face; he had hoped for a different response. "I thought you wouldn't tell me what to do."

"And I won't," Merlin said, continuing his pacing. "But I want to understand. The heart of Glevum is the feasting hall of the most powerful man in Britain—and he'll do anything to put you on a spit and roast you alive."

Merlin paused behind Artorius and placed his hands gently on his shoulders. "You look a lot like your father, you know."

"I … didn't know that."

"What reason do you have to go there?" Merlin's voice was soft, but Artorius could detect an undertone of desperation.

"Because it's the right thing to do."

"And fighting the Picti is the wrong thing?"

"No, just the lesser good. If the heart of Britain falls, then Rheged will be smashed between the might of the Saxenow and the guile of the Picti."

"But Vortigern?"

"I've thought this through," Artorius said. "If we don't stop the Saxenow—Vortigern or no Vortigern—there won't be a Britain left to be High King of. When I read the parchment calling for the muster at Glevum, I realized how focused we've been on Rheged's own little problems, and I was proud that Uncle had finally called us to help in the south. I guess I was wrong."

"We have nothing against the south — "

Merlin said these words with conviction, but Artorius could feel how empty they were. Action is what matterred now, not good will. "I know that, Tas. But the time has come to lend our aid. The kingship — "

"Please listen to reason," Merlin said. "Vortigern is getting old. When he dies, you will have the perfect time to act. Not now."

Peredur coughed. "Vortipor is his heir and will be High King after him, Merlin. Vortigern's death won't change anything. In fact, it might make it harder."

Artorius stood now, mustering up as much authority as he could scrape together. It felt strange, though, to be speaking against his father, but he had resolved to go south, and he had to speak.

"And all of this is up to God. Isn't that what the abbot would say? I've wanted to help in the south before, but the only news we've ever heard is that each year Vortigern retreats and the Saxenow take more and more land away. Well, that time is at an end. I know my purpose now."

Merlin looked away and then back, making eye contact. Finally, he sighed and sat down. "And which name will you go by?"

"Artorius, still, I suppose. It's the name I'm used to, and it can serve me a little longer. It's odd, but I had a dream last night that helped prepare me for this news — a woman with black hair called to me. Only she called me 'Arthur', not 'Artorius', and she wanted me to come to her. Before you told me the truth, I didn't understand, but now I do."

The blood had left Merlin's cheeks. "A woman ... with black hair?"

"Yes."

Merlin said nothing for the space of three heartbeats. "The woman you saw ... was Mórgana, my sister. I advise you: Do not go to her. She's worse than Vortigern, and has been trying to kill you and me ever since we fled Kernow."

Artorius crossed his arms. "I didn't sense any evil."

"It doesn't matter what you sensed — she's deceiving you. Please trust me."

"There was nothing to be afraid of," Artorius said. "I know this."

Merlin swallowed and looked sternly at him. "We'll talk about it later."

"Aye," Peredur said, rising. "We've wasted enough daylight. That creature may not have come alone."

Merlin sucked in his breath at this comment and looked around, studying the woods for a long moment. Only then did he proceed. "There's one thing to do before we go," he said. "Long ago, when you were still a child, Artorius, and we were fleeing from Vortigern, Colvarth gave me the job of leading." Merlin drew his sword and presented his blade to Artorius. "I now give the leadership to you, for I swore an oath long ago to your father, and now I swear it to you:

I beseech thee, High King,
and deign thee to bless with thy right hand —
The fealty of my mouth,
that I may speak well of thee.
The fealty of my heart,
that I may follow thee.
The fealty of my arms,
that I may fight against thine enemies.
And the fealty of my legs,
that I may go where thou commandest."

Merlin paused, swallowed once, and then finished:

"For all my days will I serve thee and defend thee,
along with thine heir, and all that is right under Christ,
on the Isle of the Mighty."

Artorius stared, shocked to hear such an oath, not just because it was to him as the High King — something he had never fathomed before this strange night — but also because it was from the man he had always considered his father. He received the sword with trembling fingers and asked him to rise. "No, you can't swear this oath," he said.

Still on one knee, Merlin looked up at him, tears shining in his eyes. "I can, and I have."

And then Peredur knelt and did the same, followed by the solemn Culann and the smiling Dwin. As each one swore his fealty to Arthur as High King, he blushed. He could hardly stand it. Did his friends really have to do this?

Merlin thought so.

But now that it was done, the weight of it finally hit him. For Artorius, this wasn't about authority as much as *responsibility*. His decisions could bring about any and all of their deaths. Was he ready to accept that? What if Dwin died? Culann? Peredur? His own father? Could Artorius live with that?

But there was no choice anymore. He had met that demon in his night of indecision and had vanquished him. Whatever happens, he had to do what was right.

Hesitatingly, Artorius spoke. "I ... accept your fealty. May God bless it."

Dwin grabbed his sword and stood. "Then we go to Glevum?"

"We go."

They mounted their horses and rode off. The adventure had begun.

Once the sun had risen high enough for Merlin to see clearly, he remembered the blade he had tucked into his belt — the one from the grotesque half wolf.

Looking at it carefully, his suspicions flared again. The shape was identical to the ones that his father had forged for the soldiers serving Tregeagle in the village of Bosventor. The blade was like that of a Roman gladius, but thinner and with a few design touches that were unique to the Britons.

Turning it over, he looked at the side of the pommel — and gasped.

The mark was there: *OAG*, his father's initials, Owain An Gof.

How had this half-wolf who had attacked Arthur come into possession of a blade that Merlin's father had made?

As the truth sank in, Merlin began to tremble.

Mórgana.

———+———

Holding forth the orb, Mórgana commanded it to show her the half-tongue. Purple fire flashed from her palm, and the image inside the orb dulled, brightened, and then clarified into an image of him lying in a pool of congealing blood.

"Is he dead?" Mórdred asked, a slight smile at the corner of his mouth.

"If so," Mórganthu said, "then the fool's plan has failed."

"Perhaps," she said, "but I need to make sure, and also give instructions to my servants. Wait, and watch."

She commanded the orb to take her to the half-tongue, and it began to grow in her palm. Scales formed on its surface, and soon it was so heavy she had to set it down. Larger and larger it pulsed until its skin ripped open and blade-like teeth appeared. The mouth gaped and Mórgana threw herself inside. Down, down the slimy throat she swam until darkness overtook her soul and she appeared, ghost-like, within a rocky glade. The sky was full of haze, and the air dry as death. Nearby smoked the ruins of a campfire, and before her lay the body of the half-tongue.

Mórgana pushed him with her foot on his chest. His body rolled and fell back into place, his clothing making a crinkling sound.

"What is this?" She reached inside his tunic and pulled forth a rolled parchment, small, but of good quality. Upon it was written a message, which she read.

The fool thought to warn Arthur! Laughing, she tore the message into bits and threw them into the remains of the fire.

And although he was astute enough to guess some portion of her secrets, the traitor's warning had failed. But even if he'd succeeded, it would've made no difference. That was the beauty of the Voice's plans — no matter what happens, he *always* wins.

The half-tongued man let out a gurgling groan, and Mórgana stepped back.

"I must do something about that," she said. Turning to the woods, she called to her servants, who were nearby waiting for her signal. "Approach me, my warriors!"

From the woods came three hulking shapes. Each wore the same kind of cloak as the half-tongue, and they threw their hoods back and howled, for though they possessed the bodies of men, their faces were like wolves with full snouts, fangs, and yellow eyes.

"Greetings, my warriors. You have done well hunting our stray wolf. Kill him now, and then continue following Arthur's trail. You remember what I require?"

The lead wolf-head nodded, leapt forward, and soon the half-tongue was dead, in a way that only a wolf can kill.

Mórgana curled her lip in a wide sneer. "Good-bye, Dyslan. I swore I would kill you, and now I have. Life is that simple."

It was early in the morning on their fifth day of traveling, and Merlin yawned as he goaded his horse down a rocky gulley over-grown with brown, dry scrub. The others rode in front of him, and that was fine as far as Merlin was concerned — he hadn't slept well the night before, having heard the prowling of some animal out-side their camp. He *had* asked Arthur if they could stay in the city of Mancunium, but Arthur wouldn't have it, saying that they had fresh supplies and that he'd fallen in love with the open country and sleeping under the stars. Giving over leadership had its downsides.

Though as a leader, Arthur gained in confidence each day, tak-ing hold of his role yet asking advice from Merlin and Peredur, even Culann and Dwin at times.

But they weren't in a battle, only traveling. And they hadn't encountered any serious challenge or delay ... yet. One thing Merlin worried about was bands of thieves attacking them, for these unoccupied lands lay thick with danger.

And then there was the constant fear that gnawed at Merlin — fear that more of Mórgana's wolf-headed warriors were loose in the land. And the creature prowling around their campsite last night put Merlin's senses on a raw, ragged edge.

At the bottom of the hillside they joined an ancient road leading from Mancunium to Deva. This sped up their progress only marginally, for the drought had made most of the wetter lands passable, and the roads less necessary.

A short while later, the trees began to thicken, and Dwin, who had the best vision, noticed a man in the far distance wheeling his horse around as if undecided which way to ride. When the stranger spied them approaching, he took off down a deer track into the fastness of the trees.

Merlin put his mask back on. As much as he hated to wear it, he didn't want word spreading of someone with a scarred face carrying a leather-wrapped harp through the land. Vortigern knew him well enough to go hunting if he heard such a tale.

Soon the forest began to encroach upon the path itself, and Merlin urged his horse closer to the others, eventually settling in beside Arthur. When he rode in the rear, as he had been, every rustle of a squirrel and every dart of a bird became in his mind a wolf head ready to leap out and pull him from his horse. Down into the bracken he'd go, where the creature would open its evil teeth, and … But he tried not to think about it.

His nervousness increased as the forest became ever darker and the trees more ancient. Everywhere the leaves were gasping for lack of rain, and many fell, spiraling in a last dance of death before their corpses collected on the forest floor.

Ahead they heard the jingle of tack, and Merlin exchanged a worried glance with Arthur. So far they had met no one on the road, and the deepness of the woods made Merlin worry about bandits. When they crested the next hill, he saw a man on a horse pulling a small wagon, with two other riders beyond. They traveled at a leisurely pace, and Merlin and the others soon overtook them.

The road was narrower here due to the strangling tendrils of the forest, and Arthur held a hand out to slow their approach.

Just ahead, the wooden cart was attached to the back of the horse by long boughs. It had only two wheels, and it was covered in a greased-leather tarp. Hanging from its sides were various pots, pans, and tools that made a soft clanking as the cart bumped down the road.

Peering past the rickety cart, Merlin was shocked to see the size of the horse pulling it. Such raw power was normally used for plowing, but this horse was clearly not meant for such work. The long, feathery hair above its huge hooves had been braided, with little bells attached to each tassel. Likewise, someone had groomed the sleek black mane and woven it through with beautifully colored ribbons.

And it wasn't just the horse that was of unusual size, for the man upon him was massive, with a torso nearly as wide as the ancient tree trunks that lined the road, and with thick limbs and solid hands. Compared to his body and the horse under him, however, his legs appeared out of proportion: strong, yes, but slightly short for one so large.

The man turned in his saddle to look at them, his suspicious eyes blinking in the dappled light. Upon his boulder-sized head sat a pointed, blue-dyed woolen hat with swinging tassels tipped with decorative spikes made of shiny pewter. His hair topped his head like gray and brown thatch, and he had the thickest eyebrows Merlin had ever seen. His white beard hung down past the man's waist despite the fact that it was finely braided into a rich tapestry of knotwork and threaded with pewter beads. His tunic was dark-gray under an old brown oil-cloth cloak strewn with patches that had been sewn on using thick sinew thread. His boots were leather, but the heels were made of pewter, and the pointy toes as well.

"Are ya thieves?" the man said, looking directly at Merlin and his mask. "If so, I hain't seen ones like ya round-about." His voice was deep, but had a melodious quality to it.

"We aren't thieves," Merlin answered, "and you have nothing to fear from us."

After studying them for a few moments more, the giant of a man appeared satisfied and faced forward. His horse continued its slow gait.

Not seeing an easy way past the huge man and his cart, Merlin became impatient. "If you would be so kind to stand aside," Merlin called, "we have urgent business to the south."

The old man ignored him and began whistling.

Merlin cupped his hands, wondering if the man were going deaf. "Kindly stand aside, I said."

The giant directed his horse over to the side of the trail, turned in his saddle once more, and waved them on. "Pass, pass, ma young masters, even ya in the mask. The road, and all upon it, are free."

Arthur compelled his mount forward, and Merlin kept pace, just behind. As he passed the giant, he was shocked to find the man's belt was at eye level. Truly this man was even bigger than the Eirish giant he had fought in his father's blacksmith shop so many years ago.

After passing, they encountered the two other men in front, blocking their way.

Merlin's hand went nervously to his sword.

CHAPTER 9

CHILDREN OF THE GIANT

Merlin shared a worried glance with Arthur and began to slowly draw his blade, hoping the giant behind them didn't notice.

Each of the two men in front, their backs turned, were dressed like the giant, but they were much smaller — in fact, probably about Merlin's height if not slightly shorter. They wore the same pointed woolen hats with tassels and decorations.

The man on the left had a green hat, with pewter moons and stars on the tassels, and the one on the right had a red hat with ... pewter hearts? He turned and pulled off his hat, revealing ... long, blonde, magnificent hair.

A woman!

Then the one on the left took off the green hat, revealing long, reddish-blonde hair.

Both women smiled at Arthur, who let his reins slacken.

Merlin slid his blade back in and let out his breath.

Both women were young and pretty, and their faces enough alike that they could be twins. The one holding the green hat wore a light leaf-colored tunic with beautiful embroidered flowers down the front. The one with the red hat wore a white tunic with scarlet lacework.

"Hello," they said, almost in unison. Green-hat giggled and said something to her sister.

"Why do you laugh at strangers?" Arthur asked.

"Because," the red-hatted one said, "because we're afraid of the woods. We met a man who told us about thieves, and we were just hoping someone would come to protect us."

"You're not thieves, are you?" the green hat said, a worried look on her face as she glanced at Merlin.

"Oh ... ah ... no," Arthur said.

"I don't trust the one with the mask."

Arthur shook his head. "He's my father, and he's a bard. We all know a bard isn't a thief."

Red hat looked suspicious of this. "How do we know he didn't steal the harp?"

"Tas, play it for them."

This was preposterous. Merlin wasn't going to risk the harp just because they didn't like his mask. "Not now."

Green hat grimaced at Merlin, but then smiled at Arthur. "I suppose since all of you aren't wearing masks, we can probably trust you to protect us."

Merlin looked back at the giant. "Surely he could protect you."

"Oh no," red hat said, a serious expression on her face. "Do you really think Father could do that? He's quite old and slow, you see, and wouldn't last a minute. Imagine ... a whole band of thieves and only him as guard! Will you protect us?"

Merlin frowned. "What are your names, and where are you from?"

"Names?" spoke the giant behind them. "In yar tongue I'm named Gogirfan Gawr map Llŷr. Some call me Little Crow, but I prefer Gogi. Gogi the bogey, haha, but that is only a jest. And, since ya're so nosey, we aren't from anywhere ya know."

"Somewhere else, then ... down south?"

"Ya don't understand. We're from nowhere and everywhere all at once." And then he began to sing in his low voice:

We live in our own tents — Don't pay anyone rents.
We set our temples high — up in the blue-bright sky.
We find our soul's blisses — Beneath starlight's kisses.
And live in our own tents — Don't want to pay house rents!

And when he concluded, he gave a friendly smile to Merlin. "We are Walkers, ya know, and that is what we are."

By now Culann had ridden up. "So then why are you riding?"

The giant harrumphed as if this were a grave insult. "But my *horse* is walking, ya know. And the point isn't that we *walk*, but that we are *Walkers*."

Merlin pondered this. He had heard tales of folk who wandered the land — nomads without a home. Sometimes they had even come through Bosventor where he'd grown up, but he'd never met any himself.

"Oh, please, Papa, that is not the point," green hat said, and then turning to Arthur, she took in a deep breath and blinked. "My name is Gwenivach, and we really are afraid."

"Aye, aye," the other said, looking to Culann. Her voice was just as sweet and musical as her sister's. "And I am named Gwenivere. The tales about this forest are very frightful, and we need — "

"An escort to make your journey safe?" Arthur asked.

Both girls nodded.

"Well, my name is Culann, and since we're traveling the same road, I don't see why we can't slow our journey a little to assist you. What say you, Artorius?"

Arthur had a grin on his face, and Merlin thought this whole thing was silly. Any delay heading south would make it that much longer until he could be with his family again.

Gogi coughed. "And it would be much appreciated. I may look big way up here, but ma legs get stiff and I don't come down very easy 'less I fall, and that, as ya know, would hurt. Very hard for ma to be a proper guard."

So they rode through the woods at a slow pace, the path wide enough that only Arthur and Culann could ride near to the girls, leaving Dwin back with Merlin, Peredur, and Gogi.

Though Merlin considered the whole thing to be a waste of time, he thought that he should at least be civil, and so he introduced them all to the giant, and then asked some questions.

"So, if you're always traveling, Gogi, how do you make a living?"

"I do not make a living," he said. "The living makes ma. I'm a tinsmith by trade, ya know, and that is what I am. In fact, we are on a holy pilgrimage to visit the site of the founding of ma trade, the Island of Tinsmiths."

"And where is that?"

"South and west. Always south and west."

"And who is the founder of your trade?"

"Why Josephus, ah course. Nah doubt you 'ave heard of him?"

Merlin shook his head. "No ... I haven't."

"A pity, ya know. Everyone should be tinsmiths. Or at least *buy* from us, ya know."

"I'm from Kernow, and they mine tin all around. Have you been there?"

"We've been everywhere except upon the road to whar the sun sets, and I'm not ready to go yet, ya know. Kernow is a goodly land, that. Not so many of ya Britons about, with lots of open space, and the grass is soft for ma big head."

Merlin was confused. "You're not a Briton?"

"Briton? Nah, nah." And then he began to sing again:

We travel and tarry — we go and make merry.
Not Picti, nor Britons — who share but a pittance;
Not woebegone talkers — for we are the Walkers
Who travel and tarry — to go and make merry!

"If you're not a Briton or a Pict, where did you come from? You're not Roman, so ... are you Eirish?"

"Eirish? Haha. Nah, nah, once more yar wrong. Ya see, we owned *all* this land before the Romans or even ya Britons came, a very long time ago it was, aye. Ya Britons killed us, stole it from us, and now we are vera few. We're the first people, and our bones have been here since the island made us."

Gogi lifted his chin and called to his daughters. "Wengis! Gweya deena sa kalpe grof stradictin! Difin sgwher gweya nak sgreat."

Merlin couldn't remember ever hearing speech such as this, said without accent but entirely puzzling nonetheless.

Gwenivere was talking to Culann at the time, and didn't respond to her father, but Gwenivach answered without looking back. "Revy noosa, grapap. Seb shapent. Gweya veha sgooks grot stesa reeha."

Gogi nodded and then turned to Merlin. "Ya see, we have a different language, aye ... and ya thought we were Britons! Haha!" And he laughed so much that his horse shook under the tremors.

Merlin acted ambivalent, but he disliked the fact that they could talk without him knowing what they said. It reminded him of the feelings he'd had when the Picti had first made him a slave.

"And by the way, what would it cost ma to buy that un's horse?" Gogi said, pointing at Arthur's black stallion, Casva. "I've noticed how old he is compared to yar others. He won't last much longer, ya know, and I'd take him off yar hands, so to speak."

"Artorius's horse is only nine — "

"Ah, but he's too broken-down for such a fine, hearty lad. When they get to being useless, I even make things from 'em: sinew, leather, horsehair for weavers, hooves for combs, bone for needles. Ya can always make something to sell."

"I thought you were a tinsmith, not a ... horse ..." Merlin tried to bring the word to memory.

"Knacker?"

"But you don't *eat* the horses, do ya?" Peredur asked, a sick look on his face.

"Nah, nah. We're with ya Britons, on that one. Horseflesh should nah be eaten. Even if the Picti eat the eyeballs as a dainty, ya know, I'll never do such. But I do make a meager bit buyin' and sellin' live ones too. A man's got to get money to eat, ya know. In fact, I'll trade for just about anything I might be able tah sell. For instance, would any of ya be interested in this?" He pulled from a sack what looked like two pewter cups, strangely shaped, and tied together with a long leather band.

"What is it?" Dwin asked.

"Why, ya don't know, do ya? Well, that goes to show the ignorance in these parts. It's tah catch the drops of tears from the eyes of yar horse. If ya gets any, ya drip 'em around yar campsite each night for good luck."

Merlin looked, and sure enough, Gogi's own horse had a tear-catcher tied under its eyes.

"Not interested, eh?" he said. "Well, how about this?" And he pulled out a flat piece of pewter polished to a smooth finish.

Peredur cocked an eyebrow. "Don't tell me ... it's for catching the tears o' the sun, and — "

"Nah, nah, young talker. It's a mushroom checker. Ya hold it up to a 'shroom and see what color ya see. If it's green, then the mushroom is safe tah eat. If it's brown, then it's gone rotten. If it's red, then it'll kill ya, aye, just like that." And he snapped his meaty fingers.

"And what does yellow mean?" Dwin asked in a slightly mocking tone.

"Yallow? Ah, that means ya should cook 'em with butter."

"I don't think I'd trust your methods," Merlin said, thinking about how dangerous mushrooms could be. A boy Merlin had grown up with found some wild mushrooms, ate one, and died.

"But ya have to buy somethin', ya know. We're a poor, poor, family, an if ya don't buy something, then ma and ma daughters'll starve, aye, it's true."

"Do you have anything more practical?" Merlin asked. "Something useful?"

"Aye, aye. Here's the thing." And he pulled out a large leather sack with pewter rivets around the top.

"And this is — ?"

"A dung hauler. The most practical thing I sell for those that keep horses. Ya shovel it all in here, and then haul it where ya want to dump it, an yar hands never touch it. Like to a garden, say, or into yar enemies boots. Normally, I'd charge six coynalls, but for ya, just for ya, ya know, I'll drop the price to one screpall. An it's even stitched tight with me own handcrafted sinews, so it'll never rip and spill, or else I'll give ya yar screpall back."

Merlin hesitated. He really didn't —

Gogi sucked his cheeks in. "Remember that we'll starve afore we get much farther. Aye, we're *that* low on rations, an I got nah money to buy more."

"One screpall?"

"One. And it can even be bent or scratched, ya know. I care not."

Merlin clenched his teeth. He really didn't need this ... thing. But if it helped them not to starve, then it was kind of like charity, wasn't it? And maybe giving them some coins would free them from the boy's false obligation to protect the girls. Merlin could only hope.

"Sure ... I'll ... take it."

Gogi smiled, showing the gaps where a few teeth were missing, and a little broken one on the bottom.

Merlin handed him a screpall coin, and Gogi tossed him the dung hauler. Unfortunately the thing had already been tested in its ... purpose. He turned his nose away and rolled it up, tying and tucking the reeking thing behind his saddle. Maybe someone back home could use it.

Mórgana stood on a rocky headland overlooking the fortress of Dintaga, and the waves crashed in chorus behind her. The smell of salt tainted the air like a hint of blood, and before her stood five hundred or more warriors, each with a steel sword belted over his plaid.

"What do you think, Loth? Are they ready?" She turned and looked to her husband, who had just returned from Lyhonesse, having completed the construction of their new fortress. His long black hair blew in the wind, and his rugged, handsome features made her smile.

"Ya have performed a wonder, my queen. I canna' even fathom their power, nor the destruction they'll pour upon our enemies. When shall we set 'em loose?"

"Soon, very soon," Mórdred said. "Am I right, Mother?"

"Exactly so."

Mórganthu strode forward, his gait uneven and his hair unkempt. "But I grow impatient with this Voice of yours. Why has he not commanded their release?"

"You have touched the Stone, grandfather, and its power felled you long ago, remember?"

"Yes, yes."

"The Voice's power is much greater than the Stone's."

Mórganthu coughed over the sound of the surf. "Yet I have only heard the Voice *through* the Stone. To me, they are one and the same, yet you tell me they are not. And I myself have not heard the Voice in all these long years. How am I to believe you? Why should we not release these warriors now?"

Mórgana looked at him and sighed. Oh, how Grandfather had aged. So pathetic and frail, with his hair completely gray now. He had once been vigorous, yes, but as his strength had waned her own power had grown. No wonder he was impatient: he would soon die and his spirit would depart his lonely body. He wanted to *see* his vengeance. *Taste* it.

Ah, but what paltry insolence he chose to offer up to the Voice. Did he think he would please such a one? No, he would not. Perhaps, after all these years, it was time for her to call the Voice and ask him to appear to her grandfather. Then the old man would be silent and do as he was told. Such an annoyance. As well, these unruly warriors that Gorlas had provided for her could use a taste of fear to keep them in line.

And Mórdred? Yes, the lad could use a taste of fear.

"Well, then, Grandfather," she said. "Why don't you ask the Voice yourself?"

Placing a hand upon the fang sheathed at her belt, she snapped the fingers of her other hand. Her voice cried out then, and Loth joined her in the chant:

Voice of blood, Voice of Nudd, come now to us.
Lord of air, dark despair, walk among us!

And this they kept chanting until the winds began to swirl around them. The waves crashed higher, sending gray ribbons of water and spray to dash upon the rocks. The clouds grew dark, curling and boiling with great black tendrils. Lightning shattered the sky and shook the ground, striking an ancient willow that stood nearby. Its trunk exploded with searing white light. Mórgana shut her eyes as bright spots burned inside her head. Thunder crashed and crackled through the air, shaking and almost toppling her. Flaming bark flew through the air as the tree split completely open and caught fire.

"Behold!" Mórgana screamed. "The Voice, whom you doubt, appears!"

All of the warriors fell to their knees, but her grandfather's legs seemed locked in place, imprisoning him upright. His staring eyes protruded, and his open mouth hung slack.

A dark shadow stepped out from the charred center of the tree.

CHAPTER 10

THE BROKEN TREE

After some time creeping down the road at the snail's pace set by Gogi's massive draft horse, Merlin and the others arrived at a small, muddy stream with a clearing beyond, and they stopped to water the horses. During this delay, Arthur, Culann, and the girls talked some more and decided it was time to have a quick meal.

Gogi didn't protest, but Merlin had to bite his tongue. He looked at the sun — it wasn't even midday yet. What was Arthur thinking? Ah, but he knew. He just had a hard time stomaching it.

In the center of the clearing sat a huge, twisted oak that had been struck by lightning. The bark was ripped open down one side, and there was a large hole about halfway up. In its shade, Gwenivach spread out a plaid blanket of black, white, and burgundy, while Gwenivere searched their father's wagon.

"There's nah food there, Gweni, but we can at least rest the horses while these good men eat."

A look of alarm passed over Arthur's face. "No food? How can you — "

"We go without food all the time," Gwenivere said as she returned to Arthur's side. "That's part and parcel o' being a Walker. But we're hopin' tah sell a few things at Deva's faire and fill our empty ... ah ... buy some food there."

Culann stepped up. "We have more than enough. Don't we, Artorius?"

Arthur nodded, exasperating Merlin. It was one thing to share money with Gogi, but Merlin was concerned that their own scanty rations might run out soon.

Merlin dismounted and found a safe, soft place to set his harp. A bee flew in his face and he swatted it away.

Dwin dismounted and untied their food bag. He was making straight for the blanket when Gwenivere stepped in his way.

"Oh, we couldn't take yar food, nah. But we thank ya very much."

"We insist," Arthur said as he took the bag and opened it. Culann was already sitting down on a corner of the blanket, and he drew in a deep breath when Gwenivach sat down close beside.

Arthur, Gwenivere, and Dwin also sat on the blanket, with Merlin and Peredur choosing a shady spot on the dry grass. Gogi, who was still on his horse, was rebraiding part of his beard.

Arthur passed out the food: hard bread, dried goat meat, slices from a half round of rather smelly cheese, along with some dried apple slices. Once, his hand briefly touched Gwenivere's, and she blushed.

Merlin looked away and wanted to roll his eyes. This was not supposed to be the purpose of their trip south.

Gwenivach paused her loud crunching on the bread. "Are ya coming, Papa?"

Gogi nodded, grabbed a lone low-hanging branch, and stiffly swung his leg over. Then he began to slide down, but the branch snapped off with a loud crack, and he collapsed to his knees.

Arthur hurried over to help Gogi to his feet, waving away several more bees that flew from the trunk near the broken limb. The insects buzzed around the draft horse, which trotted off to the other side of the clearing, the wagon bumping after it.

Gwenivere joined the two men and dusted off her father, who towered a full two heads taller than Arthur.

"Look!" Gwenivere said, pointing at the tree. A long thin line of golden honey had leaked from the hole and traveled halfway down the trunk. A few bees twirled around it before flying back inside.

"Oh, Father, can I have a taste?"

"That ya can, me great Gweni!" the giant said, and he reached up to his tallest height and touched the very end of the golden streak. He brought it down and Gwenivere dabbed some off and tasted it.

"Mmm..." she said, closing her eyes and sucking a deep, blissful breath in through her nose. "I would *love* some for my bread! Can you reach the hole, Papa?"

"Nah, nah, and nah. Someone agile would have tah climb."

Culann jumped to his feet. "I'll do it."

Arthur followed suit a moment later. He leapt over to the tree and started to climb first — but the trunk was too thick and he couldn't get enough of a grip.

"Ya could use some rope," Gogi said, "if ya had any."

Culann was already at his horse and had pulled a rope from a bag. "I've got one," he called.

Arthur ran to his horse and checked his bags, but didn't find any.

Someone tapped on Merlin's shoulder. It was Dwin. "Do either of you have any rope?"

Merlin looked to Peredur, and both of them shook their heads. Dwin sighed.

By this time, Culann was trying to throw one end of the rope over a high branch, but it kept falling short.

Arthur cracked off the thick end of Gogi's fallen branch and tied it to the end of the rope. "Here, let me try." He spun it in the air and threw it straight up ... and over the high branch.

Culann frowned.

Pulling the broken wood from its knot, Arthur threaded the other end of the rope through and pulled on the rope until it was secure on the branch.

"It's my rope. I get to go," Culann said.

"I threw it!"

Merlin was annoyed at both of them, but principles were at stake here. "Culann," he called, "come here ..."

The young man looked angry, but stepped over. He was taller than Merlin, even taller than Arthur, and he had handsome features, with a straight, fine nose between inquisitive, dark eyes. His hair was a wavy brown, and it fell down carelessly to his shoulders.

"Arthur is your king. I think you should —"

"Horse hooves! If I'm going to —"

"Things have changed, Culann. Use that cool head of yours and think about the future."

"I *am* thinking about the future."

But he said no more, for Arthur had begun to climb and was soon halfway up.

Gwenivere and Gwenivach cheered him on, their claps, whistles, and calls filling the glade.

Arthur pulled himself up, feet on the trunk, swaying back and forth. Step over step, hand over hand on the rope until he reached the hole where the honey lay. Once there, he locked his legs around the rope and, with one hand, pulled out a large wooden spoon from the bag at his belt. He carefully reached the spoon into the hole as the bees began to buzz around him.

He scooped the spoon down, and then hundreds of bees swarmed out.

Augh!" he yelled, and had to pull his hand out, leaving the spoon behind. He began swatting at the bees, but they crawled over his face and neck, stinging him.

"Augghh!" he screamed as he slid down the rope, the bees chasing him. Everyone scattered.

Arthur ran off to the little stream as the bees thinned and

returned to their hive. When he came back, he had smeared mud on his stings, which covered most of his face, neck, and shoulders. Merlin almost laughed, but held it in.

Culann jabbed Merlin in the ribs and whispered, "I think you were right: always let your king go first." And he began to chuckle — until the girls ran over to Arthur.

"Oh, that must hurt terribly!" Gwenivach said.

Gwenivere hung on his arm. "You were so brave! All to get me a little honey."

Culann sighed, and Dwin looked on, longingly.

"Now we'll never get the honey," Gwenivere said. "Climbing is just too dangerous, though it was very kind of you to try."

"Hey!" Dwin called. "Two of our horses are missing!"

Neighing came from down the path, and then the sound of galloping.

"Thieves!" Merlin shouted.

Mórgana stepped back as her grandfather gaped. The Voice had come: what would the old man do? He had been such a fool to question the Voice's decisions. Grandfather had stewed this pot of reckoning, time and time again. Now Mórgana would let him eat his own soup.

The Voice towered over them, his dark cloak snapping in the salty spray, and a blue radiance lighting his body. With each step, fissures split in the rocky ground, and up from the cracks groped human fingers, pawing and trying to grip the sharp edge. Screams resonated from below, and the Voice slammed his massive boot down. The ground boomed and shook, the fingers disappeared, and there was silence once more.

Loth and Mórdred fell to their knees.

And, Mórgana noticed, the Voice's face had changed from the last time she had seen him. Hadn't he looked like her father? But now he was different. His beard was gone and his chin had lengthened.

And were his eyebrows more arched? His ears had grown smaller, and they were lacerated with bloody scars, as if the Voice scratched them incessantly.

There were, however, two things the same — his eyes were still pits of blackness with no end to their depth, and the old scar was still there on his forehead, nearly hidden by his red hood. The jagged scar ran upward — as if his cranium had been smashed once, but had since healed.

Without warning, the Voice swept down with a giant hand and picked Mórganthu up off the ground. The old man sucked in his breath, his face contorted in terror.

"Arch druid," the Voice whispered. "Do you remember me?"

Mórganthu shook his head. "I . . . h-have never seen you, my lord. B-but I . . . know the sound of your — "

"Then why do you question my commands? My servant, your granddaughter, stands before you, relaying my instructions. Are you not to honor her?"

"Y-yes. Yes."

"Then why," the Voice asked, "have I been disturbed to speak to you?"

Mórganthu said nothing, his lips trembling.

"Do you fear me?"

Mórganthu nodded.

"Rightly so, but I will show you just why you should fear me." He reached forward, ripped Mórganthu's head from his body, and though the man's limbs went lifeless, Mórganthu's head started screaming.

The Voice brought the head upward until the two were eye to eye. "Silence!"

Mórganthu's head shut its mouth.

"Good. Now listen. You have been given a task, and in that task you have done well. Have you not raised up and trained a throng of new druidow and sent them throughout the land? And these warriors before you, are they not also ready to do my service?"

Mórganthu made a noise of assent, but his face was turning blue.

"Through the host of druidow you have raised, I am bringing the Pax Druida back to my land. The Romans are gone, and now I shall rule through Mórgana and the druidow, who are mine. But my plan cannot be accomplished when *you* think it best. The army may not attack until exactly the right moment. Any sooner and it will not have the desired effect. Any later would be pointless. Do not question my orders again. Is this clear?"

The arch druid nodded, his face now green.

The Voice slammed Mórganthu's head back onto his body, gave it a double twist, and dropped him, whole, onto the ground. Mórganthu coughed and cowered down to hide his face.

The Voice laughed as he faded away. By the end, all that was visible of him were the pits of his eyes, and these, too, finally disappeared.

Loth stepped over Mórganthu's shaking legs and called out to the men. "Arise, warriors!"

The army stood to attention.

"Shall we have victory?" he yelled.

The warriors shouted and grunted in response.

"Shall we have revenge?" Mórgana shouted.

The warriors howled now from their wolflike snouts, and the very air seemed to grow colder.

The plans of the Voice would succeed, and Britain would never be the same.

CHAPTER II

THE BROKEN PATH

Merlin jumped onto the nearest horse and galloped after the thieves. Two others were right behind him, but he didn't turn to look. The thief, or thieves, were ahead, and Merlin caught site of a man's brown hat as he hunched over his horse and held the reins of two more.

Behind him, he heard a shout.

Merlin turned just in time to see Arthur go down. His saddle had slid sideways, and the young man fell from his horse. Next came Culann, who almost ran right over Arthur. Yanking the reins, he swerved his horse to the side just in time, but ran into Arthur's horse.

They both crashed in a heap.

Merlin urged his mount forward, faster, and made gains on the thief. It was a lone man, right? What if there were more hiding in the woods, ready to cut him down? He checked to make sure of his sword and rode on.

He gained on the thief, who had to handle three horses instead of one. Merlin would soon be in striking distance, and goaded his horse faster.

But the man rode to the right where a sapling bent down into the path. The man maneuvered the horse closer to the branches, unleashing the tree from some hidden peg, and it shot upright just after he passed, pulling a rope taught in Merlin's way.

But Merlin's horse had been well trained, and leapt without hesitation. The sound of the pounding hooves stopped. Merlin's body arced backward. The forest tilted. A jolt, like a hammering, rippled through the horse's front. Merlin jerked forward, grabbing the mane.

The black mane ... he should have known. This was Arthur's stallion, Casva. The best of them all. The horse took off again and overtook the thief, who snarled at Merlin, accentuating a thick scar across his chin.

Merlin started to draw his sword, but realized the man was too far away, with a horse running between them. Instead, Merlin pulled his horse close, reached out, and grabbed the reins of the nearest stallion.

The man tried to yank them back, but Merlin had a firm grip.

That was when Merlin's saddle began slipping and just like Arthur, he went down.

The world slowed. Neighing. Black, thundering hooves. Dirt smashing into his face. His legs slipping down. The ground ripping the fabric covering his knees. Skin scraping away. Yelling.

He held on to both sets of reins with all his strength, and the horses, their heads pulled downward toward each other, came to a slow, painful stop.

Merlin stood, out of breath and spitting dirt. His saddle hung sideways, with the girth strap partially cut through and partially torn. His knees were bloody, and he kicked a nearby rock in frustration.

The thief had sabotaged their saddles and had now escaped with one of their horses.

The party continued through the forest, short one horse. Thankfully Gogi had a good store of sinew with which to repair their saddles' girth straps and make them whole once more, or else the five of them would have been riding bareback. Merlin even bought some thinner sinew to sew the fabric of his breeches back over his knees.

Poor Dwin ... his horse was the one stolen, and he rode double with Culann.

It was now that Merlin grew most impatient, for the day was getting on, and still Arthur, Culann — and Dwin behind him — rode slowly, conversing with the girls. They needed to reach Glevum and either begin earnestly strategizing on how to defeat the Saxenow, or else forget the whole thing and get back home. Merlin didn't come on this trip so Arthur and his friends could spend time courting young lasses.

But it seemed that Glevum was the farthest thing from Arthur's mind.

The forest thickened even more, and Merlin's sense of isolation grew. Gogi lost his interest in talking, answering in a dirge-like humming. The only noise was the constant jangling of bells, which not only grated Merlin's nerves but made their presence conspicuous to any thieves who might be hiding in the darkness of the woods.

At length, a muddy, muck-filled riverbed began to follow the path to their right. It was wide and shallow, most of its water having finally succumbed to the heat plaguing the land, leaving only a few pools to seep into the muddy bottom.

And it stank. The longer they followed alongside, the stronger the stench grew. Fish lay bloated on its shore, their heads staring at Merlin with white, lidless eyes.

To top it off, the dung hauler that Gogi had sold him attracted a bevy of flies that swarmed around Merlin's back, biting his neck and buzzing in his ears. He would have chucked the bag in the mud but for Gogi's feelings.

Eventually the road curved to cross the riverbed — and they were met with an ancient bridge whose timbers were so cracked and rotten that many had fallen through. Arthur called them to halt. Dismounting, he stepped onto the bridge to test the nearest board. Bouncing up and down produced a great cracking, and the wood shattered. Arthur caught one of the rails and pulled himself up.

"I don't think we should risk it, but I don't see any other way across."

Indeed, the river was completely mud at this point, and Merlin hadn't seen anything better farther back.

"Ah, but we've come this way quite often," Gogi said with a hearty chuckle, "and we always walk the horses across the river tah the left o' the bridge. It's a bit muddy now, o' course, but not deep, and nothing for ya tah worry about, ya know."

Arthur looked at the riverbed dubiously. "I'll go first. The rest of you wait here until I find a way across."

Merlin groaned inwardly. "No, my ... Artorius," he said, almost calling Arthur "lord" in front of Gogi and his daughters. "I want the honor."

Arthur narrowed his eyes. "Are you sure?"

Merlin gulped. "Yes." It wasn't right for Arthur to go first.

After handing his harp to Peredur — just in case something went wrong — he urged his horse to the edge of the riverbed. Did he really want to do this? Gogi had said it wasn't deep, but did the giant really know? Did Merlin trust him?

"Merlin?" Arthur called.

That was all the prodding it took. The others must have a good example. But did this have to be his first act of service to his new lord? Really?

He nudged his horse forward. The animal responded and trotted out into the mud. Though the surface was slippery, there *was* something more solid underneath. For the first ten feet, at least — then the mud deepened, and the horse began to leap to prevent its hooves from getting stuck. About halfway across the horse began to sink. It tried to jump, but it just dug itself deeper in the mud. At first Merlin lifted his legs to keep his feet from the muck, but then he had to stand on the horse precariously, and couldn't reach the bridge.

"Gogi!" he yelled, almost falling. "You're responsible for this!"

"Didn't ya hear me tell ya to ride farther to the left?" the giant bellowed. "Ya must be deaf, that's what I say. It's not sah deep over there. Does anyone have a rope?"

Dwin rode forward. "Our only was left on the honey tree."

"If ya had a stout rope, ya could haul the horse out ..."

Merlin judged that if he jumped, he could grab onto one of the timbers. Carefully crouching on the horse's back, he leapt. Four fingers of his right hand caught hold, and he gripped tightly ... but fell. At least it was a soft landing. He floundered through the mud, sinking ever deeper as he lunged back to the horse. Grasping the reins, he pulled himself closer, but not before smearing the stinking mess all over his tunic.

He pulled himself up onto the saddle, and then the sinew repair of the girth strap came loose and the saddle slipped sideways. Merlin fell back into the mud.

"GOGI!"

But the giant ignored him as he rummaged in his wagon, soon producing a short rope of woven sinews no longer than six feet or so. Arthur and Dwin took it and walked carefully to the center of the bridge and drew Merlin up and out from the slime.

"You stink," Culann said when he made it back to shore.

Merlin wanted to give him a verbal lashing, but held his tongue. Instead, he turned to Arthur. "So now what do we do? We're down two horses."

"We ride double, buy some rope, and come back."

"There's a village," Gogi said, "not two leagues from here, ya know, and we can buy some there."

"But the bridge — ?"

Just then, they heard the sound of a horseman coming from the other direction. He emerged from the woods, hailed them, and then proceeded to cross the bridge. Sure, he went slowly to avoid fallen and cracked boards, but the bridge only shook the slightest bit.

"Never mind," Merlin said.

One by one they crossed, walking their horses to spread out the weight evenly. Finally Gogi crossed with his wagon, vowing many times over that in all their travels through this forest he had never once seen a horse cross the bridge successfully.

Before they rode onward, Merlin attempted to clean himself. Untying his bag, he set it and his belt aside. Then, using a broken stick, he scraped as much of the mud off as he could. Finally, he washed his hands with a few drops of their precious water.

Before they rode off, Merlin took one last glance at his horse, sad and snorting in the middle of the riverbed, and he vowed to come back and free it.

They rode for some distance at the same agonizing pace as before, and Merlin's thoughts slipped away north to Natalenya. A wave of homesickness rolled over him, and he reached for his bag, seeking the keepsake bit of skirt, only to find the satchel missing. It had been covered in mud and must have blended in with the ground back at the bridge.

Biting back a curse, he tapped Peredur, who was in the saddle in front of him, and explained his predicament.

Peredur nodded. "We're ridin' so slowly, I'll walk while you ride back."

He dropped from the horse and Merlin slid into the saddle.

"I'll return as quickly as I can."

"Don't worry. We'll be on the trail, and won't be far."

Gogi overheard their conversation. "Ah, young masked one, we'll never make it tah the next village, ya know, if ya slow us down."

Merlin ignored him, kicking the horse to a gallop. At least he was riding fast, even if it was in the wrong direction, and the breeze rushing through his hair felt good.

He arrived back at the bridge in no time at all.

But a man was standing on the bridge, and he held a long rope tied in a slipknot. He was dropping it over the head of the horse that was stuck in the riverbed. Merlin's horse.

"Ho, there! What are you doing?"

The man answered with a casual air. "Ma horse is stuck, and ah'm gonna pull him out."

Merlin stopped.

The same brown hat.

The same scar across his chin.

The thief.

Natalenya sang a ballad her grandmother had taught her as she finished packing some food that she and the children could eat at the waterfalls. White clouds had finally hidden the hot sun, and besides, Lord Ector's wife, Aunt Eira, urged her to get out more.

Natalenya knew Eira was right. Though the memories of the home invasion had left her uneasy, nothing strange had happened since that night, and she was beginning to wonder if she should have the door fixed and move back. What held her back was that the horse herders hadn't been able to successfully follow the confusing tracks of the intruders. Maybe the ground was just too dry to leave a clear trace, she told herself. Anyway, she wanted to forget the about it and provide some normalcy for the children.

Passing the satchel of food to Taliesin, she took Tinga's hand and led her out the door.

"C'mon!" Taliesin said, running ahead. "The water'll be dried up by the time we get there!"

"I'm not *that* slow!"

"Yeth you are," Tinga said.

Natalenya gave her cheek a good-natured pinch, then shouted ahead to the running boy, "Tal, did you bring the fishing line?"

He nodded back at her without slowing his pace.

It was a short distance to the falls, so Natalenya slowed the children down to enjoy their walk, for even amongst the dead grasses a few hardy wildflowers had sprouted up. The stream joined them alongside the path, and here the grass grew green. They passed the high, conical rock and the stairs that climbed up to the fortress. This was where the valley narrowed and the stream rushed downhill to become a little waterfall.

Taliesin chose a spot on a flat rock next to one of the small waterfalls, and there Natalenya spread out her plaid cloth. The water wasn't much, having thinned to one-third of its former flow, but it still gave a refreshing bubbling refrain.

Below them, farther down the falls, stood the crennig where the guards kept watch behind the thick timber wall. This wall had been concealed on the outside by rocks and brush in such a way as to keep their valley hidden from outsiders. It wasn't a great secret among the people of Rheged, but they definitely didn't want the Picti to know where the kingdom's horses were raised.

Tinga waded in a sandy spot while Taliesin started to unwind his fishing line. Natalenya caught him and tickled him playfully. "We'll eat first, yes?"

"Can't I fish?"

She slipped a crock out from their food bag and set it in the middle of the blanket. "I have your favorite."

Tinga jumped up and down, splashing the water. "Grouthe pie! Grouthe pie!"

"Settle, now — we have to thank God first."

Taliesin set his fishing line down.

"O Lord, thank You — for You are the provider of this feast. May You cleanse our souls even as we enjoy the bounty of Your provision. Thank You for making the clouds to shade us, the stream to run, and the trout to leap. Amen."

Taliesin's eyes popped open to survey the falls. "The fish aren't leapin' right now, Mammu."

Natalenya sniffed teasingly. "Well, they will be soon."

"Hopefully so. Can we eat?"

Natalenya smiled and cut a thick slice of grouse pie. She handed it to him along with a smaller one for Tinga. While they ate, Taliesin pulled off his boots and tossed them to the grass. He promptly plopped down and slid his feet into the water. Natalenya did the same, sitting between them, breathing deeply, feeling alive.

"Aren'th you going ta eat, Mammu?" Tinga asked, her mouth full.

"I am," she said.

"Here, Mommu." And Tinga cut her a ragged piece of the crispy-crusted pie filled with layers of sheep cheese, greens, and tasty grouse. The birds had been given that morning by one of the horse tenders who had gone hunting, and Natalenya and Eira had prepared them together.

Natalenya ate, smelled the weedy freshness of the falls, and swished her feet through the cool, swirling water until her toes tingled.

Taliesin ate another huge piece, pulled out his fishing line, and stuck some grouse meat on the bent copper hook. Finding a good spot not too far from his mother, he threw it in.

Tinga took the net and tried to catch fish farther up the falls.

"Be careful," Natalenya said, and then she pulled her feet from the water, lay back on the blanket, and closed her eyes. Soon the splashing and humming made her sleepy. She dozed.

She was awakened by Taliesin shaking her shoulder. "There's no fish here. Can we go to the pool?"

Natalenya had to think about that. The pool was just outside the gate. But what was the harm? There were always warriors on guard.

"The fishin'th better there," Tinga said, hopping up and down.

"Yes, I know. We won't stay long?"

Taliesin was already winding up his line. "Just so we can catch a fish."

"All right." Merlin loved fishing with them, and Natalenya sensed their determination was tied to missing their tas.

She packed up, and, still barefoot, they hopped the stream before walking down the path to the guard's crennig. The clouds had thinned some, though the sun didn't reach into the gorge at this time of day, leaving the stones cool on Natalenya's feet and the air moist.

And as usual, the guards were lying about, two of them napping beside old Brice, the porter, who was knitting with deft, gnarled fingers.

"And what are you making today?" Natalenya asked him.

"Ah, sumtin' for ta missus." He had one of the thickest Rheged accents, causing all his vowels to be drawn out slowly.

"Well, now, have you replaced that rusting hinge yet?"

"Ah ... nooo."

"And what about the cracked bar? Have you gotten a new one?"

"Ah ... I dooon't think so ... Nah yet, nooo."

"And the weak part of the gate ... Have you had the smith make some new plates to strengthen it?"

"Ah ... lemme check." He stood, shuffled over, craned his head at the gate, and shuffled back. "Ah ... no."

Natalenya tapped her fingers together and stared at him.

"I'm right sorry, Missus Ambrosius. I'll see to it ... next week."

Natalenya raised her left eyebrow.

"Right awa', then ... right awa'."

"Thank you, Brice. Now, we would like to fish in the pool outside, if—"

Brice nodded and kicked the nearest guard where he slept with his hat over his eyes.

"Logan, get up! And you too, lazy-knees!"

The two jumped up to help and had the gate open in no time. Uncle Ector normally kept five guards with the porter, but what with the warriors riding to help Urien, they had a shortage.

"Call if you need us," Brice said as he closed the door most of the way.

The pool was just a little way down and to the right, shaded and almost hidden by a few pines. Merlin loved to take the children here, and they almost always caught a few of the good trout that congregated in the deep, cold water.

But there was a curious object resting at the edge of the pool, a sort of case made from horn. Someone must have lost it here. Natalenya picked it up.

"What is it?" Taliesin asked.

From inside she fished out a shaving razor. The iron edge was oiled and quite sharp, and its handle was made from bone, and ... there were symbols carved into its side.

Natalenya sucked in her breath and closed her mouth.

She hadn't seen scratchings formed like that, since ... since she had been a slave.

It was Pictish!

With shaky hands she put the razor back in its box, tucked it in her belt, grabbed the children's arms, and dragged them back to the gate. After they squeezed inside, she shoved it closed and called for the guards. There, with a thrumming pain coursing through her head, she leaned upon the gate's old timbers — and moaned.

CHAPTER 12

THE BROKEN HOUSE

The veins in Merlin's neck began to pulse and his breathing quickened. The thief was trying to steal another of their horses!

The man cinched his rope tight around the head of the horse stuck in the riverbed and then turned to look at Merlin.

His face went white.

With the fragility of the bridge, Merlin knew he couldn't ride Peredur's horse across with any speed. Therefore he leapt off, laid his harp on the brown grass, and ran up the bridge.

The man frantically tried to get the rope loose, but couldn't. By the time Merlin closed the distance, the man had drawn his knife.

Merlin halted, rethinking his plan to grapple him, and drew his sword instead.

The man lunged at Merlin, his blade seeking Merlin's sword hand, but a broken board made him lurch and miss.

"Get away!" Merlin yelled, swinging to force him backward.

The man held his ground but ducked, causing Merlin's sword to cut a slice in the top of his hat.

Still holding the coil at the end of the rope in his left hand, the man threw it at Merlin.

The rope hit Merlin in the face, stinging his left eye and blinding him momentarily. He swiped to keep the man back, but the thief was already running down the opposite side of the bridge.

Merlin tripped on the rope and fell on his side to the boards. The one under his shoulder groaned, cracked, and snapped. Merlin fell, and he landed on his back in the mud. The putrid, stinking mud.

A dead frog popped out from the ooze and its toothless mouth gaped at him.

It was a long time before Merlin was able to extract himself from the muck and, with the help of the thief's rope and Peredur's horse, pull his horse free from the mess.

About that time Arthur, Culann, and Dwin came riding back to find out what had happened.

Merlin told them the story, and they cheered at the recovery of Merlin's horse, even if it was covered in mud and had a torn saddle strap.

"Where are Gogi and his daughters?" Merlin asked.

"They went on ahead."

"Good riddance," Merlin said under his breath.

Arthur heard him and glared. "What's wrong with Gogi?"

"He's bad luck, with worse advice."

"You should have ridden farther to the left."

"I never heard him say that. He made that up!"

"No, he didn't!"

Merlin cleaned off some of the mud coating his saddle. "Well, it's not Gogi you like, anyway. It's Gweni-what's their names."

"Don't bring them into this."

"Why not? You've been talking to them all day."

"Well ... they're nice. At least they speak to me, unlike the girls back home."

"Perhaps, but Gogi's daughters don't know when to keep their mouths shut, either."

"What happened wasn't their fault."

The hurt in Arthur's voice cut Merlin's anger short. He clenched his teeth together and drew a deep breath through his nose — a mistake, considering the filth. He'd spoken too rashly. Whether or not the boy acted like a king, Merlin owed him the same respect he would have given to Uther.

Placing a hand on Arthur's shoulder, he met the boy's gaze. "I'm sorry."

"Let's get moving." Arthur said, shaking off Merlin's hand and mounting Casva again.

Merlin was careful not to forget his bag with the scrap of Natalenya's skirt. Slinging his harp behind him, he climbed onto his horse and rode it bareback. At least they could stink together.

By sundown, their party still hadn't located Gogi, Gwenivere, and Gwenivach. It was as if the three had simply disappeared. Arthur, Culann, and Dwin searched all along the trail, and if so many other horses and wagons hadn't come through, they would've been able to track them. As it was, they wasted too much time trying to interpret the muddled signs.

Although they passed through the promised village, they found no sign of the Walkers, and pressed on until the light began to fail. As much as Merlin didn't like the giant and the girls, he began to worry that something bad had befallen them. Thieves did roam the forest — he knew that now — and visions of the giant slain and thrown in some ditch floated at the back of Merlin's conscience. Three times that night he sat up with a start, thinking he had heard the distant scream of a girl. But the woods were always silent and dark, and he was forced to wonder if he had imagined it.

Merlin awoke to Arthur shaking his boot.

"Time to get up. I want to get on the trail early."

Merlin sat up and rubbed his right shoulder, which still hurt from his tussle with the thief. "Do you forgive me for yesterday?"

"I do."

"Maybe we'll catch up to them farther on."

"We should have found them yesterday. They can't have just disappeared."

Dwin, who was already up and packing his horse, called frantically from near the woods. "Arthur! Come look at this!"

Merlin and Arthur ran over, leaving Peredur and Culann to wake themselves.

"What is it?" Dwin asked.

Merlin looked, and there in the horse manure was the print of a wolf, though larger than any Merlin had ever seen. Looking more closely, Merlin saw something else — the print was more elongated than it should have been, almost as if the pads had been stretched.

"Is it one of the wolf-heads?" Arthur asked.

"I don't know. I've never seen a wolf this large."

They broke camp quickly and in silence.

Not once that day did they see a sign of Gogi and his daughters. Arthur even asked a party of traveling merchants if they had encountered them farther down the road, but they had not.

After a brief stop on the outskirts of Deva to purchase a new horse for Dwin and to repair Merlin's saddle, they continued on, and each day thereafter was the same. No word. No sign. And as they traveled south toward Glevum, it became hotter and drier. The trees were emaciated, the grass nearly dead, and it became almost too hot to breathe. Sweat soaked Merlin's clothes, and though this helped to keep him cool, it was the most miserable traveling he'd done in many a year.

How long would the drought last?

Merlin had thought it bad up north, but this was like nothing he'd ever seen. And the suffering made it worse. The crops were already withered and the cattle had nothing but dry grass to eat. One village they passed had been completely abandoned, and Merlin found out why when they tried to draw water from the village well — it was completely dry. Dead sheep lay on the hills, infested with worms and devoured by flies.

And this made Merlin worry for their horses. As much as they let them drink, they seemed to need even more. Thankfully, only ten leagues south of Deva they found a path that led them along the western bank of the Habrenaven River. The water was low, stale, and brown. But at least it was water.

The journey took six more hot, arduous days before the land began to slowly drop and the river to swell from other tributaries. They were approaching Glevum. Merlin advised Arthur to cautiously approach from the forest rather than the open road along the river.

"What's there to worry about?" Arthur asked. "He doesn't know I'm even alive."

"Many of his warriors knew your father, and they may see the resemblance."

"Do I really look like him?"

"Bedwir says so. I never saw your father clearly myself."

"You were still blind then?"

"Yes."

"What about my mother? Tell me about her."

"She was kind to me, and your sisters were sweet … tender, I'd say. They had an innocence about them that told me your mother had shielded them well from the wars your father had to fight. It must have been hard for her. All I ever did was share a meal with them."

"I should have liked to have done even that."

Merlin smiled. "You were there too."

"Too young to remember. Except in my dreams."

"One day you'll meet them. One day."

"I know, but it doesn't seem real. You tell me I'm the High King, and I try to be … I try to lead, but I'm just me. Dwin treats me differently, sure, but I don't think I like it. At least Culann hasn't changed."

"He will in time," Merlin said, but his words fell on deaf ears. He could tell Arthur felt lost, here at the edge of the unknown. Vortigern. His father's murderer. Saxenow invaders growing stronger each day. The fate of Britain. And only a part day's ride until they would arrive at Glevum, the place where all of these fears twisted and coiled together.

"I had another dream," Arthur said, interrupting Merlin's thoughts. "The woman with the black hair appeared to me again and called my name — Arthur. She's the only one beyond the valley of Dinas Crag who knows my name."

"I told you what I thought before."

"That she's some phantom of your sister."

"Yes."

"I don't have any fear when I dream of her."

"She's — "

"Yes, I know. Don't accuse me. I'm not that shallow."

"But are you looking deep enough? Anyone can talk smoothly."

"All I sense is sadness. A longing to know me."

"And to kill you."

Arthur's eyes hardened for a moment. "I don't believe that."

Merlin said no more.

That night they camped in the woods, as he'd advised. The moon was full, sending black shadows of trunk and bough across their sleeping forms. And the forest was strangely quiet. A gray hush, and then nothing. Like something waited, fretting quietly and plotting. Merlin could feel it. And when he finally fell asleep, men with the heads of wolves lurched through his dreams, each one dragging away the corpse of a man he had killed.

Merlin awoke with a start. It was still dark, but a slim line of red showed that dawn wasn't far off, so he built the fire up a little and baked an early breakfast of oatcakes for the party. As the sun rose, the light was dark red like that of a raw wound, and Merlin knew something was wrong.

By the time the others awoke, it was obvious that Glevum, just over the horizon, was burning. They ate in haste, mounted, and rode toward the city, where the scent of smoke filled the air.

A man came running down the path toward them. He still held his sword, which had been shattered, and his bloody tunic had been ripped across the front.

Merlin pulled up his mask and jumped from his horse just in time to stop the man, who was shaking. His eyes darted left and right, up and down, yet he wouldn't look at Merlin.

"Ru-run!" the man said. He wrenched his arm free and tried to get away.

Merlin wrestled him down. "What is it? What's happened?"

The man punched Merlin in the jaw. "Attacked! I'm attacked!" he yelled. He flailed and thrashed as Arthur and Culann joined Merlin in restraining him.

"Who? Who attacked?" Arthur asked.

"You! Lemme go!"

"No! Who attacked Glevum?"

"Glevum … Glevum …"

Arthur changed his tone and made an effort to meet the man's wild eyes. "Who are you? Just tell us who you are."

The man hesitated, and his gaze seemed to focus on Arthur's face. "Mabon … I'm Ma-mabon."

"Mabon, then … Tell us where Vortigern is."

"The High King's … gone to Dinas Marl to f-fight the Saxenow … He's not here!"

"Tell us what happened …"

The crazed look returned, and Mabon began to thrash again. "Wolves!"

At this, Arthur looked up at Merlin.

Merlin shrugged, but this word sent a chill across his back. Or could Mabon have meant something else? "Do you mean sea wolves — raiders? Did someone attack from the river?"

"No ... no ..."

"Saxenow?"

"Gorlas!"

Arthur looked confused. "Gorlas? That sounds like a British name."

"He's the king of Kernow," Merlin said. But what did Gorlas have to do with this man's fear?

"Lemme go! Gotta get away!"

Merlin released him, and the others did the same.

They watched Mabon run off toward the deeper parts of the forest.

"The last I knew, Gorlas was loyal to Vortigern. Why would he attack Glevum?"

They mounted and rode toward the city, keeping to the thicker parts of the forest as long as they could, but the woods suddenly ended and they were forced out onto open farmland. An old, rustic Roman villa lay before them in the final stages of burning to the ground. Behind it, barely visible through the smoke, lay a stone bridge that crossed the Habrenaven River with the walled city of Glevum beyond. It too was burning. The smoke filled the entire sky, reducing the sun to a sickly, red disk.

Arthur stopped short, surveyed the scene, and then rode hard for the villa. "Whoever's done this ..." he yelled.

"As if it wasn't hot enough!" Dwin shouted.

They rode past a farm worker's body lying facedown in the field. Blood had dried on his tunic, and Merlin didn't see him breathing.

When they arrived at the villa, they found its interconnected houses were almost completely destroyed. A large stone archway still stood, though, allowing entrance to the center atrium, and Arthur took it at full speed with Merlin right behind. Surrounded by burning buildings, Merlin began to choke, and had to pull his cloak up and breathe through its thick fabric. A wide mosaic pavement lay in the center of an ornamental garden, and that was where they found the heaped bodies of the inhabitants. A large pool of blood surrounded the pile, and a lone red-legged crow defied the smoke to lap at the moisture.

When Merlin saw the bodies, he turned and kicked his horse until it fled back outside. This was his very worst fear, for each and every person had had their throats torn out, the way a wolf instinctively kills its prey.

Merlin felt faint, and he had to clutch the mane of his horse and close his eyes. Deadly lights spun in his head, and his horse felt like it was rearing up, though he knew this wasn't true.

"Are ya all right?" Peredur called.

Merlin retched, vomiting out his breakfast over the the shoulder of his horse. Sweat began to drip from his forehead, and a chill took hold of his neck. His tongue thickened and felt like it was about to suffocate him, while his throat pulsed an evil beat.

It was too much. Too much.

Mórgana's wolf-heads had come.

CHAPTER 13

THE BROKEN CITY

Still battling weakness, Merlin followed the others across the stone bridge over the Habrenaven and rode toward Glevum's west gate. As they approached the thick stone entrance, Arthur read out the inscription carved there:

COLONIA NERVIA GLEVENSIUM
LEG II AUGUSTA

"The Second Augustan Legion built this?" Peredur asked.

"Under the orders of Emperor Nerva, whom I've only heard a little of," Merlin said. "Colvarth also told me the village of Gloui existed before the Romans came. This was the best crossing of the river for leagues and leagues, and so when the Romans saw its strategic advantages, they made it their staging area to invade Kembry."

"Is that why Vortigern made it his home?"

"Yes and no ... seventy-five years ago his grandfather, Vitalinus, was the *legatus* here, and when he assassinated Constans, the High Kingship came to him."

"And so Vortigern rebuilt it, didn't he?"

"The city? No. Nothing but his grandfather's feasting hall."

"Do you think it's still standing?"

"We'll see."

They passed under the stone arch of the wall and came to the wooden gate, which was closed and barred. Arthur banged on it, but no one answered.

"I can climb over," Dwin said, and Culann helped him up. With his great agility and toeholds on the wall, Dwin climbed easily, pulled himself over, and dropped. When he unbarred the doors and they creaked open, he wore a solemn expression. A pile of thirty or more bodies lay near the gate — people who had apparently attempted to flee but had been prevented — though by whom?

Merlin tried not to look, but couldn't pull his gaze away. They were killed just like the people in the villa. Women and children were among the corpses, and quite a few men, a few of whom were warriors. Gold and silver coins were scattered across the bloody, cobbled road, and the fingers of the dead clutched at their treasures and valued possessions. One woman, however, clung to nothing but a cross, which hung reverently between her hands even as she lay in death.

What has Mórgana become? Merlin wondered. *Is she really capable of all this destruction? Is her soul so consumed by evil that all remorse and hesitation are gone?* And if that were true, was Merlin somehow responsible? Doubts gnawed at him, and every corpse seemed to accuse him, saying, *"You didn't love her enough! You abandoned her! You were so fond of Arthur that you forgot your own sister!"*

The smell of smoke assaulted them as they entered the burning city. Arthur led them along the wall facing the river where the smoke was lighter thanks to a slight wind pushing from the southwest.

Besides the hissing and popping of flames within the ruined buildings, the city was silent, unnerving Merlin. Were some of Mórgana's wolf-heads spying on them even now?

"By the looks of it," Arthur said, "it must have been attacked last night while we slept."

Merlin silently thanked God for Gogi and his accursed slow horse. All of the buildings made entirely of wood had burned to piles of smoking ash. Those left standing were of stone, but even they had had their thatch roofs burned away, and their empty walls gaped upwards to the parched, smoke-filled sky.

The wall that they followed curved southward and led them to an unexpected overlook where they could see down into a lower plane of the city. A long quay ran along the river, and there, next to the quay, stood a walled fortress within the city. In the center of the fortress was a large central building of wood and stone, and its ruins were still in flames.

"Do ya think?" Peredur asked.

Merlin nodded, and with Arthur's agreement they rode down and passed into the fortress's open doors, whose iron hinges creaked in the wind. Just inside the gate stood a carved stone bearing the words *DINAS VITALINUS*. There were barracks and various other military buildings around the outside walls of the fortress, and these were all burned to the ground. The nearest one, a former stable, contained the remains of many horses, and at the side was a great pile of dung amongst the burned animals.

Arthur led them past all these to the ruins of the huge central building, which, Merlin could tell, had been built with ornamental stonework, now fallen, scattered, and shattered at the base of its blackened walls.

After opening the doors, Arthur and the others viewed the interior, confirming that this had been Vortigern's feasting hall. Down the central aisle of the building, underneath all the black, broken, and smoking timbers, lay a long, once-splendid hearth where his warriors would have reclined and feasted after a victory. Far down the hall, upon a bronzed dais, stood an intricately carved wooden throne, now charred and cracked in half by a fallen timber.

Arthur entered the hall as Merlin and the others followed. With the roof gone, the smoke didn't overpower them. Still, they had to step over piles of still burning wood, and the air felt hot.

All around the floor lay the bodies of warriors with the golden lion of Vortigern's reign pinned to their cloaks — their throats rent and torn, and their bodies burnt.

Merlin wanted to leave, but Culann called from the side. "Here's a different sort of warrior."

Merlin picked his way over. This one lay facedown, but it was clear he was clad differently ... with a tartan of indigo, white, and teal, and a more crude, less Roman-like armor.

"He's one of Gorlas's men," Merlin said. He rolled him over, expecting to find a wolf-head, but was shocked to see that the man had a normal face.

They searched the feasting hall further and found sixteen similar warriors, and none of them were wolf-heads. They also found the bodies of women and children in the rooms along the side and back of the feasting hall, possibly members of Vortigern's household.

"How many warriors would it have taken to capture the city and fortress?" Dwin asked.

"With Vortigern absent," Merlin said, "I'd guess a thousand or more," He'd seen the size of the city, the stoutness of the walls, and the number of warriors and people they had found dead along the way. "But Gorlas doesn't have that many. Sure, he's the king of Kernow, but his fortress at Dintaga, though nearly impenetrable, is fairly small."

"Could he have raised them?"

"To commit this atrocity? I doubt it."

"So what now?" Peredur asked. "The muster isn't to happen fer two weeks, yet we find the city destroyed and Mabon tells us Vortigern's gone to Dinas Marl."

"Back home," Merlin answered, hope rising in his heart that Arthur would forget the whole thing.

"Or we could go find Vortigern." Culann said. "His feasting hall's gone and he needs to know what happened."

Merlin spat. "Let someone else bring him the news. You think you'll get a reward for telling him what's happened here?"

"Yet he needs our help," Arthur said. "Even more than ever. How can Britain survive with invaders in the east and her own people stabbing from the west?"

"True, true," Dwin said, nodding.

Merlin pushed his doubts away and scowled. He didn't care what happened to Vortigern. As far as he was concerned, the man got what he deserved. If Merlin hadn't suspected that his own sister, Mórgana, was behind the attack, he wouldn't have even blinked.

"I'm for going back home," Merlin said. "Let Vortigern cook in his own fire."

"And you think we'll be safe up north?" Arthur asked. "Ector understood the danger, and he told me so. Maybe you've been spending too much time with King Urien, eh?"

"You know why I go there —"

"The last few years, I've hardly ever seen you for more than a week or two before you're off again."

"And Ector is the one who sends me. You know that."

"What I know is what Ector taught me. If there is no freedom in the south, then the north cannot hold out for long, and we'll be squeezed between the Picti and the invaders like a fish ready to be gutted. Are you prepared for that?"

"Ector despises Vortigern."

"And that lessened his worries?"

Merlin bowed his head slightly. It was true what Arthur said, even if it hurt.

Arthur approached and lowered his voice until it was almost a whisper.

"I know you hate Vortigern, and I understand why. They were *my* parents. But I don't remember them, and I still have you and Mother. You've been the best parents — you've been the best father that I could have hoped for. But for the good of Britain, let us resolve here and now to save her if at all possible. Please … please. I need your help."

Merlin felt conflicted, pulled, and stretched. He had spent his life running from Vortigern, and now this? Did they really have to go find Vortigern and step right into the monster's arms? And what galled him most was being told to do so by Arthur, the man who should hate Vortigern more than anyone.

Really, though ... Merlin and Natalenya hadn't fostered any special loathing for Vortigern in the young man. In fact, they had done their best not to talk about the High King or the southern part of Britain. Had all that created in Arthur a curiosity for the south, and now a desire to save it? Created a spirit that could readily come to the aid of a despicable man he hardly knew?

And what *was* best? Coming south meant Merlin might be able to visit his boyhood home in Bosventor, Kernow, even though that home was all but gone. Burned up by the flames of the Druid Stone. His father dead, yet his mother ...

He had grown up thinking she was dead too. And then he'd found her changed into a water creature by the Stone and bound to Lake Dosmurtanlin. He had been forced to leave her in order to save Arthur's life. All these years he had longed to see her again and had stuffed his feelings down.

And what had he done instead? Duty. Protect Arthur. Fight the slave-taking Picti. That was all he knew. Someday in the future, sure, he was planning on leading Arthur south to his destiny, but in his mind that was always in the future. Never *now*.

But what of all the countless other fathers there who hugged their children before bed? What of all the mothers that baked bread for their families? What of all the little boys, the little girls ...

But this was madness. The voices of the innocent clamored in Merlin's head, pounding him as he imagined the Saxenow killing them and driving them from their villages and taking their homes. Their weeping cursed his name as real fathers, real daughters, real sons, and, indeed, real mothers paid the deadly price of Merlin's inaction. Of Vortigern's incompetence. Of the steady decline of the British people and their waning strength.

Was it true? Had Merlin been so content in the north that he had betrayed the south? Betrayed himself? Betrayed every Briton who had died under the axe of a merciless Saxen invader? Betrayed those here at Glevum who had died under Mórgana's evil attack?

He had to face it.

Arthur coughed, breaking Merlin's thoughts. He held his hand out and spread his fingers to reveal five golden lion pins that he must have lifted from the dead.

"Each of us needs to wear one of these," he said. "Not as a sign of loyalty to Vortigern, but of our loyalty to Britain and her people."

Each of the others took a pin until there were only two left in Arthur's palm. One for Arthur. And one for Merlin.

No, he couldn't even touch it. If he did, he would smash it under his boot.

The blood on Vortigern's hands!

But wasn't blood on Merlin's hands? Blood that had been shed by his delay? Here he was, with practically the entire kingdom of Rheged eating out of his hand, and he had done nothing but hide and try to stop the northern slave raids. Yes this was important work, but was it his real work? The day of Colvarth's death came back to Merlin, and the words of the dying bard stung his ears:

"Merlin ... come to me," Colvarth had choked out. His face was puffy, his eyelids thick and red, and he was always out of breath. He'd been ailing for weeks, and none of the healers could help him.

"Merlin, I know this seems very rash ... but I've been feeling ..." And here he coughed for a long time. "No, not feeling ... for God Himself has shown me over the last year ... that the time has come to declare Arthur the rightful High King ... and raise up an army from Rheged and Kembry ... and all that will join our banner to fight against Vortigern."

Merlin had considered the words. He really had. But then Colvarth had died within the hour, and Merlin's busy life had moved on, and Arthur seemed so ... so young. The root of it, though, was that Merlin was afraid.

So, yes, he knew what he needed to do and had ignored it. Blood was on his hands. Could he hold Arthur back now?

"I'll go with you," Merlin said, and each word, though true, tore at his heart. "And I will support you in everything, but I can't wear a sign of allegiance to Vortigern. It will make little difference." Merlin felt the black mask that covered his face. "I wouldn't last long in Vortigern's presence wearing this, eh?"

Arthur embraced him.

Outside they heard the neighing of a horse, and turned in time to see a man dismount and apprehensively peek inside. He had a richly colored cloak and a wide hat pinned upward on one side. The man's face ... Merlin looked twice, but there could be no mistake. Fodor, Vortigern's envoy, had returned to his master's house.

Merlin ran at the envoy, and before the man could remount his horse Merlin pulled him down and pinned him to the ground.

"You! What are you doing here so soon? You were headed north."

"Get him off! Get this man of unknown parentage off of me!"

Merlin wanted to punch him in the jaw, but held back. "Answer my question, or I'll — "

"I knew you were reprehensible! Let me up, for I will not answer questions of a masked man!"

"There's a stable by the gate, and I saw a nice dung heap surrounded by dead horses. Maybe if I tossed you in there, mouth first, it would loosen your tongue."

"No! An esteemed emissary of the High King will not be abused in such a way." And here he took in a deep breath. "If you keep me and my garments clean, I will answer your simple questions."

"Tell me what's happened in the north — "

Fodor nodded. "I was heading to King Urien, and have come south with grave news."

Merlin's grip increased along with his anger. "Tell me!"

"An envoy's news is for his king's ears alone. Even the Wild Huntsman couldn't drag it out of me."

"Peredur, help me drag this man to the dung heap."

They picked him up, face down, with Culann and Dwin on the legs and Merlin and Peredur on the arms. Arthur stood back, watching the proceedings with a smirk.

"No!" the man yelled, but they ignored his struggles and marched him down the street toward the stable.

"You have three more chances," Merlin said, and at his signal they rotated the man around and began to swing him back and forth so that his face came progressively closer to the pile of dung. It had been freshly shoveled, and its overpowering odor had attracted countless flies.

"Put me down!" the man yelled. "A great-grandson of Firsil is not to be treated in this manner!"

They brought him back, and began counting as they swung him forward. "Yahn ..."

"I will not stand for this!"

Once more they swung him toward the dung. "Tahn ..."

"Vortigern will hear of this!"

And the last swing was the biggest of all. "Tethera!"

Fodor shot forward, yelling, "Stop! I'll talk I'll talk I'll talk!"

They tightened their grip and prevented his headlong descent, but it was too late for his hat, which flopped artfully into the sloppy dung and slid down into some liquid that had leaked out from the bottom.

They stood him up again, and the man cowered before Merlin, who tried one more time. "Tell me what you know of the north."

"I ... I rode to Luguvalium, after your uncouth chieftain so ungraciously threw me out, but I never made it inside Urien's fortress."

"Why?"

"Because the Picti had laid siege to it."

Luguvalium under siege? That was impossible. The Picti only raided for slaves ... didn't they?

"I don't believe you. How many Picti were there?"

"Thousands, and one of their scouts caught me, the oaf. He brought me before their High King. He let me go on oath that I bring a message to Vortigern."

There was one way Merlin thought of to prove the man a liar. "Tell me, then, about this High King."

"Necton Morbrec mac Erip. Red hair. Lots of blue paint. Two torcs, both very impressive. Imposing fellow, and, though a tad ill-mannered, he knew his pedigree, he did."

Merlin's legs went weak, and he closed his eyes.

While the others showed Fodor the remains of the feasting hall, Merlin sat on a chunk of rock, alone. If Luguvalium fell, then what would happen to Dinas Crag? Could it remain a secret if Necton destroyed the northern kingdom of Rheged? Merlin doubted it.

He reached in his leather bag and took out the torn piece of skirt that Natalenya had given him. It was so soft under his fingers, and it comforted him. She was so loving, so needed, so alone. He wasn't complete without her. And Taliesin and Tinga ...

He prayed for them — but while he prayed, something strange happened. The softness of the piece of skirt became gritty under his fingertips. What was this? He looked, and where the piece of skirt had been clean before, now it had become strangely dirty ... while he was holding it. Maybe he was confused, so he checked the inside of his bag and it was clean as he remembered. Even when he'd fallen in the mud twice, he'd been meticulous about making sure the inside stayed clean and dry.

The dirt didn't make sense, but Merlin prayed all the more earnestly.

It had been many days since Natalenya had found the Pictish razor by the stream, but a part of her was still shaking with a fear that twisted her insides. Even staying in her aunt Eira's house hadn't helped. Her breath was always tight now, and chopping wild onions and horseradish for drying didn't help either.

Once the news had spread that their valley had been discovered, a meeting had been called, attended by the remaining warriors, the horse tenders, and all the heads of families. With Ector gone, a temporary leader needed to be chosen, and to her surprise, Natalenya had been selected. Aunt Eira had suggested it, and everyone agreed, knowing her wisdom and how vigilant she had been through the years to keep the valley safe.

And so, with this new responsibility, Natalenya had personally overseen the stocking of food and water to the top of Dinas Crag by all the families. However, with the drought there wasn't as much to put up as she had hoped.

She had also made sure that an inspection was made of the fortress's outer wall, which surrounded the top of the steep hill as close to the edge as the ancient builders could place it. They found numerous weak points, which she set the men to repairing.

And the central tower — oh, how she wished it had been made of stone, but the walls must have taken all the available stone, and since timber was plentiful, the original builders had made it from that. Sure, it was stout, with thick walls and four levels including a lookout, but its construction worried her.

The weakest point, of course, was the gate, which was made of iron-banded wood. Its doors were so heavy that she could hardly push them open, but they were wood all the same. And no, the steepness of the path approaching them didn't comfort her.

What she wanted most of all was Merlin. His strong, calloused hands rubbing her shoulders and telling her it would be all right. His tender eyebrows promising her protection. But he wasn't here, and nothing could comfort her given the signs of danger all around. Tinga would look at her with her big, hopeful eyes, and Natalenya tried to be strong for her, but in private could barely hold back the sobs that welled up in her throat.

And Taliesin had tried to cheer her on more than one occasion by showing her how sharp the tip of his blade was. "No worries," he'd say. "Any Pict that attacks will be a dead Pict. He won't get past me."

Though nothing eased the worry, Natalenya found herself turning more and more to practical busywork like preparing and preserving vegetables for the crag.

"Keep chopping, dearest," Aunt Eira said from across the culinar. "I've scrubbed a whole pile here and you're getting behind. Thinking about him won't bring him back any faster."

"Your Ector will come home first, I know that now."

"And thank God."

Natalenya bit her lip.

"I didn't mean it that way. My thought is only to the war band. We need all of them now that we may have been discovered."

"I know. I'm just worried about Merlin and Arthur. I had thought they'd be back by now. He's either still looking for Arthur or else is going south with him. I don't know which I fear more."

Natalenya returned to her knife work, but nearly sliced her thumb when shouting sounded from outside. Someone began banging on the door. Goffrew, the hound, stood and bayed, her two pups looking around in confusion.

"Oh dearest, oh dearest, what could that be?"

"Ector?"

"I do hope so."

Natalenya walked across the hall and began to unbar the door, but thought better of it.

"Who's there?"

A muffled voice came from the other side.

"Who?" she yelled.

"… Caygek …"

Natalenya stiffened, then yanked the bar upward in a hasty arc. Pulling the door open, the former druid burst in. His beard was streaked with blood, and he was completely winded.

"The Picti!" he whispered, sucking in air. "They'll be … at the outer gate before long … a thousand at least."

"You didn't lead them here?"

"No ... they've besieged Luguvalium, so Bedwir and I spied ... overheard their ... rear guard discussing plans."

"Father, preserve us," Eira murmured.

"Sound the alarm." Natalenya ran from the hall, the sharp, dry grass pricking her bare feet and the hot air making it ever harder to breathe. There was a bell tower on the northern end of the main stables, and Natalenya ran to its rope, untied it, and pulled. This bell was only allowed to be rung in the direst of emergencies, and everyone in the valley knew what was required.

Down she pulled. *Clang!* The rope jerked upward. *Clangk!*

Again and again, the bell pealed across the valley, resounding from the mountainsides.

Soon there was commotion everywhere. Women and children emerged from their crennigs and ran toward the fortress with as many essentials as they could carry. The men ran to the fields to gather the horses. Natalenya knew that these would be taken south, away from the fortress, through the secret mountain passes in hopes of saving them. All of the sheep would be left behind in an effort to fool the Picti and delay them long enough to get the horses away.

Only once before in the memory of the elders had this evacuation been required — when a British king had attacked from the east. Then it had ended in disaster, with only a few of the villagers surviving. The horses were captured and never returned. Replenishing the stock and rebuilding Rheged's power took many long years.

Natalenya ran back to her uncle's hall. She scooped up the hand of the crying Tinga, holding tightly to the little squirming female puppy, Gaff. Aunt Eira and her servants had gathered the last of the foodstuffs while Caygek recovered his breath, and together they made a run for the stairs leading to Dinas Crag. Taliesin carried Gruffen, the little male puppy, and the mother hound followed behind, sniffing the wind as if some odor defiled the air from the direction of the lake.

Farther down the valley flowed the waterfall, and at the end lay the gates that would now prove fairly useless to defend. Designed to conceal them at best, and stop a small raiding party at worst, the gates would never withstand the power of an invading army. The valley's inhabitants would now have to rely on the hill fort.

And from below, old Brice cupped his hands and called upward from his lookout. "They've come! Everyone, to the fortress!"

Bedwir joined them from where he had been resting. There was a bloody gash on his left arm, and a scratch across his forehead.

But Natalenya's breath was short, and her legs felt numb. She tripped on Tinga's blanket. Falling headlong, she twisted to the side and fell into the dirt, jerking Tinga down as well. Aunt Eira and Caygek helped them up, but her skirt was horribly dirty.

"C'mon!" Taliesin said.

Placing one shaky foot upon the first step of the stair, Natalenya began the long, difficult ascent to the fortress. And as she did so, a quiet wail escaped her lips. With so few warriors to defend the walls, there was no way they could hold out against the Picti. And so her deepest fear had caught her and was dragging her down with its painted, sinewy hand.

She would be a slave once more, along with her children.

PART TWO
TERROR'S GRASP

Battle, noise, and dust: the young one fighting;
Holy, pure, and strong: the good God calling;
Spirit, hand, and heart: the white path choosing;
Gauntlet, shield, and torc: the kingship taking;
Skinned in death, there the moon will rise.

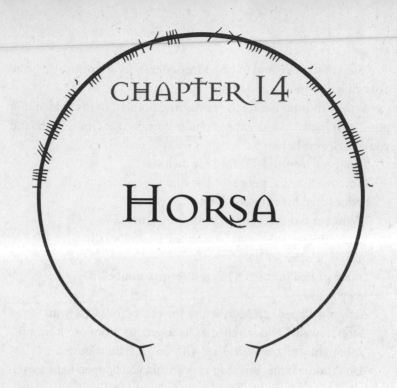

CHAPTER 14

HORSA

As Merlin remounted his horse, he saw Fodor astride his own and looking angrily at his soiled hat. He held it out with one hand and pinched his nose. "How in a Saxen spring am I supposed to carry this?" he asked.

After untying the knot holding Gogi's dung hauler in place behind his saddle, Merlin threw it to Fodor, who caught it. "Here, put it in there ... it's the perfect place." And then he laughed, but it was hollow, for he didn't feel mirthful.

Fodor warily sniffed the dung hauler and threw it down in disgust. Instead, he pulled two woven strings from within his hat and tied the filthy thing to his saddle.

Together they rode out the east gate of the ruined city.

"I'm not going with you," Fodor said.

"Fine," Dwin said with a smirk. "Then we won't smell your hat."

"A son of Fercos is not to be scoffed at."

"Nor sniffed, apparently," Culann said.

"Stop that! I demand to be addressed only by Artorius. He is the only civil one among you boors."

Arthur rode up beside the envoy and pointed to his golden lion pin. "Well then ... we're riding to join Vortigern at Dinas Marl, and you're welcome to join us."

"Not even tempted. I'll find my own way."

"You saw how the people of Glevum died, didn't you?"

Fodor lifted his chin and looked away.

"Whoever did that may be hiding anywhere."

"Quite improbable." But he glanced around warily.

"You'd be safer with us."

Fodor sniffed the air. "That is utterly in doubt."

"As you like."

Arthur galloped off. Merlin and the others followed him.

"Stop ... wait!" Fodor yelled as he urged his mount to keep up.

"I thought you weren't riding with us," Merlin shouted.

"Don't address me. But as to your insult, you happen to be traveling my way, and I might as well keep you out of trouble."

They rode out Glevum's south gate, as Merlin had directed, refilled their waterskins, and abandoned the road to cut across open country. Their goal was to find the trader road leading from Aquae Sulis to Dinas Marl, and the fastest way was to head east. En route they crossed another road, the ditch-dug Fossa, a Roman road that went from Corinium to Aquae Sulis and all the way down to Isca Difnonia, but this road didn't suit their needs either, and they continued eastward.

The fact that fighting had come so close to Glevum worried Merlin. Had the Saxenow already taken so much? After awhile, curiosity got the better of him and he turned to Fodor.

"With the Saxenow fighting Vortigern at Dinas Marl ... what of Lundnisow? Does it still stand against them?"

Fodor shook his head and trotted his horse faster.

Merlin kept up with him.

"If we're going to help Vortigern, we need to know what we're up against. What of Lundnisow? Have we lost it?"

"What concern is the port city of the Romans to you? Your accent shows that you have no heritage there, and we do *not* call it Lundnisow — a despicable, provincial name. It is called Londinium by all who know its luxuries."

"Londinium, then. No news has come north to us. Please ... I need to know. Does it still stand?"

"If you must know, the great city fell last month."

The words smote Merlin like a spear.

"But don't think it was a massacre. The fine citizens survive and even prosper, for their excellent upbringing has given them the wisdom to cooperate — "

"You mean *capitulate*."

"It was that or die, most likely."

"Those that capitulate with the Saxenow most likely *will* die. Ignore that to your peril."

"I never capitulate."

"And those that *cooperate* with those who do will also likely die."

"Fuss, fuss."

In the course of the hours of travel, Merlin extracted other pieces of information from Fodor, and guessed at much more. Such as the tenacity of the Saxenow advance. Sixteen years ago they had started small, with only a few villages in the southeast, but each year more of them came ashore and took land, like a snarling dog that refuses to let go of a bone. But their real trick was never overreaching into lands they couldn't hold.

Vortigern, the simpleton, had only slowed their advance rather than drive them out of Britain completely. Year after year, the Saxenow pushed Vortigern back. Based on what Fodor told him, Merlin sensed in the past this had been more for show — a game. But now that the Saxenow approached closer and closer to Glevum, Vortigern had begun to fight in earnest. But it was too late. The Saxenow had grown too strong.

And Dinas Marl? Fodor confirmed Merlin's own knowledge, passed on from Colvarth, who had required exhaustive memorizations about the strengths and weaknesses of Britain. Dinas Marl was one of many important hill forts that protected the ancient trade route that ran along a spine of hills crossing the south of Britain like a belt, from northwest of Lundnisow all the way to the edge of Aquae Sulis. Unfortunately, the walls of the fortress were made only of tall wooden staves, and they hadn't been maintained properly.

It took two days to find the forest road, and as they traveled east Merlin noted that the land was even drier here. The sun blazed, and the sky looked perpetually burnt, as if the two had conspired together to suck the very life from the world. What had once been verdant fields, peopled and happy, were now brown and dead as far as the eye could see. The land had been abandoned, save for mocking crows and razor-beaked vultures who slit the thin, dead cattle into strips and gulped them down.

Early one morning, Merlin spotted in the distance a great gathering of birds sailing and circling in greedy anticipation of a gory feast. There was a battle afoot, and Arthur seemed invigorated as he led them to a high hill where they could survey the scene.

At the base of the wooden walls of Dinas Marl stood rank upon rank of British warriors, perhaps three thousand men. The front line was a great mass of foot soldiers with spear and sword, followed by chariots and horsemen. The sun glinted sharply from their weapons, and their red and yellow cloaks flapped in the hot wind.

Against these, about thirty paces away, stood an army of Saxen warriors. Each was bare chested, with brown leather leggings, tall boots tied up below their knees, and broad belts with bright buckles. Their army was organized like the Britons, with their foot soldiers in front, followed up by a line of chariots. Overall, they had fewer horsemen, but many more foot soldiers, perhaps five thousand, with their small shields and their long spears.

At the very front of the British forces, a lone, gilded chariot rode out to the middle. The man riding it was wearing the purple, and his magnificent steeds were dappled brown.

"That would be Vortipor," Fodor said, causing Merlin to stiffen. "Britain's best battle chieftain."

"He has a peg leg!" Dwin said, clearly seeing farther than Merlin could.

"He lost his foot three years ago fighting horseback. But he always leads them to victory, he does."

Arthur whistled. "Against so many Saxenow?"

"Ah, yes, but one with such an illustrious ancestry can't lose, can he? And look, there he is — the Lion of Britain, protector of both fortress and city, Vortigern — looking down upon his future victory from the glorious battlements of Dinas Marl."

Indeed, Vortigern leaned over the wall to survey the coming battle, along with a large number of advisers and archers. His hair was almost white now, showing his advanced age. Like Vortipor, he also wore the purple, only his cloak was more audacious, and his polished torc sparkled golden in the sunlight.

"What kind of a fortress is this?" Culann asked, for the wooden wall was ill-maintained and some parts of the outer defenses sagged where the wooden supports had rotted.

"Yes, it could certainly use a few repairs," Fodor said, "but it has a long and famous history, Dinas Marl does. My great-grandfather once fought there, and he told me — "

Culann swore. "Vortigern's really going to try to defend that dump against so many?"

But movement down the field of battle drew their attention away. The Saxen ranks parted, and two chariots rode forth, each pulled by white horses. These men were larger than most of the other Saxen warriors, and over their forearms were worn long gold bands that matched their yellow hair.

As the two chariots rolled forward, the warriors began to slam their shields together in unison, and the sound filled the valley and roared up the hillside.

The two met Vortipor in the center, and the parley was hardly more than a series of violent gestures. After a short period of this,

Vortipor and the two Saxenow circled each other twice then rode back to their own warriors. The battle was about to start.

Arthur began to cinch up his scaled leather armor. "Let's get down there."

Culann, Dwin, and Peredur did the same.

Merlin unwrapped his harp. His role would be different here—to lift up the men in prayer while he felt with his soul and hands the beat, pluck, and tune of the battle. It was a true story unfolding before him, and his fourfold goal, as Colvarth had taught him, was to glorify God with all the skill he could muster, preserve the battle in the memory of the people for all time, remember the courageous men who died, and to praise the skill of those who lived and fought skillfully.

Even in regard to Vortipor, he supposed, his skills would need to do him honor.

Arthur drew his sword and looked to Merlin, son to father still. He winked.

"Let's go!"

And he led the way, galloping at full speed down the hill, heedless of the danger and death that waited below. Always Arthur, always reckless.

Merlin prayed.

Excitement pulsed though Arthur's limbs as he rode downhill, and the tension made him want to squeeze Casva's sides tightly with his knees, but he relaxed instead as he had been taught. Balancing, he let his body flow with the horse, feeling the steed's God-given power as it stretched forth its front legs, floated for an instant of precious time, and—full contact. A shock. They connected, like a statue with the hard, dry earth, and then the muscles rippled beneath him and the cycle repeated itself. Fast. Faster. Until the world was a blur and all he knew was the hot breath of the wind biting his face. Arthur held to the reins, the mane, and the neck in breakneck descent to the valley below. Casva could break a leg at any moment and send him hurtling to his death — and this is what made it all worthwhile.

But the descent was soon over, and the time to race had come. Power. Speed. Shouting. Pulling his shield from where it bounced at the horse's side. Drawing his sword. The valley floor fell behind him as the armies crashed, clashed, and struck each other. The warriors loomed larger and larger, closer and closer. Upon the exposed left flank of the Saxenow he attacked, with Culann and Dwin at his sides, and Peredur behind.

Arthur used Casva as a weapon, as the stallion had been trained. Crashing into the man in front, the horse rode the enemy down. The man's long spear, pointed at the foot soldier in front of him, couldn't be turned fast enough. But there was a man to Arthur's right, and he slashed him in the head, and he fell, screaming. The next man turned too late, and he fell too. And now Culann was on Arthur's left, and Dwin on his right, and they cut the men down, one after another.

A spear came thrusting toward him from his right, past Dwin, who was swinging at his own warrior.

Arthur had to lean back to avoid getting hit in the jaw. The spear jerked away and came back again, this time lower.

Arthur used his blade to shove it forward and away, and then Dwin delivered a fatal blow to the spearman.

Culann lunged his horse forward, next to Arthur, a whirl of blades, for he had discarded his shield and now swung and blocked with a long sword as well as a short. With these, he was able to dispatch many warriors and even break the tips of their spears off in a double cut.

On they plunged, a terror to the Saxenow, who didn't expect an attack from two sides at once and perpetually had their long spears pointed in the wrong direction.

A growing, rumbling roar filled Arthur's ears, the sound of horses galloping, of wheels crunching and jolting on the hard earth. The foot soldiers parted to avoid the onrush, and Arthur found himself in the middle of four chariots — two each from the opposing armies — rushing toward each other.

The British chariots contained two men, one bearing a shield who controlled the reins, and the other a warrior, while the Saxen chariots contained only a warrior who had the reins tied to his waist so he could free his hands at will if needed.

"Turn!" Arthur yelled, and he pulled his horse until it reared up and to the right.

The chariots nearly collided in front of him, their horses veering to the side just in time. But it was the Saxen warrior who was victorious, for his spear sliced through the shield bearer's shoulder and then gutted the British warrior with a blow so fierce it came right through his armor.

The shield bearer fell down, clutching his wound while the other convulsed on the spear point.

Arthur tore his gaze away from the carnage just as a Saxen warrior made a jab at him. Almost without thought, he shoved the spear point away with his sword and then kicked the man in the face. Sheathing his sword, Arthur grabbed the man's spear, turned toward the victorious charioteer, and threw the spear at his chest.

The spear missed.

The man wrenched his own spear from the dead Briton and turned to face Arthur, his lip curled in a snarl. He turned his chariot straight toward Arthur and snapped his reins.

Strength pulsed in Arthur's limbs as he kicked his horse forward.

The Saxen leveled his spear, the deadly tip vibrating through the air as the horses pounded forward.

Arthur drew his sword, ready to strike, and raised his shield. There was a great crash. Arthur was floating. The sky was white. The clouds dripped blood. Culann's face appeared, sideways. Dwin's shouting dimmed in his ears. The neighing of horses. A shock of pain smashed through his upper back. He gasped for air. The hooves of horses slamming the ground next to his head. He had fallen from his saddle!

Casva reared up and then bolted off into the battle.

Arthur tried to stand, but he was dizzy, and sucked in air.

"Get up!" Peredur yelled. The three of them surrounded him, driving back the Saxen and buying Arthur time.

"Stand ... stand!" he told himself, but his words didn't avail him. He lay back, breathed, and let warmth return to his limbs. Shakily, he sat up, and when he did so, his hand rested upon his blade, which had fallen next to him.

A man yelled.

He looked up and saw a Saxen duck past Culann's thrust and dive at him with a short sword. It was aimed at his throat.

He traced his hand back down his own blade, found the hilt, and gripped it. Barely in time, he brought his own blade up.

The warrior impaled himself, dropped his sword, and fell across Arthur's legs.

Pushing him off, Arthur stood and identified a small hill only a few steps in front of him. Two Saxenow held this high ground, and he rushed them, swinging his blade wildly to get their attention, then changing tactics at the last moment and thrusting its dangerous tip into the closest one's side. The other fled, allowing Arthur to step up and take stock of his situation.

Casva had galloped away, and everywhere Arthur looked there was swinging and thrusting steel, and the ground was slick with gore as the dead watered their lifeblood upon the parched soil. The line of British warriors rippled, sagged, and cracked all around him. They would push forward only to be driven back, while the charioteers and their men found success and cut deeply into the Saxenow.

And Arthur and his friends had fought themselves into the very heart of the battle, where they were surrounded on all sides by screaming, swinging warriors.

A yell caught his attention, and he turned to see a gilded chariot, along with ten British foot soldiers, drive forward into the ranks of the Saxenow. The rider wore a flowing purple cloak — Vortipor!

Arthur's heart leapt, but he didn't know why. Wasn't this the son of the man who had killed his father? But *Vortipor* hadn't done it, had he? Arthur had never heard about him. Either way, Vortipor represented all that Arthur aspired to ... leading men in battle. Bravely fighting the Saxenow. Saving Britain.

Vortipor was tall, yet didn't impress Arthur as being especially strong, and his peg leg made him unsteady in the chariot. He had brown hair under a tarnished helmet, and upon his throat he wore a thick silver torc. His nose was flat, and his dark eyes darted here and there across the battlefield. He wore his beard long, though thin, and it hung down over a coat of orange-rusted chainmail. His driver was a small man who bent over to keep out of the way, directing the horses as Vortipor yelled instructions.

Vortipor swung a long-poled axe and felled a man on his right, cutting him through the ribs. Another attacked on the left, and Vortipor hammered the man's face, smashing teeth and sending him into the dust.

Another chariot rushed from the mass of warriors. Its white steeds were slick with sweat and their black lips frothed at the sides where the bits were lodged. The charioteer felled two of Vortipor's footmen and raced alongside. The Saxenow had gold armbands, the left nearly hidden behind a small, iron-bound shield, and the right flashing as he brandished a long spear. He also had a set of javelins readily available at the front of his chariot, and these rattled in their wicker quiver.

"Horsa!" Vortipor bellowed as he swung his axe at the man. "Withdraw or I'll cut you down."

But they were too far apart, and the swing pulled Vortipor off balance on his wooden leg.

Horsa drove his horses closer and jabbed at Vortipor's bicep, just behind his shield, but the shield turned and blocked the blow.

Dwin and his horse rode forward a little, blocking Arthur's vision of the combatants.

Saxenow came screaming at Arthur. The first had a scimitar in one hand, and his other hand was wrapped in a bloody cloth. The second man held two weapons — a short sword and a bludgeon.

Arthur feigned not noticing them, and at the last moment slashed his blade out and sliced them both across their chests.

They fell, screaming and cursing in their throaty tongue.

Leaping over them, he ran out after Vortipor, who had just wheeled his chariot away from the mass of the Saxenow to retreat, only half of his footmen still alive.

But Horsa wasn't far behind. He set his spear down and pulled out one of the javelins. Throwing his body forward in the chariot, he hurled the sharp, wooden lance at Vortipor.

It struck into the back of Vortipor's neck, penetrated, and hung out from his throat.

Vortipor's eyes fluttered and his face contorted. He dropped his axe and grabbed the javelin, slick with his own blood, and fell sideways onto the driver, who collapsed beneath the weight.

The horses slowed to a stop, and a throng of Saxenow ran forward and slew the driver and horses.

Anger welled up in Arthur. Without their champion, the British line would crack, and the Saxenow would have the field of victory.

It must not be!

With Casva gone, Arthur needed a horse, and quickly.

Culann, Dwin, and Peredur fought on, oblivious to the tragedy that had just happened.

Arthur sheathed his blade and ran from them, back to the British line, where he found a horseman riding back and forth with his nose in the air.

"Give me your horse!" Arthur called.

The warrior turned to Arthur and spat on his chest. "Get your own, boy."

"You don't understand — "

"I am Cradelmass, king of Powys, and I will not abide this insubordination."

Black rage tinged Arthur's vision. There was no time.

He grabbed the man's boot and pulled.

"Stop that!" As Cradelmass leaned over to swing a fist, a look of surprise on his face, Arthur leapt up, grabbed his cloak, and jerked him from the horse.

The man fell to the ground, cursing, and yanked Arthur's sleeve.

Arthur punched the man in the face until he let go.

Grabbing the saddle, he pulled himself up.

There was only one way to avoid a British loss, and that was by killing Horsa.

He rode off into the thick of the Saxenow, blade swinging and yelling his own battle cry.

CHAPTER 15

VORTIGERN'S SON

Horsa was only twenty paces away, and Arthur kicked his mount faster. Slashing here, stabbing there, he fought his way through, and the enemy fled before him.

Finally within hailing distance, he yelled "Horsa!" and raised his sword in challenge.

The leader of the Saxenow saw him, smiled, and turned his chariot horses widely around until they ran directly toward Arthur.

Arthur's mount leapt forward, and then stiffened, thrashed, and neighed in a wild scream. A spear had been shoved into its belly, and it fell on its side, throwing Arthur. Earth and sky changed places as Arthur did his best to land on his feet.

But where was his sword? He had lost it in the fall, and couldn't see it.

Twenty Saxen warriors approached, spears leveled, eleven from the right and nine from the left.

Horsa was riding hard down on him in front.

Far behind him, he heard Peredur's voice. "Arthur! We're coming!"

But it was too late. And he would never find his blade in time.

He looked at the Saxenow warriors.

He looked at Horsa grinning beyond the deadly hooves of his horses, white like the faces of Arthur's dead countrymen. Horsa dropped the tip of his spear, preparing to gut Arthur.

The pounding feet of the Saxen warriors filled his ears. Red, glinting steel played at the edges of his vision as he focused on the white horses.

Arthur dropped his shield, slipped off his boots, and felt the grit of the dry soil on the soles of his feet. His timing would have to be perfect, and he crouched and tensed his muscles.

The white horses pummeled the ground, and unless he moved he would be crushed under their powerful hooves.

One ... two ...

Arthur stepped swiftly to the left, turned, and leapt.

A white blur of flesh passed under his hands.

He grabbed and caught hold of the tack, swollen with horse sweat.

His arms were jerked, and the shock of sudden speed made him dizzy, but he held tightly and pulled himself up. His legs hung, floating in air. With his right arm bent and tight, he let the left hand go and reached farther. Finding a side strap, he pulled harder and swung his right leg over the horse.

He was up! Sitting backward to face Horsa in the chariot — but at least he was up.

Horsa roared in anger and jabbed at Arthur with his spear.

With little room to maneuver, and no defense, Arthur kicked his toes into the horse's flank, and it jumped forward, faster than its companion, jolting and turning the chariot.

Horsa tilted, and the spear missed.

Arthur grabbed the haft with both hands and jerked it forward.

Horsa, taken off guard, accidentally let it slip away.

Holding the spear in the middle for balance, Arthur stood on the back of the white horse. His bare feet gripped the animal's thick skin, and he tried to remember all that Peredur had taught him — how to relax and lean into the horse's canter — only here he was backward, and the ground was rocky. Arthur's right foot slid, and he barely regained his balance. He needed more stability, so he shifted his left foot to the center of the horse and dropped his right over to the other horse. The harness held them close together, and this gave him more balance. But their hides were slick, and he wouldn't keep the position long.

Horsa reached for one of his javelins and cocked it back. Sweat covered his bare chest and limbs, his blond hair flapped madly in the wind, and fury contorted his face.

Arthur thrust the long spear, and in one swift instant he stabbed Horsa in the chest.

At the same moment, Horsa tried to lunge forward to throw the javelin, plunging the biting tip of the spear even deeper. Dropping the javelin, he tried to recoil from the spear. But Arthur drove it forward, and at the same time the chariot wheel hit a dead warrior laying on the ground.

The chariot bounced up into the air.

Arthur fell toward Horsa, jabbing and twisting the spear until it shoved all the way through.

Horsa screamed, clutched the wound, and collapsed.

Arthur heaved a sigh of relief as he rode out of the battle behind Culann. He wouldn't have survived ten heartbeats more if it hadn't been for the help of his three companions.

When the other leader of the Saxenow learned that Horsa was dead, he had called for a retreat and regrouping. This man's name, Arthur learned, was Hengist, Horsa's older brother.

Word of Vortipor's death had spread quickly among the British, and most of them had begun to run back to Dinas Marl in disarray.

A select few, however, carried Vortipor back on a makeshift bier made from the spears of fallen warriors, and Arthur and the others joined these.

Peredur had caught Casva, while Dwin had gathered Arthur's boots and shield. Arthur's sword, however, had been lost — a Saxen probably claiming it for his own.

When they entered the fortress, Arthur was surprised to find that a flock of nine druidow awaited. Arthur had heard tales of the druidow, and so knew a bit about their appearance, but he'd never seen one himself. Ector had never allowed them in the valley.

Well ... at least Arthur thought they were druidow. The man in front had thin bluish scars covering his arms in the shape of deer, bear, and fish, along with antlered figures, twisted snakes, and the like. The man was thick-limbed, short, and had a brown, bristly beard tinged red. His cloak was the color of a roan horse, and he wore black-checked breeches. Upon his shoulder were two pins ... one of the golden lion, and the other the heads of two dragons, one of reddish-gold and the other silvery-white. Dual loyalties? Arthur had never seen such a thing.

The druidow marched around the men bearing Vortipor's body.

"Hmm. Looks horrid," the leader said. "Which of you lug-ears is responsible?"

"For his death?" Arthur asked. "None of us."

The druid shook his head and made a sad face. "So there's no traitor to hang?"

"It was Horsa, and he's dead now."

"Hmmm ... a pity. Taranlos likes a good hanging."

Arthur laughed. "I don't think he would have cooperated."

The druid stared at him with bloodshot eyes. "Yer a fool, then, and must not know me. I am called Podrith, and I am appointed as chief druid to serve the High King's household. If someone doesn't cooperate, then I push them. That is the command of the arch druid, and I obey it."

"I see."

Podrith took out a short branch with sea shells attached to it by threads, and he shook this in circles over Vortipor's body, chanting along with the other druidow. He had just finished when Vortigern arrived from the upper wall. His cloak was fringed with the fur of wolves, and under that he wore a fine, embroidered tunic that had been ripped. His white beard was strung out, his face red and his eyes puffed, with tears streaming down. He wore a thick golden torc, but it was unlike other British torcs Arthur had seen, being of a solid tube construction with Roman eagles fashioned on the ends.

Behind him bustled a retinue of officials, scuffing their feet and biting their lips in dismay — followed by four servants carrying an ornate wooden throne. The chair was placed directly behind Vortigern, but the king ignored it and stared at his son, unmoving, with his dry lips parted and quivering.

Podrith directed that they bring the broken body before Vortigern, who embraced his son, howling, heedless of the blood on his hands and tunic. Finally, he kissed Vortipor's cheek, smearing the blood of his family line on his beard.

Arthur watched in silence. Intellectually, he wanted to hate this man, but seeing him for the first time, thus in his grief, he could not. Wasn't Vortigern his uncle, and Vortipor his cousin? These were kin.

Vortigern took note of Arthur then, and stood, his lip trembling. "You!" he said, and pointed a blood-marked finger at Arthur. "Stand before me." His voice was raw, and he gulped.

Arthur stepped forward and knelt before the High King. "My lord."

"Are you …? Are you not the … the one who has avenged my son's death? I don't know you."

"I'm named Artorius, my lord, and we arrived at Glevum for the muster — but did not find the city as we expected."

Vortigern wiped away some tears. "Was it not … more glorious? My feasting hall … my feasting hall, it is — "

"Destroyed, my lord."

Vortigern blinked, and the bristles of his beard twitched.

"Burned, my lord. Gorlas has attacked you and either driven away or slain all the inhabitants of the city."

"My feasting hall?"

Arthur nodded solemnly.

"My … my grandchildren?"

"I cannot say for certain, my lord." Arthur hesitated. "There were many slain in your hall, including children."

Just then the envoy, Fodor, who had been standing in the shadow of the gate, stepped forward and bowed before the king. "I wish I could negate his words, O illustrious sovereign of the line of Vitalinus, but it is as Artorius the Great Hero has announced. When I heard the news, I rushed to Glevum and personally found all your family and descendants dead."

"My wife?"

"Sevira has passed away, my lord. I have heard it said, however, that she preserved her purity and chose a dagger rather than be taken by that uncouth warlord, Gorlas. The warriors left behind to defend your house, they fought bravely to the end, each one killing three-score enemies before they died."

"Three-score?" Vortigern asked.

"Yes, my lord, each one — "

"Be quiet."

"But, my lord, there is more — "

Covering his ears, Vortigern cried out, "Silence! I don't want to hear another word from your flabby, flapping lips."

"But your sons …" Fodor shouted.

Vortigern blinked and took his hands off of his ears. "My sons?"

Arthur wanted to contradict these obvious fabrications, but was afraid to interfere. "As the Superb Hero of the Battle, Artorius, has postulated, your grandsons, Kedivor and Teyrnon, are no more, but they died bravely defending your hearth. In fact, your battle horn was only wrested from their faithful hands at the cost of many lives."

"My grandsons are dead?"

"And not only that, my lord, but the Painted Ones — "

"Who?"

"The Picti, my lord. Rheged has fallen to the northern barbarians, and King Urien, the brave soul that he was, has failed to protect your flank. Soon, they will march down from their frosty mountains and attack." Vortigern staggered backward and collapsed upon his throne. There he beat the back of his head against the wood, his neck tense and pulsing.

Arthur stepped forward, afraid to speak but compelled by the urgent need that pressed against his heart. "Mighty lord, God has permitted me to slay one of the Saxenow leaders ... and if I may be so bold, the time to attack is now when they least expect it. If we could slay the other leader, then the invaders would be driven back and our victory would be complete."

Vortigern shut his eyes and shook his head, a snarl slowly creeping over his face.

"Turn aside," he shouted, "and leave me in my grief. A truce ... we need a truce with the Saxenow, or all is lost!"

Arthur opened his mouth to speak but shut it when the king began fumbling at his belt near the hilt of his blade.

"My horn," Vortigern said absently. "I can hear it blowing again. *Who is the traitor?* it always demands ... always ... Will you stop it, Artorius? Please stop it up ..."

Arthur cocked his head, but heard nothing.

"Havoc ... havoc ..." the High King whispered, "... the battle is lost ..." The king stood, approached again the corpse of his son, and then turned and walked away, his eyes like glass. Yet his hand trailed for a moment on his son's boot, and then he pulled it away as if singed by an unseen flame.

The shadows of crows swept across Merlin's vision as Arthur and company rode toward the edge of the wood where Merlin had hidden himself. Earlier, Fodor had made his way down to Dinas Marl even as Merlin chose to stay and witness the battle, forcing himself to watch as Arthur and the others risked death countless times.

Though gladness filled his heart that all four had survived, he could now see their wounds and bruises: Dwin had a slice across his forehead, Peredur had taken a blow to his leg, and the armor on Culann's left shoulder had been slashed through. Arthur himself only had three scratches on his right arm yet was wearier than Merlin had seen him in many a year. The wounds would need careful tending, and thankfully Colvarth had taught Merlin well in that regard.

As they rode closer, a small raven, black and grizzled, landed on Arthur's boot to peck at the blood and gore. The young man noticed and kicked it away — but it took to the air and then dove at his face, cawing and raking its claws at his eyes. Three times it attacked him before he was able to drive it away.

As they arrived, Merlin dropped to one knee and bowed his head. "Hail, victor of the battle."

"Ah, get up," Arthur said. "I've had enough of that at the fortress."

Dwin clucked his tongue. "Truly, truly — you should have seen the ladies. Falling down and worshiping the very ground he walked upon."

"There weren't ... no ... don't believe him."

"Ah, but you wished for them," Culann said. "I saw you looking around."

Merlin stood, smirked, and hugged Arthur. "Vortigern didn't know you?"

"Not a screpall."

"Are you sure?"

"Yes."

"And Vortipor ...?"

"Dead."

"And the fortress grieves?" He wanted to say Vortigern's name again, but it was so acidic on his tongue the first time, he couldn't even stutter out the word.

"That's not all," Arthur said, bitterness coloring his voice. "With Glevum destroyed, the Picti attacking in the north, and his son dead, Vortigern has called for a truce."

"What? After you saved them from losing the battle?"

Arthur sighed, dismounted, and checked Casva's bit. "He's asking for peace with the Saxenow so they'll help him fight the Picti. They've set a meeting tomorrow night at Hen Crogmen."

"The old stone gallows? That's a pagan place."

"Vortigern has druidow advising him."

Merlin raised his eyebrows and shook his head. "No surprise."

"It's five leagues, so we should leave immediately, unless you want to travel with Vortigern in the morning."

"Are you sure this is the right course?"

"Vortigern requires my attendance."

Merlin spat. "He does, does he?"

"As the victor of the battle —"

"He wants to parade you around."

"I don't think so. I killed Horsa, one of the Saxenow leaders. That would only enrage them."

Merlin thought for a moment, trying to sift out the right course from the clamor of his conflicting desires. "I don't like this, and I advise you not to go."

Arthur shrugged. "It's already been arranged. Besides, Fodor told me Vortigern makes peace with the Saxenow every few years."

"This may be different. In the past, Vortigern was only admitting that the Saxenow could keep the land they had taken, which was in and of itself a travesty. From what you say, it sounds like he's giving up."

"You think so?"

"You said it yourself. Glevum is destroyed. Vortipor is dead. No help is coming from the north. How can Vortigern fight on?"

"The people would never surrender. The kings and chieftains would never —"

Merlin looked away, afraid anger could be seen in his eyes. "They *have* allowed it. Farm by farm ... village by village ... hill fort by hill fort."

"And you think us running away will fix it? The Saxenow will just leave?"

"I didn't say that."

"We're going."

Merlin had to chew on this. Nothing seemed right. He didn't want to be here, didn't want to go to the Stone Gallows, didn't want to help Vortigern.

But Arthur did, and no matter how rancid the bite, Merlin had to swallow it.

They traveled south that day and camped in the fastness of the woods. After the sun had set, taking along with it the dismal heat, a half moon appeared high in the western sky, fringed with the hint of flames. And far off in the southwest, amongst the Dobuni hills, there came the sound of wolves howling.

Merlin, with fear in his heart, pulled out the scrap of Natalenya's skirt. Folding it in his hands, he began to pray for her. Almost immediately, the fabric became wet. He looked up through the trees; there was not a cloud in the sky, and no rain could have fallen from the stars that burned above him.

So why was the fabric wet? He checked the bag it had been kept in and found it perfectly dry. Once more he prayed for her in perplexity.

Taliesin stood next to his mother at the wall, his heart burning with anger as he looked down at the desecration enacted by the massed army of the Picti. His mother had told him to expect an attack the day before, but it had not come, and this had confused him ... until now. Apparently the Picti had sent chariots and horsemen down the valley and had caught the horse tenders and brought back all the horses that he'd thought had escaped.

And now they were sacrificing them to their gods.

Each horse was brought before a hastily built altar of stone, and there they slit its throat. Soon the river in the valley ran red, and Taliesin's breakfast convulsed within his stomach until it threatened to crawl up his throat. The little foals that he loved to rollick with and pet were killed, one by one. The older horses died too, and only the young geldings, mares, and war-worthy horses survived that butcher of a priest's blade.

His mother began to cry, and though he tried to comfort her, she sat down and looked away. Pulling the long edge of her skirt up to her eyes, she bunched it together and used it to dry her face, but the tears wouldn't stop.

"All our long work is being undone," she whispered, and the words took his breath away.

With a hot hand he unsheathed his blade once more, the blade his father had made for him, and, oh, how he wished now that the edges had been sharpened like the tip. The blacksmith had moved some of his tools up to the top of the fortress, and Taliesin set off to find him. Maybe something could be done to make his blade more deadly.

CHAPTER 16

THE PLACE OF THE DEAD

D o you know the way to Hen Crogmen?" Arthur asked. His legs were sore from riding, and Merlin and the others looked equally weary beside him.

The man turned, set down his ragged sack, and looked up to reveal a gap-toothed frown jutting out from a sun-browned, wrinkled face.

"Aye. Ya got some'un to hang?" he asked.

"No, that's not our purpose," he said, groaning inwardly. Twice before when he'd inquired about the way, people had asked whether or not they had someone to hang.

"Right. Well, ye'd haf trouble finding a spot wiffout cuttin' an old one down first — "

"Do you know where it is? We were told it was down this way."

The man pointed a gnarled finger down the path. "Turn at de old oak, cross de river, and keep to de paf. Not far, not far."

Arthur led the way, and soon found the oak the man spoke of. Dead and dry, its roots curled from the thick, barkless trunk and twisted down into the ground like massive worms. Beyond the tree, a path forked away and wound its way slowly downhill through a stand of ghost-like plane trees.

Eventually they came to a brown stream, shrunken from the drought, and there, at the edge of the mud, knelt an old woman. Sobs welled from her chest, and her hands scrubbed a blood-stained tunic, reddening the water.

Arthur wanted to ask her who had died, but as she looked up at him, her weeping only increased, and he was embarrassed for disturbing her task. He pressed his horse forward until it sloshed through the stream and mounted the far bank. The others did the same.

After a league or more traveling southwest through an oak forest, they entered a wide clearing and found Hen Crogmen, the largest roundhouse that Arthur had ever seen. It was nearly one hundred and fifty feet across and built within a broad ditch and bank enclosure that surrounded the site. The outer wall was built from pairs of bluish-gray stone pillars topped with a stone lintel of similar girth — the set of three stones together measuring about ten feet tall. Inside this circle was an inner circle of twenty-six foot-tall stones. The network of lashed roof timbers angled up from the outer wall and rested on the inner to form a cone, but some of these timbers had fallen and the old thatch roof was dilapidated.

From what Merlin had told him, the site predated even the druidow, and its original purpose had been lost in the obscurity of time. Around two millennia ago, lore said, the order of druidow came to be formed and they adopted the site, used it for ceremonial purposes, and maintained it. And only now, as the disrepair showed all too well, did the fall of the druidow from favor begin to reveal itself — what with the Romans having killed many of them and most of the people turning to Christ.

One thing known, however, was that the druidow and the locals both used it to hang people — thus earning its ancient name, "The Old Stone Gallows."

From inside the building came the cawing of crows, and Arthur, curious, rode his horse into the large open door before him. Although it took a few moments for his eyes to adjust to the gloom, his nose was instantly assaulted with the overwhelming stink of death. There, between each and every pair of standing stones, hung a dead body. Many were old ... so old that nothing but their skull and spine were left hanging from the rotting rope, while others were fresher. One man to Arthur's right, in fact, looked like he had been hung only that day, and this is the one the crows fought over. His tunic was missing and he had a slice through his right ribs that let blood down his side and leg until it had finally clotted in the dirt below.

"Why would Vortigern want to hold a truce here?" Arthur asked, his strong voice swallowed up in the cavernous building.

Merlin rode his horse forward and surveyed the scene. "It's an ancient idea, and can be found in the words of the oldest scripture. When God made a covenant with Abraham, He told him to bring various animals and cut them in half and arrange the pieces opposite each other. Then God promised Abraham that unless all the vows of the covenant were fulfilled, then He, God, would die like the animals. Abraham understood what God did because this is how the king's of old made vows with each other."

Arthur turned to him, a little confused. "And God — through Jesu Christus — died because *we* failed, correct?"

Merlin nodded. "In that sense, the covenant was different than the ones between men."

"So by holding the truce here, Vortigern is saying that if either side breaks the truce, they'll become like these ..."

"Yes."

Merlin advised them to make camp in a hidden little clearing just beyond the line of trees. It was a place where he could stay without being detected while Dwin, Culann, Peredur, and Arthur joined the army for the truce meeting. Arthur, due to his bravery in battle, had been invited much closer than the others.

And so when evening came, and Vortigern finally showed up, Merlin was left alone to pray. He sat upon a fallen log, its bark missing and its hard flesh crisscrossed with the hungry trails of ants. After spending a long time thanking God for their protection thus far, Merlin turned his thoughts to Natalenya, Tinga, and Taliesin. Pulling out the piece of skirt Natalenya had given him, he held it against his cheek to feel the softness.

Before he could remove the fabric, however, he heard a distinct ripping sound and felt it shift beneath his hand. He jerked it away — and the material had torn.

Baffled, he prayed fervently, hoping his family was safe.

Taliesin smelled the smoke and cursed the Picti, so far below him. They were burning the roofs of the village houses and demolishing their stone walls. Even the great stable was on fire, and its roof shone bright in the darkening shadow of the setting sun. Worst of all was seeing his own home destroyed — the place that had always felt safe to him. It was gone so quickly, and it made him want to scream.

"Taliesin!" a man called from farther down the rampart. It was Bedwir. "Join the others carrying rock."

"To throw at the Picti?"

"Go!"

"That sounds fun," he said. He wanted to hit every one of 'em in the noggin for destroying their beautiful village.

Bedwir marched over and placed a hand on Taliesin's shoulder. "There's nothing fun about it. This is life and death." The scratch on Bedwir's forehead had faded some, but the ugly wound on his arm wasn't getting any better.

Licking the dryness of his lips, Taliesin nodded. "I know."

"Then get to work."

The evening breeze felt cool on Taliesin's shoulders as he ran down the wooden stairs and joined the others. Everyone who could was helping, from little Tinga carrying smaller rocks collected in the fold of her dress, to old Brice and his wife, who carried a basketful of the larger ones between them. Lacking men and weapons, they needed every possible means of repelling the Picti.

Most of the rocks were being gathered from the base of the central tower. Taliesin found an empty basket and chose a spot next to his mother to pick through the pile for those that seemed right for throwing.

His mother gathered her rocks from near the broad, oaken door, and her face was lined with a determination that Taliesin had rarely seen before. He knew more than anyone to steer clear of her when she was angry, but this was different. A desperate sort of look.

Her basket full, she turned and patted him on the shoulder. "Thanks for helping."

Taliesin nodded.

She left to carry her rocks to the wall, but the edge of her skirt became caught on a loose nail and tore. She pulled it free with a look of frustration and continued on.

Withel, a boy three years older than Taliesin, came up and bopped him on the head with his fist.

Taliesin spun to find the boy sneering down at him.

"Thanks for having rocks in your head, harp-boy."

"Leave me alone." Heat rose up Taliesin's neck, and hovered just below his ears as he finished filling his basket.

"If there was another horse pie up here, I'd drop you in it again."

As the boy turned away, Taliesin took a large, jagged rock, dropped it down the backside of the boy's pants, and ran off with his basket. "Thanks for having rocks in your pants, lion-face!"

"Hey!" Withel tried to fish the rock out, but it slipped down one of his pant legs and got caught at the place where it narrowed just behind his knee.

Taliesin laughed as he ran to the wall.

Withel hopped noisily after him, shouting and pumping his fist.

When Taliesin got to the top of the stairs, though, all thoughts of being chased died. The people stood still, watching something over the wall with solemn concentration. He ran to his favorite spot where a stone section was a little lower and from there he surveyed the valley below. A mass of Picti were marching up the path toward the fortress, and though it was getting dark, there was still enough light to see that most of them carried spears.

Withel joined him, holding the rock he had fished from his pants. "What's going on?"

"Don't know."

As the men climbed the zigzagging, steep path toward the gate, they would sometimes drop from view behind a boulder and then reappear somewhere else.

Mother and Great-Aunt Eira came to stand about ten feet from Taliesin. Tinga nestled in their mother's arms, her little face twisted in a frown.

When the Picti were finally within hailing distance, Taliesin caught his breath to see a monk among them. He was wearing a simple brown woolen robe, just like Brother Loyt who served the inhabitants of their valley. Only this monk had a coarse bag slung over his shoulder, which he held protectively. But this wasn't one of the valley's monks, for he had sandy-red hair and was slightly stout, with a plump if resolute jawline. And he was old. He had to be nearly thirty winters.

There was a bound man with them as well, stooped low, with a bag tied over his face. Guards stood behind him with short spears, and beyond them were fifty or more Picti on the path ready to fight.

The party came to stand before the gate, above which stood Bedwir, Caygek, and Brother Loyt, ready to parley, it seemed. They forced the bound man to kneel, and there they tied his feet tightly with rope.

Strangely, the fair monk had faded red ochre designs painted on his face and forearms. Red was the paint that the western-coast Picti used, Taliesin had heard, and this didn't match the blue paint of the other warriors. All of this confused Taliesin … A Pictish monk? After all, he had red hair …

One of the Picti was a full head taller than the rest, and his clothes were much showier. Over his bare, painted upper body lay a royal blue robe with a fur collar, and below were red-checkered breeches. At his throat lay a beautiful golden torc with the ends fashioned like two hawks. The man's bright red hair was long, immaculately braided and banded with rings of gold. He had a long nose, and though Taliesin couldn't see the man's eyes closely, he thought they must have been green based on the way the sun glinted off of his predatory gaze.

This one barked an order in a dialect Taliesin had never heard — sort of a twisted, throaty form of their own language. Two of the warriors snapped to attention and poked their spears into the monk's back, forcing him to step forward and look up at those on the wall. His left eye had been bruised badly, and the puffy bag of skin hanging under had turned purplish-green.

"To those inhabitin' Dinas Crag, I have been brought before you unwillin'ly to translate the demands o' Necton Morbrec mac Erip, High King of the Picti."

At these words, Mother screeched, startling Taliesin. What did she expect the monk to say?

She pushed her way across the rampart until she stood over the gate with the men.

"Garth!" she called, and the monk squinted his good eye back up at her, the sun partially blinding him.

"Who … who is it?" the monk asked. "Who knows me?"

Taliesin's mother looked at Brother Loyt, Bedwir, and Caygek, and then back at the monk.

"Garth! It's me … Natalenya!"

The monk blinked and swallowed, a look of desperation on his face. "I'm sorry, Natalenya. I didn't know you and Merlin were here. Necton's come to destroy this fortress and take you all captive."

"How did you — ?"

"Come to be his prisoner? I've been a missionary to the Picti on the coast for three years. There's a settlement on the Molendinar River, and we've even built a church. Necton knew I could translate for him, so he took me."

Necton grimaced at Garth, grabbed his hair roughly, and wrenched him forward until he fell to his knees beside the man with the bag over his head. "Mungo! Thusa tellha ris openidha dunstuck gatesi!"

Garth was forced to look up at the fortress, and only spoke after he was slapped in the face. "Necton commands you to open up the gates . . . or else he'll kill this prisoner."

One of the guards untied the bag over the man's head and pulled it off.

Taliesin jumped and slapped his hand to his mouth. Despite the blood dried dried onto the man's face, Taliesin knew him: his great-uncle Ector.

CHAPTER 17

THE FEAST OF THE DEAD

When the truce meeting actually began that night, it was with the lighting of ten bonfires and the preparation of a glorious feast. Arthur's stomach turned at the thought of eating in that odious building, — surrounded by the dead, but he gritted his teeth and attended Vortigern as commanded.

Vortigern's retinue had brought wagonloads of woolen mats, upon which reclined the men privileged enough to be chosen by Vortigern and Hengist to attend the feast — almost a thousand in total. Besides the two kings — who were each allowed their personal sword — all of those inside were weaponless, in the spirit of the truce.

Outside and eating less sumptuous fare sat the two armies — on opposite sides of the building, with Vortigern's men to the west, and Hengist's to the east.

But the truce inside was a friendly affair: the Saxen leaders had brought great vats of wine and, intermingled with the British nobles, passed the cups back and forth, drinking deeply.

At the same time they gorged on meat, soups, and flatbreads, all roasted and baked in the bonfires. No less than thirty deer turned on spits, and the aromatic smoke rose to the top of the old roof structure and escaped through the smoke hole and the numerous roof sections that were now drooping or missing.

Vortigern and Hengist found their seats upon two wooden thrones, and then the proceedings began. Nine druidow entered, amusing Arthur until they brought forth wooden trumpets and sounded them while marching in a circle with a shuffling, jerky dance. He had to cover his ears discreetly, for the trumpets sounded like nine rats dying. Next the druidow lit a ceremonial flame and flicked their curved brass daggers in and out of the flames, chanting:

Hear now a rede from olden day ... When druid fires blazed bright.
The people came to Hen Crogmen ... To dance the ancient rite.
And so today we bless this peace ... 'Tween Saxenow and Brit.
Within this place, this sacred space ... Today it shall be writ,
Turn not from us, nor from our kin ... The men who do live free.
Come nigh to blessed oak array ... Our gorseth ye shall see;
There worship we our primal gods ... Tread not the paths of men.
Through smoke and fire thy oaths fulfill ... At rarest Hen Crogmen.

When the druidow finished this ritual, they retreated to cluster behind Vortigern's throne, with Podrith standing directly to the High King's right. Then, with grunts of disapproval from the druidow, the priests of the Saxenow strode forward to perform their rites. Four of them came first, each in a red robe with a white sash. A fifth man approached leading a beautiful white horse. All of them began to make neighing and whinnying sounds as they danced around the horse, until they startled Arthur by grabbing the horse's neck and pulling it down to a short stone pillar and slicing it open.

Arthur began to feel sick as the horse thrashed and fought while its blood drained upon the makeshift altar. Apparently the other Britons felt the same, for a great murmur of disapproval arose from the crowd.

"Cease!" one of the Saxen priests shouted in the Britons' tongue. "We who serve the Men of the People require silence!"

At this the Britons murmured all the louder until Vortigern raised his hand. They quieted, but nothing could change the seething anger written on their faces.

When the shameful sacrifice was done, the horse was brought to the fire to be cleaned and roasted for the reprehensible gluttony of the Saxenow — and Arthur cursed them and their ways. *Why would Vortigern make peace with such a people?* Arthur wondered.

Vortigern and Hengist then began talking with one another, but their interaction was subdued. The bags under Vortigern's eyes were puffy and red, as if he'd been crying and drinking all day.

And then there was Hengist — *proud* Hengist — whose face was a mask of guarded mirth, for he would only smile when Vortigern was looking. His pale hair was slicked back and his golden armbands reflected the light of the fires so that his skin appeared ablaze.

There was a young woman who feasted next to Hengist, and Arthur found her vehemently staring at him on more than one occasion. Her hair was like long, golden flax, braided with cords of red and brown leather. Upon her head lay a slim golden diadem, and her finely laced dress was a multicolored plaid of brown, tan, and white. If she had not been a Saxen and a pagan, Arthur would have considered her to be a great prize.

But then a strange voice entered his head … a voice that was not his own:

Stare not at me, slayer of my uncle!

What you behold is not for a beast like you.

If it were not for this feast, I would slit your throat and toss the globes of your eyes into the fire.

The girl arched one of her brows and bared her teeth.

Do not be surprised I can speak to you thusly.

I am a prophetess among my people, and the god I serve, Wotan, has given me many powers.

Fear me, murderer!

Arthur turned away from her, shook his head, and tended to his duty of waiting on Vortigern. But he could feel her glare burning into him, and the urge to flee beat into his chest like dark waves upon a storm-tossed shore. He pushed against these feelings, and finally vanquished them as he focused on what Vortigern was saying to him.

"Artorius," the high king said with a vacant stare, "fill my goblet once more."

As hero of the battle, Arthur had been required to be the personal and esteemed servant of the High King. *Why have I been elevated to such a role?* Arthur asked himself more than once, and the only answer he could surmise was that his presence would aggravate Hengist. What good purpose this could serve, he didn't know.

He went quickly and returned with a decanter of one of the finer meads, one scented with plum and the flowers of clover.

Soon after, Vortigern made another request. "Artorius, my son, take this bloody venison and have the cooks roast it until the edges are charred ... and bring some oil for my beard."

But it wasn't the oil of gladness Arthur gave him, rather the oil of mourning. The tales of Vortipor's entombing the night before swirled amongst the British warriors, and Arthur picked up that Vortigern had wept and screamed. The man's lineage was at an end, and Arthur couldn't help but think of how Vortigern had tried to end Uther's years ago.

Arthur was out of earshot for a time, waiting on a cook to make a special vinegar sauce the High King delighted in, and when he came back, bearing the golden vessel, Vortigern and Hengist were holding hands ceremonially — in a pact of truce, Arthur guessed.

But he was wrong, for it was *more* than a truce. Both kings stood, and Vortigern spoke with much halting and coughing, though soon his voice grew stronger.

"British ... and Saxen nobles ... I announce to you that we have forged a lasting truce ... between our peoples ... one that shall never be gainsaid ... a truce that we will, together, fight the invading Picti in the north and rebuff the ... the ... threat of Gorlas from the west."

Here Vortigern paused, as Hengist withdrew his hand and replaced it with the hand of his daughter, who had stepped forward.

Vortigern cleared his throat and continued. "Furthermore, to seal this truce, I announce to you my ... immediate marriage to Hengist's daughter, Reinwandt. Thus shall join two great peoples. Thus shall peace be preserved. Thus shall the loss of my house" — and here a tear leaked unbidden from his right eye — "the loss of my wife ... children ... and grandchildren ... be restored."

Arthur sucked in his breath as a stunned silence filled the room — from both Saxenow and Briton alike. Reinwandt curtsied to Vortigern and then looked up at him with unblinking eyes set in a stern, emotionless face.

And of all who could have protested this unholy alliance by marriage, the only one who stood up was Fodor. The envoy shook his head and then bowed before the High King.

"My majestic, illustrious, most noble lord ..."

Vortigern closed his eyes and took a deep breath. "What is it now?"

"My illuminated, majestical sire ..."

"Out with it!"

Fodor's chin began to quiver. "It is your lineage, my lord. If you marry this Saxen ... uh ... princess, you will sully your children's pedigree, and the bloodline of their children's children, and then — "

Vortigern drew his sword and pointed it right at Fodor's upturned nose. "Be silent!"

The envoy clamped his mouth shut and drew his twitching lips inside.

In the next moment a disturbance came at the back of the room, near the gate. One of Vortigern's warriors marched forward with a spear pointed at a man dressed in black — and not just dressed in black, but with a black mask over his face and a wrapped harp hanging from his shoulder.

Merlin ...

196

Mórgana, having traveled with Loth, Mórdred, and Mórganthu to their new fortress in Lyhonesse, sat in its ornate upper throne room. A fire burned on the hearth under a small, skewered boar, whose dripping fat fell and sparked the flames higher, filling the room with a luscious, salty aroma.

Mórdred banged the door open and threw his dusty cloak over a low table. Mumbling something, he scuffed his way to the fire and sliced off a long slab of boar meat.

Mórgana paid little attention to the him, for the orb held her interest much more.

"The hunt was useless," he said, stuffing his mouth. "Did you hear me? The only deer I saw escaped into the brush, and I swear it was the only thing alive on Lyhonesse besides the rodents!"

"Really?" Loth said vaguely from where he stood behind Mórgana's throne. He, too, looked into the orb.

"Not a single, nasty deer ... not even a paltry partridge. Why did we come here?"

From where she sat on her carved, wooden throne, she lifted the orb higher so both Mórganthu and Loth could see. Inside swirled images of British men as they stealthily climbed down from a high mountain fortress in the dark. Below them lay the campfires of Picti warriors.

"So," Loth said, "they think they canna' escape Dinas Crag sae easily? They think they're goin' to come back with help? Ha!"

Mórdred edged closer and peered into the orb to see what was going on.

Mórganthu turned to Mórgana. "What ... what will you do? Will you use the fang upon them?"

"Yes, of course. I have already traveled there to alert Necton about their secret valley, and I'd rather not intervene in that way again right now. Besides, I've been waiting to use the fang upon those that have been hiding Merlin and his brood, and its power will make sure that they die."

197

She pulled the fang from its sheath and held it up until its green fire merged with the purple flames of the orb to form a strange blue blaze that danced between them.

Mórganthu reached out with his only hand and brought his fingertips close to the blue fire. "This joined color reminds one of the flames of the Stone, does it not?"

Mórgana looked at him and lifted her nose in the air. "Has your old age made you a dotard? Do you not know that the supremacy of the Stone is the merging of two great powers? Thus it was before Merlin impaled the Stone, and thus the Voice has decreed it shall be again."

"One can only hope."

Mórdred snorted at his great-grandfather's remark.

"There is no need to hope," Mórgana said. "It is as certain as the death of these British runaways."

She plunged the fang down toward the closest man inside the orb, and he screamed. As the fang came back up again, some smoke sizzled from its tip. Again and again she plunged the fang down until every man who had tried to escape lay either bleeding upon the cliff face or had slipped and plunged headlong to his ruin.

The fang now smoked so powerfully that Mórganthu backed away.

Mórgana swayed as strength drained from her. The room spun, and she would have pitched forward had Loth not steadied her. Using the fang like this taxed her to the core, and she would have to rest for a long while before she could use it again. But when she was strong enough, she vowed, she would inflict disease upon the inhabitants of Dinas Crag. She laughed. "Before long, yes, very soon," she said, finding her voice, "Merlin's litter will be slaves again!"

"But more importantly," Loth said, "the fall o' Luguvalium combined with the capture and slayin' of Rheged's vaunted horses means that our enemy's power in the north is almost broken."

"But we hate the Picts!" Mórdred said. "Didn't they destroy Grandfather's kingdom?"

Loth spat. "Nay, it was *Merlin* who destroyed my father and his kingdom, and his helpin' Rheged angers me sorely. Luguvalium was always a broken crutch to my father, and I'll never mourn their downfall. Our kingdom is in the south now ... with our queen." And here he bent and kissed the back of Mórgana's hand.

Mórgana smiled, pulled her hand away, and gave a little laugh. "You want to be king of the south, you say? That will only be true if Vortigern can be dealt with."

She took a deep breath and stood tall once more. "Let us look, then, upon him ..." And as she passed her hand over the orb, the scene inside shifted to reveal Vortigern seated on a throne, and next to him, Hengist and Reinwandt.

"You see?" she said. "I have made his heart to be a sweetcake in my hand. The fruition of our plan is almost complete."

But then the shadows in the orb shifted, revealing Merlin's face. He stood before Vortigern and bowed.

"What?" Mórgana shrieked. "He is *not* supposed to be present at the feast."

Mórganthu pushed his head in closer and squinted at the orb. "Will this ruin our plans, my daughter's daughter?"

Mórgana gnashed her teeth, finally pausing to take a little sniff. "No. I think not. And if there is any danger of that, then I will intervene — even if it costs me dearly. The planned course must not be disturbed, and I will make sure my pawns carry out their orders."

The wind blew strongly in Taliesin's hair as he gripped his basket of rocks. Far below, Necton was trying to force his great-uncle Ector to talk.

"Speaksa!" Necton shouted, and when Ector didn't respond, he slammed his fist into the back of the man's head.

Great-Aunt Eira gasped.

Taliesin picked up a rock. *If that Pict does that again, I'll —*

But Ector shook his head, strained against the bonds with his trunk-like arms, and finally spoke to those on the wall.

"I'm supposed to tell you to open the gates," he shouted. "To beg for you to save my life. But I will not! Hold the fortress as long as you can, and don't give in to these filthy, horse-killing dogs—"

Great-Aunt Eira, called out, "No! Ector, no!"

Ector stared at her. "Hold fast, Eira! Don't fear!"

Necton pointed a spear at Ector's back, his lower lip twisting angrily as he spoke. "Openidha!"

Taliesin cocked his arm back, ready to throw. "Leave my uncle alone!"

Necton looked up, trying to see where the voice came from.

"I'll open the gates," Great-Aunt Eira shouted, her hair blowing wildly around her. "Just don't kill him!"

Taliesin looked at her, confused. Should he throw his rock? Or should they give up? But there were just too many Pictish warriors on the path below Necton ... if they opened the doors to try to save Ector, they'd all die or be slaves.

"No!" Ector said. "He'll kill me anyway. *Don't open the gates!*"

"Openidha!" Necton yelled once more.

Great-Aunt Eira swooned to the side and Taliesin's mother supported her. Tears ran down Mother's cheeks, but she said nothing, only wrapped her arms around her aunt and hugged her tight.

"Openidha!"

The spear in Necton's hands tensed, and Taliesin knew the time had come.

Ector struggled against his bonds, then ceased, closed his eyes, and gritted his teeth.

Taliesin threw his rock. Like a good water-skipper, it was— flat, and sharp edged—and it sailed down in a perfect arc toward Necton's head.

Necton set his jaw and brought the spear back to strike.

Eira screamed.

A gust of wind blew, and the rock shallied to the side. But it still struck the Pictish king in the shoulder, leaving a wound that began to bleed.

Necton twisted to the side in pain, and his spear missed.

Taliesin clapped, yelling.

More rocks flew from the heights, and the Pictish warriors with Necton began to back away.

Necton shouted at them and raised his spear once more. Garth grabbed it and tried to shove it to the side, cracking the butt of the spear into Necton's mouth.

Necton backhanded Garth in the face.

The monk slipped on the loose shale, and fell.

Taliesin picked up another rock, this one heavier, and threw it, but it went wide.

Necton spit blood out, kicked Garth to keep him down, and then stabbed the spear into Ector's back.

Ector collapsed, his visage wracked in pain.

Taliesin screamed. His uncle couldn't die, he couldn't!

A flurry of rocks rained down now, and Necton ducked as he jammed the spear deeper in.

Ector fell to his side and writhed, finally spasming and then falling still.

Necton grabbed Garth, lifted him up as a shield, and backed down the mountain.

When the Picti were far enough away, Eira was the first to open the gates and run screaming to her husband. Mother, Bedwir, Caygek, and Brother Loyt ran out after her.

But Taliesin didn't go. He couldn't go. It was too horrible — an evil dream that he wanted to end but that wouldn't go away. He wanted to cry, but Withel was standing next to him, and so he held the beastly tears back, sucked in his breath, and let his soul burn instead.

CHAPTER 18
THE PROPHECY OF THE DEAD

Arthur gulped as his adoptive father was prodded forward. The vessel of vinegar, which Arthur had not yet delivered, felt suddenly cold in his hands, and the room began to roll under his feet. Arthur lurched to the side and caught himself on a nearby standing stone. Thankfully, with everyone's eyes on the stranger being marched to the front, no one noticed.

"What is the meaning of this interruption?" Vortigern said.

Reinwandt dropped the High King's hand and briskly returned to her chair.

The warrior with the spear stepped to the side. "I foun' him, my lord, hidin' in the woods. If it tweren't for him crackin' a branch, I'd'a never noticed him, the sly fellow." The warrior used the butt of his spear to shove Merlin forward.

Vortigern straightened and looked down his nose at Merlin. "Take off your mask."

Merlin dropped his hood to his shoulders, pulled the mask off, bowed slowly, and then looked Vortigern squarely in the eye.

The king's face paled. He mouthed Merlin's name, but no sound came from his lips.

"Yes, it is I, Merlin, come back from slavery and exile."

Vortigern began to shake, and he rasped out, "And the child? Where is the … the child?"

Arthur narrowed his eyes. The High King was asking about *him*, but didn't seem to realize how close the two stood.

Merlin looked fiercely at the king. "I saw the boy die."

"He died?"

"Yes."

Arthur's first reaction was that Merlin was lying, but soon realized that this was a subtle truth. He felt the old, thick scar through his tunic and a flash of pain and fear from his deepest past assaulted his mind.

Vortigern lurched forward and grabbed Merlin by the collar. "I don't believe you."

"It is the truth."

Vortigern slapped Merlin across the face, and Arthur winced. Merlin had been right all along: the king really did hate him and wanted him dead, and the reality of this slipped into Arthur's soul like a cold knife.

Hengist placed a hand on Vortigern's shoulder and spoke in his halting British, "Ef you need to verify de truth, Reinwandt can do such. She will be your wife before de night es over, so you may command her."

Vortigern looked to his young bride for confirmation of this, but she was glaring at her father.

"Come … my bride!" the High King said. "I must know the truth of these words."

Reinwandt rose from her throne with a pout on her lower lip and strutted like a cat over to Vortigern.

"What do you desire, O betrothed?" she said, but there was ice on each word.

"Tell me … does this man speak the truth?"

She turned to face Merlin, and though she was shorter, the malevolence of her presence could be felt from across the room. Merlin shifted his weight backward ever so slightly.

"Hold him!" she said to the warrior, and the man took hold of Merlin's arms.

She placed a hand on his forehead, and though he tried to jerk his head away, he could not. "Tell me the truth," she commanded, "did the child die, the one of whom Vortigern speaks?"

Merlin's eyes rolled back into his head, and he appeared to fall into a deep sleep.

Arthur held his breath as Reinwandt began to chant in the language of the Saxenow. Would she discover the truth by reaching into Merlin's mind using her evil, pagan power? Perhaps only moments remained before Vortigern would have Arthur hung on a stone gibbet. He could almost feel the rope being cinched around his neck as the dead corpses hanging behind Vortigern's throne swayed in the draft.

And then to Arthur's surprise, Reinwandt's lips began to move silently, mouthing the same words over and over, until finally Merlin's voice came from her own throat. "The boy died ... the boy died ... the boy died ... *the boy died!*" And then she screamed as small wisps of smoke began to ooze from her hair, her arm, and the hand that lay upon Merlin.

She tried to pull away but could not.

Merlin opened his eyes. "You have asked a question of me," Merlin said, "and now I will ask a question of you. Tell me, will there be peace?"

She screamed again, but did not answer.

"*Will there be peace?*" he demanded.

She looked up at him, her eyebrows twitching and her mouth open wide. "Yes ... there will be ... peace!"

She finally jerked her hand away and fell to the floor.

Arthur gazed at his father in wonder. Merlin's eyes were aflame with a holy light, and he looked at her grimly. "Now in the name of Jesu, leave me alone, witch."

Reinwandt crawled away from him, and then, rising, ran to her father and into his protective arms.

Vortigern grabbed Merlin once more by the collar, and gave him a last, searching look, suspicion etched in every line of his face. "So he died? You're sure of this?"

"Yes. I saw it happen with my own eyes."

After glimpsing no lie in Merlin's face, Vortigern relaxed and the air went out of him. He let go of Merlin and returned to his throne, collapsing upon it.

Arthur tried not to move a muscle even though his insides were shaking.

Merlin still stood before the two kings, who looked at each other as if they had no idea what to do with such a one. And then Merlin did what Arthur had seen him do hundreds of times. It was so familiar, in fact, that it did not occur to him at first how much of a revelation it was to those that watched. Merlin pulled his harp from off his back, unwrapped it, slung its leather strap over his shoulder, and lifted it before the assembly of warriors.

The druid, Podrith, snarled from beside Vortigern's throne, but Merlin ignored him.

"Behold!" Merlin said. "I make known to you that which has been hidden for many long years. Witness the Harp of Britain!"

All eyes turned to glimpse the beautiful instrument, made from wood so ancient that it seemed even older than Hen Crogmen itself. Delicate designs adorned its rich surface, and Arthur never tired of seeing their profound and mesmerizing patterns. And the strings! The strings of purest gold fairly glistened in the light of the bonfires.

"Thief!" Podrith yelled, and the other druidow joined him. "Return the harp to us, for it belongs to the druidow."

Merlin turned to face them, and his voice held an authority far above anything Arthur had ever heard. "Do not pretend, Podrith, chief dunce of Vortigern, that you are unfamiliar with your own laws. In light the harp was made, and only in light may it be given. It is the law of the land that the Harp of Britain may be passed down by the chief bard to the successor he chooses. Only if he dies without having freely given it does it return to the gorseth of brihemow, to be bestowed upon whom they choose."

"You stole it!" Podrith cried, spit flying from his mouth.

"Not true!" Merlin said. "Bledri mab Cadfan, Chief Bard of Britain, chose me by prophecy and gave the harp to me. He is the one whom you have perjured and named Colvarth."

Podrith hissed at the name and covered his ears.

"And as final proof of my right to bear this peerless instrument, behold the song of a true bard."

Merlin smiled at Arthur, shifted his black cloak and the silver brooch pinning it in place, and began to play, bringing forth music so beautiful and poignant that all those present listened with amazement. And as his fingers flashed upon the strings, Merlin walked slowly back and forth in front of the thrones, locking gazes not only with the warriors, nobles, and provincial kings who sat there, but also with Vortigern, Hengist, and the fearful Reinwandt.

And this is what he sang:

Come see the sputtering candle as it gathers forth its flame,
And hearken to this long-lost tale of Gowan's greedy claim.
One hundred years ago it was, at Dyfed by the sea,
When Peul Prydain and his girl capsized upon the key.
Now Peul was a warrior brave who'd slain a giant green;
The little girl, hiding in brush, the battle she had seen.
Vile giant, with a coat of leaves, had madly swung his axe,
Yet Peul deftly struck him down, so bold were his attacks.
Then burying his wife, now slain, they did not fail to weep,
And Peul took the green, stout, axe and sailed across the deep.
But when their boat came near the shore, it swiftly met its doom,
And up they climbed, weary and cold, to fortress dark in gloom.

Here Merlin deepened the timbre of the notes, and continued.

There was a man, Gowan by name, who met them at the door.
Fancy his clothes, bright were his shoes, and eating roasted boar.
"O please, kind sir, give us good fare, and warmth beside thy fire,

206

For we are lost and wet and froze, our need of thee most dire."
Gowan did laugh at their sad state and would not help at all,
But then he saw the bright green axe — so sharp, so grand, so tall —
And in his heart did crave this thing, and want it for his own.
"Grant me the axe, for food and warmth," he said in deadly tone.
Sad Peul turned, looked on his prize, for this he could not do.
It was his quest to show his lord, and he would see it through.
So he refused and said they'd go to find a nearby farm.
Inflamed, Gowan did seize the axe, and swung, intent to harm.

Merlin's notes became piercing as he struck the strings quickly with his nails. Arthur felt the tension tighten within his chest, as if the song itself had reached inside with a mighty fist and squeezed his living soul.

Then Peul pled with grim Gowan, and made an offer fair,
That Gowan could cut off his head, if he would truly swear
To take good care of his daughter, for one year and a day.
Then he'd return to take her back, and claim her straight away.
Gowan did mock at this fine joke, and vowed and pledged and swore,
Then he cut off the poor man's head, and felled it to the floor.
So Teleri Prydain did weep, and mourned her father's death.
She buried him within the hall; it took away her breath.

Merlin played this last stanza with deep sadness, and right as he sang of Peul's death he struck a high note so loudly that the gold string broke, and its demise reverberated through the hall. Merlin paused a moment, and then continued.

A year, a day, the time did pass, but Gowan was so cruel.
He beat her hard, he locked her up, and only gave her gruel.
Yet in that year she grew so tall, and beautiful as well.
He promised if she'd kiss him then, he'd free her from her cell.

Merlin took a deep breath and then sang on, successive hints of sorrow, anger, and finally hope touching his fine, strong voice.

But she refused and suffered hard at Gowan's calloused hand.
On final day did Peul's son appear upon the strand,

And Gowan mocked the youth so lean, and sat upon his throne
With bright green axe fixed o'er his head, a prize held on the stone.
But Peul's son was not dismayed, and said in voice so loud,
"Murderer, thief, and fraud art thou, and death shall thee enshroud."
And then he stamped his foot upon his father's grave so cold.
The axe, it fell, cut Gowan's neck, and then his proud head rolled.
The girl was free, the people glad, and Peul's son was king.
They held a feast, splendid and fine, that year in sunny spring.
In justice did he rule the land, to Dyfed's utter fame,
And we remember well the tale of Gowan's greedy shame.

Merlin stilled his fingers upon the harp, yet the final notes echoed off of the standing stones before dying to a palpable hush. "Thus is 'The Lay of Gowan and the Green Axe' when sung by all who remember it rightly."

With his eyes closed, Vortigern laughed in an uneven, quiet way, as if there were a joke in the song that only he could perceive. After awhile his mouth tilted strangely, showing his old teeth as the laugh went on.

"I have heard your ballad," the High King finally said, "and I know its meaning." Then he opened his eyes and looked to the guard behind Merlin.

"Kill him."

CHAPTER 19

✝HE PEACE OF ✝HE SAXEⴖOW

Arthur's hand moved quickly to the hilt of his blade — only to find it missing. He had forgotten that all except for the kings had been required to disarm. Culann had Arthur's blade, and there was no time to retrieve it now, for the guard behind Merlin raised his spear to strike. Arthur tensed his body to tackle the man, yet before he could move, the man sighed and fell back, dropping the point of the spear.

"Lord, I cannot do this," the man said. "He has the Harp of Britain!"

Vortigern swore. "I don't care. Kill him."

The guard knelt down. "To kill a bard is against all the laws of these isles, and he — he is the chief bard."

"Fool!" Vortigern said, slamming his hand on the arm of his throne. He stood and raised his voice for all to hear. "Who will kill him for me?! I offer a rich reward."

Arthur looked out on the throng of mixed Britons and Saxenow, and no one moved. While the British were downcast, the Saxenow watched their king.

Hengist leaned over and whispered with his daughter, then popped a thin slice of horsemeat into his mouth, chewed, and spoke. "Vortigern, do de deed yerself. Me daughter would like to see dis entertainment. After all, what is a British bard to us?"

Vortigern put on a smile for Hengist, pulled up his sagging breeches, and drew his sword. As he advanced on Merlin, Arthur knew the time to act had come.

He stepped forward and took the spear from the kneeling guard.

Vortigern saw him out of the corner of his eye and snarled.

But Arthur dropped to one knee and held the spear out upon both palms. "My lord, if I have found favor in your eyes as the avenger of your son, let me remove the bard from your presence. This deed is not worthy of you on your wedding night, nor should blood be shed in front of your guests."

Vortigern stopped short, waggling the end of his blade.

He looked back to Reinwandt, who flicked her fingers to encourage him.

He looked toward the British nobles and seemed to weigh the sour looks upon their faces.

"My lord," Arthur said, "I implore you to let me remove him from your presence forever."

"Forever," Vortigern said, a slight smile on his lips.

"Forever."

Just then, Fodor stood up from a table to Arthur's right. Arthur's hands clenched on the spear. A wrong word from the envoy and all would be lost.

"Sire! May I interrupt the proceedings?"

"Eh?" Vortigern said, turning a cold, menacing gaze toward Fodor.

The envoy nearly jumped from fright, gulped, and then spoke shakily. "O renowned ... legendary lord ... I have new information!"

"Silence!"

Fodor pointed at Arthur and Merlin. "But — "

"Say another word, and I will *wring your bumpy little throat!*" Vortigern sheathed his sword. Holding up his hands, he pretended to squeeze, wrench, and snap Fodor's neck.

Fodor squeaked, but held his tongue. Glancing at Arthur, then at Merlin, he sat down, but his face turned red with anger.

Stepping back, Vortigern slumped once more upon his throne and slapped Hengist on the shoulder. "You see, the man will die, and I don't need to get my hands any more ... any more ... bloody."

Hengist shrugged and motioned for Arthur to take him out. "Begone den, get it done."

Arthur stood, bowed, and then pointed the spear at Merlin's chest. "Out!"

Merlin, who had already slung his harp over his back once more, raised his arms, spun on his heel toward the exit, and marched out.

Arthur felt foolish pretending to force his father outside to kill him, but it had to be done. Once they were finally behind a standing stone, well beyond the campsites of the warriors, Arthur dropped his spear and opened his arms.

Merlin hugged him. "Thank you."

"To fulfill my promise to Vortigern, make sure you stay away and don't get caught again. That was quite a scrape you got yourself into."

"I'm glad we're out of it."

Arthur pulled back and looked Merlin in the eye. "We? I have to go back."

"You can't." The line of Merlin's mouth turned firm and he stared at Arthur with a steady, unflinching gaze.

Arthur tried to back away, but Merlin's hands gripped his forearms. "If I don't go," Arthur said, "Vortigern will suspect."

"But God revealed to me that Reinwandt is lying."

"Of course. The Saxenow have never kept the peace, and Vortigern knows that."

Arthur twisted away from his father's grip, picked up the spear, and ran off toward Hen Crogmen. If he didn't return soon, they would both be in danger. But the look on Merlin's face haunted him as he ran past the outer camps of the warriors. Had it been shock? Or fear?

He passed some campfires and found the place where the cooks had cleaned the deer. Dipping the spear tip in a pile of intestines, he coated it in blood and filth and then continued on toward Hen Crogmen. Finally, he entered through a gap in the outer wall and slipped inside as quietly as he could.

He soon found there was little need for his stealth. The crowd of British and Saxen warriors were hooting and hollering as they watched some spectacle near the front. Arthur rounded the nearest roof pillar and stopped himself, for Reinwandt was dancing before Vortigern. A Saxen was playing a very long flute, and the princess was slowly turning before the king in a teasing manner — catching his eye here, bowing to him there, and all the time smiling and winking at the crowd.

Soon the Saxen nobles began to clap in time to the dance, and the Britons joined in. Faster and faster her feet flew until she finally ended it in a whirling jump that landed her right in Vortigern's lap.

The king laughed, his face split by a leering smile that showed his brown teeth.

Reinwandt kissed him on the cheek, played with his hair, and turned to wink once more at the audience. Then, flicking her hand inside her outer garment, she drew forth a short, shining blade and jabbed it between Vortigern's ribs, in the direction of his heart.

Bright blood poured down Vortigern's embroidered tunic, and the king's mouth hung open, his lips moving as if he were trying to speak. Then he blinked at her, finally squeezing his eyes shut in pain. The room grew instantly quiet as he slumped over.

"*Wealas* worm!" she said, and spat in his face.

Instantly every Saxen in Arthur's sight pulled a short blade from his boot and stabbed the Briton next to him. Screams, curses, and yells filled Hen Crogmen as the weaponless Britons inside met death, either by a slice through the ribs or a deep slashing of the throat. Those few who resisted were quickly overwhelmed, and Arthur, if he trusted his disbelieving eyes, saw none of the five hundred Britons survive.

The noble closest to Arthur was slaughtered quickly, howling as his intestines spilled across the woolen mat that he lay upon.

Arthur panicked, then — for the Saxen warrior who had done the deed saw him hiding just outside the assembly and rushed at him, the knife held out before his wild eyes like a bloody trophy.

Arthur backed up, leveled his spear, and tried to strike the Saxen in the chest. But the man spun to the side and slashed out with his knife. Arthur feinted to the left then jabbed the spear back to the right and caught him in the shoulder. The man shouted as the knife dropped to the dirt. Arthur pulled the spear out and slammed the haft across the man's forehead, and he went down, clutching his skull.

Now running toward the British camp, Arthur shouted, "The High King is murdered! Your leaders are slain!"

Of the two thousand British warriors present, the closest ones gave Arthur frozen stares. One man sat at a fire and had a grouse leg hanging from his teeth. Another's arms were full of logs he was about to throw onto the fire. Yet another man was scribing a letter for his fellow warrior. In all, it took five heartbeats for the warriors to react, but it was nearly too late: The camped Saxen warriors had been waiting for a signal, and now they came rushing at the Britons in full, screaming mayhem.

The man with the grouse leg died with an arrow through his throat.

Arthur ripped a hunting horn from where it hung on a man's belt. He blew it as he backed up and surveyed the situation. It all happened so fast, yet he saw it as if in slow motion. The main force was coming from the north, across the paved entrance to Hen Crogmen, while a smaller force circled around from the south. The center was the Saxen's weak point, because the traitorous warriors from inside were only lightly armed.

Arthur sounded the horn one more time, and then yelled as loudly as he could, "To your weapons!" But something bothered him ... what had happened to the smaller force to the south? Arthur looked, and couldn't see them through the darkness. Then he knew — the horses were picketed in a large field that direction.

And there it was ... the first scream of a horse.

Arthur downed a Saxen with his spear and blew his horn once more. "To the horses!" he yelled, running as fast as he could through the chaotic battle. Many heard, but had no chance as they met a swift death at the end of a Saxen blade.

As he ran, Arthur heard pounding feet beside him. Turning his head, he expected an attacking Saxen but found Culann running next to him. The warrior held out Arthur's sword and passed it to him by the scabbard. Arthur smiled and shoved the blade into his belt as he ran. Dwin was just behind, and Peredur as well.

"To the horses!" he yelled again, and any British who were free of direct conflict began rallying to him. Arthur led them away from the impending onrush of the Saxenow — to the horses, just over the low bank and ditch. There they found the smaller force of Saxenow busily slicing the hamstrings of their horses.

Anger flared and Arthur screamed, slamming his spear through one Saxen's throat. He then drew his blade and slew another.

The enemy abandoned their evil task and turned to run. Many of the stragglers died, Arthur killing two more himself. When some of the British chose to give chase, Arthur called them back. But it was all confusion. Other Britons had already mounted and were fleeing for their lives into the woods. Only a small force followed Arthur.

Arthur searched the clearing for Casva, but the stallion was nowhere in sight. Praying he hadn't fallen to the Saxen blades, Arthur grabbed the picket line of the nearest horse and flung himself onto its bare back. "Everyone mounted!" he called. "The battle is not yet lost!"

The other men scrambled to find uninjured horses, and soon a force of three hundred men rallied behind Arthur. If used properly, they might save many Britons who were being slaughtered.

Arthur pointed his sword back the way they had come as the men reined their horses around. Picking up speed, they rode across an ancient causeway traversing the ditch and bank and thundered down on their enemies. Thankfully it was easy to tell the bare-chested Saxenow from the British, and Arthur swung his blade at everyone near enough to strike, downing many. Penetrating through the ranks of the battle, he led the impromptu army out the other side. Arthur motioned for the mounted warriors to turn back and make another run through the battle lines, but just then a new sound shook the earth,... pounding hooves from the northeast.

Arthur turned and saw a host of mounted Saxenow bearing down upon them, with Hengist in his chariot riding at the fore. A spear was in his hand and British blood was spattered across his chest.

Ruin. Ruin and death it was, for a vision wrapped in shadow appeared before Arthur's eyes: Hengist, victorious, striding over a field of the dead then pausing to kick over the body of a Briton. It was Arthur himself, his eyes gouged out and the rest of his body hacked and torn. All the Britons were dead, and none now existed that could stem the tide of domination and destruction that would blaze across the island. One by one the villages and fortresses of Britain burned in Arthur's vision, and with it the churches and abbeys. The newly established faith would disappear unless ... unless Arthur helped a remnant survive. A remnant that could grow to oppose Hengist and his barbaric horde of Saxenow. Oppose Gorlas. Oppose the Picti.

The weight of this burden came crushing down upon Arthur so that he felt his arms weaken and his sword begin to slip.

The vision faded, and Hengist's chariot clacked closer. Arthur turned and saw the rage of imminent victory upon his visage.

If Arthur stayed to fight, then would his vision come true? Would they all die? For all his efforts Arthur had only bought them a little time, and that time was up. He needed a place to regroup, and remembered that Vortigern had left over one hundred men back at Dinas Marl to man it in his absence. Arthur would lead his remnant north — back to Dinas Marl, where he'd have time to think about his next step.

"Through the ranks once more!" Arthur yelled. "Save as many as you can and then ride away with me!"

The warriors around Arthur hesitated only a moment before turning their mounts away from Hengist and his horsemen. Onward they rushed, back through the camp and the fighting footmen. Down fell hundreds of Saxenow as spear, sword, axe, and hoof made imprints upon their flesh.

And all along the way, whenever possible, the horsemen picked up stray British warriors and pulled them to safety on the back of their horses. Arthur himself pulled up a young man with desperate eyes who must have been less than fourteen winters. The youth had a bloody gash on his side, and bare feet.

"Thank you!" the young man shouted.

"What's your name?"

"Ol, son of Olwith."

"Do you have a sword?"

"Only an axe."

"Well, use it, then!" For enemy warriors were running at them from all sides and Arthur had to hack his way through.

"Retreat! Follow me!" Arthur cried as he rode through the mob, the gore thickening upon his blade and the Saxenow falling like barley sheaves at harvest. When they reached the other side, he turned to look back and saw that some of the horsemen had perished, but there were still two hundred or so left, along with the footmen they had saved who were now scrambling over the bank and ditch to find their own horses. Merlin and Peredur were among them, and seeing his father gave Arthur the final courage to lead the retreat.

Forward he rode, turning toward the rest of their horses, and there he paused while Ol found a horse along with the other men.

He led the ragged survivors into the darkness of the night, finding a broad forest road heading west. Behind him he could hear Saxenow in pursuit, but it soon broke off. Despite this, their company rode tightly together, squint-eyed and white with fear.

Leaving was one of the hardest things Arthur had ever done, and he prayed that God would forgive him for the men who died because of that decision.

A long while later they left the road and found a clearing behind a wide knoll where they might stop and rest for the remainder of the night.

After Merlin had seen to the binding of many wounds, and the men had fallen into a fitful sleep, he moved a little bit away, laid down, and wept. Despite God's protection of Arthur and the others in their company, a great evil had befallen Britain, and the terror of it made Merlin's breath come out in great gasps. In one blow the Saxenow had duped Vortigern and had slain many of the nobles of southern, western, and eastern Britain: men from Bolgi, Kentow, and Dubrae ... of Dobunni, Eltavori, Bregantow, and Ekenia ... and even some who had escaped the fall of great Lundnisow itself.

Only the kings of Kembry and some of the old north remained. But for how long?

Merlin could see clearly how this one blow would destroy their will to fight, even for Arthur. Why should the provinces send more men? With Vortigern dead, the only High King Britain had known for the last fifteen years, and with Votipor and all their princes and minor kings slain — it was hopeless now, wasn't it? And the Saxenow weren't the only enemy: now the Picti attacked from the north, and Gorlas ravaged from Kernow. What could the people do? What could Arthur do?

It would be every village, every fortress for himself, and they would all fall, one by one.

Merlin closed his eyes and tried to shut out the screaming that even now filled his head — the screams of hundreds of men being simultaneously slaughtered inside Hen Crogmen. Merlin had tried to follow Arthur, to try and reason with him, but it had happened so fast, and he had only found time to warn Peredur, Culann, and Dwin.

What else could he have been done? Well ... he should have spoken the truth to Vortigern while he had the chance, that's what. But would he have been believed? Probably not. After all, he hadn't known what was planned ... or when. The only thing he had known was that Hengist and Reinwandt did not plan on keeping the peace with the British. Could Merlin blame himself for not shouting out such an obvious thing? And if he had, what then? Would the Saxenow have attacked immediately, killing Merlin and Arthur too?

He wanted to trust God through this tragedy, but his heart beat like a hammer and a sharp pain hovered behind his eyes. Instinctively, his hand went to his bag and he pulled forth the scrap of skirt.

Natalenya. Oh, what he would give to hold her right now. To take her and their children and sail away from this cursed island where no refuge was safe.

But as he brought the cloth up to his eyes, he felt a dry stain upon part it. He wiped his face anyway, and tasted ... blood? Sitting up, he examined the skirt in the dim light and saw a black stain across it. Checking the bag, he found it clean.

How had Natalenya's scrap of skirt come to have blood on it?

Once again he prayed for his family. Would he ever see them again?

CHAPTER 20

THE EDGE OF THE UNKNOWN

Sitting with his back to the tower, Taliesin ran his fingers absently through Gruffen's fur. The clouds had come in thick that night, and the face of the moon was hidden from the world, making this the perfect night to send for help.

The Picti had made an assault upon the fortress the night before, but the steepness of the approach had made it impossible for them to break in. However, the defenders wouldn't last long without help, his mother had said, and so here they were. Four men were climbing down the back cliff face of the mountain spur that Dinas Crag had been built upon — and one, the miller who carried a pack of supplies, was being lowered down using a rope. The plan was for them to spread out and alert all the western settlements of Ector's death, as well as of the siege so that a sufficient force might come to their aid.

Beside him sat Tinga with her puppy, Gaff. In front of him stood Caygek and, farther away, Bedwir. The two men were carefully lowering the miller down the back cliff face. Brother Loyt and his mother stood lookout upon the wall, watching the progress.

Gruffen gave a little growl from deep in his chest, and Taliesin cradled the dog closer, whispering in his ear, "There's no need to snarl at Caygek. He's our friend."

But Gaff growled too and started scrabbling her paws on the ground in an effort to break free from Tinga's grip.

It was almost as if some invisible enemy lurked nearby.

"What'th gotten into them?" Tinga asked, turning her puppy on her back and pressing a hand into her chest to hold her still.

From over the wall, a scream pierced the night.

Mother bent over, squinting into the darkness.

Another scream. And another, until the whole mountainside beyond reverberated with the cries.

"Pull him back up!" Mother hissed.

"The others ... they've fallen!" Loyt called.

Caygek kicked off his boots to get a better grip on the sandy ledge of rock, and he and Bedwir began to heave the miller back up. When the man's hands got to the top of the wall, Mother and Loyt helped him climb over. But something was wrong, for he threw the bag of supplies away and collapsed at their feet, all of his limbs shaking.

Mother knelt down and took the man's jerking head into her lap. His breath was nothing but shallow gasps of pain and quiet sobs.

Taliesin handed the now-whimpering Gruffen to Tinga, and ran to get a torch from the tower. Something was wrong, and they needed light to see exactly what.

But there wasn't a lit torch on the first floor, so he had to run up the stairs to the second before he found one. By the time Taliesin got back, the man wasn't breathing, and there was a strange smell, like burnt hair, only worse. He held the torch closer, illuminating the miller's lifeless staring as if in a final plea for mercy. And there, upon the rock, was a small pool of blood, and some of it had soaked into his mother's skirt.

Caygek rolled the man over onto the rock. A small hole in the back of his neck still gushed blood as well as a thin, snakelike trail of smoke.

"What happened to him?" Bedwir asked.

Taliesin closed his eyes, shut his mouth, and turned away from the foul smell. First Ector, and now the miller and the others.

Bedwir shook his head. "No help will come now," he said under his breath.

Tinga began to sob, set Gruffen down, and ran away with Gaff.

Gruffen sniffed and growled again, and Taliesin picked him up.

Mother ran after Tinga, catching her before she had gotten to the other side of the tower. Sitting down, she hugged Tinga, rocking her and the puppy while she sang "Tingada's Cloak."

Taliesin turned back to the dead miller and stared at him. There was something strange about his eyes ... They weren't just dead, they were glowing! Deep inside raged a small green flame, and it grew and grew until the man's pupils began to smoke.

Taliesin dropped the torch, picked up Gruffen, and ran to his mother.

He wanted to hug her, but felt foolish. Yet it was unnerving the way the miller had died, and though he had a hard time holding back his own tears, he managed to do so ... in case Withel happened to be watching from the tower or from some shadow near the wall.

Mother finished the rhyme and started it again, and her soothing voice comforted Taliesin, not that he would say so.

Tingada's cloak is pied, pied.
I made it from a wolven hide.
Once we were shackled — bang, clang!
But the time came when eight slaves sang.
Now father goes to hunt, hunt,
A club to swing, a spear to bunt.
He brings along the hounds, hounds;
They seize, they catch, in leaps and bounds.

Mother glanced over to the dead miller, and a tear slipped down her cheek, landing on Tinga's brown hair. When she continued, her voice sounded choked.

> *He'll trap fish from his boat, boat.*
> *Beyond the Falls of Derwent, float.*
> *Just like a lynx's paw, claw,*
> *He'll throw his net, and, filled, withdraw.*
> *When father climbs the crag, crag,*
> *He'll slay a roe-buck, boar, or stag,*
> *Or certainly a grouse, grouse,*
> *Some tasty meat for hearth and house.*

"When is Tath coming home?" Tinga asked. "He'd get uth out of here."

"Yes, he would," Mother said, and Taliesin saw her blink up at heaven with a sort of pleading look.

"Tas can catch anything, can't he?" Taliesin said.

"Unless it has wings," Natalenya said, nodding.

Tinga frowned. "Some o' them geth away?"

"Yes."

"I wish we had wings," Taliesin said. "Then the Picti could never catch us!" But he knew that was impossible. Bedwir was right — they were already caught, and no help would come.

Arthur held up his hand in a request for Merlin to stop speaking. The sun would soon reach its zenith, and their chance to success-fully ambush the Saxenow baggage carts was slipping away. The scouts had returned with news of the enemy's movements, and the time had come.

"Go, then!" Merlin said, stepping back. The stone walls of the inside of the blockhouse made his words resonate.

Arthur strapped on his sword and Merlin followed him outside. "I'll pray that you meet with success." He fell silent, but Arthur heard what he didn't say: *And that you don't regret ignoring my advice.*

As Arthur marched out into the daylight, he looked out over the camps of the men who now called Dinas Marl home. Many more had found their way back, swelling their ranks to just over four hundred — still a pittance compared to what Vortigern had ruled just a short day ago.

And not only that, but his own leadership of the warriors was in doubt, for other, better-known men began to vie for control and to express their own divisive opinions on their next move. It seemed that Arthur's slaying of Horsa and his elevation by Vortigern meant little in their minds, and to cement his leadership with them, he had devised his daring new plan.

So when Arthur climbed the ladder and looked out from the walls of Dinas Marl, he cringed. Far away to the south and east the land was dry and brittle. Was he foolish to use fire as a weapon against the Saxenow? Yet the present situation left little choice. Not with Hengist and his Saxenow coming to take their fortress.

Maybe Merlin is right, Arthur thought, *and I should just leave with the men. Empty the fortress and abandon these lands to the Saxenow.* But the idea smoldered inside Arthur and its fumes blurred his vision. Deep down he didn't want to concede even one handbreadth of British land to the Saxenow, and if they were going to take it by force anyway, then let it be burned. So be it.

Culann and Dwin approached, and Arthur gathered them in a circle.

"Do you know that old, broken fortress we passed?"

Dwin squinted as he scanned the vale south of Dinas Marl, finally pointing to the horizon. "You mean the one on that hill way over there?"

"You can see it from here? That's more than a league."

Dwin smiled. "Can't you?"

"It's the one with the road right below it."

Culann raised an eyebrow. "Is that the place we passed on our way to Hen Crogmen? Now that *is* an interesting spot."

"In more ways than one," Arthur said.

Dwin yawned. "Nice spot for a picnic. Too bad Gogi and his daughters disappeared."

"A picnic?" Arthur said, knocking Dwin playfully on the head. "*A picnic?* Look, I need twenty of the best archers along with twenty horsemen and the forty fastest horses we have."

"Looking for a bit of revenge?" Culann asked.

"No. I just want to defend our land."

Culann nodded and ran off toward the camp of men while Dwin went to pick the horses. Within minutes Arthur had all the men and horses he needed and they were tightening their saddles and mounting.

Just as Arthur pulled himself up onto a horse — sadly, not Casva, who had disappeared at Hen Crogmen — Merlin strolled by, whistling.

"If you die, don't blame me."

Arthur ignored him and began passing out pine-pitch torches to all the men who didn't have a bow. Once every man had two, Arthur raised his arm to signal that they were leaving.

Merlin grabbed onto the bit of Arthur's horse, looked up into the young man's eyes, and whispered, "If all of Britain burns, don't blame me. And if you survive, you think we're going to hold this gap-toothed fortress with four hundred against five thousand? You might as well just bury me here, then, right on Marl mound."

"I never said this is going to be easy, but we do have one advantage that no one's thought of."

"And what's that?" Merlin asked.

"Hengist doesn't fear us."

Merlin got a puzzled expression and scratched his scalp. "That's an advantage?"

"He won't be expecting us to try anything."

"Right."

Arthur lowered his arm and gave his horse a quick kick.

The rest of the warriors followed him out of the fortress.

Merlin swallowed a catch in his throat as Arthur left, riding out the southern gate of Dinas Marl. Would he come back from such a foolish venture? Merlin wanted to go and find Peredur where he was busy dealing with a horse that had thrown its shoe, but the man had backed Arthur's plan and Merlin would find no commiseration there. Everything had failed in the south, and Arthur's presence had done nothing more than preserve a small, ragged band that had little chance against the monstrosity of Saxen domination.

But since when did Arthur ever think about odds? He had always been reckless, even when he was little. Once, when Arthur was eight, Merlin had taken him on his first overnight hunting trip. They were supposed to be looking for deer, but encountered a large, tusked boar instead. Had Arthur shown any fear? No, the boy had run right into the path of the charging fiend and nocked an arrow. Despite his hammering heart, Merlin had run out and pulled Arthur behind a tree. And the funny part was that Arthur still got his arrow off and sank it deep into the beast's chest. Merlin would never forget that day.

But I'm not like Arthur, am I? At least not anymore. When did I lose my recklessness — my youthful idea that nothing can stop me? Was it when I was a slave and saw everyone dying? When I saw Natalenya suffering and slowly fading before my very eyes? Now I just want to go back home. It would be so easy. A few weeks on the road, and I could fall into Natalenya's hard-working, loving arms once more and just rest there in her embrace. I could go hunting again with Taliesin. I could braid Tinga's hair, so soft and tangly ...

He took out the scrap of skirt once more to pray for them all, happy that the cloth still felt clean and soft under his touch since he had washed the blood off. Yet within moments, its surface began to feel slimy.

He looked down, and there was a black liquid oozing off of one end.

He dropped it, then bent down to look more closely. The rumpled piece of cloth was clean on one end but smeared with ooze on the

225

other. *What was happening? Had the disease returned to Natalenya? The same foul illness that had long ago afflicted her while a slave?*

He closed his eyes and prayed for her safety, but even as his quiet amen was spoken, he heard a ripping sound. There, below him, the piece of skirt cloth had been shredded into three pieces.

Merlin gasped.

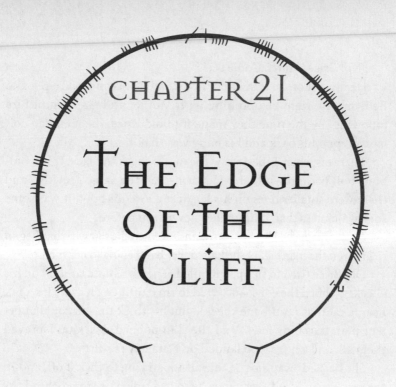

CHAPTER 21

THE EDGE OF THE CLIFF

Taliesin broke into a run along the top of the wall. He had to get to the stair. Something had happened to old Brice, and the man needed help. One moment they were keeping watch together — the old man telling him the well-worn yarn of how he had come to be a porter for the valley at age ten — and the next moment he had fallen to his knees, barely able to breathe.

Taliesin found the stair cut into the rock wall and took it, three steps per bound. At the bottom he rounded to the tower, ran in the doorway, and bump-bounced into Great-Aunt Eira, who was changing the bandage on Caygek's arm.

"Old Brice," he panted, picking himself up off the floor, "… he … he needs help!"

"Whatever could have happened?" Mother asked.

Bedwir stood from where he'd been sitting in the back of the room, looking alarmed. "Are the Picti climbing back up for another attack?"

"No! Brice is hurt. Come see!"

He ran out of the tower and up the stairs once more. Caygek and Bedwir were right behind him, with Mother and Great-Aunt Eira following. By the time they made it to old Brice, the man had collapsed upon his back and his body was shaking.

That was when Taliesin saw the man's cheek. A black, thick, bulbous boil had grown there. His arms had the same growths, and there were smaller ones on his leg, just above his boot. It was some sort of sickness that Taliesin had never seen before.

Natalenya pushed her way through, but when she saw what had begun to grow on the man's skin, she halted, her hand going to her mouth.

Old Brice tried to sit up, but failed. Then he found the boil on his cheek, grabbed the edge, and tried to rip it off. "Get it awa'! It's a rat, I say, a rat that's eatin' me cheek!" But his thick fingers couldn't get a grip on the shiny mass, and the skin popped. Black pus sprayed them all, and a huge glob landed on Natalenya's skirt.

She backed away along the wall-top, trying to flick it off, and in the process knocked over Tinga, who had stolen up from behind. As she fell near the edge of the wall, Gaff, her little puppy, barked and jumped from her hands.

"No!" Taliesin reached out, but he was too far away. The pup landed on the top of the stonework — and then slipped over the edge.

Tinga shrieked.

Taliesin sucked in his breath as the dog fell headlong down the massive, slanted wall. Halfway down, one of the stones jutted out and Gaff hit the outcrop, spun, yelped, and continued plunging down until she landed in a dry, brown bush.

Tinga began sobbing. "My doggie! My doggie! Get my doggie!"

Mother scooped her up and hugged her. "Are you all right? I'm so sorry! I'm so sorry."

And down the hill, just then, they heard the blast of a war horn as the Picti began climbing the hillside for another assault upon the fortress. There was little time before the mount would be swarming with invaders intent on killing them.

Gaff began whimpering from below, and Taliesin knew what he had to do.

The first thing Arthur did when they arrived at the foot of the ruined hill fort was to find the fastest way up along the western side where the jut of land was more gently sloped. The Saxenow would pass through a valley on the east, exactly under the fort's watchful eye.

Here, Arthur placed the archers under Culann's leadership, instructing them to wait until the first supply wagon was ablaze, and then to fire on all within range of the cliff. Arthur then positioned his men in hiding around a ridge of land toward the south, a place where they could spy on the enemy ranks of warriors as they passed ... until the slower supply wagons brought up the rear.

When the first Saxenow emerged from a forest track far away, Arthur whooped with excitement.

Dwin shushed him.

"They can't hear me," Arthur said, resentful at the rebuke.

"Best not to assume," Dwin said.

"What ... do the screaming, axe-wielding Saxenow have you worried?"

"Me? No. And you?"

"Of course. I'm not daft."

Onward the Saxenow came, thousands upon thousands of foot soldiers. And they were all headed north to pluck the prize of Dinas Marl from the Britons like a sweet, damson plum is sucked from the pit.

Arthur's anticipation built. Little did they know that he had reoccupied the fortress and lay in wait for them.

Soon, the companies of foot soldiers began to thin, and Arthur saw his true prize: the supply wagons lumbering forward, pulled by teams of draft horses and oxen.

"Wait until I give the word," Arthur whispered back to the others, but Dwin nudged his arm.

"We can't attack," he said.

"What do you mean? The wagons are almost here."

"Haven't you noticed?"

"What?"

"The horsemen ... they're bringing up the rear."

Arthur wanted to swear, as much for the fact that Dwin was right as that he had missed it. He had counted on the horsemen and chariots passing by first and being far away when they attacked the wagons. But he had forgotten in his excitement, and now he could see them emerge from the woods and come galloping forward, perhaps a thousand strong.

"Shall we call it off?" Dwin's eyes looked hopeful.

"You mean retreat?"

"Yes."

"I'm done retreating. The taste of death I left behind last night is still bitter."

"But the archers won't shoot until one of the wagons is on fire. You told them —"

"Then I'll just have to light one on fire myself." Arthur rose, his legs poised to move.

"No! There are too many and they'll catch you!"

"Then watch me get caught."

Arthur mounted his horse and lit his two torches using their bronze box of live coals. Passing the box back to the others, he kicked his horse forward into a trot, and then a gallop.

"After him!" Dwin yelled.

They all lit their torches and rode out in a ragged line.

But Arthur felt only the wind in his hair and the thrill of challenging death. Life coursed through his veins, banishing the doubt and the waiting and the defeat of the preceding day. This was what he was made for.

"Come on, Hengist! Do your worst!" he yelled as the dry grass of the valley floor fell away beneath his horse's hooves and the nearest wagon rose up before him. Riding by, he thrust the pine-resined torch into the heart of the wagon's supplies and then drew his sword. It only took moments to slay the drovers and then he was off to the next wagon.

War horns blasted through the valley, and the earth began to shake under the pounding of the thousand enemy horsemen approaching from the forest.

Soon he set another wagon ablaze, and his men had lit six more. But they wouldn't make it if they didn't ride forward into the protection of the archers.

"Forward!" he yelled and kicked his horse until it was galloping north. By the time they came to the area below the fortress, the archers had been raining down arrows long enough that most of the Saxenow were either dying or had fled the area. This gave Arthur and company a brief opening to increase their speed as their horses dashed before the oncoming storm. Unaware of the archers, the Saxenow horsemen stampeded after Arthur and his tiny band, and many perished beneath the sharp tip of a British arrow before they pinpointed the source of the threat and swung wide.

Breaking through the long thin line of straggling infantry took little effort, and soon Arthur and his men traversed a ridge of land straight for Dinas Marl.

And then came the chase ... down into the broad valley, across the dry, grass-choked remains of what had been a stream, and then up again to the fortress. Only then did Arthur realize that Culann and the archers had never joined them. They had been instructed to ride away once Arthur and his men passed the fortress, so where had they gone?

Arthur turned and saw a small battle going on. A mass of Saxen horsemen had apparently taken a more westerly route, intercepting the archers, and Arthur saw flashes of red as the Britons and their mounts went down under the spears and axes of the Saxenow.

"Dear God Almighty," Arthur prayed, "have mercy ..." But there was none given that he could see, and Arthur ground his teeth at his own shortsightedness. Twenty men dead. If he had called off the attack instead of going ahead with it, then maybe ...

The thunder of chariots cresting the nearest ridge put an end to Arthur's second-guessing. With a shout, he urged his men forward to Dinas Marl, where they rode in just before the gate was shut.

And there was Merlin, standing alone beyond the guards, his white face and pursed lips accusing.

"Where are the archers?"

"I don't want to hear it," Arthur said, dismounting and throwing his reins to a nearby warrior.

"I asked a question ... where are the archers? And where is Culann?"

"A moment of peace is all I ask," Arthur said, and his words felt bitter on his tongue. He climbed a nearby ladder to the top of the wall, as much to get away from Merlin and his condemning eyes as anything, and looked out in hope he had been wrong. Had the archers survived? But he couldn't see any among the mass of Saxen warriors approaching.

"Everyone to the wall!" Arthur called, and the men responded quickly, already having prepared for the oncoming assault by donning their armor.

Now that Arthur had escaped, the Saxenow took their time to organize themselves and prepare for the attack. And when it came, it began with Hengist approaching in his chariot and addressing Arthur.

"Artorius," he called, waving a broad, short blade whose steel blazed in the sun. "Ye are a fool to haf come. Surrender de fortress, or I'll see dat yer head is smashed an' yer brains spilled out."

Arthur laughed at the man, but it was a nervous sort of laugh, revealing more of his feelings than he wanted. Dwin stood on his left, but the spot on his right was empty. How could he face a siege, knowing that Culann might be out there on the field, dying, alone and without help? He was a brother in all but blood, and rich in counsel. Yet there was no going for him, not while this Saxen dog kept barking at him.

"Yer High King es dead. Why fight on?"

This gave Arthur an idea. Perhaps there was a way to shut the man up. He began to pace back and forth, all the while holding up a hand for Hengist to wait, and the Saxenow warrior did so until Arthur finally turned to speak.

"You say that my High King is dead, and this is true. Yet another High King stands before you, one uncrowned as of yet but a High King nevertheless. And not just any High King, but one whose forebears have never made peace with you, and one who never will."

Hengist laughed. "Who is dis High King? All de lines haf failed and der is no such man. Or is der a Roman among ye who came across de sea? If so, den beware! De Picti killed one legion ... we Men of de People killed three!"

Arthur laughed at this. "No, he is not from Rome."

"Den let him step forth and do battle with me!" And at this he plucked a javelin from its basket and launched it at the wall in front of Arthur. It jabbed the wood between two staves, and stuck fast.

As the javelin vibrated in the wind, its sound reached upward, tilting the world strangely, and Arthur felt himself falling, floating. Hengist's jeering face was replaced by another, that of a very ancient man with a long, curly white beard who stared into Arthur's face with an unholy eagerness. A mottled fur of black and white lay over his shoulders, and under that he wore a shiny red tunic embroidered with white thread.

But Arthur felt small, young. Scared.

Was he remembering the past? His past?

And the world had become cold ... so cold that Arthur's fingers were turning blue, yet as Arthur looked down at his hands, they had changed from the rough, strong hands he relied upon and knew so well to the hands of a little boy, and there was a rope tied tightly around his wrists. He suddenly felt even smaller. Insignificant. Powerless.

All around people danced upon bloody snow, and a fear clutched at Arthur's throat like a garrote, tightening, ever tightening.

The old man bent forward, and he held out a knife to Arthur as his glistening, yellowed eyes sized him up like a cut of meat.

The knife plunged into Arthur's stomach and he screamed. The world flashed as pain pulsed upward and outward … until all his flesh was on fire, as if the edge of the knife had cut his very soul.

Yet there was Merlin, through the haze, running toward him. Fear and sorrow, agony and ache were all etched there upon his face. Yet Arthur saw something else too — an assurance of faith and hope.

And Merlin held the bowl, the shining, ghostly bowl before him, and all the world faded in comparison to the brilliance of that beautiful object.

Yet even the bright image of the bowl faded to black as Arthur felt his soul slip from his body like a grain of wheat is pushed out from a dry, lifeless husk. The pain disappeared, and Arthur looked down upon his small lifeless body. The blue lips of the child's face had ceased quivering, for his lifeblood had been poured out upon the pagan altar from his torn abdomen.

Arthur's soul flew, then, far away to the lands of the south, to another time, to another place where he felt again the fresh breeze of a marsh and heard the ethereal croak of frogs and the buzz of insects. And there before him stood the woman in the raven-feathered wrap. She looked toward him with the one eye that wasn't covered by her long, black hair, and there was a beauty and inner strength about her that amazed him. Yet she was hiding something from him. Arthur longed to know what.

"Arthur," she said, "please come … You know how to find me, for you have been shown the way in your dreams. I need you. I'm so alone here, so alone."

She knelt then before a cairn of weathered, moss-encrusted stone, and she wept.

But the vision of her was swept away by a great wind, and he beheld a tower amidst dead trees, rising like a dark sentinel in the night. Wolves howled, and Arthur felt afraid. He began running through the darkness. Lightning split the heavens, and suddenly a man appeared before him. Shadow cloaked his form, and he limped as he came.

"Who are you?" Arthur called through the howling wind.

Another blast of lightning cracked through the clouds, and the man was revealed. He wore a russet robe, and his beard was dark, though tinged with gray, and he had anxious eyes.

"I am someone of no importance, yet I offer you something ... if you will come to me."

He lifted his hands then, and Arthur beheld a torc, so beautiful to behold that it took Arthur's breath away. It was a kingly ornament, ancient and rare.

Could it be? But no, that was impossible. He wanted to look away from it, but the idea that this might be his father's long-lost torc smote him. He yearned to hold it and somehow, by touching its precious edges and whorled designs, to know the man who had forever been lost to him. But these were foolish thoughts.

And then the man holding the torc faded, and his final words were: "High King ... High King! You must proclaim that you are the High King. Reveal yourself! Reveal yourself so that I may find you."

And there was light, and Arthur breathed in the smell of smoke. Hengist stood below him once again, for the vision had gone. The Saxen leader shouted, and his words finally pierced through Arthur's fog. "Are ya deaf?" Hengist called. "I asked who dis High King is, dat I may fight him."

Arthur took a breath. The time had come, and he would not shirk back.

"I am the High King, for my name is not Artorius, but rather Arthur, son of Uther. I am the one whom Vortigern longed to kill, yet I live. I am the one taken as a slave amongst the Picti, yet I survive. Behold! I am the one who was sacrificed, yet has been resurrected to lead all of the Britons against you ... and I am the one who slew your brother. Leave here, now, or I will be your death."

The men around Arthur began to murmur in wonder, but Hengist roared with laughter as soon as the speech was done. "I jus saw ya run like de rabbit, an' now ya threaten me? Come down for de fight, an' we vill see who is de High King."

Arthur nodded, and turned to descend the ladder, but Dwin grabbed his arm. There before him stood all the British warriors with their mouths agape and their eyes reflecting suspicion, doubt, and — did Arthur imagine it? — a flicker of hope.

Dwin shook him, tearing his attention away. "You're not going to fight Hengist, are you?"

"Of course I am."

"You can't!"

Arthur met his friend's eyes. "It's the only way, Dwin. If I can kill him, we may just turn the entire Saxenow army back. I'll take that chance. Now unhand me."

Dwin let go, and Arthur climbed down, hopefully to victory, but more likely to his own death.

CHAPTER 22

THE EDGE OF THE KNIFE

Taliesin gulped as he looked down the wall—twenty feet or more—to his sister's hurt and whimpering puppy. And below the puppy he could see a mass of Pictish warriors climbing the hill to attack.

There was just enough time if he acted quickly.

Around him, confusion spread like a ripple in a pond. Caygek and Bedwir tried to help the porter. Old Brice hung limply between them, and Taliesin wondered if he might already be dead. The broken, black boil on his face had leaked pus down onto his neck and tunic.

If Gaff was to be rescued, it was up to Taliesin. He just had to keep asking himself, what would his big brother, Arthur, do? What would his father do?

As his mother scooped up the crying Tinga and headed for the stairs and the safety of the tower, Taliesin ran along the parapet to the opposite side of the fortress, where he found the rope they had used the night before to lower the miller. Grabbing it, he ran back to where Gaff had fallen. But there was nowhere to tie the rope. The wall top was smooth, and the parapet likewise. Down below, in the courtyard of the tower, he saw Withel running on some errand.

"Withel!" he yelled.

The boy stopped suddenly and looked around, not seeing Taliesin above him.

"Up here!"

Withel cocked his head just as Taliesin threw the rope down.

"Tie that to the door!"

"What?"

"Quickly!"

Withel tied it onto the iron brace that held the bar, and Taliesin tested it.

"What're you doin'?" Withel called up.

But there was no time to answer. Taliesin checked to make sure his sword was still strapped to his back, grabbed the rope, and threw himself over the wall to the outside of the fortress. His feet landed with a knee-jarring crack on the stones of the wall, and the rope burned his hands as he slid down.

Gaff whimpered below him and, far away like in a dream, he could still hear Tinga's little voice: "My doggie! Help my doggie!"

Hand under hand he dropped, making three jumps down to the ground ... only then did he look up and realize how far down he had come ... and how far up he would have to climb. Running to the dry bush where the dog had fallen, he found her on the ground, bleeding from her snout and with one ear lacerated. When he picked her up, she wagged her little tail and licked his face.

Below him he heard the Picti scrambling up the scree-covered path.

He ran back to the rope and realized his quandary: He couldn't climb back up holding Gaff. He tried tucking his tunic into his breeches, which would allow him to put Gaff inside his shirt, but the thick material was too bulky.

If only he'd put his belt on that morning.

Then an idea struck him ... the rope! It was plenty long. He quickly tied it around his waist, unlaced the top of his tunic, and gently lowered Gaff into the makeshift pouch. Her sharp little claws scratched his bare chest, but there was no other choice.

Just as he was gripping the rope to climb back up, he heard a scuffing noise behind him. The foremost Pictish warrior ran up the path, huffing at the effort and bearing a short spear. He was nearly naked except for a ragged cloth, with painted blue whorls covering his body. Even his shaved head was painted, with solid blue on the left and what looked like dried blood on the right.

Taliesin panicked, dropped the rope, and ran, but only made it ten steps before the rope, still tied around his waist, went taut and stopped him cold.

The Pict laughed at this and then jumped forward, trying to jab Taliesin with his spear.

Taliesin saw the danger just in time, grabbed the rope as high as he could, and kicked off the wall to swing back the way he had come. But there was no way he could climb out of reach in time, and so he dropped back to the ground and drew his sword.

Now the Pict laughed even louder, and the man's eyes were wild like an animal's.

A freezing fear penetrated into Taliesin's gut, making his legs shake.

The Pict lunged again with a hideous roar, intent on skewering Taliesin.

Arthur mounted his horse and set a helm on his head. It wasn't a perfect fit, but it would do. Merlin handed up a shield to him, and he slipped his left arm into its straps before choosing a good, stout spear from a selection jabbed into the ground before him. Then, after shifting the position of his sword, he rode toward the closed gate. Dwin and Peredur rode next to him, along with two other warriors.

Merlin walked beside him. "So Culann is dead and now you're going out to fight a man who is so full of deceit that his stink would make a pig plug his nose with manure."

"Do you think he'll betray me?"

Merlin shook his head. "Since he challenged you to single combat, he'd lose the respect of his men if he did. But that doesn't mean he won't fight dirty."

"If I can kill him —"

"If you kill him, then nothing changes. All five thousand Saxenow won't turn and sail back to their homeland. You solve nothing." Merlin turned to walk away.

"Merlin!" Arthur called, and his father stopped but didn't turn around. "What else am I supposed to do? I've just declared I'm the High King. I can't run from him."

"Yes, you can. In order to see your fight with Hengist, they haven't surrounded the fortress yet. We're a small force, and could ride out the back gate if we left immediately."

"Where?"

Merlin turned back, and there was a zeal in his eye. "I don't have the answers yet, *but we need more men*. Until then, let the south reap their reward for following Vortigern."

Arthur gritted his teeth against a sudden swell of emotion. "No," he said, "I don't believe that. Let all the world lose faith, but there won't be any hope if it doesn't start with me. With us."

"There'll be enough fighting no matter where we go. We need a true stronghold where the Britons can rally, and this fortress isn't it."

Arthur blinked and thought about his father's words, but bravery called him forth. There was no turning back now. "Pray for me, Tas."

Merlin reached up and grabbed his hand. "I always do. Be on your guard."

With that, Arthur raised his arm to signal the doorkeepers. The ancient doors groaned on their hinges and then opened wide. Arthur rode out into a light haze as the southern sun nearly blinded him. Here was their last chance. Just him and Hengist . . . to the death.

All but a few of Hengist's men had backed down the hill to a wide plain at the foot of the fortress, and Arthur rode out into the center, leaving his supporters at the edge.

Hengist rode around Arthur, driving his chariot faster and faster, whipping the horses into a frenzy.

Arthur kept turning his horse to keep an eye on the man, and just that quick Hengist turned and threw a javelin at Arthur. The sharpened wooden stick flew like a hawk right at his face, and if Arthur hadn't ducked quickly, it would have hit just below the neck.

Arthur kicked his horse forward, timing it such that he rode alongside Hengist. But he quickly realized his danger, seeing three scythe blades attached to the spokes of each chariot wheel.

Arthur angled his spear and threw it.

Hengist raised his shield and the spear clunked off of it to the ground.

Hengist veered his chariot to the left, directly in Arthur's path.

Arthur's horse was well rested and nimble, however, and did a quick stop and turn when Arthur pulled the reins hard to the left.

But the distraction itself was deadly, for Hengist used his own spear to stab Arthur's horse right above the foreleg. The horse screamed and stumbled.

Arthur tried to jump off, but the horse slammed to its side. A shock of pain engulfed Arthur's leg as his boot became trapped under the saddle, and his back muscles began to spasm.

Hengist circled around and aimed his chariot's spinning bronze scythes toward Arthur's head.

Arthur tried to kick free of the thrashing horse, but it was useless.

Hengist's chariot rolled faster, and Arthur could hear the thunder of the horse's hooves and the whirling of the blades. At the last moment, he flattened and covered his head with his shield.

Hengist yelled in triumph as the blades slammed into Arthur's shield.

Splinters flew. Wood shattered. Arthur's arm twisted and white hot pain tore through his shoulder. Dust choked him, as well as the smell of blood. There was a tearing sound as the shield's leather strap rent loose and his wooden protection was ripped away.

The shield became caught in the blades and its edge was rammed into the dirt. The spokes of the wheel shattered, and Hengist's chariot crunched to a stop. The king of the Saxenow untied the reins from his waist and leapt out, enraged. The darkening, smokey sun reflected off his golden armbands as he lifted a massive hammer, and his arms were so thick that Arthur had no doubt he could wield it with deadly effect.

Arthur's horse, startled by the chariot, had lifted up on one leg, freeing Arthur, who climbed to his feet shakily and drew his sword. Only then did he notice that his helm was missing and blood dripped down the left side of his cheek.

Hengist strode toward him and raised his hammer and swung it at Arthur's head.

Arthur sprang to the side, and in the moment when the weight of the hammer pulled the Saxen king's balance forward, he tried to swing at his arm.

But Hengist saw it coming and twisted his body so that the blade made only a thin red line across his shoulder.

Arthur tried to strike again, this time thrusting the tip of his sword toward Hengist's bare chest, but the man was too quick and swung his hammer up, hitting Arthur's blade in the middle and nearly flinging it from his grip. And before Arthur could strike again, Hengist had dropped the hammer and tackled him.

Arthur released his sword, finding it useless as Hengist grappled him, tying up his arms in an unbelievable grip. Arthur had been trained in wrestling, sure, but no one near Dinas Crag had been as big or as strong as Hengist, and Arthur just wasn't prepared for the ferocity of his attack. With only inches between their faces, Arthur could see the twitch of the man's cheeks and his bulging eyes as Arthur fought to free himself.

A mob of Saxenow warriors had gathered, for their foreign-looking, long-laced boots had lined up in a circle around the two.

Soon, Arthur feared, they would watch the spectacle of the High King of the Britons being beaten by Hengist. Arthur looked for British boots, but couldn't find them in the sea of trespassing Saxenow legs.

Unable to free his arms, Arthur shifted his weight and kneed Hengist in the side five times.

The man's grip slackened for the briefest moment.

Arthur twisted his right wrist free and reached for the knife sheathed at his hip.

Hengist sensed the danger and slammed his forehead into Arthur's. The world exploded in flashes of light, and the only other thing Arthur could sense was the reek of the man's smoky, sweaty hair draped across his cheek.

"British mongrel," Hengist said with spittle flying, "dis is yer last, miserable day!"

When Arthur's vision cleared he found Hengist's right hand at his throat and saw his own knife in Hengist's left — ready to plunge into Arthur's chest.

CHAPTER 23

A DESPERATE END

Taliesin screamed and swung his sword, biting into the spear's tip and knocking it to the side.

The Pict stabbed again, but Taliesin ducked and dove through the man's legs, accidentally slicing the man's breeches with the edge of his sword. If only he had thought to do it on purpose!

The Pict spun around, but the rope was between his legs now and Taliesin was already running around him the other way, always keeping his blade pointed at his foe—as Bedwir had taught him.

But the Pict found the rope with his hand and with a wicked snigger jerked Taliesin toward him.

Taliesin fell hard on his side.

The Pict advanced, keeping the rope taut and his spear ready.

"By God's grace, leave him alone!" called a voice from above.

A small rock came hurtling down and bounced off of the Pict's shoulder.

Taliesin looked up, and there on the wall above him stood Brother Loyt. Taliesin got to his feet.

The Pict shook his fist at the monk and then jumped at Taliesin with his spear. Another rock came sailing down and cracked the Pict on the head.

Taliesin ran forward and jabbed his sword in deeply just below the man's ribs. The Pict screeched, dropped his spear, and fell over.

Taliesin pulled the sword out from the man and it was slicked with blood. From inside his shirt, Gaff whimpered. Taliesin sheathed his sword, there not being time to clean it, and pulled the rope free from the man's legs. Just as he reached the wall, a mob of Picti appeared over the lip of the hill.

There was no way he could climb fast enough!

But then the rope went taut and Taliesin looked up to see Withel and Brother Loyt hauling in the line. Rocks came hurtling down on the Picti too, for Bedwir and Caygek had come, along with three other defenders.

Taliesin was lifted from the ground, and, finding a grip in the stones of the wall, he started scaling upward. Withel and Brother Loyt pulled and pulled, and soon Taliesin was over the top of the wall and on his back, panting. Underneath him the stones of the parapet felt cool on his hot neck, and above him little Gaff began to wag her tail under his tunic. She poked her head out and licked him on the chin.

He held his hand out to Withel. "Thanks ..." was all he had breath to say.

Withel helped him up and then punched him hard in the shoulder. "Good kill," he said. "We'll make you into a warrior yet."

But Taliesin thought of his father and his harp, remembering the calling upon his life. "A bard, I'm going to be a true bard."

"Ah, sure, but at least you'll be able to fight, huh?"

"Sure." Taliesin pulled Gaff fully out of his tunic and set her down carefully in a little niche in the stones, where she began to lick her wounds. Then he untied the rope from his waist, glad to be free of it.

When a hook caught the top of the wall right in front of them, Taliesin realized that he and Withel had ignored the exchange of arrows, rocks, and spears that had been going on all around them. The boys looked over the wall to see a Pict climbing the rope.

"Throw rocks!" Withel yelled, and they grabbed some and threw them down on the man, but a spear came hurtling up at them, nearly parting Taliesin's hair.

To their left, one of the defenders screamed. It was Logan, a young horse tender who'd worked with Old Brice. At first Taliesin thought he'd been injured by a Pict, but it was something else, for he fell to his knees and began scratching at his arms. At first there was nothing unusual about his skin, but almost instantly splotches appeared, and they quickly filled with black pus. It was the same thing that had happened to Old Brice!

With nothing Taliesin could do to help Logan, and Bedwir and Caygek busy knocking down their own Picti horde, he turned his attention back to the Pict climbing the rope, who was now halfway up the wall.

Withel was trying to lift the hook and throw it off the wall, but it was stuck. "Use your sword," he said. "Cut the rope!"

Taliesin drew his blade and leaned over the wall. The rope was attached to the bottom of the hook but just close enough to reach, so he slashed out, only nicking it.

An arrow cracked the stone right next to Taliesin's face, and chips of rock flew into his eyes. He swung the sword toward the rope again, and accidentally slipped forward precariously.

Withel grabbed Taliesin's tunic from behind and steadied him. "Whack it!" he called.

Taliesin sawed at the rope and cut through one of the braids.

But the Pict was almost up to him now and, pausing his climb, he pulled a hatchet from his belt and angled it back to throw it at Taliesin.

Using his free hand, Withel tossed another rock and it struck the Pict in the chest.

Taliesin swung once more and severed the rope, sending the Pict down to the stones below.

Rebuffed in their first wave of attack, the Picti retreated, and there would have been silence for a space of minutes if not for Logan still moaning and crying on the parapet. Great-Aunt Eira and Taliesin's mother were called up to help the man, and when they came, with Tinga in tow, they had their own news to tell.

Taliesin's stomach clenched at the look on his mother's face. She spoke, but she didn't make eye contact with any of them, and her mouth seemed to move stiffly. "Six just died inside with the same plague. I don't think there's much hope for poor Logan."

After a moment's pause, Brother Loyt stepped forward. "Where there is life, there is hope. Come." He gathered everyone around Logan and began to pray.

O Father, holder of the two lands,
This world and the next,
Come stand at the bridge of death
To restore Logan to us.
O Spirit, giver of the three blessings —
Grace, deeds, and pureness —
Come close and lift our brother,
Touch and mend sickly Logan.
O Christ, bearer of the four wounds —
Whip, thorn, nails, and spear —
Bring comfort to the hurting;
Heal Logan son of Ellic.

Logan gave a weak smile and nodded to Brother Loyt, but there was still fear in his eyes.

Taliesin picked up Gaff and gave her to Tinga, whose eyes filled with tears of gratitiude as she hugged her tail-wagging puppy.

Then someone shouted to them from below. Everyone but Logan rushed to look over the wall. It was a group of Picti come to parley. Their despicable High King was with them, as well as that monk fellow — Garth by name — and four warriors with spears.

Taliesin had heard lots of tales of Garth and his antics while growing up, and had always wished to meet him. The funny thing was that Taliesin never pictured him as a grown-up with stubble, but rather as a pudgy, funny boy with a bagpipe. Even Brother Loyt had stories to tell of Garth, having been a monk in the abbey of Bosventor, the town where Tas had grown up.

Taliesin had also heard tales of Necton, High King of the Picti — about how he had cruelly injured Taliesin's father and the others many times during their slavery, and how he had stolen Tas's torc. So now Taliesin had his own reason for hating him — for killing his great-uncle. What a wicked man this Necton was, what with his eyes darting back and forth like a weasel, and his huge, muscled hands clenching repeatedly as if he were choking someone.

Necton yanked Garth to the front and bade him speak — even though the monk had a swollen lip and bloody bruises covering the right half of his face.

Taliesin felt his mother's hands come to rest on his shoulders just as Garth looked up.

"Natalenya!" Garth called, "Caygek! Bedwir … and all the rest who defend this fortress whom God knows — I am bid under threat o' death to convince you to give up."

He swallowed, licked his lips, and then continued.

"Necton says if you stay inside the fortress, he's made a batterin' ram and he'll kill everyone. If you give up, he'll spare you and only make you slaves. He says to give up, for you're just a fly-dung o' a fortress, and he's tired o' your obstinacy."

Natalenya gripped Taliesin's shoulders so tightly that it hurt.

Necton seemed satisfied with these words so far, but then Garth's voice came again, louder, and filled with joy.

"But I say, no! Keep trustin' in God, who can deliver you. Never give up!"

At these words Necton's face twisted in rage and he drew a long knife. His men grabbed Garth's light-red hair and yanked it backward in order to thrust the monk's stomach out, and there Necton's blade came to rest. The High King of the Picti had a wicked grin as he looked up to the wall, and he whispered in Garth's ear.

"He tells me he will kill me if you don't surrender, just like the other prisoner. Don't do it! I knew this might happen when I went north to plant a church, and I'm prepared."

Great-Aunt Eira and Mother both looked ashen faced as they whispered to each other. Then Eira ran down the stairs on some urgent errand.

Taliesin's mother called down to Necton. "Let him go! I will pay you gold if you let him join us in the fortress!"

Garth gulped and translated her words into Pictish.

Necton laughed at her. "Thusa ghivaive up yui!" he demanded.

"If you don't let him go, I'll hide these coins in a hole where you'll never find them. But if you let him go, I'll give them to you. If you conquer us, then you'll get to kill him anyway." And then her voice turned sarcastic. "Or are you so weak that you're not able to capture us?"

Necton scowled when he heard the translation of these words and swore at her in Pictish.

Taliesin wanted to run down the stairs and hide. He couldn't watch someone else die like this. His memories were still raw from seeing his great-uncle murdered.

Necton took his knife and cut open Garth's robe ... slicing his skin enough to make it bleed.

Natalenya screamed and threw the money down to him. "Let him go, you pig!"

Necton was frowning as he picked up the bag, but when he opened it he began to smile. At a motion from him, the guards let go of Garth and Necton kicked the monk forward.

Garth fell, cut his hands on the rocks, and crawled forward until he came to the foot of the wall.

"Get the rope!" Taliesin yelled to Withel, who retrieved it and came running. Caygek and Bedwir lowered it down and soon raised Garth to the parapet.

"Thank you!" Garth said again and again as he embraced his old friends.

Mother fussed over the cut on his stomach, and he waved her off.

"It stings, sure, but it's not deep, and we have more important things to deal with."

"Still, I'll get an ointment for it right away."

Tinga cleared her throat, and when she had Garth's attention, she held the injured Gaff up to him. "Will you pleathe pray for my puppy?"

Garth smiled, wiped his bloody hands on his robe, and took Gaff up and cradled the puppy to his chest. "What's his name?" Garth asked, looking at the puppy's little face.

"It's a she, and her name is Gaff," Tinga said.

Garth placed a hand on the pup's head and prayed:

I lift my prayer to the mighty power
To the almighty power of the One
To the almighty power of the Three
To heal and protect this creation:
Brave Gaff—dog o' dogs and evil's bane.

Then, to Taliesin's confusion, he continued in a different language.

Lift I mo phraiyer ris am mhighty phoweir
Ris an tailmhighty phoweir an Oni
Ris an tailmhighty phoweir an Threhi
Airson healsa aind phrotectsa thish creishon:
Bhraive Gaifh—dogh doigshe aind eivil's bhaine.

"What did you say?" Tinga asked.

"I prayed in our language first, and then in Pictish, but it was the same prayer."

Taliesin drew his sword. "If you're not a Pict, then why'd you pray like 'em? If a Pict comes here, I'll kill him just like the other one." And there was still blood on the blade, proving his words.

Garth kissed Gaff, who gave a little grunt. "Not all Picti are like Necton. I've a church up north in the village o' Cathures. The people there have turned to God and are your brothers an' sisters in the

Lord, and you should hear how beautifully they sing. Moreover, I'm goin' back to that green valley once ..."

But his words trailed off as a great booming filled the air. The parapet shook, and Taliesin almost lost his balance.

The Picti had brought the battering ram.

Taliesin sheathed his blade and took up a rock.

"It seems my stay'll be short-lived," Garth said.

All but Garth grabbed what rocks remained and began pelting them down on the enemy. Taliesin threw his, but they all bounced off the upturned shields and fell uselessly to the ground.

Boom!

The stone shook and they heard a crack in the doors below.

Boom!

And the great bar securing the door began to break.

"To the tower!" Bedwir called.

Taliesin looked out and saw behind those with the battering ram, the entire army of the Picti climbing the mountain. Some of them held torches while all of them carried glinting weapons. And they were chanting a dirge which the valley winds carried to the top of the wall. It seemed to Taliesin to say: *Slaves! Slaves! Slaves! Slaves ...*

Garth cradled his sack in one hand and put his arm over Taliesin with the other. Together they ran down the stairs, Mother and Tinga just behind. The others followed, and then Bedwir and Caygek helped carry Logan down the stairs — for he couldn't walk, and the fearsome boils had thickened and swelled across his body.

Brother Loyt came running down just as the battering ram smashed through the center of the doors. Chunks of wood and splinters exploded outward.

Taliesin drew his sword, but Loyt grabbed him by the tunic and yanked him into the tower where all the others villagers had gathered.

Picti began to break down the fortress gate.

Everyone labored together to slam the massive tower doors and bang the double bars in place.

Outside, the yelling and cursing sounds of a Picti mob arrived, and they began to beat on the doors and hack at it with their blades.

Taliesin turned away from the doors, almost running into Tinga, who looked up at him with admiration.

He nodded to her and went to show Bedwir his bloody blade only to find Logan's dead body blocking his way. His mouth hung open and his eyes had sunken into his head so that Taliesin was forced to look away.

From the level above came the sound of screaming, and a young girl ran down the stairs and flung herself into Mother's arms. "Ten more got the sickness, an' the others died!"

Boom! Crack!

The Picti brought their battering ram against the tower's doors with shuddering force, causing dust to fall from the ceiling.

"Whath gonna happen?" Tinga asked, grabbing on to Taliesin's belt.

"We're goin' to die," he said, shaking his sword, "but we're not goin' down without a fight!"

Mórgana howled in rage as she looked out the north-facing window of her stone tower in Lyhonesse.

"Try once more," Loth said, "and if it does nay work this time, then go there yoursel' and tell Necton Two-Torc tae throw 'em from the cliff. You do want to see 'em dead, don't you?"

She stamped her foot.

"Now, now, my granddaughter," Mórganthu said. "Patience is required. Remember the Voice's plan?"

"Don't tell *me* of the plan, you fool. What I need to know is why I can't inflict Natalenya with the disease."

"The malevolent light must be stopping you," Mórdred said. "Just as you told us it did before."

"Yes, but I thought it had gone away. Now I can inflict anyone I choose, but neither Natalenya nor her children succumb."

Loth leaned back upon his throne. "And dinna forget the two

warriors. Now, it is interestin' to me that all o' those that are immune happen to have been with Merlin the longest. Do you think those warriors were with him at my father's temple?"

"Indeed, I think they were. As I recall, I arrived just in time to keep those two from cutting your throat."

"Me? Hardly. Yet I still dinna understand how Merlin could destroy the whole temple and slay my father and his household as well."

"He has a power that I do not understand."

"Are you ... are you afraid of him?" Mórganthu asked. "Dare I imagine that weakling of a brother scaring you? Ha!"

"No." Mórgana pulled forth the orb and fang for one last attempt. She had slain as many as she could to devastate their defenses, but the effort had weakened her considerably. She had just enough strength for one more attempt. This time she would try the little girl, the one with the oh-so-cute little doggie. Mórgana smiled. She hated innocence, just as the Voice did.

She held up the orb and pointed it north, hoping the alignment would improve her chances. "Show me the girl — Natalenya's daughter — heiress of Merlin, our enemy."

Purple flames burst forth from the orb, and she looked inside to see a small, upturned face. The girl was leaning against her mother and stroking her puppy's ear. And there was the horrible boy, blade in hand, snuggling in on her other side. The mother leaned back against the tower's wooden wall with her eyes closed, yet she was mouthing some words to the children. The boy soon joined her and they spoke in unison.

Mórgana fished the fang from its sheath and held it near the orb until its green flame united with the purple of the orb's. Loth, Mórdred, and Mórganthu began to chant, and she joined in. A thrill of power trickled into her arm, strengthening her for the task, for she felt so tired and empty after inflicting disease upon so many.

Finally, when the potent power of the fang was at its height, she touched it to the orb, yelling, "A curse on the girl child — a disease of death, a plague upon her flesh!"

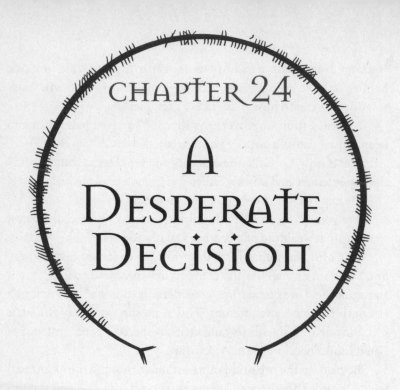

CHAPTER 24

A DESPERATE DECISION

Arthur's body clenched as Hengist brought the blade down, but the stroke never fell. The sharp edge of a sword slipped under Hengist's chin, and the man faltered, his knife hand tense and the weapon quivering in the air just over Arthur's chest.

Arthur squinted. A Saxen held the sword, and one of the man's outlandish, muddy boots was planted right next to Arthur's shoulder.

"Get off!" the Saxenow said.

Arthur jerked to see the man's face, for he spoke like a Briton. What he saw took his breath away ... Culann! Somehow he had come to be dressed as a Saxen, bare chest and all, and had slipped through the ranks of the enemy warriors to stand next to and watch Hengist's fight with Arthur.

Another blade came to rest under Hengist's nose, and Arthur saw someone from behind place one at the man's back. It seemed Culann had not been the only Briton to survive the massacre of the archers.

"Drop it or you die," Culann said.

Hengist looked out the corner of his eye at the edges of the swords, and then down at Arthur. Sweat had beaded on the man's forehead, and his golden armbands reflected his panting mouth and teeth.

There was silence for the space of a few heartbeats before the enemy Saxenow stepped forward with their spears and swords pointed at Culann and his companions.

Culann tightened his sword against Hengist's throat, eliciting a barked order from the Saxen king. His men backed off, muttering. Hengist dropped the knife to the dirt and slowly, ever so slowly, removed his fingers from Arthur's throat, though the look of hatred remained on his face. Then he rose and backed away.

Arthur sucked in a few breaths. The smell of smoke was thicker now, but he barely registered it as he looked in wonder at Culann and then stood on shaking legs.

Shouts came from the back of the Saxenow horde, suddenly, and the ranks began to break, with men running everywhere and in complete confusion.

Finally Arthur saw it. From the distant hill, where he had attempted to burn the Saxenow supply wagons, came a roaring wall of flame and smoke.

Without moving, Hengist shouted orders to his men, some of whom ran madly for their horses.

Arthur shouted for Culann and the others to follow him.

But Culann shook his head and pointed his blade directly at Hengist's chest. "I'm going to kill him."

"He and I had an agreement, and you've already interfered enough. Look! We'll all die if you break faith!" Arthur pointed through the chaos toward an elite guard of forty Saxenow warriors who stood nearby with their weapons ready, unaffected by the chaos around them. Beyond, the wave of flames roared closer.

Culann sneered. "Don't have the guts, Arthur?"

"I don't kill defenseless men."

"You think I care?"

"Leave him. That's an order."

Suppressed rage swept over Culann's face.

Arthur picked up his sword and locked eyes with his friend.

Culann growled and shoved Hengist away, withdrawing his blade.

Hengist jumped backward and commanded his men to attack.

Arthur performed the rear guard as he and his men bolted for the gate of Dinas Marl. Thankfully, the warriors on the walls shot arrows at the Saxenow, keeping them back.

Hengist yelled after them, "I'll kill ye yet! Just wait, de time will come!"

Once safely inside, Arthur yelled for everyone to prepare to abandon the fortress, and in response the men immediately started packing supplies and weapons — anything useful that could be carried. Then he threw his arm over Culann's shoulder, trying to patch things up. "Thanks for saving me ... I don't know how you did it. I thought ..."

"Hengist was going to kill you?"

"Well, yes ... that too. But I thought you'd been killed."

"Most of the archers wanted to return right away, but I suggested we hide in a cave I'd found. Things had gone wrong for you, and I thought you might need our support. Anyway, I was out voted, and all but me and three others rode off toward Dinas Marl. They were caught, and, well ..."

Arthur closed his eyes, and the air went out of him. He had led these men to their death, and that was hard to bear. Up until now it had been *Arthur the champion* who had slain Horsa, *Arthur the hero* who had saved a remnant of Vortigern's men from the treachery of the Saxenow. But not anymore. Now it was *Arthur the reckless*, who, through his own foolishness, had caused these men's deaths. Arthur didn't mind risking his own life, even relished it. But to do that to another —

Arthur opened his eyes and found Culann staring at him, searching his face. For what? Remorse? Valor?

"Don't let it bother you. They made their decision."

"It was *my* decision to attack."

"We all die. Live your life before you puke, that's my motto."

Arthur changed the subject. "How ... how did you get these?" he said, pointing to Culann's Saxenow clothes.

"We waited until they were gone and rode down to the valley, stripped the dead, and put on their clothes. With you fighting Hengist, no one was watching."

"Thank you."

"Just let me kill him next time."

Merlin rode up, with Peredur and Dwin mounted next to him. They had brought two other horses.

"I suggest we leave. The fortress won't last when it catches fire."

Arthur noticed the courtyard had slowly filled with mounted men, though a few still scrambled to finish packing. But before he could give the order to open the gates, he had to be sure of the decision, so he climbed the ladder to the top of the wall.

"What are you doing?" Dwin called.

It only took one look. Hengist led the Saxenow eastward, avoiding the roaring line of flames. It was almost as if someone were pumping a giant bellows to fan a blacksmith's forge. Had Britain become that dry? Soon the fire would reach the walls, and the fortress would burn. There was nothing here to save. Nothing here to defend anymore. All of southern Britain was either burning or taken over by the Saxenow, it seemed, and Arthur felt at a loss as to how to fix it. From the coast all the way across to the broken city of Glevum, destruction reigned.

But that word stuck in his head. *Glevum ... Glevum ...*

Sliding down the ladder, Arthur strode to the horse Merlin had ready for him and stopped.

"Casva! Where did you find him?"

Merlin smiled. "Among the picket lines. One of the warriors rode him from Hen Crogmen, and we didn't know it."

Arthur took the reins and patted the horse's neck. He was dusty to the point that it almost changed his color. With joy he tightened the saddle, mounted, and borrowed a hunting horn from Peredur. He blew on it three times and led the men out the northern gate of the fortress and turned westward, away from the flames and away from the Saxenow.

After a few leagues of journeying, Merlin rode up to him.

"Where are we going?" he asked.

"Back to Glevum. Remember the muster?"

"Of course, but ..."

"It takes place in two days. Maybe some men will show up. You never know."

"And after that?" Merlin asked, but his voice seemed hollow. Distant.

"I don't know. Keep fighting the Saxenow is all I can think of. Any ideas?"

Merlin didn't answer, but just stared straight ahead toward the west, where the last light lingered in a faint gray glow. There was a strange look in his eyes, as if he sensed something dreadful just beyond the bend in the road.

Arthur rode quietly for a while, but then could stand it no longer. "I asked where we should go. Are you all right?"

But Merlin hung his head and slowly let his horse drop back without answering.

When they finally made camp, Arthur was exhausted and discouraged, and the unforgiving ground didn't comfort him any as he wrapped himself in his cloak. But before he could slip into the oblivion of sleep, Peredur squatted beside him. "Arthur, there's something you need to see."

Suppressing a groan, Arthur rose and followed to the top of a nearby hill. There the night breeze ruffled Arthur's cloak as Peredur pointed eastward, back the way they had come.

Arthur sucked in his breath and held it. There, far away, he could see that the fires still raged. The wind had whipped them across the dry, drought-stricken land, and now all the forests to the east were on fire.

"Why are you showing me this?"

Peredur stared out at the conflagration, the reddish light reflecting weirdly in his eyes. "Because everything we do, no matter how necessary we think it at the time, has a far-reaching consequence. Remember that."

Arthur said nothing, only watched the east burn. What had he done?

That night, Merlin lay wrapped in his cloak, staring at the campfire as it slowly dimmed. Finally, when darkness and silence reigned in the camp, he prayed for wisdom — and when wisdom came, he stopped praying and shut his heart to it. He knew the truth — he had known the truth for a long time — but didn't want to face it. He closed his eyes and drifted off to sleep, yet when sleep claimed him, he wished it had not.

He found himself floating down into blackness. Wind whipped at his face and clawed at his clothing. Evil, mocking laughter swirled around him. Voices in the air. Screams and the flailing of chains. Faster and faster he plunged until green, sickly lights began to swirl around him, illuminating the stone walls of a shaft. Dark archways appeared in the walls and he flew past them, ever deeper. Then he began to see red, glowing eyes staring out from the doorways. White, leprous arms suddenly began to reach out from every hole, trying to grab him. The hands had sharp claws, and Merlin pulled in his limbs to avoid them.

But the arms grew longer, more muscular, and finally one snagged his tunic and he came to a complete, jarring stop. He hung there, twirling in the air, in shock and breathless. Then just as quickly, the arm dropped him. He fell to a flagstone floor a short distance below and collapsed, moaning.

A dank, burnt smell filled the air, and Merlin sneezed. When he opened his eyes he saw that he lay on a small outcrop that was wedged between a towering stone wall and the shore of a lake. Its black surface wet the stones within a pace of Merlin, and a gloomy, unbroken stillness lay over the water as if nothing had disturbed it for a thousand years.

He rolled over and studied the wall. On the left and right were twin iron sconces holding torches that cast a pale green glow — and between them, half hidden in shadow, was a recessed wooden door with horizontal iron bands shaped like skeletal necks ending in malformed, horned skulls. Behind the door, Merlin heard a sniffing sound, and whatever it was began to scratch at the wood.

The hinges ... the door opened *toward* Merlin.

He stood and backed away from the door until his foot splashed in the oily water.

The creature behind the door roared and snorted.

Cold terror dug into Merlin's heart, and it began to thump and throb in his chest. His feet went numb and his guts constricted into a knot.

It can't be. It simply can't be ...

Behind him he heard a splash.

Whipping around, he saw the water swell and ripple. From the depths he caught a flash of movement. Something lurked there.

Merlin's breath came in rasps now as he looked for a way of escape but saw none, for the curved rock ledge that he stood upon ended where the wall met the water. There was nowhere to run. Could he climb? He ran to the wall, five paces from the door, and found a film of green slime had coated the surface of the rocks. He tried to find toeholds and rocks to grab on to, but slipped and banged his knee badly.

Could he defend himself? He searched his belt but found his sword and dagger missing. Yet his right foot pressed upon a rock that shifted. He began to pull it up from the grit and shale just as the water exploded in a cascade of black, foul-smelling drops.

A dark form floated upward.

Merlin broke out in a cold sweat as he pulled the rock up and hefted it to his shoulder. He backed up against the wall, but felt it boom and shake as someone screamed from behind the door. The beast roared and scratched at the wood. Merlin wanted to yell, but his throat had nearly squeezed shut.

The creature from the water slid closer, now just entering the torchlight.

Merlin dropped the rock and it went rolling away.

The form was a woman ... his mother! Long red hair lay wet upon a dress of the finest silver adorned by red metallic beads. She looked upon him with curiosity and sternness, and though her oval face was now older, it was still lovely beyond all that Merlin could remember. He rushed to her, splashing through the black water until he embraced her gently.

"Do not hold me, Merlin! But rather ya need ta admit the truth!" With a look of deep wisdom, she backed away, took hold of his shoulders, and, with a gentle pressing, turned him around to face the door. Roaring. Scratching. Screaming. The wall shook as the beast slammed into the wood, bulging it outward.

"Take me away from here," Merlin pleaded. "I can swim, and we can —"

From behind, she clamped a hand over his mouth.

"Shah, now. The power has been granted ta me ta take ya away from here. Ya need never face the door again, nor what is inside, if ya so desire. But ken this: There are thousands of innocent men, women, and bairns behind that door who will be slaughtered unless ya choose to challenge the beast."

Merlin shuddered. "But I have no weapon," he whispered.

His mother held up a sword with a twisted iron guard in the shape of ox horns. His sword. The sword that had been his father's. She gave it to him, and he took it. The steel hilt was heavy, the blade sharp and deadly.

"If I try — will I succeed?" he asked, but regretted the question immediately.

"It does na matter whether ya succeed. This is your destiny an' your calling — your doom, if ya will. Unlatch the door, Merlin, and face what is inside."

Every part of Merlin yearned to run and hide. But what of those being slain beyond the door? Could he let them die? Who else would confront this evil?

"Mother," he asked, "what kind of creature is the beast? Is it a ... a ...?"

"Yes. It is a wolf, sent by Mórgana, an' more deadly than any that has yet existed in the shroud o' this world. The wolf an' his army have just destroyed Aquae Sulis, Vortigern's third-most important city, and they must be stopped."

"How can I — ?"

"By overcomin' yer fears, which are set far deeper than yer scars. Yet, ya can overcome them and face the wolf."

So it was true. All his fears had united against him to become a nightmare, a walking death so terrifying that it strangled even the screams of his soul. Then a horrid remembrance of his childhood came back to haunt him:

He was shrieking, and the wolves were scratching his face, snapping at his limbs. Sharp teeth. Hot, putrid breath. And there was no one to help.

And when Merlin's father finally came, it was too late and Merlin had been blinded.

Beyond the door a child began to sob now and call for help. Merlin realized that the tables had turned, and it was *his* time to help. Just as he had hoped for someone to save him, he needed to rescue others.

Merlin stepped forward, the tip of the blade shaking.

The beast's claw rent against the door, and Merlin heard it crack.

"Pray for me, Mother."

There were tears in her eyes. "Always, Merlin ... I always love ya, an' I'm always prayin' for ya."

Merlin walked forward.

The beast began to beat against the door, shaking it and causing dust and rocks to fall from the stonework.

Merlin readied his blade and then placed his hand upon the latch. The metal was cold and wet.

The beast roared.

Merlin jerked his hand away and looked back. His mother was still there.

"I ken ya can do it. Go."

Merlin gulped as he shakily reached out again ... grabbed the latch ... and squeezed.

There was a clicking sound inside the iron handle, and the beast fell silent beyond the door. Merlin imagined it waiting, tensing ... flexing its claws. Ready to slit Merlin's skin until his lifeblood ran and his soul screamed for mercy.

He stepped back as he opened the door, the point of the blade ready.

But there was no beast. Beyond the door lay only the camp where he had fallen asleep. The moon was hidden behind clouds now and the crickets weaved their gentle, humming music. Arthur, Dwin, and Culann slept beyond the campfire.

Merlin turned once more to his mother, confused, and she urged him forward. "Go now, sweet son, and know that God is with ye. Confront yer fears, and know this: No matter what, God's love is with ya, and I'll always be prayin' fer ya."

As Merlin stepped through, the door, ledge, and lake vanished.

He took a long, slow breath, and looked up to the night sky where a star appeared, brighter than anything Merlin had ever seen — its light burrowed into his eyes like a flaming cinder. It swooped low over the camp and moved toward the southwest. Merlin squinted and saw that it was a shining drinking bowl made from the most beautiful golden glass that he had ever seen, as clear and bright as if it had been heated in the furnace of the sun itself.

The Sangraal!

Over the sleeping men it floated, past the horse pickets and beyond the vastness of the southwestern forest. Toward Kernow. Toward Mórgana. Toward all that Merlin feared. Yet it gave him hope and faith as it directed him onward.

And as it went, words filled the air, and they brought back a remembrance from long ago.

The bear will charge — with steel claw free
'Gainst hoary swell of peoples be.
All things will lose — and dead the tree,
Lest wisdom to — he bend the knee.
Hell dog will dark — the sun's bright face.
The beast will rise — from secret place.
All men will flee — to water trace,
Till sword and spear — with prayer grace.
The beast will bring — forth fetid birth,
And bear will scratch — and prove his worth.
But land will not — have new its mirth,
Till red-leg crow — be brought to earth.

It was the words of the madman, Muscarvel — and his prophecy floated away on the air like a nightingale's lament. Merlin knelt down in prayer, embracing the wisdom that he knew was right, fearful though it was. After Glevum they would travel to Kernow to fight Mórgana. She and her conspirators were the source of all that was wrong in Britain, and even if he had to fight wolf-heads to stop her, this he would do.

CHAPTER 25

ASHES OF THE PAST

The Picti crashed their battering ram into the doors of the tower once again.

Boom!

With panic ripping into her soul, Natalenya tried to breathe slowly, evenly. The ground seemed to lurch under her feet even as all that she had trusted in for the last sixteen years failed. She had been a slave of the Picti once, and had vowed that it would never happen again. Then she had carried a disease that had caused the Picti to loathe her — the same disease, from appearances, that was killing the inhabitants of the tower.

Merlin had tried to tell her that her disease had been caused by his sister, but Natalenya had never fully believed him. It just seemed so ... strange. Yet now, with slavery and disease surrounding her once again, she began to truly believe her husband's stories — seeing apparitions of Ganieda far from home, even fighting her ghost. Thankfully, their family had all been spared such evil goings-on during the last many years. Yet now, with Merlin away, they had come upon her again, like a crazed mountain bear slavering to kill.

She closed her eyes and, for a brief moment, grabbed hold of the secret dream she'd held on to throughout the siege. She imagined that she was sailing away from this hell. Sailing away south to Kernow — to Dinas Camlin — to see her mother once more. Sailing to the ends of the earth in search of her love, her Merlin. She longed to hold his face, look up into his tender eyes and feel his strong, safe arms around her.

Boom! pounded the battering ram.

Her dream faded like a phantom, and the nightmare took her once more:

Slavery. Disease. Death. Was there no way out?

Then, in a flash of insight, it all made sense. How could she have missed it? She had been protected her from Necton before when she was a slave — would God do it the same way now?

O bright Father, O holy Son, O sanctifying Spirit ... grant us your safety!

She grabbed Bedwir's shoulder. "How long will the doors hold?" she asked.

He looked at the tower doors, the bars, and the hinges.

Boom! crunched the battering ram.

"Ten more blows, I'm afraid, if that."

That's not enough time!

"Everyone!" Natalenya shouted, startling Garth and those around her. "There is a way to save ourselves, but we'll need more time! Is there anything to brace the doors?"

Caygek shook his head. "Nothing."

"Anything! Please!"

Crack!

And one of the door hinges bent.

Garth ran to her. "I can slow 'em down! I know a tune ... it's about their greatest king. If I play it, they'll stop to listen!" He reached into his sack and pulled his bagpipe out — the same one he had owned when he was a young orphan, the one he'd inherited from his father.

Natalenya smiled to see it after so many years. "Run! Up the stairs! On the third floor there's a window facing the gates ..."

But Garth was already bounding up the steps while fitting the drone pieces on.

Boom!

Parts of the lower bar shattered, sending splinters into Natalenya's hair.

Taliesin patted her on the shoulder. "Can I help?"

She turned to look at him. He had blood smeared on his cheek and there was fear in his eyes, but a maturity and determination too that Natalenya had never seen there before. "Yes." She ran her hand through his hair, pushing it out of his eyes. "Protect your sister. Take Tinga and the pups to the third floor. Help Garth."

"But — "

"Hurry! Now!"

Taliesin grabbed Tinga's hand and ran upstairs with Gaff and Gruffen. .

Boom! The post on the right side started breaking away from the wall.

Natalenya called everyone over and began instructing them.

A sound interrupted her, a skirling sweetness raining down that could only be Garth's bagpipe. The man's fingers played a low, complex, and mournful tune that immediately tugged at Natalenya's heart.

The battering ram stopped its swinging, doom-filled rhythm.

Natalenya forced herself to focus once more, then finished her directions and sent everyone running to their given tasks.

But halfway through the preparations, while Natalenya was running up to the second floor for the third time, Garth's bagpipe faltered in squeaks and honks. He'd run out of air. Natalenya sent up a supplication urging God to give him a second breath.

Then she smelled smoke.

Taliesin came bounding down the stairs. "Necton was mad that the men stopped hittin' the doors, an' so he lit them on fire!"

"Help me!"

Taliesin did, and when they made it down to the first level, once more the flames were shooting through the door. Smoke began to fill the room.

Garth started playing again, weakly, and yet he provided enough distraction to hold off the Picti until Natalenya and the others had completed their task, coughing and choking through the smoke.

When it was done, Natalenya ran up to the third floor with Taliesin and the others, legs weak and lungs burning.

Garth's face was deeply red, and his poor bruised lip was swollen even more.

She nodded for him to stop.

When he caught his breath, all he could say was, "... Outta practice ... way outta practice ..." And she gave him a hug.

"Hey!" Taliesin reported from the window, "Necton's got piles o' tinder against this side o' the tower, an' the fire's climbin' higher!"

And then the battering ram boomed once more.

Crack!

Natalenya sat down with her back to the wall, pulled Tinga close, and called Taliesin away from the window.

He came, bringing little Gruffen.

Loyt led them all in a prayer for protection, and Natalenya and others joined him, for it was the twenty-third Psalm, which they had been memorizing:

The Lord God, my Good Shepherd, sates my hunger
And gives unto me verdant fare on the heaths,
Where I may feed my soul.
The Lord God, my True Chieftain, quenches my thirsting
And gifts unto me crystal streams in the glens
Where I may fill my spirit.

And now Taliesin joined in, and Tinga snuggled closer with Gaff.

The Lord God, my Just High Priest, slakes my longing
And grants unto me righteous paths on the heights,
Where I may praise His name.
The Lord God, my Stout Shield Arm, guards my lifeblood
And walks with me through the vale of deathly shades,
Where I must fear no more.

Boom!

The whole tower shook.

Tinga whispered in Natalenya's ear, "Mammu, why do I see Tath's drinking bowl when I shut me eyes? An' I feel funny too, like little happy angels are danthing on my skin."

Natalenya hugged her closer. "I don't know, honey. I don't know."

Loyt raised his voice to continue the psalm, and Garth joined in.

The Lord God, my War Hammer, clouts my haters
And lights hearth fires with sumptuous meat on the spits,
Where I may mock my foes.
The Lord God, my Great Delight, makes the honey
And fills unto me bowls of drink from the vats
Where I will join the feast.
The Lord God, my Torc Bearer, gilds my own neck
And runs after me to goodly joy on high,
Where I may always dwell!

Boom! smote the battering ram, and Natalenya heard the doors below burst inward amidst the shouting, angry Picti.

Outside, flames licked as high as the window, and Natalenya began to cough as rolling smoke poured across the ceiling.

Garth called out for them to sing a hymn in these, their final moments.

"What can stop them?" Tinga asked. Her face was pinched up in a scowl and her hands shook.

"Only the dead can stop them. Only the dead."

She pulled both children close and let the silent tears flow.

Mórgana screamed as she lifted the fang from the orb. A searing pain shot up her arm, and what did she get for her trouble? Natalenya's little girl was *still* unharmed. Mórgana hated it ... hated *her*. In fact, she hated all young girls, including her own, brief childhood. The Voice had taught her to despise her former innocence. To kill off all childish, girlish desires. To be willing to sever all ties and familial love unless it advanced her master's plan. To serve no one but him.

"Is the girl sick yet?" Mórdred asked.

"No, the little beast."

"Perhaps she is sae protected because she's your brother's daughter?" Loth asked.

Mórgana swore. "Blood has nothing to do with it. Merlin has no relation to the two warriors standing there, but they are protected as well."

"What ... what are those warriors waiting for?" Mórganthu asked, his question ending with a wheeze and a cough.

"They await in futility to attack my servants, the Picti," Mórgana said, returning the fang to the safety of its sheath.

Mórdred peered eagerly into the orb. "Have they finally broken in?"

"I do not know, but even if the Picti fail to break down the doors and smite the inhabitants, the flames will devour them more surely than the moon can conquer the sun."

The image in the orb shifted to the Picti below, and Necton Two-Torc, their High King. They heaved the battering ram back one more time and slammed it into the tower doors, which burst and shattered, the right one falling off of its hinge.

Mórgana snapped her fingers as she looked into the orb. "They've broken in! They've broken into the tower!"

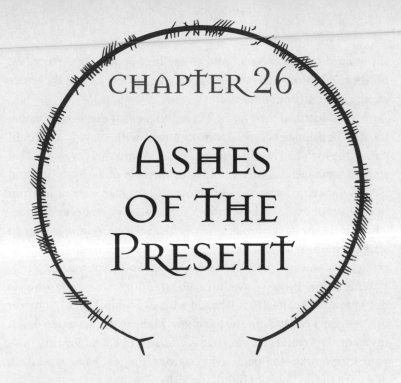

CHAPTER 26

ASHES OF THE PRESENT

Merlin awoke to Arthur's hand pressing his shoulder. The slanting rays of the sun blinded him, and the camp stirred with the sounds of breakfast.

"'Morning. Did you get good sleep?" Arthur asked as he turned to wake Dwin.

Merlin stood and stretched his legs. "None worth mentioning."

"So what do we do? You never answered me yesterday. I'm out of ideas."

"Let's gather everyone," Merlin said. "We need a council of war."

Arthur agreed, and the word was spread throughout the camp that anyone could come share his opinion. At Arthur's direction, several fallen logs were placed in a circle near the center of the camp, and the men selected five warriors to represent them, though all were allowed to speak.

Merlin brought his harp concealed in its leather cover — not because he planned to play it, but because he wanted the men to think hard on who he was, and to see his support for Arthur. He positioned himself to Arthur's right as the leaders sat and the entire camp gathered around to listen.

Merlin scanned their faces. There he saw sadness, anger, curiosity, and hopelessness spread among them, with varying shades of pain. One man had lost his hand and the stump was covered with a stained bandage. Another stood with the help of a crutch. Beyond him was a warrior who had lost an eye. All the men were filthy from many days of battle and they stank of sweat, dirt, horse, and blood. These were the survivors of one of the greatest calamities ever to strike Britain, and Merlin could feel their fear and frustration gathering like a storm — ready to beat upon the rock that was Arthur.

"My fellow Britons," Arthur said, standing, "for those who do not know me, I came from Rheged with my companions in answer of Vortigern's call to fight the Saxenow. Many of you have heard that my name is Artorius ... but that is a false name, and for this I ask your forgiveness. As I declared yesterday, my real name is Arthur, and I am the lost son of High King Uther."

Murmurs spread, and it was obvious that not a man among them was unfamiliar with Arthur's declaration at the fortress wall. A bearded man stepped forward, a seasoned warrior wearing grimed scale armor with a notched battle-axe hanging from his belt. His arms were thick, and his bald head shone in the morning light.

"I am Percos mab Poch, and I speak for the rough-blade lads ... right?" He turned around and raised his arms as the men behind him hooted and jeered. Turning back to Arthur, he spat on the ground and then smeared it into the dirt with his boot. "And we heard yah, an' have been followin' ya for the last day... But ye can hardly grow a beard yet ... and where's the proof? No one here's heard bone or breath of Arthur in nigh a score o' years."

Arthur opened his mouth, but it was clear he didn't know how to respond.

Merlin stood and raised his voice. "Legends live again," he said. "They walk among you. Behold the Harp of Britain, which has lain

272

in hiding all these long years!" He unwrapped the instrument and held it before their eyes. None of these men had witnessed his ballad in front of Vortigern.

"I am Merlin mab Owain, heir of Colvarth, the chief bard of Britain and bard to High King Uther mab Aurelianus. It was I who took Arthur away to safety and hid him from the world until he was old enough to reclaim the torc of his father. If any man dares question my testimony or Arthur's claim to the High Kingship, let him speak."

But Percos spat again, and this time the glob landed halfway between him and Merlin. "If a piece o' wood makes you the chief bard, then my axe can make me the high blacksmith!"

The crowd roared in laughter, and the nearest man slapped Percos on the back.

He took another step forward and thrust his chin out. "And how're we to know you didn't kill ol' Colvarth and steal the harp? Maybe you're the one who killed Uther too!"

The crowd went silent at this accusation until a man to Merlin's left stood and cleared his throat. He wore a thick leather jerkin, and his face was weathered and lined, centered with a reddish, pitted nose. His long pepper-gray hair was pulled back and tied with a leather thong, and he had a thick sword at his belt.

The man jostled through and found his way to the center of the gathering. He stepped close to Merlin and peered at his face, then he turned to Arthur and did the same. The man's eyes were watery, and he blinked many times.

Finally, he turned to face the crowd.

"You all know me, for good or ill. I've seen each one of you join the war band as fly-catching fools with yer thumbs still in yer mouths. Yes, I'm the eldest o' you all, and you know that I used to be a war chieftain under our *goodly* king, but then lost my position when my sight went bad."

Here some of the warriors smirked, and one of them called out, "You mean you gutted Vorty's horse wit' a spear!"

The men laughed.

"Ah, well, sure, but that was a tough battle, and yer changing my tune. What I'm here to tell ya, you see, is that I was one of the very few in strict confidence with ol' Vorty, and I know a sight more about him an' his dealings than anyone else alive. An' when he took my position away, I threatened to tell all o' you the truth."

Merlin began to recognize the man's voice. Had he heard it somewhere before?

"An' do you know what ol' Vorty did? He threatened to kill me. To take my guts an' feed 'em to his pigs. To poke out my eyeballs and stuff 'em up my nose. Called me a sot, he did!"

"You *are* a sot, Rewan," called a voice from the crowd. "So sit down and shut up!"

And when Merlin heard that name, a memory came back to him. Rewan was one of the battle chieftains that Merlin met that fateful day in Uther's tent ... so long ago. Rewan had been the bloodthirsty one, and Merlin had recoiled at the man's advice. Taking a step back, Merlin sat down on a log to give the man room to speak, but part of him shuddered with worry that Rewan might lie.

"Well, I am a sot, but so are you, Tethion, and I'm not going to be quiet anymore."

Tethion swore, but Rewan ignored him.

"I let Vorty kick me in the shins an' sew me mouth shut, but I'm done with it. Here's the truth, so open yer ears wide, my lads."

Merlin held his breath.

"The truth is that Vortigern is a traitor and a murderer. He slew High King Uther in cold blood and blamed the druidow. He even had the man's daughters slain. I ... I ..." And here he faltered, allowing Merlin to exhale.

Rewan studied his own dirty boots for a long while. "I ... helped Vortigern do it. We shot 'em both with arrows, an I could'a stopped it, ye see? I did it for gold and the gold is all gambled away, and all I've left is the guilt, see? An' this Merlin, what with his marked face, he was in fact a sworn and faithful servant of Uther. I met him myself sixteen years ago and heard Colvarth declare that he would teach Merlin to be a bard."

Rewan gestured to the whole crowd. "But there are others who have more shame on their head than me in this bloody business, and it's my hope they're right sorry and'll confess it."

"An' just for all o' you scoffers," Rewan said, pointing at Arthur, "this one is the nose-to-nose image o' his father — of High King Uther."

Arthur blushed slightly.

Rewan looked around. "None o' you ever met Uther? Percos, how about you? Well I did, an' he was a *real* High King. And the hoof of it is that there's no one else in all the world who could be his son except that one there. This man is Arthur — true and truest."

Rewan fell to his knees before Arthur. "An' I beg you, Arthur — real and rightful heir of two High Kings, Uther *and* Vitalinus, to forgive me for my drink-lovin' tongue an' my gold-lovin' fingers. I'm not worthy to be yer warrior, but if you'll have me, then I'm yer man. If not, then just kill me quickly, for I've the innocent blood of your sisters on my hands." He set his sword down in front of Arthur and lay prostrate on the ground.

A range of emotions flickered across Arthur's grim face, but Merlin couldn't sense his feelings.

Arthur picked up the sword, and set the sharp edge upon the back of the man's exposed neck.

"Rewan," Arthur said, "the price of murder is ... blood for blood. That is the law of the land, and also God's law."

The man caught his breath.

"And so I now exact the blood debt from you."

Arthur cut a thin line across Rewan's neck, just deep enough to bleed. Then turning the blade, he cut another one across it to make the sign of the cross.

"Now rise, Rewan, rise with the Christ and with his forgiveness upon you, for you've been found faithful today to the truth."

Rewan began weeping. "I will not rise until I swear fealty to you as I once swore to your father ... and I promise you that I will keep this vow." Here he spoke the old oath, just as Merlin had done weeks before.

When Rewan was finished, Arthur helped him up, and they embraced. Other men followed, each swearing fealty to Arthur. Eventually Percos bowed, and soon more than half of the men had done likewise.

Those that would not — the prideful ones, as Merlin thought them — quickly packed their belongings, mounted their horses, and rode off northwest, toward Kembry. The core of these men served Cradelmass, the king of Powys, who had not been present at Hen Crogmen when the nobles were slain, having departed early on an urgent summons.

As it was, Arthur had less than two hundred men now.

Against five thousand Saxenow.

They traveled most of the day, making excellent progress toward Glevum, but still had another day of travel before they arrived. Their campsite was placed in proximity to a spring that still gave out a thin trickle of brown water. It tasted to Merlin like rotting, bitter oak leaves, but their waterskins were nearly empty, and thirst can make even foul water seem refreshing.

In the morning, Rewan was found dead.

A rag had been jammed into his mouth and an arrow shoved through his right eye deep into his head. Arthur called everyone together and questioned those who slept near Rewan, yet neither they nor the guards who kept watch around the camp had noticed anything unusual during the night.

This troubled Merlin. Was there treachery against Arthur in the works? Or was this just some personal spat? Arthur acted like it didn't bother him, but Merlin saw the tightness in his jaw, especially during Rewan's burial.

After a hasty breakfast, Merlin called the men together for a final meeting before they set off for Glevum. After the men gathered, he stepped to the center to speak. Now that half the men had left, revealing their weakness, it was time to lay before Arthur and the men the plain truth of their predicament.

"Faithful warriors of Britain! Loyal warriors of the reign of a new High King! We are small, but not without strength. We are adrift, but not without guidance from on high. I declare to you that the source of our troubles is not Hengist and his Saxenow, but rather the secret power that has arisen in the west — in Kernow."

The men stared at him blankly.

"Some of you have no doubt heard of the full-fledged Picti invasion in the north. All of you know the bitter blades of the Saxenow. And a few of you know that King Gorlas has attacked. But few of you know the full extent of what is going on in the west. He has not only destroyed Glevum, but Aquae Sulis as well. And his devastation will not stop, for a secret power is driving him on, and the men under him are enslaved."

Merlin paused to let his words sink in as he slowly circled within the clearing, making eye contact with as many as he could.

"Think of it ... we are giving our very blood fighting for Britain when our own countrymen are stabbing us in the back! It cannot be borne. These men should be helping us, not hindering us!"

"What do you suggest we do?" Dwin asked, his brow knotted and his eyes squinting.

"We do not have the strength to fight the Saxenow. We do not even have the strength to fight the Picti. But we *may* have the strength to fight Gorlas."

Percos stood. "You want us to kill our own brothers?"

"Not to kill the warriors, although I know that some will likely die. The plan is to kill Gorlas and the powers behind him, if possible. Then his men will be free and be able to think clearly. And, by God's grace, they may join us in our fight against the Saxenow."

"How many of them are there?" a man called from deep in the crowd.

Merlin bit his lip. Of this he was not fully sure, but with what he knew of Gorlas and his men from his time in Kernow, and with what

Colvarth had taught him, he thought he could make a reasonable guess. "At least three hundred men. But hear me! If your friend is fighting you, you must first make him an ally. Then you can battle the real enemy with strength."

"We have only two hundred to fight them, if that," Arthur said.

Merlin spread his arms out and turned slowly around. "Our only other options are to either die at the end of a Saxenow spear ... or run away without honor. But there is *some* hope, for today is the expected muster at Glevum, and when we arrive at the ruined city, we may find men willing to join us."

Another man stepped forward from behind Arthur. He was broad, with a long beard dyed red on the left and black on the right, and tucked into his buckled waistcoat. He walked with a bronze pike in his left hand. "Neb mab Kaw stands before you and requests the right to speak."

"If your words are shorter than your beard," Merlin said, "then, yes, you may speak."

The man bowed. "And I will abide such a request as long as Merlin the Bard keeps his answer shorter than *his* beard!"

Merlin rubbed his rough-shaven chin in an obvious way while feigning to think of a response, causing the men to hoot and chuckle.

But Neb raised his hand for silence. "Rumor has come that Glevum was sacked by wolves. Some even say they're in the shape of men with wolfish pates. What do you say to that?"

"That what you've said is true. As I stated before, there are — "

"*It is true?*" the man bellowed. "And you expect us to fight bewitched men? That's not for me, no, no."

"To Kernow. We must go to Kernow," Merlin said. "Arthur ... you support me in this? Surely *you* can see the truth of my words?"

Arthur looked pensive and said nothing.

Culann, sitting at Arthur's right, scowled. "You think we have enough men to fight wolf-heads when those same creatures have destroyed two Roman cities? You're a fool, Merlin. I've heard some call you that behind your back, but now I see it in full daylight, and I'll say it to your face." He stood and looked Merlin in the eye. Culann was taller than Merlin, and he had a way about him, if not menacing, that could be alarming.

"You're a fool, Merlin. This cause — any cause — is hopeless. *We need more men.*"

Merlin looked to Arthur, hoping for support, but the king avoided his gaze.

"All right," Merlin said, a bitter taste on his tongue. Then he turned to Arthur and said under his breath, "Think on what I have said, please ..." He picked up his harp and walked off, pushing his way through the crowd.

Merlin took his harp into the woods, found a fallen log, and kicked it. Finally sitting, he wanted to rip at the harp strings until his hand bled, but didn't dare touch the instrument in such a way. He could speak, he could advise, but could he sway the hearts of men?

Did Colvarth have the same frustrations throughout his life? How many times had the man advised Aurelianus — advised Uther — and had them choose a different course? Had them make bad decisions in the face of the truth?

Merlin thought back to his first and only time advising Uther. The king had taken *most* of his advice, but Vortigern had twisted it to his own ends, which led to the death of the royal family. And like a hammer to Merlin's skull came the memory of his failure at the Druid Stone. Uther had been tied and laid upon its craggy, glowing surface, and Vortigern, dark traitor that he was, came to the clearing to slay the king. And though Merlin was half blind at the time, he would never forget —

Drawing his dirk. Rushing headlong toward Vortigern's shadow.
The strange blue flames of the Stone burning Uther.
Vortigern poised to slay the king.
The sound of his own yelling. Swinging wildly. Blindly.
The shock of their blades meeting.

Vortigern slamming him on the head with his pommel.

Pain. Collapsing. Choking for air.

And then the nightmare of Uther ... screaming ... dying.

The blade through the king's chest.

Merlin had failed. Totally failed. And it had all begun when his advice had been ignored. Could he survive such a calamity again? If Arthur died, Merlin might be driven mad by his sorrow. One mistake. One failure. One poor decision. Hadn't Arthur nearly died already? Thrice?

But none of this was under Merlin's control. What did God want of him? To somehow go and battle Mórgana and Gorlas alone? Could Merlin even attempt such a thing?

No sooner had the thought come to him than he knew it was true. If Mórgana and the Voice were the real force behind the oncoming destruction of Britain, then any time spent battling the Saxenow or the Picti was foolish.

Merlin grimaced. Why had Culann galled him so? It wasn't as if the boy wanted something stupid ... more men would be welcome, certainly. It was that Culann couldn't understand the direness of their situation. The more they fought the Saxenow, the weaker they became. The weaker they became, the more powerful Mórgana became. She was like a deadly snake, sneaking up on them from behind. And if Arthur wouldn't support him and move to cut off the snake's head, Merlin would have to do it.

Alone.

His feelings of fear and failure engulfed him. He set the harp down and wept. And there, alone and in need of comfort, he took Natalenya's torn skirt scraps from his bag and held them lovingly between his palms. He could envision her as if she were right there with him, her eyes flashing with love and mischievousness. Her chin held just so. Her kiss — as only a true and faithful wife could kiss her husband.

Except that the pieces of skirt began to feel hot ... so hot that Merlin almost dropped them. Soon he had to separate his hands and blow to cool them off. The smell of acrid smoke stung his eyes, and like a blacksmith's bellows, his breath seemed to fan the scraps into flame. Soon all the material blazed bright and searing. The palms of his hands were singed, and still he held on until the pain became unbearable and he dropped the precious scraps, flaming, to the rocks.

The glow faded and went out, leaving nothing but ashes. When the next gust of morning wind blew, the white powder swirled away into the air — and was gone.

Merlin screamed.

"Natalenya!"

PART THREE
NIGHTMARE'S GALLOWS

FASTER THAN CROW, THE BLEAK NIGHT COMING;
BLACKER THAN COAL, THE DREAD OATH BINDING;
STRONGER THAN STEEL, THE GREAT CLAWS GRIPPING;
SHARPER THAN FLINT, THE LONG TEETH GNASHING;
SWORD AND STONE, THERE THE PROPHET OUTCRIES.

CHAPTER 27

THE ABDUCTION

Merlin packed his saddlebags for the ride to Glevum, but he fumbled at the straps with numb fingers. He could only see Natalenya's face. He would go to Kernow, he told himself, but his heart was in the north, if anything — anyone — still lived there. If Natalenya and his family still lived.

He choked back a sob. How could he go on living, moving, and breathing when terrible things must be happening back home? Why had his divine mission called him south just when he was needed most in the north?

Taliesin ... Tinga ... *Natalenya*!

Arthur blew a horn, and the men mounted.

Merlin climbed onto his horse, his limbs wooden and his head so heavy that his neck bent down and his back ached. Peredur fetched his harp and handed it up, but Merlin hardly cared. "Leave it behind," he wanted to say, but his tongue felt thick and he couldn't speak.

Peredur looked at him with pity and concern, his lips tight and his eyes sober. "Can I help?"

But Merlin couldn't tell him what was wrong. What good would it do? Nothing the man could say or do would solve the dilemma Merlin found himself in: bound to the task of going forward to confront what he thought was his worst fear, only to find a greater worry dogging him from behind. Beset on both sides with crushing nightmares, how could he survive? How could he *not* go home now?

Around and around his thoughts chased, until the rhythmic jostling of the horse jumbled them and they fell away into the dry scrub. All manner of sanity fled.

Gorlas is coming... Gorlas is coming...

Mórgana is near ... Mórgana is near ...

Mórgana's waiting...

With a baited blade ... And a ghostly breath ...

Crows flew overhead, and then all the land grew silent.

Merlin began to see things. Snouts sniffing the air from behind massive trees. A hairy paw sticking out at the back of a boulder. Wicked eyes glaring at Merlin from inside the slim opening of a cliff-cave. Yet whenever he blinked, the wolf would be gone, and the forest empty.

Am I seeing things? Am I going mad?

The warriors around him seemed oblivious.

Merlin kicked his horse into a canter. He had to scout ahead. Maybe Gorlas was laying a trap for them and had a large force hidden in the woods. He rode past Culann and Peredur, then Dwin and Arthur at the lead.

"Merlin!" Arthur called. "What —?"

But Merlin made the motion for silence and rode on ahead, keeping his eyes open and his wits about him, addled though they were. Soon the path led up a broad hill that blocked his view of what lay beyond, and Merlin approached the crest cautiously. When he reached the top he found a red-legged crow sitting in the path ripping at a dead squirrel with its blood-red bill.

Merlin rode closer, but the bird only turned its head and eyed him suspiciously. When his horse's hooves were finally upon it, the crow shrieked at him and flew up into the air, flapping at his face. He covered his eyes with his hand, but the bird raked him across the forehead before it flew off into the woods, cawing.

Merlin rubbed the welt, let out his breath, and spent a good while studying the woods nearby ... but noticed nothing unusual.

Continuing down the road, he turned a bend and saw a man in the distance lying on the ground next to the path. Merlin drew his blade as he rode his horse nearer. The man was very large, and had blood on the side of his head ... and ... did Merlin recognize him?

The man stirred, glanced at Merlin, and pulled himself up with great effort.

It was Gogirfan Gawr! The giant!

"Goodly stranger, ya have come in my great need!" he said. His left hand was scraped and bleeding and his clothes were all disheveled. Merlin looked, but the man's stout horse was nowhere in sight, and neither were his daughters.

Merlin wanted to hail the giant, but Gogi didn't seem to recognize him. Then again, Merlin wasn't wearing his mask and hood anymore. Now that Vortigern was dead, there was no need.

"Ma daughters! They've both been abducted by a ruffian! Can ya please help me save 'em?"

"Where?" Merlin asked.

"In ma tent ... just down this path, ya know! The thug means to harm 'em. Please help ma!" He pointed down a thin trail that snaked off into the woods.

The sound of men and horses drifted toward them as Arthur, Dwin, and Culann rode up over the crest of the hill, the army behind them.

Recognition flashed in Gogi's eyes, and then the color drained from his face. "Ahhh ... I didn't know it was you! An' I thought ya were alone ..."

Merlin called back to Arthur. "It's Gogi! Gwenivere and Gwenivach are captives!"

Arthur and Culann raced their horses down the hill and pulled them to a fast, hard stop.

"Well ... maybe ah can handle it!" Gogi said, and he patted a little knife at his hip. "Ah didn't realize I still had me trusty blade. No need — "

Arthur leaned forward. "Where are they?" he asked, his words quick.

Merlin explained, while Gogi grew more agitated. The giant started backing down the trail. "Ya got's a big group here, an so's ya can let ma handle it."

Culann drew his blade. "Stand aside, man, and let me through."

"But ya all might scare the ruffian! He might kill 'em then, ya know!"

Arthur found a gap between the trees and rode his horse past Gogi.

"Let me pass!" Culann said.

As Gogi turned to see Arthur thundering off, Culann slipped his horse into the gap, pushing the giant aside.

Merlin followed, with Dwin close behind.

Gogi shook his head and ambled behind.

Merlin rode fast to catch up with the others, who were dismounting outside the tent. It was a strange sort of pavilion, with large, embroidered flaps, a central pole, and two smaller tents protruding on either side to form wings.

Arthur drew his blade and was about to run in when Merlin called to him.

"Caution, Arthur! That may not be the best ..."

Arthur took one look back and ran into the tent as if he hadn't heard. Culann and Dwin were right behind.

Merlin entered last ... and sucked in his breath when he saw the situation. In the rear of the tent stood a brown-hatted man with a knife to Gwenivere's throat. Gwenivach lay on her side, bound, with the man's boot on her head.

"Get back or I'll kill her!" the man yelled. He looked wildly at the four of them, and he jerked the blade closer.

Gwenivere screeched.

Arthur didn't back up, but didn't advance either. "What do you want?"

"Three gold pieces ... and a horse tah ride away on ... and I let 'em live."

Arthur searched the bag at his side.

Culann kicked out the central pole of the tent.

The ruffian looked up and panicked as the tent fabric began to float down on him.

Culann lunged forward, grabbed the man's knife hand, and pointed his own blade at the man's face.

The man gave up and dropped his knife.

Dwin pushed the central pole back up, giving Merlin a better view. That was when he recognized the man, who had a thick scar across his chin ... and that brown hat! There was a cut through the top. This was the same horse thief that Merlin had fought on the bridge. The same one that had stolen one of their horses.

Merlin's stomach clenched like he'd just swallowed a rock, and he drew his own blade and placed it next to Culann's. Knocking the man's hat off, he grabbed his hair, jerking him back.

Gwenivere fell from his grip, screaming. "Don't hurt him! Don't you dare hurt him!"

For a heartbeat all three rescuers stared at the girl. Then Gogi ducked into the tent, huffing. "Don't ... don't hurt him!"

"What's going on here? Who are you?" Merlin shouted, as much at Gogi as at the stranger.

With two blades in his face the man didn't dare move, but he slowly turned his gaze up at Merlin.

Gogi spoke first. "He's ... he's me only son, ya know!"

Merlin stiffened and felt his hands tingle.

"Aye, I'm his son — Melwas mab Gogirfan!" the man said. And though he had neither his father's height nor girth, Merlin saw the resemblance now: the roundly shaped ears, the slightly bulbous nose, and those bushy eyebrows.

He let go of the man's hair and pulled his blade away.

Gogi fell to his knees before them, yet his head was still level with Merlin's chest. "We were trickin' yah," Gogi said. "To give us gold and a horse. I only tell the story tah riders I thinks are alone. I didn't know it was you all, or I would've never tried, ya know." He took his sleeve and wiped what Merlin had thought was blood from his hand. There was no wound.

Culann reached down to help Gwenivere stand, but she pushed his hand away and found her own feet. Gwenivach slipped out of her loose knots and stood next to her sister, teeth gritted and eyes glaring.

The giant bent his head down, his eyelids drooped, and his lips formed a pout above his finely braided white beard. "I'm full sorry, Gogi is, and I admit that I've been trying to take your horses from the moment I met ya. We people — we Walkers — are a poor lot, and we fairly starve come late winter."

The urge to slap the man came over Merlin, but he held his arms tight to his sides. "Where's Dwin's horse, then? Give it back to us."

Gogi's eyes brightened. "Ya know, we tried to sell 'im three times, but haven't found someone willing to part with enough coins ... so we still have him. Melwas ... go get the chestnut, and be quick about it."

Melwas stood, slipped from the tent, and came rushing back in. "There's warriors out there!"

Arthur led the way, then, and they all stepped out.

Percos, Neb, and a few other warriors had come with their weapons ready.

Arthur nodded to them as Melwas stepped into the woods and swiftly returned with Dwin's horse, which nickered at Dwin's gentle touch to its cheek.

"I never thought I'd get you back!" he said.

"Well, while we're all here," Gogi said, "why don't we make up a big pot o' soup and — "

Merlin held up his hand. Just thinking about it made his ears throb. "We have to go," he said curtly. "And I hope we *never* have the pleasure of seeing you again." He stared sternly at Arthur, but the young man looked away to steal a glance at Gwenivere. The girl sat with her eyes downcast upon the burnt remains of their campfire, over which a skinny, charred bird was spitted.

Merlin mounted and the others followed suit wordlessly. Once they were riding back down the trail, though, Arthur trotted his horse up to Merlin.

"Why'd you leave so soon?"

"Go ahead. Give 'em Casva and be done with it."

"I'm serious. Gwenivere — "

"Tried to steal your horse."

Arthur huffed and rode ahead.

"And my horse, remember?" Merlin called after him. "If they'd had their way, we would have all walked the entire length of Kembry!"

A short ride brought them to the Fossa, but they ignored the dusty road bed to head cross-country toward Glevum.

Merlin rode near Arthur the rest of the day, but the two didn't speak. So it was a relief when evening began to descend and the setting sun etched the sky with brass and burgundy, heralding their arrival at Glevum. They rounded a ridge of trees and beheld smoke still hanging over the city. After passing through the east gate in silence, the small band wound their way toward the ruins of Dinas Vitalinus, hoping to find those who might have gathered for the muster.

As they approached, a figure dashed into a large stone building.

"Hey, there!" Arthur called, but no one answered his hail.

By the time they arrived, the man had run out again with ten other warriors, all holding spears.

"Halt!" the man said, looking from Arthur to Culann to Dwin, and then to the long line of warriors beyond. "Who dares enter Vortigern's city unheralded?"

When Merlin rode up, he saw that the man was mostly bald, and what was left of his brown hair hung down, unkempt, past his shoulders. He wore a black tunic and a thick leather belt adorned with a whip, a long dirk, and a flagellum.

Arthur laughed. "And who is foolish enough to guard a ruined city with ten men?"

"I am Rondroc, chief jailor to High King Vortigern, and the highest official still alive in the city. State your names and your purpose — or get out."

Merlin's mouth fell open ... Rondroc was the name of Natalenya's older brother. They had heard nothing of him since the day he'd gone off to serve Vortigern sixteen years ago. Merlin searched his face for a resemblance ... perhaps the nose and forehead. Could it be him?

"Vortigern and Vortipor are dead at the hands of the Saxenow," Arthur retorted, "and we are all that's left of his army."

Rondroc blinked, took a step back, and tightened the grip on his spear.

Percos rode forward. "It's true, Rondroc ... there's been disaster on the trail, as well as here, I see."

"Then who is this one leading? I owe no man my — "

Merlin gave his harp to Peredur and dismounted. Stepping around from behind Arthur's horse, he interrupted the proceedings. "Hear me, Rondroc of the house of Tregeagle, brother of my wife. The man you are speaking of is High King Arthur, the son of Uther, come back from both death and slavery."

When Rondroc saw Merlin's face and scars, he flipped his spear around and waved the cudgel end threateningly at him. "Ol' birdscratch, eh? After all these years! I think we have an old score that needs settling!" The man's neck turned red and his nose twitched.

Merlin held his hands out in a gesture of peace. "I'm not here to fight you, Rondroc. I paid for my deed at the end of your father's whip, remember?"

"Oh, I remember it well," Rondroc said with a scathing tone, "because *I* wanted to be the one to flog you. But my father refused me, and now's my chance to even it up."

Merlin looked to Arthur, who had a smirk on his face. "Here," the king said, "take my spear." And he tossed it to Merlin, who caught it.

Rondroc swung at Merlin, who backed up just in time.

"Hey," he said, "you can see!"

"So you noticed." Merlin held his own spear out in a defensive stance. Memories came back to him of his former fight with Rondroc. Merlin had been just eighteen winters old, passing by Tregeagle's house with Garth and his bagpipe.

Thwack!

Rondroc lashed out, and Merlin barely blocked the blow.

"Peace, Rondroc. We're not children anymore."

Rondroc swung again, this time overhead, and Merlin raised his spear to block it, but just as it hit and bounced off Rondroc swung it lightning fast to the side and cracked Merlin in the shoulder.

Merlin reeled back, his arm stinging.

"You're right!" Rondroc said. "I'm a man now and ol' Ronno's going to take you out, one way or the other." He flipped his spear back, and now the steel tip gleamed in the sunlight. His forearms rippled with strength, and there were many scars and burns crisscrossing them. "This time you'll stay down. Dirty villager. Not paying my tax."

Merlin's memory drifted back to his first encounter with Rondroc again. Garth had distracted Rondroc for a moment, allowing Merlin to crack Rondroc over the head with his staff. Merlin had been blind then, but now what was he to do? Fight his brother-in-law?

Rondroc lunged forward with the tip of his spear.

Merlin failed to block it fully, and the tip missed the right side of Merlin's chest by two handbreadths and ripped through his cloak.

Merlin grabbed the middle of Rondroc's spear with his right hand, and with the haft of his own spear in his left he hit Rondroc over the head.

Whack!

Rondroc didn't flinch.

Again Merlin hit him, this time across the forehead, cracking his spear.

But Rondroc only smiled. He was missing a few teeth, and the rest were rotting — but it sure *seemed* to be a smile.

Then Merlin noticed that the man wasn't fighting to free his spear and had let it go slack.

"Ha-ha!" Rondroc said, and then he hugged Merlin, patting him on the back. "I've heard you've taken good care of my sister since you married her. Welcome to Glevum!"

"But ..."

"Ah, I just had to test you for ol' times' sake. Mother's twice visited me in secret and told me about you all — even about Arthur — and I've kept my mouth shut all these years. Wasn't easy, to tell the truth, but what else are family for, huh?"

Merlin was stunned. Rondroc knew?

"Hear, hear!" Arthur said, clapping, and all the men joined in.

Rondroc bowed. "And welcome, High King, to your field of spoil."

"Spoil?" Culann asked, raising a dubious eyebrow at the charred ruins surrounding them.

"Well ... I'm actually *not* the jailor ... not in a strict sense, anyway. If you and those you trust most will follow me, I have something to show you."

Merlin exchanged glances with Arthur, and the young king nodded.

Arthur dismounted and asked Culann, Dwin, Peredur, and Percos to join him. Rondroc led them into the building on the left, which was a massive stone structure with only tiny arrow slits for windows on the upper floors.

"This is Vortigern's jail and dungeon here in Glevum. Not the kind of place invaders pay attention to, at least not at first."

As they passed deeper into the structure, Merlin caught the faint sound of someone singing far away. It was a sad sound, but Merlin couldn't tell where it was coming from. A little deeper in, and the song disappeared altogether.

Rondroc grabbed a torch from the wall, led them to a cell, and unbarred it. Inside, he went to a moldy wooden wall where prison chains hung. Pulling both of the chains in an alternating pattern caused some mechanism to click inside the wall, and a wooden door, cleverly hidden, opened on the left. Rondroc took them through the doorway, which led to a precipitous set of crudely cut stone steps.

Down and down they went until the air turned musty and Merlin's nose itched. Water dripped from the ceiling, making the stairs slippery. As the walls began to close in on them, a nameless fear grew in Merlin that they were descending the throat of some giant, eyeless frog, and soon it would swallow them down into its sluicing belly where they would die and never again return to the light of day.

But their echoing footsteps went on and on until finally the stairs ended and Rondroc led them through a passageway. Along the sides lay ancient dungeon cells whose bars were slimed with rust and whose wooden doors had long ago rotted to uselessness. The torch-light would sometimes slip into these cells, revealing skulls Merlin felt were staring back among scattered piles of refuse and bones.

"Where are we going?" Percos asked, his low voice filling the darkness.

Peredur, who had been bringing up the rear, sidled up to Merlin and whispered in his ear, "I don't like this. Rondroc's men ... do ya think they've followed us?"

Arthur put a hand on Rondroc's shoulder, and the man spun to face them. The flickering torchlight reflected red off his eyes, and the shifting shadows accentuated his rotting, jagged teeth.

He brought his hand up into the light, revealing a sharp dagger with ancient etchings on the blade.

CHAPTER 28

OATHS FORSAKEN

Rondroc jabbed the dagger at Arthur, who stepped back and slammed into Merlin. Merlin caught himself by grabbing the slimy, rusted bar of a dungeon cell, which broke free from the rotten wood. They both would have fallen if Dwin hadn't steadied them.

Rondroc pulled back, cackling. "Made you jump, huh?"

He turned to face a dungeon door — this one intact. "I told you I wasn't a jailor. Well ... I'm actually the treasurer, and those wolf-warriors didn't have enough brains to find what ol' Vorty squirreled away. As you are the new High King, I present to you my captives — one and all."

He popped the pommel off of the dagger, and a large gold ring dropped into his palm from within the hollow handle. But the ring was strange, as it had a protrusion that was bent and had a raised pattern on it.

"This is an old Roman key," he said. "The very key of Vitalinus, and of his grandfather before him. And as you, Arthur, are his only living heir, Ronno's going to give what it guards to you." He pushed the bent end into a hole, pressed it downward, slid it to the right, and the door clicked open. The old hinges groaned and squealed as Rondroc pulled the heavy door open.

Merlin squinted, but a deep shadow lay over the room.

Rondroc handed the torch to Arthur and beckoned him forward.

Arthur raised it and entered the room. Before him sparkled two small open chests of gold and silver coins mixed in with gems of every hue.

Merlin almost bit his tongue. He had never seen such treasure — the cream skimmed from the top of an impoverished island.

"Vortigern's been saving this for a long time — and stole half of it from Uther, I'm told. The plan was that once Vortipor became High King, Vortigern always said, he planned on sailing to Brythanvy and living on an estate he'd purchased for himself. This treasure was his new life, and he wanted to get away from these Saxenow, he did. Well, it looks like they got to him first, huh?"

Merlin put a tentative hand on Rondroc's shoulder. "Why are you doing this? Your father — "

"My father! Hah. He's a greedy, brutal madman. And I was greedy too ... back then. I joined Vortigern because I thought I was cruel and that I'd enjoy killing people. I sure wanted to kill you back then."

Rondroc sighed. "But here ... here I saw *real* cruelty, and if it weren't for my oath, I'da run away many a time. Well, now I am free, I guess, but I won't be going anywhere. Not with my charge to take care of for you, huh? Vortigern liked hiding his treasure in the dungeon so he could check on it when he questioned the condemned for information. You might wonder why Hengist and Horsa hated Vortigern so, but know this: over three hundred Saxenow were viciously slain here. So I've worked here all these years pretending to be a jailor, watching the real jailor's brutality, witnessing injustice, and all the while Vortigern never knew I guarded *your* secret too ... something more precious than all his rotted jewels."

He turned then and looked on Merlin and smiled. "Now I can see Natalenya again."

Merlin nodded and tried to smile back, but a lump as big as a rock gathered in his throat and stuck there. How could he tell Rondroc his fear? Tell him that Merlin had failed her and his family by coming south? If only ... Arthur handed the torch back and looked to the others with wide eyes. "Now we have enough to raise a new army, don't we?"

Culann nodded with a satisfied smile, while Dwin wore a look of disbelief.

"Take what you need right now," Rondroc said, "and I'll be waiting for when you need more. I'll keep the secret, you can be sure of that."

Arthur selected enough silver coins to pay the men with him, and then adequate gold to recruit more men from the chieftains of Kembry and Kernow. After counting them out, he poured the gold into Merlin's bag for safekeeping and kept the silver himself.

Then Merlin shook Rondroc's hands. "Thank you," he said, "you've given us a chance."

Rondroc locked the door again and led them back up the stairs. The torch was sputtering now, and they barely made it back up before the flames thinned and died. Rondroc secured the secret door and then barred the cell where it was hidden.

As they trudged back toward the outside, Merlin began to hear snatches of singing once again. He turned his head but couldn't tell which side passage it came from.

Catching up to Rondroc, he asked "What happened to all the prisoners?"

"Well, the true jailor ran away when the attack started, and I doubt I'll ever lay eyes on that coward again. So then I took charge of all the prisoners, and with everything destroyed and the citizens either dead or gone, I knew I'd have a hard time finding food to keep 'em alive. So ... I let 'em all go. They were shocked at my kindness, I'll tell you, and many made pledges to me in thanks."

"But I'm still hearing someone singing," Merlin said.

"Ah, him! He's no Saxenow. That's Mabon—a guard who went mad after the siege. He came back to the city. Roaming the streets at night crying and shouting, he was. Didn't know what else to do with the fellow."

"Mabon!" Dwin said.

"You know him?"

Arthur looked to Culann, who raised an eyebrow.

"Take me to him," Arthur said. "We need every man we can get."

Rondroc rolled his eyes. "But you don't want *him*. Someone not right in the head, huh?"

"Let's find out."

Rondroc turned them around, led them down a side passage, through two locked doors and to a cell. Mabon came to the bars, and his tongue was bloody, as if he'd bitten it.

Arthur approached and leaned in. "Mabon, do you remember me?"

Mabon studied his face. "Yes ... you ... you're not a wolf."

"I'm Arthur, and I met you outside the city."

"O-outside there are wolves."

Arthur nodded. "But we can kill them, yes?"

"Have you killed any?"

Merlin raised a hand. "I've killed one. Remember me?"

"You can kill them?"

"Yes we can," Merlin said. "Do *you* want to kill them?"

"Give me my sword back ... th-they took my sword!"

"I'll let you out and give you your sword," Arthur said, "but you'll have to promise to follow me and help fight."

Mabon backed away from the bars. "I'm afraid. Who ... who are you?"

"I'm Arthur, the lost son of Uther, and I've come back."

"Uther? You're Uther's son?"

Arthur smiled. "Yes."

"I swore allegiance to your father. A long t-time ago."

"Will you swear it to me?"

"Y-yes."

Arthur lifted the bar from the door and set it aside.

Mabon stood there, cracking his knuckles. His lips were moving as if he were speaking, but no sound came out.

Beckoning him to come, Arthur reached out and took his hand. Mabon followed.

"We need your help, Mabon. We need to save Britain."

"I'll h-help."

Rondroc gave back the man's sword, which was hung from a peg in the passageway, and led them outside.

"The muster?" Arthur asked. "Has anyone come?"

"Adding mighty Mabon to your army isn't enough, huh? Well ... to my knowledge no one's come. And with the city destroyed, it doesn't surprise me."

Culann muttered something and turned away to check on his horse.

Merlin closed his eyes. Without additional men, the chance Arthur would agree to go to Kernow was very unlikely.

After shaking Rondroc's hands once more, Arthur remounted his horse, and Merlin was about to mount as well when he realized he had something to do first. He had made a decision, and regardless of what Arthur did, there was no turning back.

Taking his harp, he placed it in Rondroc's hands.

"Can you keep this safe? And if I don't return ... see to it that it gets to my son, Taliesin." Unable to speak his deepest fears, Merlin left no further instructions, and Rondroc accepted the harp with a gracious nod.

Merlin finally mounted, and soon they were all riding through the city, Mabon on Dwin's extra horse. It didn't take long to verify that Rondroc was right — either no one had come or no one had stayed for the muster. The destruction they had witnessed before seemed even worse this time, for the city lay in decrepit shadow, and the stench of the corpses covered it like a repulsive fog.

Along the way a warrior directed them to a bake house that supplied Vortigern's campaigns, where they found a large cache of unspoiled dry bread. Out back were mud-daubed storehouses for grain, and they filled many bags with barleycorn, wheat, and rye. Two cisterns were also nearby, and though their level was low, there was enough for everyone to refresh himself and his horse, and to refill his waterskin.

Finally Arthur led them back out the east gate of the city where the wind brought fresh air and relief from the stench. The sun was now fully set and the men made a camp with a great bonfire in the center. After everyone had eaten, Arthur stood and addressed them.

"Men of brave deeds ... heroes of Britain!" Arthur called, "You now know our plight fully, for none have come and stayed in answer to the muster. We simply need more men before we can ever hope to defeat the Saxenow and drive them from our shores."

Many of the men nodded in assent. "And not only that," Arthur said, "but now you have seen the destruction of Glevum and what Gorlas has wrought. Our countrymen have become our foes, and we are stabbed in the back even as we shed our blood for their freedom."

Arthur began to walk amongst the men passing out the silver coins, one to each man. He made sure to look into their eyes, pat them on the back, or shake their hands.

"And so the question remains ... where are we going next? We stand, my friends, at a juncture. To the southeast lie the Saxenow, a foe who is now too powerful for us. To the northwest lay Kembry and her clans, who live in peace and ignorance of the events happening here. To the southwest is Difnonia and Kernow, lands shrouded in darkness, mystery, and suffering."

When each man had a coin, Arthur returned to the center. "And so I lay before you two choices — Kembry or Kernow? Do we take the easy path, rest, and gather more to our cause? Or do we, as men of deeds, go to meet a dangerous foe that grows stronger by the day? Either choice may result in death ... death for us, death for the innocent ... or both."

Percos stood and Arthur nodded to him.

"To me and the rough-blade lads, our choice is obvious. How many o' you were sickened by the murdered o' Glevum? How many o' you want to make sure that doesn't happen to your own family? We're all for Kernow!

"That's 'cause you're from there!" someone shouted from the crowd, and others jeered at him.

"And you're all a bunch o' lazy rats!" Percos said, slamming his fist into his palm. "Take your precious posy-time *after* we stop the killin'!"

Neb stood up on the opposite side of the circle, tucked his half-dyed beard back into his waistcoat, and spoke. "Percos, I can't call you a coward, no, but I *can* call you a dupe. If an army of wolf-heads can destroy Glevum — by driving out or killing the guards and citizens — what do you think they'll do to this little tinker of an army? It can't be done, and that's where I stand!"

"Well, you're standin' in muck then." Percos said, stepping toward Neb and shaking his fists. "Do ya got the guts to join us, or are you Kembry lads too skeared o' the little pups to save the kin o' yer Kernow cousins? My wife an' bairns are down there!"

"Ah, you're nothing but a clam-head!"

"Rabbit-tailed coward!"

Neb beat his chest. "You take that back, Percos!"

"Never!"

The two men ran at each other with raised fists, and Arthur had to step away from the bonfire and get in between.

"We solve nothing by fighting!" Arthur said. "Each man back!"

Neb took a swing at Percos, but Arthur shoved him and the blow didn't land.

Percos tried to get past Arthur, but Culann grabbed him from behind and jerked him backward.

"Hear me!" Arthur called. "We must not quarrel, but must speak in peace. And know this: every man will be bound to my decision. If it is to Kembry, then each man will go to raise warriors as quickly as possible. If it is to Kernow, then I will need each and every one of you in order to defeat this enemy."

Here he paused, looking Percos and then Neb in the eyes.

"And there will be no fighting among ourselves. Understood?"

The two men nodded curtly and sat down.

"Does anyone else who has not already spoken have an opinion?" Arthur asked.

Merlin burned to speak, but felt he had already spoken his heart.

No one else stood to speak, and an awkward silence covered the camp, the men looking to each other, but no one responding.

"Well, then," Arthur said. "If no more opinions are to be had, then my decision is made." He turned to walk away, but called over his shoulder, "Be prepared to ride out in the morning at the first light of dawn."

Arthur passed through the crowd, and was almost out of sight when Merlin realized that Arthur hadn't said what the decision was. He rushed after and stopped him.

"But where *are* we going?" Merlin asked.

Arthur turned, and there was a light in his eyes that stunned Merlin—a reckless determination, a longing—something so inscrutable and strange that it sent a paralyzing sting down Merlin's spine.

Arthur looked off to the night sky and stared at the moon, half shrouded by a black cloud that caressed and smothered its sallow light. "I'm going to meet the woman in the raven cloak."

"In Kernow? You're taking us to Kernow?"

"Yes."

A nearby warrior heard this and spread the news.

Merlin took hold of Arthur by the shoulders. "Take care, Arthur. You've chosen the right path but for the wrong reason. I fear Mórgana's bewitched you."

Arthur squinted. "We're going to fight Gorlas. Be content—it's what you wanted. But I'm going to meet *the woman from my dreams* as well." He emphasized the words as if to imply that she was not Mórgana. "She's in Kernow too—I know it."

Culann ran up, his cheek twitching and his teeth bared. "What's this I hear? You're taking us to *Kernow*?"

"Yes."

"Are you mad? You and your father … you're both so gizzard sure of yourselves that you'll lead us all to our deaths. *We need more men!*"

Culann turned on his heel and stalked off, and Merlin watched him go. Before he knew it, the king had already walked off in the other direction.

Merlin would have to keep a close eye on Arthur and find some way to convince him that Mórgana had deceived him. But there was something even more pressing: the possibility of treachery against Arthur. So he called Peredur, Dwin, and Culann to talk privately. Culann agreed to come, but only grudgingly.

"In light of Rewan's murder, I believe we need to set a guard over Arthur through the watches of the night."

They agreed, and Dwin offered to take the first watch, followed by dour-mooded Culann. The following night it would be Merlin and Peredur to trade off.

But when Arthur got wind of their plan, he put a stop to it.

"I need each of you well rested. No special watch, hear me? I won't allow it."

And so that night Merlin tried to stay awake and keep watch, but failed. The white carcass of the moon had begun to sink when Merlin drifted off to sleep. He dreamt of wolves sniffing his clothing and dripping their saliva onto his throat. One time he startled awake to see a floating, ghostly claw scratching at his eyes, and he nearly yelled out as he frantically waved it into nothingness. Then he tucked the bag of gold coins more tightly inside his cloak and fell back asleep.

Sometime near morning, before the sun had risen, Merlin jerked awake to the sound of a horn blowing. He rubbed his face, wiping the sleep from his eyes, and began to gather his things. When he reached for Arthur's bag of gold, he found the leather thongs cut where it had been tied to his belt. The bag had been stolen.

Merlin's hands began to tremble.

He quickly found Arthur, who was engaged in tightening Casva's saddle.

"The money's gone."

"What?"

"The gold ... the bag was stolen while I slept."

"That makes two missing at the same time."

Merlin's brow furrowed. "What else is — ?"

Arthur stared at the ground. The skin around his eyes was tight and he took a slow, taut breath. "Culann. He rode away in the middle of the night. He's broken his oath, Merlin ... He's broken his oath."

Mórgana, sitting on her throne, placed the orb back into her bag and snapped her fingers.

Loth entered, bringing a wooden trencher with a bowl of boiled-boar and cabbage soup, and next to it a dish of honeyed parsnips mixed with mint and chestnuts.

"The moment has come," she said. "Prepare to leave Lyhonesse."

"Is it sae, already? Arthur and Merlin are comin' to Kernow?" he said, placing the trencher in front of her.

She twirled her finger in her hair and leaned back. "Yes, although I'm not sure why. Merlin did not influence them as much as I had expected. Arthur made the decision himself."

"That is surprisin'."

"Quite."

"What will we do?"

"Exactly what we planned. We leave tonight."

CHAPTER 29

A SLEEP OF DEATH

For Merlin, their journey southwest was fraught with a heavy heart and a sense of deep foreboding. He had gotten his wish, hadn't he? And now he regretted each plodding, jolting, hateful step of his horse. For every league meant he was that much farther from Natalenya and his children. From saving them ... But who was he kidding? He knew the truth, and it bled his heart till it could bleed no more. Until all feeling left and the long road stretched out before him like a noose of his own making.

He was dead, wasn't he? The nightmare would consume him. Rend him of limb, lungs, and laughter. Yet the laughter remained even when he could hardly breathe, for he was Merlin the laughing-stock. Merlin the lost. Merlin the lonely.

And in that kind of death an anger arose. A righteous anger. A seething, teeth-cracking, gut-aching anger at Mórgana — at the Druid Stone and the power behind it.

All of Britain would bow, the Voice had said — and that monster had meant it, for the backbone of the island was nearly broken. Arthur had led Vortigern's tattered little army away from the heartland, leaving it no defenders. Even great Lundnisow had fallen. Hengist and his dirty, treacherous brood could sack and raid to their spleen's content, and no one would stop them. It made Merlin sick.

Yet the Voice was behind Hengist's invasion. Merlin knew this. He had ignored it year after year after comfort-filled, peace-loving year. But he'd finally stepped out — and for that he had Arthur and Peredur to thank. He patted the hilt of his blade and squinted at the hills on the horizon.

The time is now, Mórgana. I'm coming. With my sword sharpened and with steel in my soul. Beware, Mórgana! You who have slain all that I hold dear . . . you have not yet slain me!

And if God wills it, I will prevail. And you — Mórgana, the Voice's servant — will die.

But could he kill his own sister? She who had shared his porridge bowl? His childhood home? The very blood in his veins? Or was there a way to rescue her, to pull her away from the Voice's talons? He didn't know. And this uncertainty rusted through the armor of his bravado, letting the black cockroaches of fear crawl in so that he fairly shook and scratched to get rid of them.

As the journey wore on he stopped eating his share of the rations. He stopped shaving. He stopped washing his face and hands. And mostly, he just stopped talking. At night he would rub ashes on his skin to kill the fear. To confess his sins and lack of faith.

Believe the gospel, he kept telling himself. *Just believe the good news that has already been given, and trust in God's power . . . Please, Father, don't let go of me!*

And he would pray. Hours and hours he spent praying.

Peredur looked on him with pity mixed with sadness.

"Eat, Merlin," he would say. "You have to eat. Look how thin you're getting!"

But Merlin needed a different kind of strength, so he only shrugged and tightened his belt.

Peredur did win out on one thing, however: he found some extra scale-and-leather armor and finally pestered Merlin until he took it. But the thing stank of sweat and sour mead, and one buckle had been ripped off. Merlin wore it only under protest.

While fasting, Merlin found his strength from drinking water … that was life to him. Life to his bones and burning soul. And whenever his waterskin ran dry between the few acidic springs that still gurgled out their dark liquid and the shrunken ponds and marshes, Merlin would begin to slowly die inside. For the once green land of Difnonia and Kernow had become a wasteland due to the drought.

No rain had fallen, and all the trees were dead and the grass but a lie.

The villages they passed were empty, their crennigs like skulls and their windows empty eye sockets. Mocking him. Laughing out their noses as the dust-filled wind blew through the doors and swirled their death sentence upon the streets. Animal carcasses lay where they had fallen, nothing more than feeding grounds for clouds of massive horseflies. Once, the evil creatures attacked the traveling party and jabbed their blade-like teeth into their flesh until the men were all bleeding and yelling.

Some of the men begged that they turn back then, but Arthur refused to let them go. Who could blame him?

"Every man must stay," Arthur told them, and this was true, for none knew what lay ahead, or how many men would be needed.

It took the better part of a week to travel the fifty or more leagues between Glevum and Kernow. Merlin had wanted them to take the coastal road, which led directly to Dintaga, but Percos had advised the interior route that led them through the moors.

"Less likely to be noticed, that-ways," the man had said.

Arthur had agreed with him. "We need to surprise Gorlas at all costs."

But Merlin wondered if that were possible with Mórgana's demonic powers. His past experiences showed her to be able to follow him wherever he went … even as far as the lands of darkness across the sea. Could *any* precaution help them?

"We should turn northeast toward Dintaga once we get to Dinas Hen Felder," Percos had said, and Merlin agreed. This was a good spot, as it marked the border between Difnonia and Kernow and was near to Dintaga. The plan was to then slip over the coastal road of Kernow unseen and approach through the woods so that they might surprise Gorlas at his sea-bound fortress and prevent his escape.

"And when we've whipped Gorlas," Percos said, a broad smile on his face, "we can visit old Pelles one-ear, the chieftain of Dinas Camlin. Now *there's* a strong fortress if you need a place to hole up in! And the feasts … oh, the feasts …" So after passing through the dead villages of Brewodwyn, Trendrine, and Penmoor, they finally approached Dinas Hen Felder on the outskirts of Bosvenna Moor. The sun would soon set, and the dusty road led down into a shadowed, deeply wooded vale where the gaunt branches rattled in the wind.

Percos had told them that the Dowrtam River lay in the bottom of the valley, and from there it flowed southward to the sea. But their chosen path went on and on, down and down, and Merlin saw no sign of the river.

Wolves howled from a far hill, and Merlin shuddered.

He asked Arthur if they had taken a wrong turn, but the king just shook his head. Beads of sweat had formed on the man's youthful brow, though the air had cooled to almost a chill. Arthur loosened the blade in his scabbard, alarming Merlin and sharpening his senses.

From then on he began to catch the sound of someone or something walking through the wood, but he never saw what it was. When the sound grew louder, Merlin called for a halt to listen, but the impatient warriors behind him could not keep silent, and in frustration he agreed to move on again.

Then, out of the corner of his eye … he saw her.

A woman dressed in black walking between the trees. She held in her hand a dagger, pale as bone, and her eyes burned in the gloaming with a purple flame.

Merlin blinked and she was gone.

A crow circled overhead.

Call to me! Call for me! the bird seemed to say. *Claw! Caw!*

The creature flew above the trees and down into the valley.

Merlin's horse started to have tremors — but then Merlin's hands began to shake too, and he knew that the trembling he felt was not from his horse. It was his own. He swallowed and tried to concentrate. The trees swam before him and tilted. It wasn't until Arthur placed a hand on Merlin's shoulder and shoved him up that he realized he'd been leaning in his saddle, dizzy and about to fall.

He shook his head. He had to focus. *Everything is fine ... everything is fine ...* he told himself, but knew it wasn't. Within forty paces the path turned and dropped more steeply. At the bottom of the trail, Merlin and Arthur emerged onto a level plain traversed by the thin, shallow remains of the Dowrtam River. Like a mockery, a broad bridge crossed the tiny trickle. And there, on the other side, stood an army of foot soldiers. The sun was sinking behind them and the horns of the moon lay above them.

Arthur rode forward to a point just beyond the woods and blasted his horn. The men behind came rushing down the path and formed a long line, two horses deep, to face the army before them.

"Ride forward with me, Merlin, to see what challenge this may be," Arthur said. His voice was void of all emotion save a grim determination.

Merlin nodded, and the two approached the river. From the other side, a single man walked forward and stepped onto the bridge. He wore a leather doublet covered with gold rings, and the helm hiding his face was of burnished steel with a plume of sea-blue feathers on top. He wore woven plaid of indigo, white, and teal, and his spiked gauntlets were of blackened leather. His breeches were the color of blood, and the sword at his side was finely crafted, both sharp and beautiful.

If Merlin's quick estimate was accurate, behind him stood an army of more than five hundred men. All of them were on foot, but well protected by armor. Their ready weapons glinted in the fading light.

Merlin shifted in his saddle. "Who obstructs our path? Name yourself and your right to bar the way of the High King of Britain."

"High King?" the challenger said. "You mean the rubbish-spawn of that pig, Uther." The man laughed as he pulled his helm off... and it was Gorlas, the king of Kernow. He was older and balder than Merlin remembered him, but his sunken eyes and unkempt black beard told all. At his neck he wore the same silver torc, yet the tips of it were now red as blood. But for all that, there was something strange about the man that Merlin couldn't distinguish...

Gorlas gave a menacing smile and looked at Arthur. "I am Gorlas, King of Kernow. And you are nothing but the son of a coward — for my love was faithful to me, and Uther tricked her!"

Arthur leaned over and whispered to Merlin, "So this is crazy Gorlas? I thought you said they were wolf-heads... *These men* can die with the simple thrust of a blade."

"Mórgana is here ... beware."

"Ah ... and *Merlin*," Gorlas called, "I see you've come as well — Arthur's ridiculous counselor and chief bard of hot air. Tell your brat that he can go home and suckle his thumb. This is the land of true kings, and he's not even worthy to step on our precious soil."

Merlin felt his cheeks redden, and if he could have spit bile at Gorlas, he would have.

"Turn aside your wrath," Arthur said. "We've come to ask for your aid against the Saxenow."

"The bastard of Igerna speaks! Let's see how well his voice works with this lodged in his gullet." Gorlas drew his sword and called his men forward.

The Kernow warriors sprang to action and came rushing toward the river, which in its current state presented no more of an obstacle beyond splashing and mud.

311

Arthur and Merlin drew their blades at once.

"To battle!" Arthur shouted, rearing up his horse.

The warriors behind him shouted and rode forward, trotting at first, but then riding headlong toward Gorlas and his men. The ground shook and Merlin found himself in the middle. He kicked his horse forward, but it backed up instead, snorting at the chaos before and behind.

Two of the Kernow ran toward Merlin, and he briefly clashed blades with the first until his horse reared and kicked him down. Merlin grabbed the saddle with one hand and held on to the reins with the other to avoid falling. By the time the horse came down, the other man was upon him, and Merlin slashed out, cutting into his scalp before the warrior could stop his blade.

The man swore and shoved Merlin's blade back at a strange angle, hurting Merlin's arm. Then he readied his blade to strike.

Peredur rode forward and speared the man in the chest.

He fell screaming to the ground.

Peredur jumped off his horse and stripped the man of his shield, which he threw to Merlin.

"You'll get yerself killed without that."

"I might get killed with it!"

Arthur fought nearby, with Dwin, Percos, and Neb supporting him. Gorlas and a score of warriors fought against them, as blood and bodies began to cover the ground.

All around Merlin the battle raged, and the charge of the horses dealt a deadly blow to Gorlas's men. The open ground worked in their favor as the horsemen rode through and out the other side of the lines, only to turn and rush again at the foot soldiers with blade swinging and spear stabbing.

Another man attacked Merlin, this time with a spear.

Merlin deflected the blow, dodged to the side, and sliced the man's arm nearly through at the bicep. More warriors ran forward to take his place, and Merlin and Peredur were beset on all sides.

But as the disk of the sun set behind the hill bearing the fortress of Dinas Hen Felder, a murky fog arose in the valley, seemingly from nowhere. Merlin squinted, but in the gray half-light he could barely see who he was swinging at.

A shrill horn blew in the distance, and suddenly the man he was fighting had run off.

"To me! To me!" Arthur called from the right, and he blew on his horn.

All around him, men took advantage of the respite to bind wounds and retrieve lost weapons. Merlin had a bad gash on his left arm, which Peredur bound with a torn cloth. After this was done, they joined the others around Arthur.

"Our enemy has run off to their fortress," the king said, "and by the look of it, two-score of our brothers have fallen. Let's find them in the fog, help the wounded, and bury our dead."

"But Gorlas is fleeing like a rabbit ..." Percos said. "Let's run him down!"

"Gorlas isn't going far," Arthur said, "and if he does, then he can go back to hell where he belongs, for all I care." Neb joined Percos by raising an angry fist. "But Vortigern wouldn't have let his enemy get away. This is —"

Arthur heeled Casva forward so he was eye-to-eye with the two men. "I don't care what Vortigern would have done. If we're not fleeing for our own lives, we will tend to our men first!" Arthur dismounted and hurried into the fog. Soon Merlin heard him calling for help in pulling a horse off of a fallen warrior.

Grumbling, the others joined him in the task, and Merlin found himself helping a warrior who'd been speared in the gut. The man was moaning on the ground with his head resting on a smooth stone from the river. Merlin lifted the man's shirt, and swallowed the words he was going to say.

The man's cheeks were pinched in what seemed a permanent grimace of pain. "It's bad, I knows. When them innards don't stay *innard* ... Me brother died the same way last fall."

"Tell me, do you know the love of Christ?" Merlin asked.

"Don't know. Thought about …" And a spasm wrenched his body, so he pulled his left knee up with his hands and shook until it passed. The tears had streamed down his cheeks, and he looked to Merlin with desperation.

Merlin grabbed the man's hand and held it tightly. "Do you want to be with God?"

"Ahh-h!" the man yelled, and now the blood poured even faster from his wound.

"Call on the Christ! Call on Jesu!"

The man gasped, choked — and in a strangled exhale, he died.

Merlin held his hand for a while, the fog thickening around him. Finally, he closed the man's eyes and prayed over him.

May the power of the mighty Threeness,
May the presence of the loving Oneness,
May the grace of the God of Jacob
Be yours as you stand in judgment!
May the holiness sent by the Father,
May the sweetness given by the Spirit,
May the pardoning blood given by Jesu Christus
Be yours in abundance forever!

Forgive him, Father! Please receive, by grace, such a one as him into Your kingdom.

Merlin dragged the man's body to the center of the field where all the dead were soon buried under a cairn of stones from the riverbed. Overall, twenty of their men had died, with thirteen injured. As Merlin moved away from the cairn, intending to find Peredur, the soft sound of neighing horses and the slight jingle of bells called his attention to the woods behind them.

Merlin turned to face the trail they had come down, apprehension jabbing him like a splinter. Down the hillside rode a large horse pulling a wagon. Upon the horse sat Gogi, as big as ever, and just as unwelcome to Merlin, who felt his throat go dry. Behind him rode his two daughters and son, the last pulling along a group of mangy, tethered horses.

"Well met!" Arthur said, going to greet them. Dwin joined, and together they shook the giant's hands and gave courtly bows to the daughters. Melwas said nothing, but Merlin noticed the man eyeing up their horses like a fox would a clucking chicken.

Gwenivere rode over to Arthur and gave him a big smile. Her blonde hair had been freshly braided, but her eyes looked tired, and there was a smear of dirt across her cheek.

Arthur beamed at her.

"Where's Culann?" she asked, looking around.

Arthur's smile faltered. "He's gone."

"He went back home," Dwin said.

"Oh."

"But I'm here."

She smiled at Dwin, but Merlin could tell it was forced.

Gwenivach rode up and held her hand out to Arthur, who took it and gave a slight bow of his head. Her eyes glistened in the mist, and she had doffed her green hat to reveal locks of exquisitely long, flowing red-blonde hair.

But Merlin had seen enough and stepped forward. "Well met indeed, Gogirfan," he said with as much sarcasm as he could muster. "However, as you can see from the dead and dying, we've just had a battle. For your own safety, I suggest you leave as *quickly* as possible."

"Ooh, haha!" Gogi said, surveying through the thick fog the wounded men and the corpses that still remained from Gorlas's army. "Is it all over?"

"We've had only one skirmish," Arthur said, "and our foe has retreated to a fortress on the farther hill."

"A fortress, ya say? So you'll be besiegin' it then?"

Arthur looked to Merlin, who didn't know what to say, and so shrugged. This was one part of the plan Merlin hadn't thought through, for they hadn't come prepared for such a task, although it could be attempted, he supposed.

"Ah, well ... ya could scale the walls with some ropes, ya know?"

Dwin shook his head. "I doubt we have enough."

"Ya don't? Well, ya can make some of horse sinew! And I just happens to have a good stash of it, ya know. We could braid lots and lots —"

"You do?" Merlin asked. "Funny you didn't offer that *before*, when my horse was stuck in the river bed."

"Well, ya know, this is now and that was then. And to help make amends we can sell ya some pitch fer making torches. Very useful at night when you're besiegin' a fortress. And not only that, but we'll make ourselves useful by watching your horses while ya attack yer enemy. Mind now, this is rare generous on our part, it bein' so late and all —"

Each breath Merlin took was deeper, stronger, and angrier than the last. Finally it was either kick Gogirfan's shin or speak his mind. "Get out of here!" he said. "If I ever see your miserable, horse-thieving hide again, I'll have the men strip you bare and throw you off a cliff! Go! You, your daughters, and your thieving son!"

The giant looked surprised, his jaw hanging at a funny angle. Then he brought his large lips together in a pout and touched his finger to his chin.

"Well, then ... *it's obvious we're not needed*. Wengis! Elmwa! Seth stribogs rega gnob denfrily sot gussa. Stells sug feally dans gebo dri fop methem!"

Gogi snapped the reins of his horse and trotted right past Arthur. He held his heavy chin high and looked straight ahead.

Melwas followed directly, with the girls bringing up the rear. But the two looked back upon Arthur and Dwin and fluttered their fingers in good-bye.

Arthur looked at Merlin incredulously. Finally, he called after the girls, "Where are you going?"

"We're off to the island of the tinsmiths, as ya already know," Gogi said, bunching up his lips. "And you *won't* see our horse-lovin' hides again — that I can assure ya. And may ya be stricken down this night for yer inhospitality to thoughtful strangers."

CHAPTER 30

A SLEEP OF RAVENS

For the next several hours, Merlin focused on binding wounds alongside the team Peredur had organized. Other men had brought horses for the injured, and each warrior was helped up. Most of these men would die, Merlin knew, but they wouldn't be left behind.

"How many o' Gorlas's men died?" Peredur asked.

"Over a hundred," Percos said, spitting. "If they hadn't run, maybe we'd ha' kill't them all."

"And how many prisoners?"

"Fifteen," Arthur answered, "and they'll survive here until Gorlas can fetch them."

Neb wrinkled up his nose. "That fright-footed beast? You think he'll care enough to come back? Hah!"

Merlin was glad to find no sign of Gogi save the wagon tracks as they followed the trail up the opposite hillside toward Dinas Hen Felder. They curved around to the left and found themselves at the foot of the fortress on a high, conical hill. Torches burned inside,

317

and a guard patrolled the thick, staved walls. The only way to reach the gate to the fortress was through a stair that climbed the southern side of the hill between two walls. And the stair was so narrow that only two abreast could approach, making any attackers easy targets.

Merlin took one look and realized Gorlas's wisdom. Their horses, which had given them a great advantage on the field, were useless in besieging Dinas Hen Felder. Arthur would need an army of a thousand warriors or more to raze such a strongly defended fortress.

"We need to wait till morning," Merlin said.

Arthur agreed, looking almost as weary as Merlin felt. A rush of concern swept over him. So much had happened; Arthur had risen so fast to the kingship, to responsibility — much faster than Merlin could have ever anticipated.

He put a hand on the young man's shoulder. "You need rest. We all do."

Again, Arthur nodded. "Do you think we can draw them out to fight in the open again?"

Merlin looked back at the fortress. "We can try. His hatred of your father could cause him to take risks."

Arthur passed word to the men that they would camp just to the south on the nearest hill, but would travel west at first and then double back so as to conceal their exact nighttime location.

They slipped away and eventually found their way to the top of the hill Arthur had chosen. There they made camp. Guards were assigned different watches of the night, and Peredur personally saw that they received strict instructions.

Thankfully, an old well with a deep shaft was found next to the ruins of a farmstead, allowing them to water their horses and replenish their waterskins. A hasty meal was prepared of dried fish and bread, but they lit no fires in order to keep their location a secret.

That night the stony ground made Merlin's bones ache, and he slept fitfully. Broken images of a sneering Gorlas flashed through his dreams, each time with skin more blotchy, and teeth longer. Then the man laughed in Merlin's face — a long, barking sort of laugh. He drew his sword, challenging Merlin to a duel. Their blades clashed, and Merlin fought him away until Gorlas broke apart into a thousand bats and flew away.

Then Merlin wandered alone in the dark, all the stars smothered by thick clouds so that only the crescent moon slipped through the black void like a jaundiced, winking eye. A wind rose and tore its fingernails at the branches of the dead trees — and yet Merlin was not alone, for a raven, red-legged with a beak red like blood, had followed him. It cawed at him from the ground, and then strangely grew until its wings were eight feet in length. Though he ran and ran, he could not escape the sight of its hungry eyes or the sound of its razor-sharp bill snapping at his back. A mountain appeared before him and he ran upward, panting, lungs burning. He came upon the camp in the darkness, but no warning sounded, as all the men were asleep, including the guards. Though Merlin tried to wake them, he could not. One by one the raven began to slay anyone in its path, with Merlin just steps beyond its reach. He ran to where he thought Arthur had been sleeping, but the king couldn't be found.

Merlin came across his own bed, tripped, and scrambled back to his feet.

Then the raven laughed, and Merlin turned to face it, his blade ready.

It was Mórgana. With blood on her hands.

Merlin tried to move, but his whole body froze. His legs wouldn't lift. His hands lost their strength so that his sword fell to the earth. He couldn't even scream.

Mórgana ignored him, gathered up the weapons of the sleeping warriors one by one, and dutifully dropped each down the well. Spears. Axes. Swords. Bows. Quivers. All went down the throat of the mountain until every man was unarmed.

And all the while, Merlin fought to move, to stop her, to call out, but could not.

Finally, Mórgana strolled over to him.

"Well, brother, it seems you are powerless against me. Just as I like it. And for your sword? I will take it as my very own ... in memory of our father, whose death *you* caused."

These last words burned like poison in Merlin's ears, and he fought to speak — to refute her lies — but stood mutely.

Mórgana picked up Merlin's sword and twirled the edge near his throat. "Will you give in, then, even now? Will you do my bidding? Before I force you ... or force Arthur? It will not be pleasant, I assure you."

She snapped her fingers, and Merlin was able to cough, and his words came out tasting of ice and blood. "I will not ... do your bidding ... I will fight you ... and with God's grace ... I will prevail."

She slapped him sharply across the cheek so that he jerked away and closed his eyes. When he dared open them again she was still gloating over him.

"Just as I expected," she said. "Well ... it will at least be fun to watch now, won't it?"

Then, with a gleam of triumph in her eyes, she turned back into a red-legged raven and soared into the night sky, cawing.

Merlin stared after her, and only then did it dawn on him that he wasn't dreaming. The blood on his tongue was too authentic. The sting on his cheek was genuine.

This is real. She was here!

A wolf howled in the distance ... and then a multitude of other wolves joined in. All around the mountain it came, sending a violent tremble down Merlin's legs. For a moment his sight dimmed, and he lurched to the side, dizzy.

Arthur was next to him in an instant. "What's happened?" he asked, buckling his armor.

The wolves howled again, and then Merlin saw an army of men streaming up toward their camp, but there was something strange about them ...

"Wolf-heads!"

Arthur blew his horn to wake the men, and within moments they were on their feet, grabbing for their weapons.

Arthur reached for his, but it was missing.

The men began to yell, asking where their weapons were.

"Mórgana ... she's taken them — " Merlin rasped.

Arthur wasted no time. "To the horses! Bring the wounded!"

They ran to the side of the hill where the horses had been picketed, but it was too late, for all their tethers had been cut. The animals had caught the scent of the wolf-heads and were in a frenzy of rearing and thrashing. Some of the men tried to calm them, but it became a dangerous stampede. Two warriors took blows to the ribs as the horses panicked to escape. And when the wolf-heads came within a stone's throw, the central mass galloped down the hill and away.

Arthur swore. "Get knives, branches ... anything!" he yelled.

But his words were unnecessary, for every man had already found makeshift arms, ready to fight.

Merlin and most of the others had short dirks, but none of them had their longer, more deadly weapons. They gathered, shoulder to shoulder and back to back on the mountainside.

The wolf-heads came upon them with startling speed. Their muzzles were varied colors of gray, brown, or black, with streaks of white, and their eyes blazed yellow as moonlight and full of wrath. The rest of their bodies were furless and human. None of them had weapons, and they needed none ... for the sight of their teeth made Merlin's arms stiffen and his ribs constrict.

A gray wolf-head ran at Merlin, and it leapt through the air and vaulted over him with its teeth directed at his neck.

Merlin ducked and jabbed with his knife, but its fangs slashed his cloak and cut the skin over his collarbone. Merlin winced and whirled around, barely in time to avoid the slavering jaws again. As the wolf-head lunged at his throat, Merlin grabbed onto its tunic and shoved it back.

The wolf-head snarled, straining forward. Its teeth and curling black lips were so close that the foul smell of its breath clouded the air.

Merlin jabbed his blade toward its throat, but the wolf-head slammed its forearm down onto Merlin's head.

The pain instantly reverberated down to his hand, and Merlin's dirk missed. Time slowed, and with perfect clarity he heard screaming, grunts, and the slashing of blades. He fell backward — his head lolling to the side — yet it felt like floating, and he had no sensation of hitting the ground besides seeing the dry plume of dust lifting up and obscuring his vision for a moment. When the dust cleared, he saw the warrior next to him, dead, his throat ripped out and his lifeless eyes staring.

No! It can't end this way! The wolf-head lunged at him. Merlin yelled and flailed his dirk out, finally slamming the hilt against the creature's temple.

The creature shook off the blow, and within moments its form pressed against him, pinning him to the ground. The wolf-head opened wide, and the ridged roof of its maw and curved fangs snapped forward.

Merlin thrust his dirk upward, cutting deeply into the beast's throat.

The wolf-head screamed, a gurgling, roaring wail that was matched by the chaos around them.

Merlin shoved the dirk deeper — and the beast fell still.

Pushing the dead weight off, Merlin stood to take in the creature, and gasped. The creature had turned back to a man who wore the plaid of Gorlas's warriors. Yet he was young, not much older than Arthur ... and Merlin had killed him.

Mórgana, you've bewitched them ... May God judge you!

There were so many wolf-heads and warriors screaming that Merlin wanted to cover his ears. Dead littered the field, and Arthur's previously injured men had become the first victims.

Mabon came running toward him through the thick of battle, and Merlin grabbed his collar and pulled him close. "Fight with me!"

The man's lips quivered, and there were blood and scratches on his neck. *"He's coming ... he's coming!"* Mabon yelled, and his gaze was locked on the ground.

"Who?"

Mabon shook his head and wouldn't answer.

From the east came a piercing howl that made fear gurgle up and fill Merlin's throat.

Mabon cowered down.

As one, the wolf-heads ceased their killing and ran toward the howling.

Merlin was left speechless as he viewed the carnage left behind ... over half Arthur's men lay dead, with less than ten men in Gorlas's plaid slain. The exposed stones of the mountain had become slick with blood, and Merlin nearly gagged.

But there was no time. The dark shadow of the howling beast now approached with his wolf-head army. Unlike the others, he was covered from head to foot with reddish-brown fur, and even when hunched over he still stood a head taller than Merlin. At his neck lay a silver torc with blood-red tips, besides that he wore no clothing.

This was no wolf-head. This was a *werewolf.*

Merlin's heart thumped and his skin began to writhe. He ran to find Arthur.

Dear God, let him be alive!

And there Arthur was, standing with his back to a pine and his foot on the body of a former wolf-head. He watched the oncoming beast with open-mouthed horror. Peredur and Dwin, both white-faced, stood next to him as guardians.

"Run!" Merlin yelled. "It's a werewolf! We can't fight it without weapons!" He dashed westward down the mountain, toward the slice of moon spying at them through the clouds.

I have to get away ... get away! I can't face it!

Arthur yelled for the men to follow, and they did so without hesitation.

They ran for more than a league, with the wolf-heads at their heels. Merlin had trouble keeping up with the younger men as his body was weak from fasting, but his fear drove him forward, foot over foot, breath after empty breath, and hill after endless hill ... until a cramp formed in his side.

He was near the back now, and couldn't run much farther. He needed to rest. Behind him came the panting wolf-heads, with their white teeth shining in the moonlight — and at their vanguard loped the werewolf. The creature's claws clicked on the rocks, and its red fur bristled at its neck as it ran.

Onward they ran, though slower. Sometimes the werewolf would run alongside them and try to attack a straggler, who would run quickly into the thick of the group and they would all change direction. Sometimes this happened on their left, and sometimes on their right, for the beast was tireless and determined. Only one man was caught by the werewolf, and his life ended so quickly that Merlin could do nothing but let bitter-tasting tears streak down past his scruffy cheeks. And continue running. Always running.

Overall, their course headed roughly toward the moon, angled sideways in the sky with dagger-like horns stabbing upward toward the stars and inky clouds blowing past.

Their route turned downhill once more, making the ache in Merlin's side ease up, and he tried to breathe as evenly as he could to alleviate the pain. Unexpectedly, his feet splashed into water ... they had found a shallow, thin stream in the wilderness. Merlin scooped up the water as he dashed across and gulped it down, bringing some relief to his burning throat.

As he ran up the opposite hillside, a strange thing happened ... the sound of the wolf-heads' pursuit stopped. Merlin turned and saw that the werewolf at their lead had halted at the stream and would not enter it. Howling in rage, the beast shook its head and gnashed its teeth as Merlin followed the others away.

"Look!" Merlin called to the others, and they saw too. The word was passed to the front, and soon the whole group stopped and fell to the dry bracken, their lungs heaving.

The werewolf yowled and led the pack northward.

"They'll look for a bridge," a man next to Merlin said, "and when they find it, they'll — "

Merlin knew the man's voice, and he turned to him. "Peredur!"

"I've been next to ya the whole run, and ya didn't notice me?"

"I — "

Peredur held out some crusty bread. "Here ... I saved this. Ya need strength."

Merlin took it and began to eat.

"Up, my men!" Arthur called. "We run or we die!"

CHAPTER 31

A SLEEP OF STONES

Merlin pulled himself up on all fours. His knees ached and his lungs had only begun to recover.

But Arthur was fuming at the men's inaction and pulled Percos up by the back of the tunic. "We have to keep running or they'll catch us!"

"How far?" he asked.

"I don't know. We need weapons ... or an island. Preferably both. We run or we die. Up!"

Something in Arthur's words struck Merlin, and he closed his eyes to think. *An island ... an island? Where are we heading?*

He looked to the moon and, just as Colvarth had taught him, he found its two points and drew an imaginary line down to the horizon. This point was south ... therefore the moon was in the southwest, which meant that they'd been running ... where?

The men began to stand. Arthur was prodding them to run again.

Merlin searched his memories. Where was Dinas Hen Felder, the place they had set out from? Named "Old Watchful" by the locals in Kernow, he had heard the name all through his childhood, but couldn't think where it was positioned on a map.

He pushed himself to a squatting position, and finally stood. As they set off once again — legs aching, lungs tired, and throat raw, he finally realized what lay ahead ...

Bosventor.

The village where he'd grown up. Where his father had kept a smithy until that fateful night when the sword had been thrust into the Druid Stone. The events flashed before his eyes, each one appearing with the rhythm of his feet —

His father cried out on the floor in pain. Mórganthu gloated above him with the sword of the High King in his hand.

Left, right.

Merlin ran at the druid, cutting off his hand. Mórganthu screamed and ran from the smithy. The Druid Stone roared in anger ... blue flames so high.

He leapt a ditch. Left, right. Left, right.

Fire. And Natalenya! She was trapped behind the Stone. He tried to drive the sword into the Stone with his father's hammer, and failed. The flames burned his hands.

Merlin ducked a branch, his strides quickening with the flood of memory.

Natalenya reached in, strengthened his grip. He tried again, only to have lightning lash at him from the Stone. The vision. He hammered again.

Left, right.

The flesh on his hands burned away ... Dear God, help! He slammed the iron head down. The blade pierced the Stone and he drove it through and out the bottom.

He nearly stumbled, but kept going. Left, right.

An angel healed Natalenya. Healed him. But his father lay dying.

Dead. Merlin buried him under a cairn of rocks and tears. His old life was gone. Ashes.

Bosventor.

The realization was so shocking that Merlin ran without breathing, and the effort nearly killed him. They might go to Bosventor! If they could keep the path, and not be pushed off course by the werewolf, then they could find the marsh beyond the village. And in the marsh was an island.

Inis Avallow. The Isle of Apples.

There, alone in all this dead wilderness, was refuge from the werewolf and his snarling wolf-heads. A plan kindled in Merlin, and he doubled his speed until he caught up to Arthur.

"Keep running toward the moon!" he said, panting. "There's an island ahead in the middle of a marsh. We can swim there!"

"Will there be enough water?"

"There should be enough ... it's fed by many springs."

Arthur nodded as he turned his head and glanced at Merlin, a glimmer of hope in his red-rimmed eyes.

Bosventor!

They ran for the better part of a league, following the moon, and all the while Merlin listened for pursuit, yet none came. The land began to drop, the trees thickened, and though the ground became stony they found themselves running on a thin path that snaked downward.

"Water!" someone shouted ahead, but then there was a scream.

The men in front came to a sudden halt, and Merlin had to press through to get to Arthur.

"Wolf-heads!" someone yelled.

Arthur looked to Merlin, as if unsure what to do.

"Forward!" Merlin shouted. "We have to cross the water!"

Another scream, and the men began to trample backward. Someone's shoulder shoved Merlin, and he tripped on a rock. He tried to climb up again, but there were so many loose rocks that he couldn't find a grip before another man fell over him.

"Rocks!" Merlin called. "Throw rocks!"

Arthur seconded the call, and order was soon restored as the men armed themselves.

Merlin got to his feet, three rocks in his left hand and two in his right.

"Forward! It's only a few of them!"Arthur called, and the men surged toward the water, throwing rocks at the wolf-heads until the creatures blocking their way had fallen back, howling. The men rushed through the gap across the stream. The water was hardly over Merlin's ankles when the man just behind him screamed. Merlin had one rock left, and he threw it at the wolf-head who was pulling the warrior down — who was Mabon! The rock solidly hit the creature in the side, but it didn't let go. Merlin grabbed his dirk and stabbed the wolf-head low in the back.

The creature screamed and fought back, scratching his human-looking hands at Merlin's face, jabbing him in the left eye.

Merlin kicked his knee into the wolf-head's stomach, and it finally fell, twisting, into the water. Mabon slammed a huge stone upon it, ending the creature's life.

Some warriors helped their injured companion to stand and together they rushed across the stream to dry ground.

Behind them, the werewolf himself arrived with the rest of his army and bellowed in a rage, his shoulders shaking and his teeth snapping.

They ran, slower, for another part of a league until finally Arthur's strength gave out. He halted them near a mound of large, flat granite boulders. Arthur climbed up and lay down on one as if it were a bed, his chest heaving and his legs splayed out in exhaustion.

Merlin was more than glad for the rest, as his left eye felt swollen and his lungs were like burning embers from his father's forge.

His father's forge.

His father …

Oh, that his father were there — alive and still working in their family's blacksmith shop! Was someone else smith now? What had happened to Troslam and Safrowana? To Allun the miller? To all the good people of the village?

What of Dybris and all the other monks? Were any of them left in the village?

But Arthur was up once more and pushing the men.

"It's not far," Merlin told him, "Maybe one more league, and ..."

"An island. You're sure there's an island?"

"Yes."

Soon they came to a cross-path. Rushing into the woods beyond, they arrived at a clearing, which Merlin entered at first with uncaring, unseeing eyes. Then the realization of where he stood brought him to a standstill. It was the Gorseth Cawmen — the druid circle just outside Bosventor. The stones towered above him against the trees, and silent as a grave. Uther's grave it was too — for here the High King had been murdered by Vortigern. Memories from the past flooded Merlin's head.

Druids chanting. Drums pounding. His father's failed fight with Mórganthu. Brother Dybris yelling as he was captured and thrown into a wicker cage with the other monks.

Mórganthu's call for the people to bow and worship the Druid Stone. His yell for the crowd to burn the monks:

Flames blaze and burn the witches!

Fire! Flames! Destroy the witches!

Caygek planning with Merlin on how to save them.

It all came back.

"Run!" Dwin yelled, waking Merlin from his thoughts. The man grabbed Merlin and yanked him along.

The circle passed behind him like a dream. Like a nightmare. They descended the hillside where the pines began to thin and were replaced by beeches. Down they went, faster and faster until they came to the Fowaven River.

As they splashed across, Arthur yelled, "Rest a moment! We're safe once more."

Merlin knew the truth. "There's a bridge to the south where the wolves can cross. Run!"

Across the moorland Merlin dashed, and soon came to the withered shore of a once-broad lake, now much reduced in size. He stopped. Lake Dosmurtanlin, the water where he had once thought his mother drowned. Yet it wasn't so, for she still lived beneath the surface — changed forever by the Stone into a water creature. Merlin longed to —

"Run!" Arthur yelled, for the great werewolf surely had crossed the bridge and, howling, would soon be upon them.

Merlin regretted it, but he started running and left the lake behind. He longed to call out to his mother in hope that she might hear him, but his ragged breath prevented speech. To his left rose the Meneth Gellik — the mountain upon whose southern side his village was built — yet here on the northern side he could see only a hint of the fortress on its western spur. So close, yet he couldn't stop as the ground descended toward the marsh. Some of the men had already reached it and were swimming for the island.

Most of the reeds on the receded shoreline were dead, and there was a stronger stench than Merlin remembered. Safety was so close. He ran past the dead skeleton of a deer, its skull stuck in the dry mud, through the rattling reeds, and dove into the water. Its warmth enveloped him and filled him with such joy at finally being safe.

The swim across the marsh was farther than he had remembered, and his right calf began to cramp up so that he had to float on his back for a long way, sculling with his hands. His leather-and-scale armor weighed him down, and he was tempted to pull it off, but he persevered and finally reached the rocky shingle of the northern landing. He pulled himself ashore: wet, tired beyond the frontiers of exhaustion — and safe.

It seemed a long time before the last man made it ashore, and many had to be dragged from the water half dead.

Then, across the water came the roaring of the werewolf. The sound sliced through the air and set Merlin's teeth on edge. And only after Merlin collapsed shivering and laid his head down on a stone to sleep did he remember the fishing boats over at the village.

If the werewolf found them, then nowhere was safe.

Not even the island of Inis Avallow.

Nowhere.

Merlin forced himself to rise and look for Peredur, but he couldn't find the horse master among the men. Desperate, he called for him, but the man simply wasn't present. Somewhere along the trail he had slipped from the group and been lost.

Merlin fell to his knees and pulled on his hair, wanting to rip it out. Peredur — his brave and loyal friend. How could Merlin not have noticed him falling?

To the east, the sun began to trace its lonely finger across the horizon in a streak of red and gray. And with the coming of dawn, Merlin prayed for Peredur's safety, and that they all might have one day of rest and preparation. *Just one day ... just one day ... keep him safe ... please keep him safe!*

Sleep overtook Arthur so quickly and profoundly that when dreams came he didn't remember where he was. He was flying — flying across a land bespeckled with verdant hills and flowing rivers, where wild roses were knit together with sweetbriar, and the cowslips grew among the violets. A land of peace, where no sword needed to be drawn.

Arthur watched as all these beautiful things passed by, his eyes wide and mouth agape in startled ecstasy.

And then she was there.

The woman in the iridescent, blackbird-feathered cloak ... and she was flying behind him. Whenever he turned to see her, she flew just out of his sight, and a dark hood hid her face.

"Do you see all this?" she asked.

"Yes."

"It can all be yours, Arthur. Imagine with me a land of peace and safety. It is within your reach, but you must take hold of it and never let it go."

"How can I?"

"I will show you ... yet how does any king reign? How did Uther reign before you?"

Arthur's pulse quickened, and he turned to glimpse her. "Did you know him? Did you know my father?"

She paused, and hid her face from him again. "Yes ... in my own way. It was long ago, Arthur, and there is no going back. I have learned that. You must go forward, and listen to my advice, whatever it costs you."

"You ask much of me."

"Nothing more than what I have already paid."

"Who are you?"

"I am she who lives in secrecy." With that the woman arched the flaps of her black feathered cloak and swooped upward into a cloud, and was gone.

Arthur longed to follow her, for she was beautiful — yet against his will he was taken back to the island, and there he awoke. It was still early morning and, though his bones ached and his muscles were cramped and sore, he rose with a strange expectation in his soul. A thin mist had arisen on the marsh, low though the water level was, and Arthur wandered away from the sleeping forms of his warriors.

Southward he walked across the length of the island as if in a daze, and his feet found an old, thin trail that snaked through a stand of pine, rowan, and ash, and soon the trees gave away to emaciated, almost skeletal apple trees. Their fruit was stunted, yet Arthur plucked one and took a bite, only to choke and spit it out. Tiny white worms had filled the inside cavity. They slithered and twisted out onto his hand, and he threw the wretched thing away, wiping his palm on the smooth bark of its parent.

Farther down the path he came to the ruins of a fortress whose old stones had been weathered over the many lives of his forefathers.

Moss and vines had overgrown their northern faces, while the sun-bitten southern sides were dry and pitted. The stones were massive, much larger than any man could lift. Yet they had been thrown about as if some giant had destroyed the walls and buildings long ago.

At the far end of the ruins stood a tower of stone, still mostly intact, although the roof was entirely gone and some stones from the top of the western side had fallen out like old, forgotten teeth. A window survived near the top on the eastern side, and on the north gaped a dark doorway three feet off the ground. Whatever steps had once existed were now gone, for empty socket holes showed where the railing and posts would have been wedged. And though the tower was forgotten and dejected, surrounded as it was with the wind-blasted remains of long-dead apple trees, someone had cared enough for the place to drag a few flat rocks underneath to make access easier to the door.

But all of these details entered Arthur's mind like a haze of smoke, and they were soon forgotten as he wandered aimlessly south to the very tip of the island. There he looked out upon the brooding reeds and sulking, silent water veiled in mist.

Then he heard a woman singing from somewhere across the marsh. And though he couldn't catch the words, he could sense that they were sung mournfully. He sat and let the song fill his soul as the beauty of her voice enthralled him.

And then she herself appeared ... in her cloak of black feathers, balanced upon a narrow skiff and propelling herself with a long, thin pole. Thusly she passed like a dark ghost through a bank of reeds, and they bowed to her as if she were the very queen of the marsh. Her song was unbroken, and now the words themselves fell clearly upon Arthur's ears, sinking into his soul where they would haunt him, he knew, to the very end of his days.

O where is my love, lost long ago?
And where's the harp, plucked sad and slow?
Forlorn am I, and filled with woe,

For he's gone north, to land of snow.
And will he come, a bold hero?
Or will he die, his blood to sow?
Forlorn am I, and filled with woe,
For my sure love, he'll never know.
Arthur, Arthur, yourself do show,
Or all will be, yea, food for crow.
Forlorn am I, and filled with woe,
For who can fight, and who the foe?
All land will die, and moon will glow.
The shade of night, so tall will grow.
Forlorn the land, and filled with woe,
For who will make, the deadly blow?
O come, loved one, lost long ago,
And bring the harp, strummed sweetly low.
Forlorn am I, yet all aglow,
For you've come south, to land of woe.

She had poled to the very edge of the island now — and stepping ashore, she threw back her hood to stare knowingly and unemotionally at him from the one eye that wasn't hidden by her raven-hued hair.

Arthur's breath caught in his throat, and he stood as if he had no control over his legs. She was so close! His heart began pulsing and his throat went dry.

A hand grabbed his shoulder, and Arthur was spun around.

Merlin stood there, his eyes bloodshot and his face lined with fear.

"Do not look at her!" he hissed. "It is Mórgana!"

CHAPTER 32

A Sister's Wrath

Arthur was torn. His heart had leapt when he first saw the woman in the black feather cloak, yet Merlin pulled him backward in terror.

"Let go!" Arthur cried, jerking away from his father. A strange longing urged him to embrace her, as if somehow, deep in his heart, he knew her.

"She has bewitched you!" Merlin cried as he drew his dirk and lunged at her.

Arthur, off-balance, tried to grab his father but slipped on the gravel and fell.

Merlin lifted his dirk and slashed it down.

The woman didn't flinch, but faster than Arthur thought possible she slipped two thin blades from her belt and crossed them, catching Merlin's dirk in mid-strike. Before he could react, she turned sideways and kicked him in the stomach, knocking him down.

"Arthur!" Merlin yelled, but there was no time to respond.

She leaned forward and slipped her blades downward so that the tips came to rest on each side of Merlin's head — at his temples, where his pulsing veins lay just a hairbreadth from being sliced open.

"Do not attack me again, O heir of Colvarth!" she said. "Or Britain shall have one less bard to count among her blessed number, and that would be a great and tragic shame."

Merlin dropped his dirk and she kicked it away.

Arthur saw then, as she leaned over, that her hair covered one side of her face intentionally, for her left eye was missing. The skin had completely healed over the wound so that no eyelid was even present — only unbroken, slightly scarred flesh under a dark eyebrow.

Arthur fell to his knees to get a better look, and deep was his wonder, for he had never met anyone who had endured such a wound and yet lived.

"Who are you?" he asked.

She turned to look at him with her beautiful hazel-green eye, and there was a slight quiver to her lip.

"I am one whom few men fish for, and those who do never see my face again. Do you trifle with me, Arthur?"

Arthur stood. "But your name — what do men call you?"

She pulled her blades away from Merlin's temples, stepped back, and swallowed.

"I?" she said. "It has been many long years since anyone has said my proper name. To myself, I am Abransva, but to the locals I am known as Muscfenna."

"And to us? Who are you to us?"

I have to know, he thought. *There is some secret here ...*

She took a deep breath, licked her lips, and then spoke.

"To God, firstly, I am known as Myrgoskva, the daughter who lives under the shadow of the Almighty — prophetess of God Most High. But to you ... to you I was once known as Myrgwen ... but that Myrgwen has died and is no more."

"Myrgwen…"

It was a name he hardly dared to breathe.

It was a name he'd only recently connected to himself and his own history.

Is it true… Is she alive?

Understanding grappled with his soul, and he spoke the words aloud. "You're my sister."

She sheathed her blades and looked at him with uplifted chin, a sad smile on her lips. "And you took a long time to come visit."

"But…"

She poked him in the chest with her finger. "And that's for not even knowin' who I am!"

Merlin stood and dusted himself off, understanding replacing the confusion and shock on his face. "This was my mistake," he said soberly. "After we settled in Rheged, Colvarth and I sent an inquiry about you and Eilyne. We intended to bring you north, but the news came back of your deaths and Troslam and Safrowana's disappearance. I never dreamed…"

Tears came to Myrgwen's eye, and her voice cracked. "Vortigern slew my sister and injured Troslam. He lived but was ill, and finally died during my sixteenth winter. We had all lived on an island away in the western marsh for safety, but eventually Safrowana left with Ymelys to stay with relatives, and then Muscarvel, my protector, died too. I've lived alone ever since."

"You never left Bosventor."

"No. I was afraid… afraid you'd never find me."

Arthur reached out a hand to her and she took it.

"All these years…" he said. "We never knew."

"I've known," she said, "and I've been waiting for you. God told me…"

"What… what did He tell you?"

"Come with me first." She pulled away and began walking northward toward the ruins. She led them to the doorway of the old tower and motioned for Arthur to join her.

Merlin stayed back, and Arthur cast him a grateful look.

"Enter now," she said, "and weep with me."

Arthur climbed up onto the sill of the doorway, turned to take her hand, and together they entered. An earthy scent met him, and it took a moment for his eyes to adjust to the dimmer light. What he saw amazed him. Where he had expected dead earth and stones to fill the interior, he found a lush garden instead, with green bracken, sweet-smelling fairyglove blooms, ivy, and a type of flowering nettle that was soft to the touch.

"It's beautiful," he said, discerning the care it would take to keep the plants watered from the marsh during the drought. But then he stepped back, for against the wall were two modest cairns, both about the size of ...

"Is this ... is this ...?" was all he could say.

"Yes. Mother's buried here ... and Eilyne too."

He squeezed her hand as they approached the twin graves. They knelt. Moisture began to cloud Arthur's vision, and soon the tears began to flow. All these years, lost to him. All these precious people, lost to him. But now he had Myrgwen, beyond all chances and beyond all evils. Blood of his blood and bone of his bone. True family. Yet just below these rocks — so close, yet so forever far — lay his mother and sister. A violent longing took hold of him to see them in the flesh, to be a child and sit beside them at a cozy hearth. Just share a single meal. *Why can't I do that? It's so simple, God, why is this denied me? Why were I and Myrgwen stripped from their arms? I don't understand ... I don't understand!*

His mother and sister had both died as part of Vortigern's evil plot to steal the High Kingship. A sudden urgency took hold of him. "Father ... where is my true father buried?"

"In a cairn near the druid circle. I'll show you, but not now."

"Why? Why not now? You have a boat, and we could ..."

"You must prepare for your enemies."

"Prepare? We're safe here. The men need to rest."

Without another word, she stood and left the tower.

Arthur followed.

Merlin, who was resting on a rock, stood to join them.

Myrgwen addressed them both. "Your enemy was revealed to me last night in a dream. I knew something was deeply wrong in the land, but I did not know what until I saw them. Until I saw *him*."

"Gorlas?" Merlin asked.

"Yes. Once the sun dies and the moon rises ... they will come. They have already secured boats from the surrounding area and are even now making rafts. They will cross the water, and you must be ready for them."

Arthur shook his head. "But our weapons are few ... How can we fight?"

"You must make bows."

Merlin looked at her, confused. "But we have neither string nor arrows. You're asking the impossible."

"You'll find the answer at the king's hearth."

"I don't have one," Arthur said. "Certainly not on this island."

"Come and see."

She led back north toward where the warriors slept. As they approached, Arthur saw a trail of smoke in the sky and smelled roasting meat. One of the warriors must have woken and caught some game.

But when they stepped out of the woods and into the clearing of their makeshift camp, Arthur stopped. On the edge of the clearing of men — before a roaring campfire — sat Gogirfan Gawr. And next to him sat Melwas, Gwenivach ... and Gwenivere herself!

Dwin sat between the girls, smiling and roasting two ducks.

Myrgwen walked directly to Gogi, placed a hand on his big shoulder, and, turning to Arthur and Merlin, announced, "This is the man who will save you."

A thrill shot through Arthur.

Merlin's mouth fell open. "What are *you* doing here?"

"I've come to the island o' the tinsmiths on holy pilgrimage, ya know." He wiped his greasy hand on a little napkin he pulled from his waistcoat.

"But—"

"This is the very place I've told ya about since the day we met in Kembry, don't ya recall it, ya daft-wit? Old Joseph built the fort and tower and introduced the craft tah us poor folk. All this moorland used to be ours ... Long, long ago it was, and we had been pushed here from the coasts even then. Yet ya Britons took this land away too, ya did—so ya could feed the Roman greed for tin—and now we are Walkers, with no land o' our own."

Gogi turned to Myrgwen with a strange expression. "And what'd ya say, lass?"

"I said that you are the man that will save all of Britain. You will help them make bows and arrows."

"Me?" he said, spitting out a duck bone. "But I'm good fer nothin' but bein' stripped and thrown off a cliff." Here he glared at Merlin. "An' besides ... I doesn't make weapons for mah enemies, the *Brythons*." Here he slurred the word on purpose as if it were a foul thing.

Arthur stepped up and nodded to the smiling Gwenivere, catching her eye. "Gogi ... could you make them for your *friends*?"

Gogi stiffened his lips and pulled at the long plaits of his beard. He looked to his daughters, then, and Arthur saw something in the girls' eyes.

Gogi sighed. "Yah ... I suppose I could do that, ya know. What do ya need?"

Myrgwen pulled her cloak tighter and spoke to Arthur. "The giant can pour arrowheads from pewter, and his sinews can be fashioned into strings for the bows. The men can cut down branches for bows and the shafts of arrows, and the pitch—"

"Now just how do ya know so much about me?" Gogi asked, scratching his beard and puffing out his chest.

"I have seen it," she said.

Gogi stood, his brow creased and his head cocked to the side.

Arthur looked up at how tall the man was, and a genuine fear entered his heart. This was *not* a man to fight hand to hand.

"And how much are ya goin' to pay me for all o' this?" Gogi said, shaking his fists. "I swear by me own guts that I'm not stuffed with coins, and ya know it better than anyone!"

"I've got gold that I can pay you," Arthur said. "But ... I don't have it with me."

"Ahh! That's what everyone says." And then Gogi wiggled his fingers through the air and made his voice high-pitched. "I'll pay ya next week for a pigeon pie today! Oh my! How about that horse for payment tomorrow? Oh, no! I doesn't have my money with me! Hah-hah!"

"Honestly, I do," Arthur said — but how could he convince the giant?

Gwenivach stepped forward and took her father's arm. "Papa ... if we don't, then we might all be killed."

Gwenivere stood and looked on her father with a serious expression. "I know Ambrosius has been cruel to you, but none of the others have. In fact, they've been more than kind considering. Please, I think we can help them."

"Ohh!" he said, looking from one to the other. "Do I haff-tah?"

Melwas stood up, and he squinted at his father and stamped his foot. "Are you really goin' to help 'em? They beat me and tried to kill me, and took our hard-won horse away, an' we're already that much poorer for knowin' em!"

Gogi looked from Gwenivere to Gwenivach, and then back to his son. "Melwas ... I know yer thoughts, but ya know I've got a big heart in this here boot" — he thumped his chest — "so I'm goin' to help 'em. An' if he fails to pay me *two* gold coins, then I'll let ya steal as many o' his horses as ya can get."

"I'll pay you three!" Arthur said.

Gogi pursed his lips. "Even better. Ya will agree to this, yes? Both of ya nod, then."

Melwas nodded, and Arthur did too ... but there was something in Melwas's eyes that Arthur couldn't read. Pride? Anger? Or was it hatred?

"But now we's gots another problem," Gogi said. "You can't make the arrows fly right without feathers. We've got these ducks here that I caught, but the feathers are mostly burnt."

Myrgwen stepped forward and bowed to Arthur. She removed her feather cloak, revealing a thin, white cloak underneath. She held out the feathered one. "At my God's direction I have stitched a cloak for this very day — the day your kingship has come to Kernow, and for the end of our sundering. I had thought it was to be for your glory, but now I see that it is instead for your protection. Take every feather for the arrows, and may God strike each one into the eyes of your enemies."

Arthur took the cloak, amazed at its beauty and the care with which his sister had stitched it. How many birds must she have caught in order to make it? How many hours of work went into it? It seemed almost irreverent to destroy it and pluck the feathers from this thing of majesty — but there was no choice.

Arthur raised his horn and blew it to wake the late risers.

All that day the men worked to find suitable wood for both bows and arrow shafts, and though nothing ideal existed on the island, they found enough that was acceptable to fashion a bow and set of arrows for every man.

Gwenivere and Gwenivach worked tirelessly to soak and braid their father's stash of sinews into bowstrings, with loops on each end. And Gogi, along with a grudging Melwas, melted pewter in an iron pot and cast hundreds after hundreds of small arrowheads using simple molds that the men had carved from wood.

Myrgwen herself fletched many of the arrows using sinew, helped by a small group of deft-handed men. Another group tied on the arrowheads. They were crude creations at best, but each one was capable of killing a wolf-head, and for that Arthur was thankful.

When everything was ready, the men gathered for a meager evening meal, and afterward Merlin stood to speak. His thoughts returned to

343

the dying man he'd held after the battle at the river, and he cleared his throat. Things needed to be said that had gone unsaid for far too long.

"Men of Britain!" he shouted in his clear, strong voice. "Are you warriors?"

The men called out and stamped their feet in a sudden cacophony that startled a host of sparrows from a nearby tree.

"Are you Arthur's men?"

They whistled and raised their fists.

"Are you armed?"

The men cheered and lofted their bows and bundles of arrows.

Merlin quieted his voice. "But how many of you are ready to die?"

The men looked at each other. Some nodded. Others looked down or away.

"And of those ready to die ... how many of you are ready to stand in judgment before a holy God?"

Everyone became quiet. Sober.

"You are warriors ... and heroes!" Merlin called. "But God isn't counting your victories. So, if you are a warrior, then be Arthur's man. And if you are Arthur's man, then be prepared to die, for we fight a powerful foe this night. And if you are prepared to die, then do so with your conscience clear and with the blood of Christ covering your life ... cleansing you of all sin. In the sixteenth Psalm it says something like this ..."

Because I know that thou hast been faithful to thine own Holy Son; yea I know it full well that even in death I need not fear, for never shalt thou disinherit me, nor shalt thou throw me to the dogs.

For in time long past thou shewest unto me the safe highland path — even now I tread upon it to thy mountain court.

There will I see thine happy countenance and thou shalt sit me down as thy champion, and I will joyous be, and feast, and merrymake forevermore!

"So then I say to you, call upon Jesu, and he will take you on the safe, narrow mountain path to his kingdom, and there you will eat at the wedding feast of the Lamb of God. *Do you want this, men of Arthur?*"

The warriors nodded, grunting in agreement, and Merlin prayed out loud for them that God might give strength for the coming battle and prepare their hearts to walk in newness of life in His presence.

And when he was done, he bade Gogirfan to stand next to him.

"Warriors and fearless men, you know the enemy that we are up against. But now we're armed, and I want to both apologize to Gogirfan, and thank him, for he's given us a chance — "

But Gogi interrupted him, placing a hand on Merlin's shoulder and raising his voice. "But ya know … if ya want to increase that chance, then I have a way to improve yar arrows a bit. This is what I've got."

He walked over to Melwas, who sat tending a large iron pot at a nearby fire. Gogi picked up the pot and took off the lid. Tearing a strip of cloth from a rag, he tied it just behind the tip of the arrow and then dabbed it in the pot, which was filled with melted pine pitch.

"Hold this to a torch, and ya've got a flamin' arrow, ya knows! And most helpful against wooden boats, given ya a chance to sink 'em, or at least make the warriors swim."

"Hear, hear!" Merlin said, and all the men cheered.

But the evening had gotten on, and the light was beginning to fade. Merlin looked westward and saw that the thin form of the moon had appeared.

And from the woods, across the water, the werewolf howled.

CHAPTER 33

MERLIN'S NIGHTMARE

Merlin followed Gogirfan's instruction and quickly prepared his arrows by tying cloth behind each tip … but he had to rip off both sleeves of his tunic to get enough material. Sixty men. Twenty arrows each. Was it enough to fight off the wolf-heads? Most of them weren't bowmen, and the thirteen that were had been organized by Tethion into an elite group that Arthur would use to make the deepest strikes at the enemy.

The other men set to, ripping up their tunics when they had no other choice. Each man brought his bundle to Gogi and Melwas, who applied the softened pitch to the arrows.

Gogi also prepared a number of torches specifically for lighting the arrows — one for every pair of men.

And yet they were barely ready by the time the wolf-heads appeared, howling upon the far shore and dragging boats and rafts down to the opposite bank.

"Tethion … take the best bowmen to the front!" Arthur called. "Everyone else, do not shoot until the wolf-heads are halfway across."

"Wolf-heads?" Gogi asked. "I didn't know ya were fightin' wolf-heads! I thought 'twas the same warriors ya fought at Dinas Hen Felder!"

Arthur coughed and then nodded. "They are the very same."

"Ahh," Gogi said with a nervous laugh. "That's a bite more serious. And, I suppose, it makes me even prouder ta have helped. And 'tis a good thing our horses and wagon are on the western shore of the marsh! We always hides 'em over there when we come on pilgrimage … No need fer a Brit to steal us out o' home and horse, ya know."

Arthur gave the word. Tethion and his men lit their arrows, nocked them, and let them fly across the marsh toward the wolf-heads on the far eastern shore. It was hard to see across the water, yet the moon gave Merlin just enough light, and he saw one of the wolf-heads get hit directly in the chest and go down.

The wolf-head shrieked and thrashed about as the burning pitch caught his tunic on fire.

Tethion and the archers lit new arrows and launched them, but this time none of them found their mark, and two fell short and plunked hissing into the water.

Merlin had hoped the arrows would light fires on the far shore, but the land exposed by the receding marsh didn't have quite enough vegetation amidst its mud and gravel.

By now the first wave of wolf-heads had launched a set of boats, with more preparing just behind them. Eight boats were coming, with four or five wolf-heads in each, and they all paddled with flat boards chopped from the trunks of trees so that they didn't need to touch the water.

The archers shot again, and one arrow struck a boat directly in the prow. There were four wolf-heads onboard, and the foremost leapt backward, knocking another into the water, and he screamed and thrashed in terror.

As the boats rowed closer, the archers fired again, but the only arrow that hit did so in the cloak of a wolf-head, and he flung it into the water before it could catch fire.

All the while Merlin could see the beast — the red-furred were-wolf with glowing, yellow eyes striding up and down the far shore, now hunched and clawing the earth, and next standing to roar out guttural, barking commands to his cohort of wolf-heads.

Onward the wolf-heads paddled through the flaming missiles. Only a few hit, setting two boats on fire. This sent the wolf-heads into a furious roaring as they fought each other to get away from the flames. Some fell into the water.

Merlin lit an arrow of his own now. *How easily the creatures could put the flames out if only they weren't afraid of touching the water!*

The other six boats drew closer, and behind them a new set had launched. Tethion and his archers shot at the far boats, while the other men aimed closer in.

Merlin set his sight on a boat, and then adjusted his bow upward to account for the distance. He let his arrow fly, and though it flew fast and straight with roaring flames, his shot landed in the marsh just beyond the boat.

Another, and another arrow he shot — both missing. The last came so close, however, that it would have struck a wolf-head in the shoulder if the creature hadn't ducked.

The others nearby were more successful, and six wolf-heads jumped screaming into the water after being struck and having their clothing catch fire. Another boat was also set aflame, but the wolf-heads on board used their paddles to splash water up to wet the wood and keep it contained.

Faster they paddled, and soon they were only moments from shore. Sweat dripped down Merlin's forehead, and he felt the blood pulse in his neck. *They can't come ashore! They cannot!*

He lit three arrows simultaneously and shot them off in quick succession, one striking a wolf-head in the neck, and another in the forearm.

Ten wolf-heads leapt onto shore ... and Merlin had only time to let one more arrow fly, missing.

He handed his arrows to the man beside him, dropped his bow and pulled out his dirk. Grabbing a torch with his free hand, he ran at the wolf-heads, yelling. Others did the same, including Arthur, while many held back, readying arrows.

Please, let the archers be quick!

Three men died instantly, the wolf-heads lunging past their weapons and ripping out their throats.

A wolf-head with dark brown fur across its face attacked Merlin. The creature ran forward, flipped through the air, and landed next to him with its teeth snapping.

Anger surged through Merlin, and he slammed the flaming torch at its maw. "No!" he yelled, jabbing the dirk toward its chest.

The wolf-head yowled, bit the torch lower down, and yanked it out of Merlin's hand.

Merlin backed up and swung his dirk to keep the beast back.

A flaming arrow punctured the creature's ribs just below its armpit. The wolf-head screamed and fell to its knees, grabbing at the shaft and trying to pull it out.

Merlin turned to find another wolf-head to fight, but ... every one on the island was either dead or was thrashing on the ground with arrows piercing its flesh.

A small cheer went up along the shore, but it was short lived. More wolf-heads were paddling across, this time with ten larger boats, holding at least six wolf-heads each.

Arthur ordered every man to either collect fallen arrows or to move forward with their bows. Soon they formed a great line along the shore, and Arthur instructed them to only shoot when the creatures were closer. Too many arrows had already been lost, and they couldn't afford to waste them. Gogi, Gwenivere, and Gwenivach ran behind them and replaced the fading torches with fresh ones for lighting the arrows.

This time, not a single wolf-head made it to the shore in any shape to fight.

On the opposite side, the remaining wolf-heads hesitated in launching a new flotilla of rafts. Were they afraid? Why did they wait?

Merlin dropped to his knees on the gravel and gave a short prayer of thanks, caught his breath, and steeled his soul, if that were possible, for whatever might come next.

Mórgana rolled her eyes when she heard Mórganthu and Loth curse. Yes, the wolf-heads who had attacked the island had failed and died. Didn't her grandfather know anything? Didn't Loth trust her?

But Mórdred was silent beside her, and his face showed sternness without despair. A boy after her mother's heart — did he understand what was at stake? What the true plan was? The four of them stood behind a thick stand of pines watching the proceedings, and oh how she wished she were close enough to see Merlin's face when he learned what she had planned next.

"Loth!" she said. "Tell the warriors to bring the wagon forward."

"Is that wise, my queen? They canna do much against Arthur and his men —"

"Of course. And afterward you must go to the rendezvous point and hide. The appointed wolf-heads may need to be reminded of their final task. Now do as I command." And she snapped her fingers.

Loth bowed and ran off into the dark.

She leaned against the pine and imagined what would happen, unable to suppress a wild grin at the thought. Her foes had all been such simpletons, hadn't they? Did they really dream that they could escape the grasp of the all-seeing Druid Queen? She could predict exactly what Merlin would do. For she knew her brother — heart, mind, and soul.

Oh, yes, it was true that the Voice's older plans had been thwarted, yet just as he had promised, it only sweetened the final victory tonight and made it more sure. *Hah!*

Turning to Mórganthu, she took his hand and patted it. "Go now ... you and Mórdred must prepare a place for our guest."

"But I want to watch," Mórdred said, creasing his brow.

"The other side of the mountain is not far, and it is too dangerous for either of you here. We must be ready when the moment arrives, true?"

Mórganthu nodded. "I know ... know very little of this *moment* you speak of, but I will obey."

"Do you remember our other guest ... the one we caught last night? Make sure he has not escaped. This will be the grandest pleasure of all. Loth and I will join you both very soon."

"We will do as you say." Mórganthu bowed and limped off into the night, leaning upon Mórdred and mumbling to the young lad.

Soon she heard the wagon rumbling from the north. Loth didn't see her at first, and so she stepped out to meet it. The horses whinnied in dread to be so near the wolf-heads, but Mórgana gave a singsong and stroked their cheeks, putting them into a stupor. Leaving the horses to loll in their sleep, she walked to the back of the wagon where her prisoners lay — tied up and brought here just for this occasion.

Her army of wolf-heads turned to see what this new thing was, and Gorlas himself, her werewolf, came lumbering over. His claws hung low to the ground, and saliva dripped from his teeth as he sniffed the nearest prisoner.

"What do you think?" Mórgana asked him. "Shall we make a snack of them?"

The werewolf looked at her with his wild, agitated eyes and snarled. With one claw, he scratched at the side of the wagon.

"Not yet ... and if that time comes, you must only eat a little. You don't want to be slowed down in the fight, do you?"

The werewolf roared at her and snapped his teeth.

"Back!" she yelled. "You have a special task to do. Do you remember it, my *Gourvlyth* ... my Gorlas?"

The werewolf looked at her menacingly, his nose twitching and his fangs bared.

She reached into the bag at her waist, pulled out her green, glowing fang, and raised it threateningly before him. "Do you need *help* remembering? At the utter end of the fight, what must you do?"

At the sight of the fang, he cowered down, nodded, and slowly backed away.

"Good. And do not forget … you must conduct the entire battle *exactly* as I have instructed you. No matter what happens, *you must obey me.* And if you do not, I will release Gorlas's soul from the orb and then you will be thrown out of the world once more. Do you want that?"

The werewolf shook his head.

Now it was time for Mórgana to select which prisoner. Ah, what fun. Who should she choose? A warrior? One of the young? They could all serve her purpose, and Merlin would know the truth no matter who she chose. But why not the one prized by both Merlin and Arthur? Yes, the one whom she had failed to slay before.

Mórgana climbed up into the wagon, found the one she sought, and undid the gag. Natalenya's long, dark hair had covered her face, and Mórgana pushed it back to reveal defiance set deeply in the woman's eyes and lips stiff with rage.

No matter … that look won't last long.

"You'll not break me!" Natalenya said.

Mórgana laughed. "You are *so* dimwitted — even if you were rather clever at Dinas Crag. You may have escaped from my gullible and fearful Picti by piling diseased bodies on the lower level of your fortress, but you cannot escape me, especially when you foolishly flee to your mother — so close to the center of my power! Know this, ridiculous girl, that I captured you on the shore of Dinas Camlin for an entirely different purpose than you could *ever* imagine."

She untied Natalenya's legs and arms and lifted her to a standing position within the back of the open wagon.

"Where am I?"

"Are your eyes so dull that you cannot recognize the land of your childhood? You are north of Bosventor. Before you lies the marsh, and within it, Inis Avallow."

"Those men on the island … is that …?"

"Yes," Mórgana said, her voice turning sarcastic. "It is your precocious Arthur and your beloved Merlin leading powerful, well-armed warriors. They are ready to liberate these lands, but we can't let them do that now, can we?"

Mórgana turned to the werewolf, who was hunched over to the rear of the wagon. "Take this one," she commanded.

The werewolf howled in delight and scuffled over.

Natalenya saw the beast for the first time and screamed.

Mórgana smiled. Just as she had hoped.

The werewolf reached for her, curling his black lips and revealing fangs as long as Natalenya's fingers.

Natalenya fell backward, screamed again, but then grabbed one of the loose ropes that had been used to tie her up. Standing quickly, she turned on Mórgana, threw the rope over her head, and tightened it around her neck.

Mórgana was taken off guard. The werewolf should have made the girl cower, twitch, and beg for mercy, but this … was … unexpected. Natalenya tightened the rope, and Mórgana suddenly found it hard to breathe. She gasped, and tried to twist away, but Natalenya was stronger than she expected.

"Call your beast off or I'll kill you."

Anger surged in Mórgana, and she shoved a palm into Natalenya's chin, pushing the girl back. With her other hand, she took out her fang and cupped it in her fingers. It only took a moment for power to pulse within her arm, and then she slammed her fist into Natalenya's shoulder.

The girl yelled and collapsed, letting go of the rope.

Mórgana pulled the rope off of her neck and sucked in a few angry breaths.

"Take her!" she screamed, her voice raw.

The werewolf loped forward and scooped Natalenya up.

The girl struggled against him, beating his chest and kicking furiously until the werewolf opened his maw and roared, his teeth inches from her face.

Natalenya stopped struggling and began to whimper, barely breathing.

Mórgana rubbed the rope burns on her neck. "Good," she said. "You finally see the wisdom in cooperating. And if you give any more trouble, do not expect to see your children alive again. Now take her to the shore and hold her before the eyes of our enemies."

Merlin stood beside Arthur on the shore and watched the activity across the marsh. After a period of relative quiet, the wolf-heads had again begun to mill about as if in restless expectation. Arthur raised his arm, ready to give Tethion's archers the order to fire on the far shore, but Merlin grabbed his elbow.

"Stop!"

Arthur turned. The flaming arrows wavered as the archers held their bowstrings taut.

"There's a woman in the hands of the werewolf ... Look!"

Arthur followed Merlin's gaze.

"Is it Mórgana?"

"I don't think so."

Now the woman began to scream for help. Her voice floated across the marsh and pricked Merlin's ears, swirling inside his soul until, until ... But what his heart told him his mind contradicted. It couldn't be, though it had to be true. He knew the voice too well. And just as recognition dawned on him in a blazing heat — he heard her call his name.

"Merlin! Arthur! They have the children!"

His wife! She and the children were alive! And that very truth shocked him more than the startling fact that she was here in Bosventor and in the clutches of the werewolf.

"Natalenya!" he called, but the word caught in his throat and cut him so painfully that he fell to his knees.

The werewolf howled, and his massive claws lifted her up. The reality of the situation hit Merlin like a blow to the chest. He had already counted her as dead in his heart, and now to find her alive beyond all hope ... yet in the hands of his worst nightmare!

An inner scream began in his heart — ripping, ripping — until his spirit bled and bled and he would stand it no longer.

"We've got to save them!" he yelled as he ran down the shore. Finding a boat left behind by the wolf-heads, he shoved off and paddled furiously out into the marsh toward his wife.

And the werewolf.

He would save her or die.

CHAPTER 34

MERLIN'S KING

Merlin paddled with such strength and power that the water churned and flowed as if it were time itself, each flash of wetness passing like a moment, a day, a year, a decade — until all his life slipped away and he was old, old and frail, and his wife was dying before him, now entombed, now dust, a living whisper on the wind-shaped shore.

God of Abraham, in Your mercy, take our crumbling lives and make us whole.

Save us, Lord Jesu!

Save my wife and children.

Please, don't let them die.

Merlin was dimly aware of his fellow warriors following him across the water, and he turned once to see Arthur, Dwin, and others paddling in the forefront of all the serviceable boats and rafts, each one filled with warriors. And there was old Gogi rowing his own boat, and tucked into his white belt was a big iron mace.

But none of them made any difference. Merlin felt alone in this. And the closer he paddled, the more he saw, and the more he feared. His greatest earthly treasure in the hands of the greatest horror.

Red, thick fur and rippling muscles.

Razor, slashing claws.

Eyes aflame with the fire of hell.

A tongue ready to taste Merlin's worthless, yellowed blood, and a throat ready to gulp it down.

As the cold coils of dread squeezed his heart, his paddle fell slack. His arms useless. How could he fight this beast? How could he save her? He wanted to scream, but his pinched lungs could let out nothing more than a thin wheeze.

Yet as Merlin looked helplessly upon Natalenya, his hearing sharpened and he heard a voice speaking his name.

MERLIN ...

The world stopped. Nothing moved. A flaming arrow shot from behind hung in the air to Merlin's left, its flame frozen. The drool from the werewolf hung, floating idly from his teeth.

The words came again. MERLIN, WHO ARE YOU?

"I am a warrior," he said, holding up his dirk. Blood covered the tip, and the wooden handle was cracked, but the short blade felt good in his hands. His father had made it.

MERLIN, WHO ARE YOU?

He was confused. "I am a ... a bard."

With persistence, the voice spoke once more. MERLIN, WHO ARE YOU?

"I am ... a servant of Arthur, my king."

A wind swirled, and when the words came again, they vibrated all around him. MERLIN, WHO IS YOUR KING?

"Arthur ... Arthur is my king."

The wind became furious, buffeting him, and he hunkered down lest he be blown off the boat and into the water.

The words came next like a whisper, a still, small voice speaking through the raging winds. MERLIN, WHO IS YOUR KING?

Merlin closed his eyes. Then he knew. Not only *who* was speaking to him, but why. He had forgotten, hadn't he? He had prayed for his family, yes, but it was a cornered kind of prayer, the type you say when you have no hope.

Certainly all the events before his eyes screamed for him *not* to hope. Justified him. So few warriors left alive. The powerful and numerous wolf-heads ready to attack. Very few weapons. His wife and his children half a breath away from dying.

MERLIN, WHO ARE YOU?

He hesitated, but when he spoke he knew it was true. It had always been true, for he had been chosen. Picked out.

"I am ... a servant of the Most High."

AND WHO IS YOUR KING?

"You ... You are my King. My Emperor. My Sovereign. My Suzerain."

AND WHAT DOES YOUR KING REQUIRE OF YOU?

Merlin knew the answer but could hardly say it, and the words escaped from his throat like jagged fish bones. "It is required that I follow You. Through suffering, to death ... and beyond to Your feasting hall ... to Your very throne."

BE STRONG AND COURAGEOUS, MERLIN. DO NOT FEAR THE ONE WHO CAN ONLY SLAY YOUR BODY, FOR HE CANNOT SLAY YOUR SOUL. FEAR ME, FOR I HOLD BOTH YOUR SOUL AND YOUR BODY, AND NO ONE CAN STEAL YOU FROM MY HAND.

The world around him lurched. The arrow hissed, speeding toward a watery grave, the wolf-heads howled, and the water rolled under his boat once more. Merlin paddled then, new strength in his limbs and his dirk ready at his belt.

As he closed in, he saw more clearly Natalenya's peril. Her screams had faded now and were replaced by fearful moans as the beast sniffed near her face and licked his dagger-like teeth.

The wolf-heads had arrayed themselves behind the werewolf, and farther up the bank stood a lone wagon. A light breeze blew at his back, and above him hovered a silent raven that was soon lost in the darkness.

Merlin propelled himself to the shoreline and leapt on a rock. His dirk was in his right hand and he kept the short paddle in his left for a shield. He breathed heavily and clenched his jaw in seething fury.

"Let her go!" he yelled at the beast, who stood not five paces away.

The creature howled, and all the wolf-heads joined him in a barking cacophony. Merlin covered his ears to block it out as the sound fairly shook the air.

"Merlin!" Natalenya cried, fighting and kicking to get free from the clawed hand. The beast tossed her into his left hand and held her kicking limbs away from his face. With his right hand he extended his claws toward Merlin and roared.

Merlin ran at him.

The beast lunged forward, making a swipe at Merlin's face.

Merlin dodged to the left side, jabbing into the palm of the clawed hand with his dirk. The blow had come at him so hard, however, that it knocked away his dirk and jammed his wrist.

The werewolf pulled his hand away and yowled.

Merlin threw himself toward where his dirk had landed but fell short.

The werewolf's razor-sharp nails came down.

He rolled and tried to block the attack with his paddle as a shield, yet the beast's claw ripped the wood out of his hand and cut through the scale armor, slicing him. He grabbed the dirk, slashed out at the beast, and rolled up onto his feet. His whole arm hurt now, and even his shoulder felt weak.

The wolf-head minions advanced now, and three crouched, ready to pounce on him.

Flaming arrows came hurtling in from the marsh.

All three beasts barked and screamed, pulling on the arrows that had lodged in their flesh.

Merlin attacked the beast holding Natalenya just as another volley of arrows flew past. Many wolf-heads went down, and one arrow struck the giant werewolf in the leg.

"Ready!" Arthur yelled from behind him, and Merlin saw that they had kept their boats just offshore and were using them as platforms for the archers.

Merlin took his chance and dove, trying to strike a blow to the fur-covered body.

But the creature yanked the arrow out of his bleeding thigh and flung it, still flaming, at Merlin. The tip of the arrow caught in Merlin's hair, and the burning rag started to flame up.

Natalenya screamed.

Merlin ignored it and dove inward toward the beast. The smell of burnt hair filled his senses as flicks of flame danced at the edges of his vision. He slammed his head into the creature's stomach, reached around with his left hand to anchor himself — and stabbed the creature in the side with the tip of his dirk.

But the beast's fur was too thick and its skin too tough for Merlin's weakened arm, and the point penetrated only part way.

The beast roared and threw Natalenya behind him like a rag doll. Merlin saw her hit the side of the wagon and slump to the ground.

Now with both claws free, the werewolf grabbed Merlin by the scruff of his armor and flung him back toward the shore so that he landed with his head in the water, extinguishing his hair.

Coughing and choking, he thrashed to sit up. When he did so, he was alarmed to see a wolf-head launch itself right over him and out into the water. Flaming arrows shot past, and yet more wolf-heads came running toward the shore.

Merlin turned and saw that Arthur and the others had floated too close, and the enchanted creatures were leaping and landing on the boats, taking the archers down. Roaring and ripping sounds erupted and the warriors began to scream and yell from the boats.

Merlin stood, dizzy. He still had his dirk but had lost his makeshift shield.

The werewolf lunged at him with ferocious speed. Merlin ducked, but a claw raked across his chest, piercing his armor, and he was vaulted into the air.

The shoreline flipped, and Merlin landed headfirst on the ground, making his whole body buzz and colors dance before his eyes.

He tried to move ... to sit up ... to lift his head ... to do anything, but nothing worked. As Merlin's eyesight cleared, he panicked to see the werewolf's face hanging over him, grinning with his white teeth and long, slavering tongue. The beast's nose twitched and his lips pulled away from his fangs as he opened his mouth.

The tingling in Merlin's limbs began to decrease ... too late.

The Werewolf picked Merlin up, but then the fearsome face twisted, and the beast howled in pain, throwing Merlin back to the ground.

"Leave my tas alone!" yelled a hoarse, wild voice.

The beast hesitated, confusion in his wolfish eyes. Then he snarled in rage and spun around, thrashing out with his claws.

A smirking, determined face poked around the left leg of the beast and ran to Merlin.

Merlin's heart pounded in joy and fear at the same time. "Taliesin! How did you — ?"

"Always hide a knife in your breeches!" he said, and then stabbed the beast in the calf.

The creature turned again, roared, and swung downward.

Taliesin ran through the beast's legs and back toward the wagon, snaking through the wolf-heads who were running forward and launching themselves at the warriors on the boats.

The werewolf set off after Taliesin, and Merlin yelled to warn his son.

More screaming erupted from the boats. Merlin's heart beat out a rhythm of *Doom ... Dead ... Doom ...*

He sat up, trembling, and stood. Arthur was still fighting, for he could hear his clear, strong voice calling to the men. He was Merlin's earthly king, yes, and they would both die together serving their Sovereign, for disaster was at the door, and the door was being ripped from its hinges.

The time has come for me to die, my King. Make me brave! Make my family brave! Take us to Your kingdom!

And then he heard a drum sounding from the east.

Louder now ... it was a battle drum!

The sound of thundering horses followed, and Merlin looked up to see a mounted army ride over a ridge and attack the wolf-heads, spears raised and swords slashing. And at their head rode three men — one whom he did not know with red and grayish locks and bronze armor — and two whom he did:

Peredur ... and ...

Culann!

A cheer rose from Merlin's raw throat, and the men on the rafts joined him. The wolf-heads attacking them faltered and were thrown into the water.

Arthur raised his voice in a shout and ordered the men to shore.

Dwin yelled, his exuberant voice floating over the battle.

Five hundred or more horsemen rode through the wolf-heads, cutting them down and striking deeply into their ranks.

The werewolf left off chasing Taliesin and, howling in rage, grabbed a warrior off of his horse. Swinging him into three others, he slammed them all to the ground.

Merlin ran, ducking and diving through the chaos, until he reached the wagon where his son had just finished cutting Tinga's bonds and helping her down. Together the three of them pulled Natalenya underneath where they could hide. Tinga closed her eyes and jumped into Merlin's arms, sobbing.

"It's all right, Tinga ... it's going to be all right."

"No, ith not. Make 'em go away!"

The boats landed and Arthur led the warriors in his company up the shore to harry the wolf-heads from that flank. Gogi towered above them all, swinging his iron mace and clouting any wolf-head that came near.

"Culann!" Dwin yelled. "I knew you hadn't deserted us!"

He ran toward his newly returned friend, but the raging werewolf turned, saw him, and leapt. The beast's arm swung out in a ferocious strike, and Dwin crumpled.

Arthur screamed as he rushed toward his friend. The werewolf gave an evil, barking laugh as he lifted Dwin by the throat and squeezed. Running past two fallen horsemen, Arthur picked up an ash-wood spear with a sharpened iron tip and charged.

Arthur had known Dwin for as long as he could remember, but as he closed the distance to the werewolf, the time compressed into flashes of memory: climbing trees; taking their first deer on the same day; throwing each other off of an old, fallen tree into Lake Derwent; learning to tame horses together, to ride bareback, to fight; sharing worries they couldn't voice to anyone else, talking late into the night about girls; getting to know Culann, who had moved to the valley with his family when they were fourteen.

"Let him go!" Arthur shouted.

The beast lifted Dwin up and bit into his side, ripping away a chunk of armor and flesh together. Dwin screamed until his air ran out, and then he kept screaming in silence, his lips writhing in pain — and that was the worst of all for Arthur to see.

Arthur vaulted forward, anger hot in his veins and rage stretching his neck muscles taut until it felt like they would burst. He smashed the spear point into the werewolf's left hip until he heard a ripping of fur, skin, and muscle.

"Die, you demon!" Arthur yelled, twisting the tip and shoving it in deeper.

The creature bellowed and threw Dwin down upon a large, blood-stained rock, and turned upon Arthur. Clawing outward, he caught Arthur on the shoulder with a glancing blow as Arthur leapt back to dislodge the spear.

The werewolf lunged forward again, but Arthur ducked to the

side, placing himself between the creature and Dwin's bleeding body. Backing up, his heel bumped the large rock Dwin was laying on.

The werewolf turned, snarled, and leapt.

Arthur planted the butt of the spear between the rock and the ground and angled it up toward the monster.

The creature impaled itself on the spear, the tip sliding in between two muscled ribs on the right side. In a rage it thrashed out and backhanded Arthur across the face.

There was a jolt as his head snapped to the side.

The monster's leering, gnashing teeth — crimson and white.

The skewed, sharp-tipped moon — dancing in the darkness.

The spurting chest wound of the werewolf — red and black with gore.

The world spun and Arthur fell, his hand sliding down the length of the spear.

The cold and musty gravel of the shore smashed into his face.

Howling. Shuffling feet. Horses neighing. Warriors shouting. The blare of a battle horn.

The spear quivered as Arthur tightened his grip, and then the tip fell free of the beast's chest and Arthur was alone. He pulled himself up to a sitting position, shook his head and spit out a chip of broken tooth, a molar from the upper left side of his jaw. His face felt numb. But where had the creature gone?

Dwin moaned beside him, and Arthur turned to see his friend reaching out a blood-soaked hand. Arthur took it.

"Kill the werewolf ..." Dwin rasped. "No one ... should die this way."

"You're *not* dying. Hang on, I'll wrap you up, you'll heal, you'll —"

"Arthur ...?"

"Yes."

"Take my necklace. My grandfather gave it. Remember me ..."

"You keep it. You're going to heal, see?"

"Tell my mother I love her. My tas, tell him —" But Dwin choked on his words and his body fell limp. He wasn't breathing, and his eyes ... his eyes ...

Arthur shook his friend's shoulders, but there was no response.

"No!" Arthur yelled, digging his hand into the blood-soaked pebbles and squeezing them in his fists.

"No-o!"

He laid his head on Dwin's silent chest and wept angry, bitter tears that coursed down his cheeks and into his mouth, wetting his tongue enough to curse the werewolf and all of its bloody kin.

Arthur closed Dwin's eyes, and the finality of the act squeezed his heart dry. He then slipped the cord off of Dwin's neck and placed it over his own. It was strung with the teeth of a wildcat killed long ago on the slopes of Dinas Crag. Dwin had prized it along with the stories his grandfather had told about the hunt.

But how could Arthur go on without his friend? The impossibility of it smote him. Using the spear to steady himself, Arthur stood and surveyed the battlefield. Victory was at hand. The main body of the surviving wolf-head army was fleeing north at top speed, while a small group of six wolf-heads ran away eastward.

But the beast wasn't among either party.

Arthur looked for his men and saw that all those who had come with him on rafts across the marsh had found horses and mounted: Percos, Neb, Mabon, Tethion, and all the others. All except Gogi, who was stumping slowly toward the wagon where Merlin sat.

"Culann!" Arthur called, wiping the tears from his stinging eyes. "Where's the beast?"

Culann turned in his saddle, a gruesomely spattered blade in his hand and a look of satisfaction on his face. "South," he said, pointing along the shore between the mountain and the marsh.

Arthur must have appeared confused, for Culann scowled. "Toward the village."

Arthur finally saw the creature limping urgently away.

"Chase him! We have to kill him!"

"No!" Culann said. "I saw what happened to Dwin ... I'm sorry, but we're riding after the main force of the wolf-heads." He kicked his mount forward and followed all the other horsemen.

Arthur's face heated up ... this, on top of Culann running off with the gold, was serious defiance the two would have to settle later. He turned back to see the werewolf disappearing into the darkness. The beast was wailing in pain.

Arthur looked around, and the only man left who could help him was his father — but Merlin was comforting Taliesin and Tinga, and needed to tend Natalenya.

Arthur clenched his teeth and set off after the badly wounded beast.

"Come back!" Merlin called, but Arthur couldn't stop.

I will finish this beast. Dwin begged me to do it, and I will, so help me God.

CHAPTER 35

SWORD AND SHADOW

Merlin jumped up in a panic, torn between following Arthur and tending to the rest of his family. He called after the young king again, but Arthur did not turn. Just then, Merlin heard muffled grunting emanating from the wagon above. He turned to find Caygek and Bedwir still tied up in the bottom. Focused on his family, he had missed them before, so now he slipped their gags off and cut their bonds, explaining to them the need to help Arthur and protect him.

The two were stiff from having been tied up, so they tried urgently to rouse the horses hitched to the wagon, but found them unresponsive. "Wake up!" Merlin said, patting one on its warm cheek. But the horse's eyes were closed, and their heads hung down.

Bedwir set a hand on Merlin's shoulder. "See to your wife . . . we'll go after Arthur."

Merlin locked eyes with him, and then with Caygek. Although these hardened warriors had already survived things that Merlin could only imagine, he saw fear on their countenances: pinched lines at the corners of their eyes and tight lips. But there was also a determination — a steadfastness that Merlin needed right now.

"I'll follow as quickly as I can."

Caygek nodded, and the two found some discarded spears and ran off into the night on Arthur's trail.

Back beside the wagon, Merlin lifted Natalenya into his arms and held her close.

Her lips were moving, and this little sign of her recovery melted his heart. But he had no time to stay until she awoke. He had to help Arthur, but couldn't leave his family unprotected.

Gogi plodded over and dropped his bulk down so that he leaned against the front wagon wheel. He was out of breath, and there was a bloody wound on his left hand, but other than that he was unscathed.

"Go ... after tha lad. It'll take every man ... to kill it, ya know? I'd go meself, but ... ah ... I don't have the legs for it. So then, I'll stay here and guard the little ones. I assume this is yar family?"

Merlin nodded, grateful beyond words.

"Taliesin ... stay here with this man, Gogi. He'll protect you all. The wolves are gone now, but I need you to help him keep watch."

"Yes, Tas ... Where are you — ?"

"I'm going after your brother."

"I'm coming — "

"Stay!"

Taliesin held on to Merlin's chest and wouldn't let go.

"I need you and Tinga to be strong. I'll be back very soon."

Tinga grabbed on to his neck. "Don't leave, Tath!"

"Take my dirk, Tal."

Taliesin looked up, his face tight and his brows wrinkled in worry. A lone tear hung at the corner of his left eye. "I won't need it."

"It's yours. Just in case."

Taliesin nodded and received the weapon.

Natalenya stirred and opened her eyes. "Merlin ..."

"I have to go, my love. Arthur."

"When ..." She placed both hands on his face and looked into his eyes.

"Now. I'll be right back."

He hugged her, kissing her on the lips. She coughed, and so he pulled the water bag from his belt and gave her the last few drops.

Away south, the werewolf howled. He had to help Arthur. Why did he have to choose between those that he loved? He didn't want to let any of them go. Never. He had thought he'd lost Natalenya, and now she was here, hurt, and needing him. And Arthur, loved as a son, needed him too.

He pictured Arthur fighting the fell beast in the dark. And what of Mórgana? Bedwir and Caygek didn't know what they were dealing with ...

Merlin closed his eyes, hugged Natalenya one last time, and then set her in Taliesin's arms. He kissed Tinga on the head even as the little girl clung to her mother, weeping and coughing.

Gogi stood and held out his mace. "I'm ready ta guard 'em, ya know, so don't worry."

Merlin picked up the spear of a fallen warrior, stood, and backed away. But he couldn't take his eyes from them.

A sweet family. Surrounded by darkness. Hiding under a wagon. And he belonged with them.

His whole heart. His whole life. Bone and soul.

And as he backed into the gloom, he saw them sitting close, so needful, but he had to turn away to save Arthur — whom he belonged with just as deeply — from death at the hands of the werewolf. He dashed off into the night, hardly able to see through his tears, following the shore and hoping he could find Caygek, Bedwir, and Arthur.

Arthur had no trouble tracking the creature in the moonlight, for its claws had left deep impressions on the trail and its wounds had dripped black blood upon the dry scrub and dirt. But then the path split, and the beast must have been unsure of its direction, for the trail became confused.

Following the path to the right, he found that the tracks passed a burned-down and overgrown crennig and then ended at the marsh. A set of decrepit docks stuck out into the water, and moss sucked at the rotten boards, many of which hung sadly into the murky water below.

Without finding any sign of the werewolf on the trail beyond the docks, or on either side of it, Arthur turned back to the crossroads and picked up the beast's tracks going the opposite direction. These led uphill toward the village of Bosventor, Merlin's childhood home. Over to the left, on a spur of the mountain, stood a fortress, and though there were a few flickering torchlights upon the ramparts, all was quiet.

Soon he passed a crennig whose walls had fallen in and whose thatch roof lay broken and torn. In fact, at least half of the crennigs he passed had been destroyed, perhaps by something more deliberate than decay. In Merlin's stories of his growing-up years, the place had been a bustling village. This seemed nothing like that. The path was little trod. Weeds overran the gardens, where the little plots remained at all. Field walls had tumbled down.

Arthur ran faster now, and the path turned downhill toward a distant road. The blood of the beast had poured more freely here, for it left a near continuous trail, scraped and spattered as it was by its right foot, which appeared to be dragging.

The werewolf howled ahead, not far off, and Arthur heard a crennig door creak open to his right. Two men stepped out. One of them was balding, and he held an oil lamp and a jagged iron shovel. The other grasped a poker. They both looked around fearfully.

"It's a werewolf!" Arthur called to them. "Gather help!"

"Where's it runnin' to?" the balding man asked.

Without stopping, Arthur answered, "Across the road!"

"It's goin' after the sheep an' goats!" the younger said.

As Arthur raced away, he heard the two men raise the hue and cry among whatever villagers remained. More crennig doors opened and men gathered on the path behind him. He crossed the road, sighted the trail of blood ending at a stone-stacked pasture wall, and vaulted over it to pick up the trail again. Eastward the creature had run, and Arthur set off after it, now nearly out of breath. Ahead of him lay a large crennig, and to its right came the frantic bleating of sheep. Heedless to the clumps of dung, he followed the trail of claw marks.

A scream, not human.

Arthur tightened his grip on his spear and dashed toward the sound.

And there was the werewolf, holding a young sheep. Before Arthur could get any closer, the beast had slain the sheep and was swallowing great hunks until the blood stained his snout, neck, and finally ran down his chest to drip on the broad slab of granite under the creature's feet. On the slab lay a black stone about three feet wide with a long metallic object protruding from its center — a beautiful sword. The blade was long and gray, and it had a hilt and pommel of golden bronze with inlays of red glass.

Arthur drew a sharp breath. This wasn't just *any* stone ... This was *the* Stone, the very Stone that Merlin had told him about in all the old tales. Which meant this was the sword Merlin's father had made for Uther. The last true sword of the High Kingship.

But the stories of Merlin's youth would have to wait, for the werewolf saw Arthur now and threw the sheep's body down as it swallowed its last bite. The beast's menacing gaze never left Arthur, though, and it seemed as if there was a strange recognition in the beast's countenance — perhaps it remembered Arthur was the one who had injured it.

Arthur stepped forward, spear ready.

The beast stepped off of the granite slab, its left leg shaking and weak. Blood still poured from its chest wound, but the injury did not stop the beast from swiping out with its deadly claws.

Arthur shifted his spear toward the beast's hand and sliced into it. Then, while the creature was recoiling, Arthur lunged in with the tip pointed at its gut.

But the werewolf was still quick enough to evade the blow and swiped at Arthur.

Ducking, he jabbed the spear blindly upward and heard the beast howl.

Arthur jumped to the side and saw that he'd jabbed it in the upper arm.

The beast jerked away, screaming, and then it dove forward so fast that Arthur didn't have time to react. It grabbed him by the shoulder flap of his armor and spun, lifting Arthur off the ground and throwing him through the air.

Arthur hit the ground hard and skidded onto the granite slab, his back smashing into the Druid Stone. He shook his head to focus, but it only made him dizzy.

The werewolf limped toward him.

And even as his vision blurred, he felt heat at his back. The Stone was burning him!

Before Arthur could rise, the werewolf grabbed him and lifted him into the air. Arthur tried to hold on to his spear, but it rolled off of his fingers and fell to the grass. He struggled to get away as hot, breathless panic set in, and he kicked at the creature to no avail.

The werewolf opened his jaws and Arthur saw the massive lines of sharp teeth, doused in blood and thrusting at his neck.

Arthur's whole body surged with power as he fought uselessly against the beast, and the awful, stinking maw drew closer. Arthur found himself helpless, his heart throbbing and pulsing with terror. *Dear God!*

A frantic cawing filled the air as a raven dove down and scratched at the beast's eyes.

Arthur fell to the earth with a painful thud as the werewolf sought to catch and kill the raven. The bird nipped at the beast's snout and poked him in one eye before flying to safety.

Arthur pulled himself up to his knees, found his spear, and stabbed out with it.

But the beast was enraged, and a claw grabbed the tip and shattered it off, flinging the metal into the darkness.

Standing, Arthur backed up until his heel hit the granite slab.

The werewolf pounced at him, roaring and snapping.

Arthur threw the useless spear shaft at its face, jumped onto the granite slab, and backed himself to the other side of the Stone. Now the embedded blade was between himself and the beast. It glinted in the darkness. *The blade!*

Arthur grabbed the handle and tried to pull it from the Stone — but it didn't budge.

The werewolf stepped closer, nostrils flared, lips curled in a snarl of hatred.

Arthur pulled harder, but the blade held fast.

Then everything around him blurred and changed.

Whirling, Arthur beheld an open glade edged with standing stones, and all around him stood ghostly people. The Stone was before him, yet upon it lay the semitransparent form of a bound man, with another on the ground to his left. The man upon the Stone cried out as flames burst from the sides and flicked up at his flesh.

The apparition of a warrior approached, and he was holding the blade that Arthur had just seen — the blade from the Stone. Except now it was free, and the warrior raised it up to plunge into the man whose chest lay on the Stone.

"No-o!" Arthur yelled, for the warrior with the sword was a younger, ghostly Vortigern. He jumped to push the man back, desperate to save the man on the Stone — his father.

But he fell right through the warrior and landed on the ground.

Vortigern plunged the blade in — and Uther cried out in pain.

Arthur had to look away, for it was too horrible to behold — yet in his father's last breath, he called on Christ for mercy.

Arthur pulled himself up on his knees as grief overtook him. There lay his father, dead upon the Stone, his blood leaking down and his eyes vacant and staring. The man Arthur had never known. The man who should have raised him. The man who . . .

The world shifted, spun, and swirled away all the ghostly people except for Vortigern and the Stone — and now the blade appeared, embedded in the Stone.

Vortigern leaned forward and gazed into Arthur's eyes, a mocking sneer on his bearded face. "Eeh ... didn't like the look of him dead?"

Arthur wiped away his tears. He wanted to wrench Vortigern's head off and throw it to the dogs. "Leave me alone, butcher!"

"Get up and fight me!" Vortigern yelled. "And stop yer eye-dribbling."

Fury rose in Arthur — but before he could act Vortigern disappeared and an ethereal woman took his place. She wore a cloak as black as death, and her eyes were filled with ice and bile.

"You are weak, Arthur, so pitifully weak. You couldn't save your friend. You couldn't kill my werewolf. And now you can't even kill me, a servant of the one who commanded your parents' death!"

Arthur clenched his fists, and though he tried to mask his anger, they began to shake against his will.

She laughed at him, as if his pain was the most humorous thing she'd ever encountered. This had to be Mórgana, the one whom Merlin had warned him about. Similar to his sister Myrgwen in appearance, yet an evil lurked in the depths of this woman's heart beyond what he could fathom.

His head throbbed and his throat went dry. He grabbed the handle of the blade and pulled, but it wouldn't budge.

Mórgana kept laughing until the apparition of another woman stepped from the fog, this one wearing a cloak of alabaster linen. She approached Arthur, placed her hands upon his shoulders, and offered up a simple prayer. It was Myrgwen!

By God's bright and righteous name,
I bind protection unto Arthur today:
Against all spells and wiles,
Against all hurts and guiles,
Against wizard's evil snares,

Against wounds and harmful prayers.
Protect him, O Christ of the Three!

Mórgana screeched and pulled out a long, curved fang. She held it aloft until green flame began to course up and down its length, then she jabbed it at Myrgwen.

But the instant the fang touched Myrgwen, there was a burst of light and Mórgana was thrown backward.

The vision of both women faded, replaced by Gorlas in his armor. The man's swarthy face glared at him, his bald pate and unkempt beard only added to the scorn emanating from the man.

"High King? Hah!" Gorlas yelled. "You're just the wart of a pig, and your mother will be mine, do you hear?"

Arthur pulled harder on the blade.

Gorlas leaned over, his lips quivering and his teeth strangely lengthening. Fur grew on his face, and he loomed taller, growing stronger until the werewolf stood before Arthur once more.

Arthur heard shouts in the distance.

The werewolf howled and lunged.

Arthur pulled on the blade with all his might. And it budged.

The beast's claw swiped at him, and Arthur spun to the side, keeping one hand on the hilt. When the werewolf reared back for another strike, he pulled harder, straining with his back, arms, and legs. Every muscle that he had been gifted with strove together to free the blade.

Aaghh!

And with a great sucking and cracking noise, the blade came loose.

Blue fire instantly erupted from the Stone.

The werewolf reached through the flames with a great, bloody claw.

Arthur, unused to the weight of this blade, swung and missed.

While he was off-balance, the werewolf grabbed him and pulled him upward, one claw clutching Arthur's torso, and the other clamped around his sword arm, immobilizing it.

Arthur yelled helplessly as he struggled to free himself.

The beast pulled Arthur toward its open jaws and jagged teeth.

Arthur froze, knowing this was the end. All he had tried to accomplish had failed, and there was nothing he could do. The beast was too terrifyingly strong, and Arthur's struggle was over. Like Dwin, he would die.

Death ... His family had died here.

Now he would join them, and Myrgwen would make a cairn for him too, and all the long years she would weep over it and his useless death.

At least —

But instead of ripping Arthur to pieces, the beast screamed and roared, pivoting to reveal Merlin, Caygek, and Bedwir with spears jammed into its back.

The werewolf loosed Arthur's sword arm and reached back at the three men.

"Now!" shouted Merlin.

Arthur swung — cutting off the hand that held him captive in the air.

Arthur fell to his feet on the other side of the Stone and crouched, preparing to strike again.

The creature looked at the bleeding stump of his hairy arm in mute shock.

Arthur lifted the sword, brought it back as far as he could, and swung again. This time the great arc of the gleaming blade sliced through the werewolf's neck.

The creature's head fell down upon the flaming surface of the Stone, bumped off, and rolled to the ground. The smell of burnt fur, flesh, and blood filled the air.

And still the creature's body was alive! It leaned over on its stump, lurching, and its remaining claw attacked, swiping blindly toward Arthur's throat.

Arthur stepped to the side and shoved the blade into the beast's belly, ripping it open.

"*Die!*" Arthur yelled. "*Die, you spawn of hell!*"

The body fell to the side, twitching.

"Ard Righ! Ard Righ!" Arthur heard all around him. "High King! High King!"

Arthur glanced upward, and through his haze of weariness and desperate relief at the werewolf's death, he saw that nearly a hundred armed villagers had gathered to watch, their torches lighting up the pasture.

And they were all cheering.

"Why are they calling me the High King?" Arthur asked. "How do they know?"

"You've pulled your father's sword from the Stone," Merlin said, looking at the blade with a strange delight in his eyes. "In their eyes that means you're the High King."

"But I'm already — "

"Your warriors know, yes, everyone needs to embrace your kingship and swear fealty to you. That time has truly come."

Merlin put an arm around Arthur and pulled him toward the crowd, raising a hand to get their attention. "You have declared this man to be High King because he has pulled the sword from the Stone, but what you don't know is that Vortigern and Vortipor are dead, and this is Arthur, the son of High King Uther, and rightful heir of not only the sword, but of the High Kingship itself."

"Arthur! Arthur! High King!" they shouted, and hope made their voices all the stronger.

Then a great gust of wind suddenly swept the field, and Arthur and Merlin held on to each other lest they topple over. The trees all bent, and their dry leaves were shorn loose and filled the air with dust and debris.

And just as the wind eased, someone at the back of the crowd began to scream.

The people panicked and scattered. A small contingent of wolf-heads had attacked the rear of the gathering, leaving at least one man bloody and broken.

There were six of them in all, and they ran at Arthur with astonishing speed.

Caygek and Bedwir ran in front, their spears ready. Merlin backed away, assessing the situation, yet had his own spear poised to attack.

Four of the wolf-heads ran at top speed toward Arthur, but then jumped over him at the last moment and landed behind.

Arthur spun and flashed his new blade out, but the wolf-heads were out of reach.

Instead of attacking, the creatures brought out a great leather sling with four straps, rolled the Stone inside it, and ran off with it at top speed.

Arthur, Caygek, and Bedwir chased them, but were too slow. Soon they had to give up. Arthur heard a man yell from behind and turned in time to glimpse the remaining two wolf-heads running off into the darkness with an unconscious figure between them.

Fear stabbed Arthur's heart. His father's spear lay shattered on the ground.

Arthur collapsed to his knees, turned his head upward, and yelled with what little breath he had until his voice was nearly gone.

"Merlin-n-n—!"

CHAPTER 36

REVELATIONS

The long walk back to the site of the original battle on the shore of the marsh was the most painful journey Arthur had ever made. Dwin was dead, and Merlin, the only father he'd ever known, was taken captive.

And now he had to tell Natalenya, Taliesin, and Tinga of his failure to protect Merlin. He had saved Arthur's life, and Arthur had failed him. Why had Arthur been so intent on stopping the four wolf-heads when he knew that there were two more behind him? Merlin had been left to fight them alone.

And though he had pulled the blade from the Stone, it was no consolation for the great loss he felt in his heart. He'd throw the exquisite blade away in an instant if he could trade it for Merlin's freedom. He'd give up the High Kingship. Anything. He didn't even care what the villagers said about him, and their cheers thrashed his heart like a mourner pounding on a tombstone.

And so now when he, Caygek, and Bedwir approached the

wagon where Natalenya and the others hid, he had no words. What he saw when he came in view of the wagon made it even worse, for Gogi lay near, bleeding and groaning, with Natalenya, Taliesin, and Tinga caring for him.

A prone wolf-head, its neck twisted sideways, lay next to Gogi.

"He saved us!" Natalenya said through her tears. "It jumped on him from behind, and they fought, and ..."

"Gogi!" Arthur called, kneeling down and surveying the man's injuries. His beard was covered in blood, and Arthur moved aside the thick, white braids. It was bad, with his neck critically mangled. It appeared the wolf-head had tried to shred his throat, and only Gogi's beard had saved him. But there was so much blood, and the wound raw and open ... How could — ?

"Where's ... wem Wengis?" Gogi asked, gasping. "Gweni ... Melwas —!"

Only then did Arthur look to the water and see Gogi's son and two daughters rowing toward them in an abandoned boat. Myrgwen was with them, and she looked on forlornly from the back bench.

"Father! "Gwenivach called, a hidden scream strangling her words.

Gwenivere's face was ashen.

When the boat was close enough, the girls jumped into the water, slogged to shore, and ran up the bank to fall to their knees next to their father's torn body.

Gogi tried to sit up, but could not.

The mounted warriors returned, then, their horses clopping out of the darkness and halting on the edge of the battlefield.

"You've killed him!" Melwas yelled, shaking a finger at Arthur.

"He wasn't supposed to fight, he — "

Melwas slammed a fist into Arthur's face.

He fell back, staggering as a blinding pain shot through his skull. Tripping, he fell onto Gogi's legs, the sword from the Stone trapped under his hip.

Hands gripped Arthur's throat and began to choke him.

"You Brythons! You're always killing us!"

Arthur grabbed the man's wrists and pushed unsuccessfully.

Melwas's thumbs pressed into Arthur's windpipe.

Arthur kicked and lashed out, but the attack was so sudden, he wasn't —

The stars faded and Arthur began to black out.

Melwas released his grip, screaming. A flurry of motion passed in front of Arthur's blurred vision as Caygek and Bedwir's voices filled the air.

Arthur coughed and tried to catch his breath.

"Let me go! *Midga tiwagged stoulyer!*"

Arthur sat up with Myrgwen's help, and he held on to her arm while she looked sorrowfully on.

Melwas struggled between Caygek and Bedwir, and he was so violent that he slipped from Caygek's grip and smashed Bedwir in the gut, then turned and ran.

"I'll get you, Arthur!" he yelled. "I'll stick your head on a pike, I will!"

Gogi groaned between them and tried to sit up again.

Caygek came and, with Arthur's help, rolled Gogi to his side. The big man spit out gobs of thick blood. "Arthur," he said, choking, "Take care ... o' my daughters. Melwas ... is too hateful ... ya know ... he ..."

"Father," Gwenivere said, her voice thick with greif, "You're going to get better. We won't leave you!"

"I'm so sorry," Arthur said. "I shouldn't have ..."

"Quiet!" Gwenivere yelled, her chin quivering and her teeth bared.

Gogirfan sneezed. With a great strangling, sucking noise, the giant died, his body falling limp and his eyes losing the light of life.

Gwenivere wailed and held on to her father's belt, shaking him as if to wake him.

"Do you forgive me?" Arthur asked.

"I'll never forget this. Never forgive you."

"Do you hate me?"

She spit at him. "Yes. Ever and always."

"Only me?"

"Yes and *yes* and *yes!*"

Arthur swore that until the day of his death he would never forgot the cruelty of her words.

Gwenivach lifted up her father's head and kissed his cheek.

Culann arrived then, his boots crunching tentatively on the gravel. With wide eyes, he placed a hand on Gwenivere's shoulder.

"I'm sorry."

She looked up and blinked at him through her tears.

"It's my fault," Arthur said. "I never should have gotten him involved."

But no one responded, and Arthur was left alone to his thoughts, a black leech of guilt sucking at his soul.

"Arthur ..." Natalenya said, breaking the silence. "Where's your father?"

Arthur wanted to hide. What could he say?

Natalenya stood and took hold of his shoulders. *"Where's Merlin?"*

He hugged her while his own tears began to flow.

"Is he ... is he ...?" she asked, her voice barely a whisper.

"No. He's not dead. But he was taken captive by wolf-heads. I ... I'm so sorry."

"Dear and Holy God ... have mercy," she prayed, her words trailing off as sobs overtook her and made her whole body shake.

Arthur locked gazes with Taliesin, and saw fear mixed with exhaustion there. Tinga had fallen asleep in the boy's arms, and he haltingly stroked her hair.

"You mean Tas isn't coming back?"

"We will pray," Arthur said, making every word a vow, "and though I don't know when or how, I promise you I'll find him. I'll bring him back."

Merlin moaned. The world hurt, that was all he knew. Every blasted, wretched part of it ached. What he wanted was to go back to sleep where the clouds spun in ethereal colors while glowing angels held his hands, guiding him along paths of serene beauty and flowing waters. Fruit grew there in abundance and he longed to eat of it, but their luscious, shiny ovals were always just out of reach.

And now with the vision completely faded, his back hurt, and something painful was pressing at his head. He tried to shift his legs, but they felt twisted and numb.

"Struggle, Merlin ... yes, struggle," said a woman's voice. "But it is quite useless, and there *is* no escape."

Merlin turned toward the voice and opened his eyes. He lay in a dank-smelling cave lit by a smoking torch. Before him stood Mórgana, his half sister, her eyes aflame with an unholy delight. He fought to sit up but his legs — tightly bound — thumped into a tripod supporting a large cast-iron pot that hung amidst a pile of ashes and half-burnt logs. Merlin's wrists were also tied.

"It is time for you to weep, my bardic brother, for all the plans of your enemy have come to complete fruition."

Merlin spit out a few small pebbles that had found their way into his mouth. "It's over," he said. "You lost the battle and now your werewolf is dead."

Mórgana laughed, and the voices of three men joined in from behind her. Merlin blinked and saw Mórganthu — his old nemesis — now old and wrinkled. Another was Loth, whose presence here in Bosventor shocked Merlin. The two had fought atop King Atle's mountain temple in the northern lands of darkness, and Merlin truly thought him dead. How could he be here?

The third man's hooded face could not be seen from where he stood in shadow. Shorter than Loth, he was nonetheless strong and had a dangerous-looking sword strapped to his hip.

The mocking laughter continued, louder and louder, as if Merlin had spoken some astounding joke.

Finally, Mórgana kicked him in the chin, knocking his head back. His whole skull rang, making a tender spot on the right side hurt. That's where one of the two wolf-heads had cracked him with a club.

"Did you think, my dear Merlin," Mórgana said, sneering, "that you and Arthur came to Bosventor of your own will? No, you were driven here like goats to the slaughter. Oh … and I really care nothing about the outcome of the battle, or the ultimate fate of my puny werewolf. He deserves his death for impiously flouting my commands. You see, the entire goal was for either you or Arthur to survive … and to force you by my careful plotting to pull the sword from the Druid Stone. *Nothing else mattered.*"

The Stone! Merlin had forgotten all about it since the wolf-heads had attacked him. He had been proud when Arthur pulled the sword out. It was by right the lad's blade, and it was of such fine workmanship that Merlin had always wanted to retrieve it. His father had made it, after all, and given it to Uther.

But now a new thought struck him. Had Arthur, by removing the blade, somehow revived the Stone? His stomach twisted.

"I see the confusion on your face, dear brother, so let me clear things up a bit."

"Don't listen to her," came a voice from behind Merlin. "She's been telling me lies ever since — "

"Quiet!" Mórgana shouted. "I will not have such insolence from a monk."

Merlin rolled onto his back and turned his head to see who had spoken, and the sight filled him with both joy and sorrow.

"Dybris?" Merlin exclaimed as a familiar, grim face peered at him from a dark corner of the cave. Dybris was the monk who had brought Garth to the moor sixteen years ago and had helped fight Mórganthu and destroy the Stone. But Dybris was in poor shape, now, with his right eye was badly swollen, and an infected gash marred the skin on his neck.

If Merlin were free, he could have hugged the man. "What are you — ?"

"This part of the cave is my home, and I was taken prisoner yesterday."

And it was true. This must be the storage cave behind the old, burned-down abbey. Garth had once bragged to Merlin about sneaking in here and pilfering a few snacks from the barrels. Merlin had admonished him, sure, but the boy had been proud of it. How he ever got past the locked door, Merlin never knew.

Dybris struggled, but his feet were tightly bound with rope, and his arms were tied behind his back.

"And so, my lucky prisoners, behold the Druid Stone in its last, final glory!"

Mórganthu struck his staff at a dark spot of the cave. A blue flame exploded from the Stone, which had lain hidden there. But there was something different about the Stone now, for it was larger than Merlin remembered it and its surface was no longer a weird mixture of black and silver. No, it was a translucent blend of weird, swirled colors: the black of coal, the green of algae, and the white of grub worms.

And something moved inside of it. Squirming. Writhing. Twisting. Humming.

It was alive!

"Ah, what joy to see the horror on your face, dear brother! For what has long been concealed inside the Stone is now hatching. Your error, and everyone else's, was thinking it a Stone, for it was never such. *It is an egg.* And from its glorious crust shall be born twins that shall terrorize the earth and bring ultimate power to the Druids."

At these words the humming increased until Merlin felt the stone floor beneath him vibrate and shake.

Mórgana knelt, placed her hands lovingly upon its pulsing surface, and began to sing.

O hatch thou, my master's drakes; Now break forth, ye flaming snakes.
Hewn of rock — the Voice's bud, cleft from stone — with thirst for blood!
Speed thy birth, my awful drakes; Split thy shell, ye ghastly snakes.
Break the bones — as dreadful beast; Crack and kill — for frightful feast!

O come thou, my fearsome drakes; Take and rule, ye blazing snakes.
Brood of wind — with brutal sting; Spawn of night — to slay the king!

But as her voice rose in ecstatic singing, the Stone calmed and ceased to vibrate. The itching hum fell away, as if whatever lay hidden in the Stone were listening intently. "Your sword, dear brother, prevented these two from hatching — but now that the blade has been removed by a hand that was able to claim it properly, they will come forth. Watch and tremble!"

Merlin couldn't take his eyes off of the egg, for she spoke the truth. Under her hands the shell began to crack, quiver, and convulse. Then with a jerk that surprised even Mórgana, a small section broke away and slipped to the floor. The scaly nose of a creature pushed through the hole, bubbles forming in the green, gelatinous slime that spewed forth as the creature breathed in and exhaled for the first time.

Merlin watched in horror, his heart beating so hard that it would surely burst.

The creature fought against the shell and finally broke through, its entire head slipping out into the cold air of the cave.

It was a lizard ... a dragon!

The skin was white, it had curved horns like a goat, and the tips of its teeth were sharper than needles. But there was something odd ... the dragon was missing one of its four longest fangs, and where the tooth had been there was only an uneven scar. The blade that Merlin had thrust into the Stone must have cut it off.

Soon, the rest of its snakelike body slipped from the egg.

A sulfurous cloud belched outward, and Merlin almost choked on the stench.

For the dragon's size, the creature had small arms and legs, each ending in a claw-like hand. The dragon was six feet long from the tip of its tail to the curve of its wickedly sharp fangs. On its back lay a set of scaled wings, folded now and sodden with slime.

Mórgana began petting it.

"Poor dragon ... you've been through a lot, haven't you? Now to birth your brother."

She reached into the egg and searched amongst the slime.

"Where has your brother gone?" she shrieked. "There were two here ... a white dragon and a red one. But — but — "

Loth bent down and turned the egg on its side, emptying it. "He's nay here. Are ya sure you weren't imagining it? Could you have misunderstood the Voice?"

"NO!" she screamed, and struck him in the face.

Loth fell backward with the smoking outline of Mórgana's handprint on his cheek. "Th-then ... perhaps the blade slew 'im, and his body dissolved."

"That must be it," Mórgana said, scowling. "But ultimately it is no matter. This was the larger, and shall soon be strong enough for all of our purposes."

Mórganthu stepped near, smiling as he stood over the dragon while shaking his druid stick with all its tinkling strings of little seashells. "But now — but now the dragon needs its first meal, does it not?"

"Yes it does. I had almost ... forgotten, shall we say."

Mórgana stood and glared at Merlin and Dybris.

"You, dear brother — along with the foolish monk — shall be the dragon's very first meal. This doom of yours was requested by the Voice and I have endeavored to deliver you both. Yes, a tasty snack!"

The man in shadow handed a wooden bucket to Loth, who poured its contents on Merlin's legs, torso, and head. "A wee bit o' sheep's blood to whet the appetite." The liquid was sticky and rancid, making Merlin gag and struggle against his ropes.

Next he coated Dybris with the blood and then laughed at them. "We must encourage proper feedin' for the little one, now mustn't we?"

"We'll retire now and leave you to your meal," Mórgana said. "I don't expect to find you here in the morning." And with that, she, Loth, the hooded man, and Mórganthu climbed up a stone ledge and out of the cave. Behind them they closed a stout door and slid a bar in place, locking Merlin and Dybris in. The footsteps of the four echoed as they strode down the far passage.

The dragon lifted its head, opened its silver eyes, and stared at them. From its nostrils flashed a small green flame. The dragon opened its razored jaws in salivating anticipation and gave out a purring hum.

Merlin froze as the creature began crawling closer.

CHAPTER 37

BAPTISM OF FIRE

Merlin struggled as the dragon slid closer — nose sniffing and tongue licking at the trail of foul-smelling blood Loth had left behind. All the time, a humming pulsed from its white throat, and its strange, silver-flecked eyes focused on Merlin's face.

"Dybris!" Merlin yelled, "Help!"

"Sing," Dybris said, twisting and rolling toward Merlin.

"What?"

"Sing!"

Merlin sang, quavery at first, but then stronger as he saw the dragon lift its head and pause its forward motion. The song was an old lay, taught to him by Colvarth, about a young king from the fens of Ekenia whose bride had vanished on a cold, blustery night. The man searched for her for a year and a day, but never found her. It was a sad song, and though Merlin didn't know why he chose it, he was glad to have something to sing, for the dragon completely stopped in order to appraise him.

Stretching its neck out, the creature twitched its nose as if it were sniffing the tune floating through the air. "THOU SINGEST … WELL," the dragon said, its deep voice vibrating like a drum.

Merlin kept singing as Dybris slid closer, feetfirst.

The dragon's pupils narrowed as it studied them.

"BUT WE MUST EAT …"

Merlin's heart convulsed in his chest and would barely let the words be sung.

The dragon opened its jaws, a humming hiss escaping from deep within its throat, and the long teeth shone in the torchlight.

"It's not working!" Merlin yelled, rolling backward until a sharp rock on the floor of the cave jabbed painfully into his spine, halting him.

"I'm sorry!" Dybris said, scooting closer.

The dragon lunged forward — toward Merlin's defenseless middle.

Merlin flinched just as Dybris lashed out with his feet, kicking the dragon in the head and knocking it to the side.

The dragon rolled, screaming and hissing in frustration.

Merlin swiveled his feet toward the beast and bent his knees, prepared to strike.

"Keep him busy!" Dybris said. "I've almost got a hand loose …"

The dragon spun, jerked its head in rage, and then lunged at the monk.

Merlin kicked, missing the creature's head but knocking its front legs out from under it.

The dragon fell, clunking its chin on the ground. It turned on Merlin, snarling.

"I've got a hand loose!" Dybris yelled.

"Stop talking!" Merlin said, "I can see!"

"You can?"

"Long story." Sweat began to pour down Merlin's face as he kicked again, this time slamming the creature in the snout and knocking it back against the cave wall.

"Jesu help us!"

The dragon shook its head and reared up, balancing on its hind legs and tail, with its still-damp and weak wings spread out as well.

Merlin tensed, ready to strike back with his feet.

But the dragon took in a great breath, swelling its snake-like chest to twice the size, and let forth a powerful stream of green fire.

The flames engulfed his legs, and Merlin started to scream—until he lifted his knee-high boots to block the torrent, dispersing the flames and decreasing the pain. The thick leather soles blocked most of the heat, protecting him. Still, he could feel the flames flicking at the sides of his boots, the ropes, and his breeches, causing acrid steam from the sheep's blood to singe his nose.

Merlin gritted his teeth as the heat leaked through the leather and the pain approched excruciating. Then with a whoosh, the fire went out and the dragon fell back, out of breath. If the creature had been larger and able to produce more flame, Merlin would have been roasted alive.

Dybris now had his other hand free and, reaching past Merlin, he grabbed one of the tripod's wooden poles that held up the cast-iron pot. Pulling it loose, the pot crashed to the ashes below.

With one hand Dybris swung the narrow end toward the dragon to keep it back.

The creature hissed, its forked tongue flicking up and down angrily.

Merlin rolled and held his bound hands up to Dybris, who began picking blindliy at the knot with his free hand while keeping the dragon at bay with the makeshift staff in the other.

The dragon began swinging its head back and forth, looking for a path to strike, but Dybris countered every move.

"LET US ... EAT!" the dragon roared, and then it bit onto the end of the staff and jerked backward, trying to wrest it from Dybris.

The monk grabbed on with both hands and threw his weight sideways, pulling the dragon off its hind feet. Swinging with all his strength, he threw the dragon and staff against the far wall of the cave.

The dragon slammed to the ground, stunned.

Rolling closer, Merlin held up his hands. "Dybris!"

The monk knelt down and worked desperately at the knots.

Merlin tried to calm his heart, but it banged until his throat felt like it would explode. The rope loosened much too slowly, and there were still three knots to go when the dragon leapt upon Dybris, knocking him to the ground. The beast's claws cut through the monk's robe, and his jaw snapped open, plunging toward Dybris's head.

The monk twisted his face away and reached up, blindly grabbing the monster's throat just below its spiraled horns.

"Help!"

Swinging his body over, Merlin kicked at the dragon, but was only able to hit the tail. In response the beast writhed against the monk's grip, and its snapping jaws drew closer.

Merlin yelled as he used every ounce of strength to pull his hands free from the rope.

The dragon gained leverage by wrapping its tail around Dybris's legs, then used its claws to cut into his arms.

Dybris screamed.

Merlin kicked again at the monster, this time ramming its curved horns.

The beast was knocked to the side, but quickly sucked in a deep breath, turned its head toward Merlin, and let out a stream of green, burning flames.

Merlin's leather boots began to smoke, and the rope caught on fire.

Spinning to the side and away from the dragon's fire, he rolled to put out the flames — but then changed his mind. Lifting his legs against the cave wall, he let the rope burn while straining against it.

"Merlin!" Dybris shouted.

His legs aflame, Merlin gritted his teeth as the pain jabbed into his calves and shins like white-hot pokers.

The dragon had drawn bleeding gashes down Dybris's forearms now, and the monk's hands began to shake as he squeezed at the creature's throat.

The dragon's neck bent forward, closer and closer until white saliva dripped off of its snapping teeth and onto Dybris's forehead.

"*HELP!*"

Merlin yelled as the scorching pain bit into his flesh, all the while straining against the rope around his legs until they broke away and fell smoking to the floor.

Pulling at his right hand, he yanked it out of its rope.

He was free!

Standing, Merlin grabbed the handle of the large, cast-iron pot and swung it at the monster's body.

Thud!

The dragon screamed and its tail went slack, releasing Dybris's legs.

Anger surged through Merlin as he swung the pot back and slammed it into the dragon a second time. "Get off!" he yelled. With a loud crack, the pot broke, and its iron shards scattered across the floor.

The beast went limp as Dybris threw it against the far wall.

Merlin ran to the door and slammed his shoulder into it. But it was solidly barred from the outside, and the stout oak wouldn't budge.

"Untie my legs …" Dybris called. His voice was weak, his arms bleeding, and his hands shaking.

Merlin ran back and undid the knots, keeping one eye on the dragon, which was beginning to coil up and twitch. "We have to escape! Is there a way out farther back in the cave?"

"No, but there *is* a way," Dybris said, pulling himself up onto his feet with Merlin's help. "Grab that barrel and bring it over here."

Merlin didn't understand, but obeyed. Rolling an empty barrel from the side of the cave, he carried it to the fallen tripod and jumbled ashes underneath.

Dybris limped over and accidentally stepped in the bucket of sheep blood. Kicking the foul thing away, he shifted the barrel onto the pile of ashes. Finally, he pointed up.

Merlin looked and saw that there was a wide, soot-covered hole in the low roof right above the barrel, sort of a natural, chimney-like tunnel that angled upward. Why hadn't he realized it before?

"That's how Garth used to sneak in … It leads out."

The dragon straightened itself, lifted its head, and eyed them with a smoldering hatred.

"I'll help you up," Merlin said.

Dybris shook his head. "You first — I have to get something!"

"No."

"There's a ledge … you can pull me up. Go!"

Merlin took one look at the dragon, now slithering toward them, and jumped on top of the barrel.

"THOU … WILT BOTH DIE …" the creature hummed, its eyes like the slits of a grave.

The barrel wobbled beneath Merlin's feet, but it gave him enough height to reach into the darkness of the hole, grab the ledge, and pull himself up.

Dybris was directly behind and boosted Merlin's legs until he knelt upon the ledge. Reaching down, Merlin grabbed the monk's right hand and pulled him up.

But Dybris began to scream.

"It's got me!" he yelled, kicking and thrashing.

Merlin tried to pull up against the combined weight of the monk and the dragon.

Dybris cried out in anguish for help. "Jesu! Sweet Jesu!"

Something broke free, and Dybris suddenly weighed less. Below, there was a crash and the sound of venemous hissing.

Merlin hauled Dybris up to the ledge, and squinted in the darkness to see what had happened.

"He got my boot!" Dybris said, laughing and huffing.

And sure, his left foot was scratched and bare, and the boot that had stepped in the bucket of sheep's blood was gone.

They both looked down, and the barrel had fallen and rolled away. The dragon stared up at them in furious anger, the bloody boot hanging from its mouth.

Merlin smiled and whispered a prayer of thanks.

Something metal lay in Dybris's hands, reflecting the dim torch-light from below.

"What do you have?" Merlin asked.

Dybris held it out to him. "It's Uther's torc. The night the High King died at the druid circle, I found it — just laying in the grass near the Stone. I've kept it secret ever since, waiting for you to return with Arthur. I couldn't leave it behind with the dragon. Is he here? Has Arthur come ...?"

"Yes," Merlin said, amazement and relief washing over him. "Let's get out before that thing finds a way to get up here ..."

"We need to kill it!"

"If we had swords, and if you weren't injured, we might be able to. But Mórgana could come back at any moment, and we need to be away from here as quickly as possible."

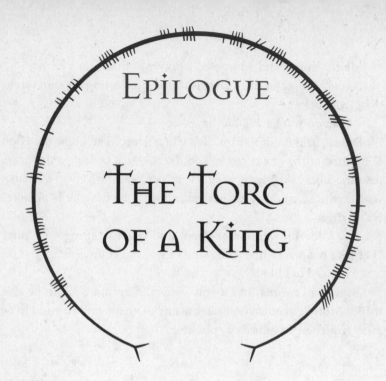

Epilogue

The Torc of a King

Two weeks later

I t was twilight, and Arthur stood on the upper walkway of Dinas Camlin's massive, round feasting hall, staring through one of the many lookouts. Although he gazed past the harbor to the fleeing clouds that had so recently buffeted the bay of Lake Camlin, all he could think about was his thirst.

And it was the kind of thirst that couldn't be quenched by the rains that had fallen upon the isle of Britain. For the first time in many months, a storm had blown in from the western ocean and its showers had drenched the long-parched land in waves of life-giving water.

Arthur sighed.

Gwenivere.

Just the thought of her name sent a longing through his bones.

And if he would just turn around, step toward the railing, and look down, he could see her sitting at the feast near one of the four hearth fires.

But Culann was with her.

And try as he might, Arthur had to sit upon the central dais at the champion's table with Merlin, old Pelles one-ear, and the newly arrived king who had rescued Arthur from the wolf-heads — Bors the Elder, a ruler of Silures and Culann's distant, puffed-up relation.

Besides these, the feast was thick with folk from Kernow, for the word had spread through the countryside that the High King had returned and slain the Great Werewolf along with his plague of wolf-heads. Also, the recent rainfall only increased Arthur's fame, for all the people saw it as a miracle. And truly it was, though none of Arthur's doing, but who would convince them of that?

The real problem for Arthur, however, was that all of these people and their cousin's crusty cat wanted to wish him well. Toast the return of Uther's son to the High Kingship. Speak with him about their petty problems. Keep him so busy that he had no time to do anything but walk past Gwenivere, make idle chit-chat, and then attend to the next interruption.

And worse was that Gwenivere always responded to him with a formality that bordered on coldness. It was clear that she and her sister were still grieving the loss of their father, and rightfully so. But why did she blame *him*? Was it really Arthur's fault? He hadn't asked Gogi to help in the fight!

Nevertheless, perhaps all his focus on Gwenivere was simply an attempt to distract himself from Dwin's death. The man's absence felt to Arthur like his right arm had been cut off, and perhaps all his pining over Gwenivere was just a lot of useless chaff.

Had it been only twelve days since Dwin's burial? And though Arthur had been the one to place the last rock upon the cairn covering his friend's body, he could still hardly believe the man had died. It seemed so unreal, yet the ghastly nightmare lurched after Arthur, ready to catch and smother him.

And the worst was that Arthur would see some sandy-headed young man walking just out of the corner of his gaze, and his heart would quicken. Until, of course, he saw the man's face and knew that he wasn't Dwin.

His best friend was gone, and Arthur was stunned. Absolutely shaken.

And the madness of all this desire and grief was the reason he'd escaped to the upper, circular walkway of the feasting hall. At least here the guards ignored him, what with their duties to watch over the fortress, abbey, village, and surrounding countryside through the many open arches.

Arthur covered his face with his hands, wiped his eyes, and shook his head. Could he conquer the tempest raging inside?

And what of Gwenivere's sister, Gwenivach? If Culann took to the former, couldn't Arthur court Gwenivach? Weren't the girls nearly twins? One like sunshine, and the other the radiance of the moon? Neverthless, their spirits weren't the same. Where Gwenivere was quiet, with a strong streak of serene independence, Gwenivach was petulant and pouty — even if she did follow Arthur around like she was his lost puppy.

All in all, Arthur was just glad to have had Gwenivere so near for the last fortnight. In his anger, Melwas had abandoned his sisters, leaving them alone to build a cairn over Gogi's body — and none of them knew where Melwas had gone. Arthur, Culann, and the others had assisted in transporting Gogi to Inis Avallow, where they held a painful, harrowing burial. Arthur had even delayed Dwin's burial because of it, but the girls were oblivious to his own suffering.

And Gwenivere had refused his offer to pay for a carved stone marker to commemorate Gogi's deeds at the battle of Bosventor.

"We Walkers do not mark our graves," she had said, blinking away her tears. "We walk in this life from under the dappled shadows to the next world — the place where the unknown King reigns over the pool of mysteries. We will never forget the woven story of our father's life and the place of his rending. Neither will this place forget us."

These memories cut him, but just as painful was his initial failure to find his father. Immediately after Gogi's burial, Arthur had led a party of warriors on horseback to try to find Merlin, but nothing could be discovered. And because of the physical needs of Natalenya, the children, and the wounded, Arthur was forced to abandon his search and bring everyone to safety.

And that meant lifting Dwin's body onto the wagon reserved for the stricken. This act almost crushed Arthur's heart, for the man's skin was cold ... cold as the never-sated grave. Yes, Arthur would come back with men to bury all of their fallen comrades, but Arthur couldn't abandon Dwin for so long.

After considering the dangers of the open country, Gwenivere and Gwenivach had chosen to come along to the protective walls of Dinas Camlin. Once there, the good Abbess Trevenna, Natalenya's mother, took the girls under her care, giving the girls words of comfort, truth, and wisdom to help their crushed spirits. Truth that Arthur prayed they nourished still.

Myrgwen had come along as well, but her demeanor unnerved Arthur and made him worry all the more for Merlin's safety. Not only did she refuse to speak, but she stared ahead, unseeing. And when Arthur looked into that one beautiful eye of his sister — a depth of fearful portent lurked there that took his breath away.

At first light they'd prepared a second sortie to find Merlin as well as to bury the fallen — but to everyone's surprise, the bard himself knocked on the gates before they could mount the horses ... even bringing a monk with him!

But their appearance was like prophets of doom, both covered in blood, with wounds and news of a dragon loose upon the land.

Arthur didn't know what to think, even now.

A dragon?

There were tales of such monsters, of course, passed down from ancient times, but no creature of that ilk had entered into the known history of Britain. What was Mórgana up to?

After washing his wounds, receiving fresh clothes, and seeing to his joyful wife and children, Merlin had led the mounted warriors to the entrance of the cave, hoping to catch and kill the dragon.

But when they unbarred its inner door, they found no sign of the beast, even after searching the farthest depths of the cave. In fact, all evidence of Merlin and Dybris's fight with the creature was conspicuously absent as well. Even the shattered iron pot was gone.

Some of the warriors began to doubt the story, but Arthur knew his father better than that.

The man's word was his bond.

And the gouges on Dybris's arms also testified to the encounter.

The feasting hall below became quiet, waking Arthur from his thoughts. Soon a harp began to play, and Arthur recognized his mother's elegant style. It was a beautiful song commemorating the coronation of Aurelianus, who was Arthur's grandfather. He had heard it many times growing up, but never understood the tune's significance to his own life.

But the song also reminded Arthur of the last time he'd heard Natalenya play: at Dwin's funeral. Arthur squeezed his eyes shut, trying to block the images out.

Thankfully, the song ended, and Arthur opened his eyes as a man began to chant — Dybris, the monk, who would be standing in the center upon the dais. The champion's table would also have been cleared away and the chapel's altar placed upon it. The man's words lifted to the upper reaches of the hall.

Sanctus, Sanctus, Sanctus — Dominus Deus Sabaoth.
Pleni sunt caeli et terra gloria tua.
Hosanna in excelsis.
Benedictus qui venit in nomine Domini.
Hosanna in excelsis!

And then a chorus of male and female voices responded by singing it again in British:

Holy, holy, holy is the Lord — the God of mighty warriors.
Heaven and earth are filled with Thy glory.

Hosanna in the highest.
Blessed is He that cometh in the name of the Lord.
Hosanna in the highest!

As Arthur turned to approach the rail to see what Gwenivere was doing, someone climbed the stairs about five paces away.

"Arthur! There you are ..."

It was Merlin, and he had a worried look on his face.

"It's time for your coronation."

Arthur paused.

"Are you coming?"

Sighing, he bowed his head and moved to follow Merlin. Though he knew he had to go through with it, he hated standing in the center and having everyone look at him. The only thing that made him follow was the fact that he would now be allowed to wear the torc of Uther, his birth father. Arthur and Merlin descended the steps while Dybris sang in Latin, followed by the chorus in British:

Sanctus Deus, Sanctus Fortis, Sanctus Immortális, miserére nobis.
Holy God, Holy and Mighty, Holy and Immortal, have mercy on us.

The singing ended as Arthur and Merlin stepped onto the ground floor at the east end of the circular hall. Dybris stood in the center, and Arthur was glad that the man's wounds had healed enough for him to lead the coronation.

There was not one chorus, but two — on the north and south sides of the feasting hall. The north was made up of the abbey's sisters, led by Trevenna. The southern chorus consisted of the abbey's brothers, and these were led by their abbot, Offyd — a monk who'd left Bosventor after the troubles with the Stone.

Arthur and Merlin stood, waiting for their separate cues.

Two boys began snuffing out the large oil lamps that had brightened the room for the feast. While this was done, the people lit small beeswax candles, one from another. The hall darkened and a hush fell over the people.

Dybris nodded to Arthur, and he knew it was time to walk forward.

But before he could step out, someone touched his shoulder — Merlin, the only father Arthur had ever known — and he was smiling with such hope, confidence, and assurance that it seeped and finally swelled into Arthur's own heart.

He could do this. He was made for this, to take the mantle of the High Kingship and, come what may, to do his best.

Arthur grinned back.

Dybris raised his hands; everyone stood and turned to look at Arthur as he stepped forward to walk westward down the candlelit aisle. Garth began to play a martial tune on his bagpipe, and the double-chanters produced an exquisite refrain that filled the hall.

From both sides of the hall came the thrilling sound of drummers.

Everyone's gaze was locked on Arthur, their expressions varying widely. Most of them had hopeful smiles spread across joyful faces. Taliesin was one of these, and he stood on his bench with his mop of hair trembling in excitement. Tinga, who peeked out from behind her older brother, had a radiant smile on her lightly freckled face.

Gwalahad, the son of Chieftain Pelles, was another who smiled. The lad was a little younger than Arthur, with white-blond hair that fairly shone in the dark. And Arthur's warriors were there to support him: Mabon, Percos, Tethion, Ol, and Neb, along with all the others. Near the aisle stood Peredur, his grin contagious.

Until Arthur remembered Dwin's absence. How could he not be here?

Others were dour, with their eyes made almost scary in the shadows of the candlelight. A few were even baleful, and these, he noted, wore finery such that marked them as supporters of Bors the Elder — of a generation that knew nothing of Uther and the good years that characterized his reign.

"... pig-snot," one even dared to whisper, and Arthur winked at the man as he passed. Warriors such as these would have to be won over by deeds — and no mere torc would convince them of Arthur's right to rule.

The bagpipe music swelled, and Arthur's heart began to beat faster with every step.

Then he saw Gwenivere, and his stride almost faltered.

She stood on the left next to Culann, and the man had his arm draped tensely over her shoulder. She looked upon Arthur quizzically, as if he were a wooden puzzle that might be solved and put away in a bag.

Arthur met the challenge of her gaze, but her stare unnerved him and he looked away.

Directly before him in the center of the feasting hall, Dybris opened his arms in greeting, a slightly lopsided smile on his tan face and gentle eyes sparkling in joy above a thick beard.

Arthur stepped up onto the dais and, as instructed prior to the ceremony, kissed the back of the priest's outstretched hand.

Garth finished the tune and expertly cut off the sound of his single drone.

Together, then, Arthur and Dybris knelt before the simple altar and its three candles.

This humble kneeling was meant to represent servitude to God Most High, but for Arthur, it was more than a show. Desperately, he prayed for the strength to lead these people. Their situation was perilous, and great wisdom was needed lest they all meet a swift death at the end of a Saxenow blade or a Pictish spear.

They both rose, and Arthur turned to face the priest.

Dybris reached into a bag at his side and pulled out a copper flask with a wooden plug. Unstoppering it, he decanted a palmful of oil and anointed Arthur on his forehead, cheeks, and bristly chin, all the while chanting:

Kýrie, eléison. Kýrie, eléison. Kýrie, eléison!

And the chorus of voices answered:

Lord, have mercy. Lord, have mercy. Lord, have mercy on us!

At this cue, Merlin began walking down the aisle, holding aloft the torc of Uther mab Aurelianus for all to see. Some in the audience gasped, and Arthur nearly joined them, for though the tale of Dybris keeping the torc secret all these years had spread like honeyed oatcakes throughout the land, this was the first time Arthur had been able to behold it himself.

But that made this moment all the sweeter.

Made of solid gold, the thick braids flashed in the dim light as if the very rays of the sun had been tamed and bent by Merlin's hands. As well, the amethyst eyes of the twin eagle heads sparkled with purple fire so that the combined effect was astonishing.

When Merlin reached the front, he bowed and placed the torc into Dybris's hands.

The monk raised it aloft, and its metalic beauty enthralled Arthur. Was this really happening? Was he about to receive his father's torc? He bit his tongue in anticipation.

"As priest of God Most High," Dybris said, "I solemnly charge you, Arthur mab Uthrelius, with the task of guarding your people, the Britons, against all enemies. Remember well that you are not the High King *of Britain*, but rather *of the Britons*. The land is not yours — rather, it belongs to God first, and is given by Him as a goodly blessing to all His children who tend it."

Dybris paused here and looked heavenward. "Your kingship, then, is a call of protection, not overlordship, and God will bless your reign if you will always remember these truths. Many will whisper in your ear to use your power for selfish gain, but heed them not! The Mighty King over you stands at the door with a great sickle in His hand, and if you but stray He will end your reign as swiftly as He has given it."

Dybris sighed, and then continued.

"So in light of these admonitions, do you, Arthur — son of Uthrelius, son of Aurelianus, son of Constans, and also of the uncorrupted line of Vitalinus — willingly accept this torc of the High Kingship?"

Arthur nodded. "Truly, I do."

Spreading the ends of the torc, Dybris placed it upon Arthur's neck.

The severe weight of it upon his collar surprised Arthur, and it was then that Dybris's fretful words were made manifest to him.

This thing did not mark him for privilege — rather it was a burden that he must bear. The heavy mantle of his father's fallen throne. The mantle of all those that had worn the purple before him.

Arthur let out his breath. Yes, he would try.

Dybris embraced him in congratulations, and then took Arthur's right hand and turned him slowly around in the dais to face all the people. Merlin stepped up and took Arthur's left. Lifting their joined hands together, Dybris and Merlin shouted:

HERE IS YOUR KING!

In silence, the people blew out their candles so that only the three candles on the altar in the very center remained lit.

And then, from the darkness came the shout of a familiar voice. It was Taliesin, standing on a bench, and his words shocked the assembly. "Look! Up there!"

Everyone glanced to where he pointed, but this was behind Arthur, and he had to turn to look out the high central archway that faced westward.

There floated something unlike anything Arthur had ever seen in the sky. It appeared to look like a star falling toward the final glow of the sunset, but it was suspended in the heavens, unmoving, with two tails — one straight, and the other curving away toward the left.

Colvarth had once shown Arthur a scroll with drawings of such celestial portents, and so he knew this was a Dragon Star ... a dread omen that had not been seen during his lifetime.

Fear swam in Arthur's gut until his legs began to shake and his eyesight blurred. The room tilted and Arthur fell upon the hard floor, his arms outstretched before the altar.

There he beheld a vision of every clan and people of Britain gathered together. And all of them — from the youngest peasant to the dusty farmer, from the calloused-handed craftsman to the rotund, vassal king of Lundnisow — all worshiped the Dragon. Yet when they bowed, the white-scaled beast betrayed them and blazed upon their backs the green flames of death. All through the land it burned, and from within the flames, untouched, came the armies of the stocky Saxenow and the painted men of the north — and these took the land as their own and killed the Britons who tried to resist.

Death. Death and destruction.

The souls of many wept, and within the flames a lone woman stood. She was Myrgwen, Arthur's sister, and in a loud voice she called out:

Woe! Woe to Britain!
For the Dragon has come,
and who will save us?

(To be continued in the Pendragon Spiral)

PRONUNCIATION GUIDE

The following helps are for British names, places, and terms and do not apply to Latin. If you find an easy way to pronounce a name, however, feel free to ignore the following. Your first goal is to enjoy the novel, not to become an expert in ancient languages.

Vowels

a	short as in *far,* long as in *late,* but sometimes as in *cat*
e	short as in *bet,* long as in *pay,* but sometimes as in *key*
i / y	short as in *tin,* long as in *bead,* but sometimes as in *pie*
o	short as in *got,* long as in *foam*
u	short as in *fun,* long as in *loom*

Consonants — the same as English with a few exceptions:

c / k	hard, as in *crank,* not like *city*
ch	hard, as in Scottish *loch,* or *sack,* not like *chat*
f	*f* as in *fall,* sometimes *v* as in *vine*
ff	*f* as in *offer*
g	hard as in *get,* not like *George*
gh	soft as in *sigh*
r	lightly trilled when found between two vowels
rh	pronounced as *hr,* strong on the *h* sound
s	as in *sat,* not with a *z* sound

GLOSSARY

Pronunciation Note: The goal is for you to enjoy reading *Merlin's Nightmare*, and so, where possible, easier spellings have been chosen for many ancient words. For instance, the word *gorseth* would more properly be spelled *gorsedd*, with the "dd" pronounced similar to our "th." This is also true of the decision, in some words, to use "k" instead of "c." The goal is readability. A pronunciation suggestion has been provided for each word. Again, please relax about how you say the names. If you are a language purest, then indulge the author, knowing he is well aware of the depth, history, and complexities of the Brythonic and Goidelic languages represented here.

Also, since this spiral of Arthurian stories begins and ends in Cornwall, Cornish has been chosen as a basis for many of the names and places. Though Welsh, Irish, or Scots Gaelic could have each served for this purpose, Cornwall is the nexus of the story line.

Historical Note: Although many of the following explanations are based on history and legend, they are given to aid your understanding of *Merlin's Nightmare* and thus are fictional. If you feel inspired, you can research Roman, Celtic, and Arthurian literature for a deeper appreciation of how they've been uniquely woven into the entire Merlin Spiral series. An asterisk has been placed next to those words that will yield a wealth of information.

Abransva — (ah-BRAWN-sva) The meaning of the word is simply "eyebrow."

Àille Fionnadh — (EYE-la fi-OH-neyg) Natalenya's pet name for Merlin, which Ector teases him with. It means "handsome hair." This is the author's version of the name Elffin*, who was the father of Taliesin in legend. Some think Elffin is based upon Aill Fion*, which means "bright rock."

Allun — (AL-lun) The name of Bosventor's miller in *Merlin's Blade*.

Aquae Sulis* — (OCK-way SUE-liss) The modern day city of Bath*, which includes hot springs and many Roman baths. This city is near to Glevum, and is Vortigern's third-most important city.

Arthur* — (AR-thur) The orphaned son of Igerna and Uther, and heir to the High Kingship. He is being taken care of by Merlin and Natalenya. His sisters are Eilyne and Myrgwen. He is eighteen years old.

Atle/Atleuthun — (AT-lee/at-lee-OOH-thun) The king of Guotodin in the far north that Merlin visited in *Merlin's Shadow*, his fortress was at Dinpelder. He is Gwevian's father and Merlin's grandfather. In legend he is known as King Lleuddun*.

Aurelianus* — (ow-rell-ee-AH-noos) the former High King, Uther's father, and Arthur's grandfather. He slew Vitalinus Gloui to revenge his father's murder.

Bank and Ditch — A simple method of making a fortress harder to attack by digging multiple ditches around it in concentric rings and throwing the dirt up on a bank. Sometimes wooden spikes are placed in the ditches.

Bedwir* — (BED-weer) A former chieftain under Vortigern, he is pledged now to help raise, protect, train, and serve Arthur.

Bélre Cèard — (BEL-rah KAIRGE) This is the "Speech of the Tinsmiths," which Gogirfan, Gwenivere, and Gwenivach speak. As a cant language*, the Walkers use this speech as a secret way of speaking with each other using a twisted form of the common language in Britain. Today it is known as Beurla Reagaird*.

Bors The Elder* — (BOARS) A king of Silures, Kembry, he is a distant relation of Culann.

Bosvenna Abbey — (bos-VENN-ah) An abbey of the Celtic church in Kernow, which was destroyed by fire in *Merlin's Blade*. Bosvenna* (or Bos-menegh) means "the abiding place of monks."

Bosvenna Moor — (bos-VENN-ah) The highland area in central Kernow, covered with forests and marshes. Before the monks came, it was known as Tir Gwygoen, "land of the woodland moor." Today it is called Bodmin Moor* and is cleared for grazing.

Bosventor — (bos-VEN-tore) The village and fortress where Merlin grew up. It was built upon the slopes of the Meneth Gellik mountain six years after the abbey. South of modern-day Bolventor*, Cornwall, an actual iron-age village and fortress existed at this exact location.

Brewodwyn — (breh-WODD-win) Modern-day Broadwoodwidger*.

Brihem — (BRIH-hem) The order of judges within the wider order of the druids. Normally spelled brithem* or brehon*.

Britain — (BRIH-ten) The land occupied by the people who speak various forms of the ancient Brythonic* language south of the River Forth*.

Brittania Prima — (brih-TAN-ee-ah PREEMA) The area of Britain bordering the southern coast, generally south of Lundnisow / London.

Brythanvy — (brith-AHN-vee) The same as modern-day Brittany*, France. This was a Celtic-populated area.

Bysall — (BY-sall) A small coin, usually a ring of brass or iron. *Bysallow* is the plural.

Casva — (COSS-vah) Arthur's black stallion.

Cathures* — (kath-OO-ress) A village of southwest Scotland on the Clyde River that began with the church that Garth planted. Modern-day Glasgow*.

Caygek — (KAY-gek) A former druid who has become one of Arthur's warriors and protectors. He is named Cai* in the Arthurian legends.

Colvarth — (COAL-varth) The former chief bard of Britian; he passed away before the beginning of *Merlin's Nightmare*. His given name is Bledri mab Cadfan, and he is known as Bleheris* in Arthurian literature.

Constans* — (CON-stans) A former High King. He is Arthur's great-grandfather and father to Aurelianus. Murdered by Vitalinus Gloui for the throne of Britain.

Corinium* — (core-IN-ee-um) Modern-day Cirencester*, and a former Roman fortress. This city is near to Glevum, and is Vortigern's second-most important city.

Coynall — (COIN-all) A single-sided coin made of silver. It is worth eight bysallow, and it takes three coyntallow to make one screpall.

Cradelmass* — (crah-DELL-mass) The haughty king of Powys, he is distantly related to Vortigern.

Crennig — (CREN-nigg) A fifth-century roundhouse. They are normally made of wooden timbers staked into the ground to form a circle, but sometimes they are made of stone if it is readily available. The roof is conical and typically woven from thatch. On occasion they are built out in a lake for easier defense. Cren means "circular," or "round." Spelled Crannog* outside of the Merlin Spiral.

Culann — (KULL-lann) One of Arthur's friends who goes journeying with him. He is the son of Llachau, and in legend he is known as Lancelot*.

Derwent* — (dare-WENT) One of the streams that runs through the Nancedefed valley, down a series of falls, and into Lake Derwentlin.

Derwentlin, Lake — (dare-WENT-lin) The lake just north of Dinas Crag. Called the Derwent Water* today.

Deva — (DEH-vah) More properly called Deva Victrix, which is modern-day Chester*, England.

Difnonia — (diff-NO-nee-ah) The kingdom to the east of Kernow, today called Devon*. Ruled by the Roman-established town of Isca Dumnoniorum (modern-day Exeter*).

Dinas Camlin — (DINN-ahs CAM-linn) A large hill fort. Old Pelles is the chieftain, and his grandson is Gwalahad. The fortress has a large, circular, two-story feasting hall. Situated on the western side of a bay fed by the Camel* River. Modern-day Padstow*.

Dinas Crag — (DINN-ahs CRAIG) A rocky hill fort in Rheged, north of Kembry, which protects the Nancedefed valley where Merlin and Natalenya live with Arthur, Taliesin, and Tingada. Merlin's father grew up here, and Merlin's uncle Ector is now the chieftain. Modern-day Castle Crag*.

Dinas Hen Felder — (DINN-as HEN FELL-der) An iron-age hill fort at the site of modern-day Launceston Castle*. In *Merlin's Nightmare* it has been given the name of "Old Watchful." Also known as Dunheved* in later times.

Dinas Marl — (DINN-ahs MARL) An aging fortress that Vortigern is defending against the Saxenow, it is built on an ancient mound around which modern-day Marlborough* sits. "Marl" means "marbled clay," and "bar" means mound, or barrow.

Dintaga — (din-TA-guh) The fortress of Gorlas, King of Kernow. *Dintaga* means "the strangled fortress," and is modern-day Tintagel*. It is on an island separated from the land by a narrow causeway that is inundated with water when the tide comes in.

Dosmurtanlin, Lake — (doss-mur-TAN-lin) A lake north of the village of Bosventor, on the other side of the Meneth Gellik mountain. Legend says that when a portion of the Dragon Star fell, it gouged out the earth, and the water filled it in, forming the lake. *Dosmurtanlin* means "the lake where a great fire came." It is the same as modern-day Dozmary Pool*. Merlin's mother, who was changed by the Stone into a water creature, is confined to this lake.

Dowrtam River — (DOUR-tamm) Known today as the Tamar*, it flows south past Dinas Hen Felder and spills into the ocean at modern-day Plymouth*.

Dragon Star — The comet that Muscarvel saw in the night sky seventy years before Chapter 1 of *Merlin's Blade*.

Druid* — (DREW-id) The order of priests within the wider order of the druidow. They also carry out the laws as set forth by the Brihem judges.

Druidow — (DREW-i-dow) The plural form of druid, this term can sometimes refer to the wider order of all the druidow, filidow, and Brihem judges combined.

Dubrae Cantii* — (DEW-bray CAN-tie) Dubrae is a city among the Cantii tribe south of Lundnisow. This is the primary area the Saxenow were invading. Some of Uther's warriors came from this area. It is modern-day Dover*.

Dwin — (DWIN) Based on the Arthurian warrior Bradwin, or Bradwen*. His name means "pleasant and agreeable."

Dybris / Dybricius* — the only monk left who still works in the village of Bosventor. He was the one who originally brought Garth, the orphan, with him from Porthloc, a small village on the northern coast of Difnonia. He is known in modern-times as St. Dubricius*.

Dyfed* — (DIE-fed) A kingdom in southwest Kembry.

Dyslan — (DIE-slan) Natalenya's younger brother.

Ector* — (ECK-tor) Merlin's uncle and the chieftain of Dinas Crag. He has traditionally been shown in Arthurian legend as fostering Arthur during his growing-up years. Ector's wife is Eira, and his younger brother is Owain, Merlin's now-deceased father. Ector and his wife are childless.

Eilyne — (EYE-line-uh) The oldest orphaned daughter of Uther and Igerna, and sister to Myrgwen and Arthur. When she was young, she and Myrgwen were pursued by Vortigern and fled into the marsh. No one has seen her since. In the legends, she is Elaine of Garlot*.

Einkorn* — (INE-corn) An ancient form of wheat.

Eira — (EYE-rah) Ector's wife at Dinas Crag, and Merlin's aunt. The word in Welsh means "snow."

Eirish — (EYE-rish) The people from Erin, which is modern-day Ireland.

Elmekow — (EL-meh-cow) A coastal British kingdom southeast of Rheged.

Erin — (ERR-in) The island of Ireland west of Britain.

Ewenna — (ee-WHEN-ah) Gorlas's companion at Dintaga.

Fairyglove — Foxglove*.

Fili* — (FILL-ee) The order of sages and poets within the wider order of the druidow. Filidow is the plural, and they are led by the arch fili.

Flavia Caesariensis — (flah-VEE-ah see-zar-ee-EN-sis) The area of Britain north of Lundnisow / London, westward to the border of wales, and as far northward as modern-day Manchester.

Fodor — (FOE-door) An envoy of Vortigern who carries news to Dinas Crag. He wears a gaudy hat and is always concerned with knowing one's proper ancestry.

Fossa — (FOSS-ah) A Roman road leading from Lindum (Lincoln*) all the way down to Isca Difnonia (Exeter*). Currently called the Fosse Way*, the road was built up by digging up the soil at its side to form a ditch. *Fossa* means "ditch" in Latin.

Fowaven River — (foe-AY-vehn) The stream that lies east of the village of Bosventor. It generally runs southward through Bosvenna Moor and, fed by many springs, it soon becomes a river, known today as the Fowey*.

Fowavenoc — (foe-AY-vehn-ock) A major town on the southern coast of Kernow where the Fowaven River spills into the sea. Modern-day Fowey*.

Gaff — (GAFF) Goffrew's female pup

Gana/Ganieda* — (GAH-nuh / gah-NYE-dah) Merlin's half sister, who became Mórgana in *Merlin's Shadow*. She is the daughter of Mônda and granddaughter to Mórganthu.

Garth/Garthwys* — (GARTH / GARTH-wiss) An orphan who used to live at the abbey with Dybris when he was young. His father, Gorgyr, was a fisherman at Porthloc in Difnonia, and so Garth was raised on the sea.

Gladius* — (GLA-dee-oos) A stout Roman-style sword, generally of medium length.

Glevum* — (GLEH-vuhm) The Roman fortress of Glevum, and the seat of Vortigern's kingdom. Modern-day Gloucester*.

Goffrew — (GOFF-rue) Ector's hound who had two puppies, Gruffen and Gaff.

Gogirfan Gawr* — (go-GIRR-fan GOW-er) A giant tinker who is the father of Gwenivere and Gwenivach. He is a Walker, and is descended from the first peoples to settle the island of Britain. Some scholars think that the name Gogirfan is related to the word for "crow." Gawr means "giant."

Gorlas* — (GORE-lass) The crazed king of Kernow, whose fortress is Dintaga. He and Uther were rival suitors for Igerna's love. In the last third of the book, it can be said that he is a merging of the traditional Gorlas* and the Arthurian character Garlwlwyd*.

Gorseth — (GORE-seth) A meeting place of the druidow, typically denoted by a circle of stones. In ancient times it would have been spelled gorsedd, the double-d pronounced like our *th* sound. In the Merlin Spiral it is spelled, like many other words, phonetically.

Gorseth Cawmen — (GORE-seth CAW-men) The stone circle northeast from the village of Bosventor. Literally means "the meeting place of giant stones." On modern maps it is shown as the Goodaver Stone Circle*, though the Merlin Spiral describes it as having larger stones.

Gourvlyth* — (goor-VLITH) An ancient word for werewolf.

Grannos* — (GRAN-nos) The Celtic god of water and healing. Represented by Saturn in the night sky. The Latin form of the name is Grannus*.

Gruffen — (GRUFF-en) Goffrew's male pup

Guotodin* — (goo-OH-toe-din) The northernmost Brythonic kingdom. It was ruled by Atle when Owain, and then Merlin, visited, and it lies between the two walls built by the Romans, just south of the land of the Prithager. Its principal cities are Dineidean (modern-day Edinburgh*), and the fortress of Dinpelder (which was destroyed by Necton and his Picti at the end of *Merlin's Shadow*).

Gwalahad — (GWALL-a-had) Pelles's grandson, he lives at Dinas Camlin. In legend he is known as Galahad* (or Gwalchavad* in Welsh).

Gwenivach — (GWEN-ee-vach) Daughter of Gogirfan, fraternal twin to Gwenivere, and sister to Melwas. She is a Walker, and has reddish-blonde hair. Nowadays, her name is more typically spelled Guinevach*. Since Gwenivach is the younger twin, she has "-vach" on the end of her name, meaning "the lesser."

Gwenivere — (GWEN-ee-vere) Daughter of Gogirfan, fraternal twin to Gwenivach, and sister to Melwas. She is a Walker, and has blonde hair. Nowadays, her name is more typically spelled Guinevere*. Since Gwenivere is the elder twin, she has "-vere" on the end of her name, meaning "the greater."

Gwevian — (GWEV-ee-ahn) Merlin's mother, the daughter of King Atle. She supposedly drowned in Lake Dosmurtanlin when Merlin was young, and her body was never found. Merlin discovered her alive at the end of *Merlin's Blade*, changed by the Stone into a water creature to serve it when it was in the lake. She is now the Lady of the Lake*, and a merging of the legends of Vivian* and St. Theneva*.

Gwyneth — (GWIN-eth) A major kingdom in northwest Kembry. It includes the isle of Inis Môn, which is sacred to the druidow. Spelled Gwynedd* in Welsh.

Habrenaven River — (ha-bren-AY-vehn) The modern-day Severn* River. In later Welsh, the word is Hafren*, which comes from the name of a legendary British princess who drowned in the river.

Hand — A measurement for horses approximating four inches.

Harp of Britain — The harp that has been passed down through the ages from one chief bard to the next, now possessed by Merlin as given him by Colvarth before he died. The druidow desire to take it back.

Hen Crogmen — (HENN CROG-men) Modern-day Stonehenge*, which some scholars think was originally a very large roundhouse. Etymological sources say that Stonehenge literally means "stone gallows," thus Hen Crogmen is a Brythonic way of saying "the Old Stone Gallows."

Hengist* — (HEN-gist) The co-leader of the Saxenow army along with his brother, Horsa. They have invaded Britain and are slowly taking over the southeast.

Horsa* — (HORSE-ah) The co-leader of the Saxenow army along with his brother, Hengist. They have invaded Britain and are slowly taking over the southeast.

Igerna* — (ee-GERR-nah) The deceased wife of Uther, she is Vortigern's sister, and therefore descended from Vitalinus Gloui, a former High King of Britain. Her children are Eilyne, Myrgwen, and Arthur. Gorlas vied with Uther for her hand in marriage.

Inis Avallow — (IN-iss AV-all-ow) The largest island in the marsh outside Bosventor. It has an old tower and broken-down fortress surrounded by an ancient apple orchard. Legend says this was built by a pilgrim and tin merchant known only as the Pergiryn. Its name means "Island of Apples," and is known in legend as Avalon*.

Jesu Christus* — (HEY-soo KRIS-toos) Latin for Jesus Christ.

Kedivor — (keh-DIH-vor) The eldest son of Vortipor.

Keelos — (KEE-los) One of Gorlas's warriors. Literally, "gray wolf."

Kembry — (KEM-bree) The land stretching from the Kembry Sea in the south to the isle of Inis Môn in the northwest. It is made up of multiple kingdoms. Modern-day Wales*.

Kernow* — (KER-now) The kingdom that lay on the peninsula of land in southwest Britain, between Lyhonesse and Difnonia. Ruled by Gorlas from his fortress, Dintaga, which is on an island on the northern coast. Kernewek is their local dialect of Brythonic. Modern-day Cornwall*.

Keswick forest — (kess-WICK) The forest just north of the Lake Derwentlin.

Legatus* — (leh-GAH-tus) The leader of a legion*, made up of approximately ten cohorts*, which in turn were made up of approximately six groups of eighty to one hundred men, each named a century*, around five thousand men total. Vortigern's grandfather, Vitalinus Gloui* was the Legatus stationed in Glevum*.

Loch Obha* — (LOCH OBE-ah) Modern-day Loch Awe in Scotland.

Londinium* — (lun-DIN-ee-um) A city taken by the Romans in AD 43 and named Lundnisow by the Britons. Because of its river and harbor, they made it the capital of their provinces in Britain. Modern-day London*.

Loth — (LOTH) The son of King Atle, brother to Gwevian, and Merlin's uncle. He was saved from death by Mórgana at the end of *Merlin's Shadow*.

Loyt — (LOYT) The abbot of Dinas Crag. He had formerly been a monk in Bosventor while Merlin was growing up.

Luguvalium* — (lug-oo-VALL-ee-um) A hillfort north of Kembry where Urien is king. Modern-day Carlisle*.

Lyhonesse — (ly-OHN-ess) A thin peninsula of land stretching even farther out to sea from the western tip of Kernow. It is sparsely settled by the Eirish. The name literally means "the lesser." Known as Lyonesse* in legend.

Mabon* — (MAY-bonn) A guard who serves Vortigern at Glevum, and formerly served High King Uther. His name can be found in the poem *Pa Gur Yv Y Porthaur**.

Magister* — (ma-JEE-stare) Literally "master," which is the title Tregeagle has adopted as the appointed official over the tin mining region around Bosventor. A holdover from the Roman empire.

Mancunium — (man-koo-KNEE-um) Modern-day Manchester*.

Marrok* — (MARR-ock) One of Gorlas's warriors.

Mawken — (MAW-ken) Gorlas's captain. Literally, "prince of wolves."

Melwas* — (MELL-was) Gwenivere and Gwenivach's brother, and the son of Gogirfan.

Meneth Gellik Mountain — (MEN-eth GELL-ick) The mountain upon whose southern side the village of Bosventor is built. Halfway up on a plateau sits a fortress and beacon, which is familiarly known to the villagers as the "Tor." The mountain is over 1,100 feet above sea level, its tallest point is 100 feet above the marsh, and it is the third-highest in Kernow. Today it is known as Brown Gelly*. Literally, "The Brown Mountain." Lake Dosmurtanlin is situated just to the north.

Merlin* — (MER-lin) The son of a village blacksmith / swordsmith. His face was badly scratched by wolves at the age of nine when he tried to protect his younger sister, Gana. This also scarred his eyes, half-blinding him. His eyesight was healed at the end of *Merlin's Blade*, but his scars remain. At the beginning of *Merlin's Nightmare* he is thirty-four years old and is living near the fortress of Dinas Crag. The Latin form of his name is Merlinus.

Molendinar* **River** — (mow-lenn-DIN-are) A river near which Garth started his ministry to the Picti. This ministry grew to become the village of Cathures*, and eventually became the modern city of Glasgow*.

Mórdred — the son of Mórgana and Loth.

Mórgana — (mor-GAH-nuh) Merlin's half sister, who used to be named Ganieda. She is the daughter of Mônda and granddaughter to Mórganthu.

Mórganthu — (more-GAN-thoo) The arch druid, and son of Mórfryn. He is grandfather to Ganieda, who now goes by Mórgana. His name is a merging of the name Mórgant with *huder*, which means "magician."

Muscarvel — (musk-AR-vel) An old man who lived deep in the marsh to the west of Bosventor. He was last seen at the end of *Merlin's Shadow*.

Muscfenna — (musc-FENN-ah) An epithet for "crazy one who lives in the marsh."

Myrgoskva — (myr-GOSK-vah) A name that means "daughter of shadow," a daughter who lives under the shadow of the Almighty.

Myrgwen — (MEER-gwen) The younger orphaned daughter of Uther and Igerna, and sister to Eilyne and Arthur. When she was young, she and Eilyne were pursued by Vortigern and fled into the marsh. No one has seen her since. In legend, she is called Morgause*.

Nancedefed — (nance-DEH-fed) The name of the valley which Dinas Crag protects. Today it is called Borrowdale*, and its entrance is so narrow it is called The Jaws of Borrowdale*. Merlin and Natalenya live here. Its name comes from Nans-Deves, which means "Valley of Sheep," being intentionally deceitful to hide the fact that they are raising war horses in the valley for Rheged's use. Nancemargh, coming from Nans – Margh "Valley of Horses," would have been the actual name if they weren't trying to hide the horses. If you look at photos of Borrowdale, Cumbria online, you will find it is about as close to Hobbiton as you will find in England.

Natalenya — (nah-tah-LEAN-yah) Tregeagle and Trevenna's daughter; she is wife to Merlin and mother to Taliesin and Tingada, and foster mother to Arthur.

Neb — (NEB) A warrior who swears fealty to Arthur; he carries a bronze pike. He is the son of Kaw.

Necton Morbrec* — (NECK-ton MORE-breck) The cruel High King of the Picti, he was Merlin and company's slavemaster during *Merlin's Shadow*. The son of Erip, he has been given the title morbrec, meaning "great." He is very tall, with long red hair.

Offyd — (OH-fid) The abbot of Dinas Camlin, formerly of Bosvenna Abbey when Merlin was young.

Ol — (OLE) The son of Olwith, a young man that Arthur saves at Hen Crogmen.

Owain* — (O-wayne) Merlin's father; he grew up in Rheged, north of Kembry as the son of a chieftain. Owain's first wife, Gwevian, drowned while they were boating on Lake Dosmurtanlin. His second wife, Mônda, is the mother of Ganieda / Mórgana, Merlin's half sister. Owain was the smith in the village of Bosventor prior to his death, and so was given the title of An Gof, which means "the smith."

Pace — The unit of measurement of a grown man's stride from the time the heel leaves the ground until the same heel touches the ground again. Typically five feet.

Pelles* one-ear — (PEL-less) The elderly chieftain of Dinas Camlin. His grandson is Gwalahad.

Penfro — (PEN-fro) A clan in southern Kembry.

Penmoor — (PEN-moor) Modern-day Penny Moor*.

Percos — (PURR-kos) A warrior who initially opposes Arthur's kingship. He is from Dinas Camlin and the son of Poch.

Pergiryn's Tower — (per-GIH-rin) All that is left of the fortress built by the Pergiryn on the island of Inis Avallow. Some say a light can sometimes be seen from its top-most window. The Pergiryn was an unknown tin merchant who, legend says, built the fortress and planted the apple orchard. Pergiryn means "pilgrim."

Picti* — (PIC-tie) The people who live in the wild lands of the north. They often raid the southern realms now that Hadrian's Wall has been abandoned by the Romans, and even more so now that the Saxenow are weakening what is left of the British army. They call themselves the Chrithane. Necton is their High King.

Podrith — (POD-rith) The chief druid under the authority of Mórganthu and Mórgana who serves High King Vortigern. He also had a brief appearance in *Merlin's Blade*.

Porthloc — (PORTH-lock) The seaside village in Difnonia where Garth grew up and met Dybris. Modern-day Porlock*.

Powys* — (POW-iss) A major kingdom in east-central Kembry (Wales).

Prithager — (prih-THAY-girr) The Brythonic name for the Picti*.

Purple/wearing the purple* — Wearing purple was a sign of being in either the upper class of Roman society, a highly regarded Roman military leader, or a Roman emperor. Vortigern and Vortipor wear purple to show that they consider themselves royalty.

Reinwandt — (RHINE-want) The daughter of Hengist, the name means "Pure Kinswoman" in Germanic. Rhonwen* from legend.

Rewan — (REH-wan) A former battle-chieftain under Vortigern during *Merlin's Blade*, he was eventually demoted due to his age, and has held a grudge for it ever since.

Rheged* — (REH-gedd) A Brythonic kingdom in the north, it is situated northeast of Kembry and south of Guotodin. This is the land Owain is from. Urien is their king.

Romans* — The sprawling empire that conquered Britain and ruled it for 360 years. They never conquered the northern area controlled by the Picts, nor Erin, the island of the Eirish. In 407, Constantine III (Arthur's great-great-grandfather) took the majority of the Roman army that had been stationed in Britain over to Gaul in a failed bid to become the Roman Emperor, and they never returned.

Rondroc — (RON-drock) Natalenya's older brother.

Safrowana — (saf-ROW-ah-nah) Mother to Imelys and wife of Troslam. They are weavers, and their family took care of Myrgwen, Eilyne, and Ganieda for part of *Merlin's Shadow*.

Sangraal* — (SANN-grail) An ancient wooden bowl found by Colvarth after Uther's kidnapping in *Merlin's Blade*. At the Last Supper it held the wine, and the Pergiryn used it to catch Christ's blood when he hung upon the cross. It is also called the Sancte Gradale, and is more commonly called the Holy Grail*.

Saxenow* — (SACKS-eh-now) An invading people group from what is now known as Germany, they landed on the southeastern shore of Britain and have been slowly taking over. They are led by Hengist and Horsa. Today know as the Saxons*.

Scoti* — (SCOT-eye) A seafaring tribe of the Irish that have settled in what is now western Scotland.

Screpall — (SCREH-pall) A double-sided silver coin worth three Coyntallow.

Sevira* — (seh-VYE-rah) Vortigern wife, and Vortipor's mother.

Solidus* — (so-LIH-doos) A gold coin of the Romans weighing approximately 4.5 grams.

Stone, The — A strange stone that was found by Mórganthu at the edge of Lake Dosmurtanlin. Everyone who sees it is enchanted by it, and so Merlin drove Uther's sword into it at the end of *Merlin's Blade* in an attempt to destroy it.

Suzerain* — (sues-EH-rain) This is an ancient term for the king of a foreign country to whom you owe fealty.

Taliesin* — (tal-ee-ESS-in) Merlin and Natalenya's twelve-year-old son, who is being trained to be a bard.

Tán Menéth Marrow — (TAN MEN-eth MARE-row) Grannos wants to send Merlin on a quest to this place. Literally "The Dead Fire Hills," it is an imaginary place invented by the author's daughter, Adele, for an early draft of one of her novels. Used here for fun.

Tas — (TASS) An ancient word for "father."

Tethion — (teth-EE-on) An archer employed by Vortigern in *Merlin's Shadow*.

Teyrnon — (TEAR-non) The younger son of Vortipor. The name means "Divine Prince."

Tinga/Tingada — (TIN-gah / tin-GAH-dah) Merlin and Natalenya's seven-year-old daughter.

"Tingada's Cloak" — (tin-GAH-dah) A song Natalenya composes and sings for her daughter. This is based on Dinogad's Smock*, an ancient lullaby embedded without explanation in the the ancient battle poem of *Y Gododdin*. The lullaby mentions the Derwent*, and thus originated from the same valley in which Merlin and Natalenya settled in *Merlin's Nightmare*.

Tor, The — The nickname for Dinas Bosventor, the fortress situated partway up the side of the Meneth Gellik mountain. It has a timber-built tower with a beacon on top.

Torc* — (TORK) A sign of authority, social status, and nobility in ancient Brythonic society. Made in the shape of a ring with an opening, it is worn upon the neck. They are usually twisted from wires of gold, bronze, silver, iron, or other metals, and have finely sculpted ornaments at the ends.

Tregeagle* — (treh-GAY-gull) The Magister of Bosventor and the surrounding tin-mining region when Merlin lived in the village. His wife is Trevenna, and his children are Natalenya, Rondroc, and Dyslan. He was enchanted by the Stone in *Merlin's Blade.*

Trendrine — (TREN-drine) Modern-day Thorndon Cross*.

Trevenna — (treh-VENN-nah) Tregeagle's wife, and mother to Natalenya, Rondroc, and Dyslan.

Troslam — (TROS-lum) The village weaver. Safrowana is his wife, and Imelys is his daughter.

Uther* — (UTH-er) The deceased High King of the Britons, he was descended from a long line of Roman governors and kings. His father was Aurelianus, his wife was Igerna. He had two daughters, Eilyne and Myrgwen, as well as his son, Arthur. His name in Latin is Uthrelius.

Vitalinus* — (vi-TAL-ee-noos) Usurper High King who slew Uther's grandfather Constans. His grandson is Vortigern, and his granddaughter is Igerna, Uther's wife. He was slain in battle by Aurelianus. In history he is known as Vitalinus Gloui*.

Voice, The — A shadowy figure that appears to Mórgana and instructs her.

Vortigern* — (vor-TUH-gern) The grandson of the former High King, Vitalinus Gloui, who killed Uther in *Merlin's Blade* due to his enchantment by the Stone. In *Merlin's Shadow* he also sought to kill Eilyne and Myrgwen.

Vortipor* — (vor-TUH-poor) Vortigern's son and now the leader in the battles with the Saxenow.

Walkers — A traveling people who were the first to settle the island of Britain long ago. Most of them are tinsmiths by trade, having settled first on the Kernow peninsula. Their language is the Bélre Cèard. Gogirfan and his daughters Gwenivere and Gwenivach are Walkers. In the modern era they would be equivalent to the Highland Scottish Travelers*.

Wealas — (WEH-lass) A Saxenow term of contempt meaning "foreigner" or "slave."

Wild Huntsman — A mysterious phantasmal being who hunts on horseback through the woods with a pack of hounds.

Withel — (WITH-el) Taliesin's friend, who is fifteen winters. His name means "Lion."

Yahn, Tahn, Tethera* — (YAWN, TAWN, teth-ERR-ah) An ancient livestock counting system. There are many variants of it.

Want to experience more of Merlin's story and world?
Go to the author's website at *KingArthur.org.uk* to
unlock exclusive content using the ogham codes around
each chapter start. Or play the Merlin's Spiral game,
request a signed copy, or simply sit around the virtual
fire and chat with other fans of the series. There might
even be a contest running where you could win your
very own Excalibur made by the author. Registration
only takes a moment, and it's all free!

BEFORE THE ROUND TABLE...BEFORE ARTHUR WAS CROWNED...
THERE WAS MERLIN.

MERLIN'S BLADE

ROBERT TRESKILLARD

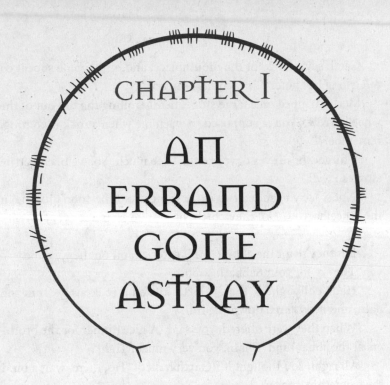

CHAPTER I

AN ERRAND GONE ASTRAY

Merlin frowned. He didn't know what he wanted more: to talk with Natalenya or to hide. After all, how many young men walked past the house of the girl they admired while pushing an overstuffed wheelbarrow? And how many were accompanied by a boy wearing a too-big monk's robe who insisted on playing bagpipe?

Wasn't the rope, wooden tub, bundle of herbs, and sack of oats quite enough to fill the barrow? Did Garth really have to add a squawking hen and a young goat too?

Merlin turned his half-blind gaze to the bobbing boy with red hair. "You told me, 'Not another thing to deliver,' and now look what we've got."

Garth's lips let go of the mouthpiece, and his bagpipe squeaked out a long last note. "How could I say no?"

Merlin tripped on a large stone, nearly rolling the tub out of the wheelbarrow. "You're supposed to warn me when a rock is coming, remember?"

"I forget those eyes o' yours can't see much. You've been gettin' along so well."

"Not since you added *two* extra things, and they don't just lie in the wheelbarrow. No, they cluck, bleat, and leap out every twenty steps."

"But they're for the abbey. We'll drop 'em off on the way and — "

"They're for your Sabbath supper."

"Hadn't thought o' that." Garth kicked a rock away from the path, and it skittered down the hill.

"When they were offered, you said, 'A nice dinner for the brothers at the abbey' and 'Thank you very much.' Hah!"

"All right, so I thought it." Garth halted. "Ho, there, wait a bit. I saw somethin' move."

Merlin stopped pushing the wheelbarrow. "What now?"

Garth knelt down and advanced into the bushes on all fours.

Merlin could see only a smudge of Garth sticking out from beneath the green leaves, and then a colorful blotch flew out above the boy's head.

"I found me a tuck snack!" Garth bounced up and placed a warm egg in Merlin's palm.

Merlin judged the egg's size to be about half of a chicken's.

"Three of 'em!" Garth said. "Oh, but how can I carry 'em? The goat'll eat 'em in the barrow, and I can't hold 'em and play me bagpipe too."

Merlin reached out, felt for Garth's hood, and dropped his egg to the bottom. "How's that?"

"Perfect. Yer clever at times, you are."

Merlin held out his hand for the other two eggs and set them beside the first.

426

Fuffing up his bagpipe with air, Garth resumed playing as he marched down the hill.

Merlin followed, and as the hill leveled out, he was better able to keep the barrow steady. But that was when his heart started wobbling, because he knew by the big blur of a rock coming up that they were about to walk by —

"Look at that house," Garth said, stopping to take a breath. "A big house ... behind those trees. Didn't notice it on the way up."

In vain, Merlin shook the black hair away from his eyes. He wished he could see if Natalenya was home. "You've only been here a month ... but you've heard of the magister, haven't you?"

"Sure. The brothers at the abbey pay taxes to the ol' miser."

"He's not old, and his name's Tregeagle. "He and his wife have two sons and a daughter."

"Those the boys that called you 'Cut-face'?"

"Yeah." Merlin scowled at the memory. The hurled insults had been followed by a goodly sized rock, which had only narrowly missed his head.

But Natalenya was different. She never mentioned Merlin's scars. During worship at the chapel, she was always polite and asked him questions now and then, almost like a friend. So when Merlin's father had asked him and Garth to get charcoal with the wheelbarrow, Merlin suggested that Garth get a tour of the fortress too. The fact that they'd pass Natalenya's house twice was a small coincidence, of course, even if it was out of their way.

The problem was that an empty wheelbarrow was just too inviting, and practically everyone had given them things to deliver. And now they had the goat and chicken as well. Out of embarrassment, Merlin almost wished Natalenya wouldn't be home.

"What does the house look like?" he asked. "Tell me what I'm seeing."

"Ornate kind of ... Bigger than the mill, I'd say, an' made o' fancy stone. The roof's got lapped bark with a real stone chimney, not jus' a hole for smoke." Garth paused. "Why does the magister's door have a bronze bird on it?"

"It's the ensign of a Roman legion. An eagle, or an *aquila*, to be precise. His family's descended from soldiers on the coast."

"Huh. Why'd the Romans come here? Nothin' here but hills, woods, an' a bit o' water."

"For the tin and copper. A little silver," Merlin said. "None of the brothers explained that?"

"Haven't had time for history, what with fishin', seein' you, workin', and eatin' o' course."

"Do you see anyone at the Magister's house? Maybe a daughter?"

"Nah ... no girl. Nothin' but a little smoke."

The sound of horses' hooves clattered toward them from farther down the hill. Merlin had just turned in the direction of the sound when Garth shoved his shoulder.

"A wagon!" Garth cried. "Out o' the road!"

The driver shouted as Merlin scrambled to push the wheelbarrow off to the side.

"Make way for the magister," the man shouted. "Make way!"

A whip snapped and the air cracked above Merlin's head.

The wheelbarrow hit a rock, and Merlin felt it tilt out of his control just as Garth ran into his back, causing him to fall, with a chicken flapping against his face. Merlin removed the feathered mass in time to see the blur of the goat leap over the tub and everything else tumble out of the barrow.

The wagon rumbled by and came to an abrupt stop in front of the magister's house.

Merlin sat up and rubbed his knees. He felt around for the bag of oats and found it spilled on the ground — a feast for the chicken and goat. At least it would keep them nearby.

The passengers climbed out of the wagon, and amid the general din of everyone walking toward the house, Merlin heard a soft, lovely voice and a gentle strumming. "Garth, is that a harp?"

"A small one, sure. A lady is holdin' it." Garth rose and brushed off his knees. "The magister ignored us, him in his fancy white robe. But did you see those boys? They'd liked to have kicked us."

Merlin pushed the goat away from the oats and knelt to scoop what grain he could find back into the bag. "How old?"

"Oh, the bigger one weren't more'n yer age, an' the other's about fourteen, I'd say."

"That's do-nothing Rondroc and Dyslan. I meant the one with the harp. Was that the mother?"

"Oh, no," Garth said. "Must be the daughter … but a lot older'n your sister. She held herself straight and ladylike. Does she come to chapel?"

"Natalenya and her mother came two weeks ago. Tregeagle doesn't let them come every week." Merlin had never heard the magister's daughter sing so sweetly before.

Garth tapped him. "Hey, look at those horses!"

Merlin rubbed his chin and closed his eyes. "Pretty?"

"Very! That yellin' wagon driver tied 'em to a post an' — "

"Must be Erbin." Merlin chuckled and swatted Garth. "But I'm talking about Natalenya. I don't remember what *she* looks like. Is she pretty?"

"Blurs don't count for seein', huh? I guess y*ou'd* think she's pretty. Long brown hair and green dress, but *I* don't go for that. The horses look fine, though. White, with such shiny coats — an' so tall they match that fancy wagon. Me father's old wagon just brought fish to market. Sure woulda helped us gettin' the charcoal if I still had it."

Garth paused for a moment, and Merlin remembered that the boy's father had drowned in a storm not six months before while fishing on the Kembry sea. Twelve winters old, and Garth had already lost both of his parents.

After clearing his throat, Garth continued, "But *this* wagon's a real beauty, with a wide seat up front. The back box is fine for sittin' too, though you *could* just haul with it." The chicken jumped on Merlin's shoulder, and Garth swatted it away. "Get off, you!"

Merlin stood. "Better deliver these things and get the charcoal."

He righted the barrow, and they refilled it. He could still hear Natalenya's voice filtering from her home, and he wished he had something for her.

"Psst," Garth said. "Those nasty boys are comin' over."

Merlin turned toward the approaching footsteps and extended his hands in greeting, only to have them ignored.

"What are you doing here? Spying?" Rondroc said as he stepped up to Merlin. The older of Tregeagle's sons, Rondroc stood slightly taller than Merlin. His dark clothing lay on him like a shadow, and from his side protruded a short black scabbard.

Dyslan, the younger brother, wore reds and blues, with what looked to be a shining golden belt. He yanked on Garth's voluminous robe. "What's this for? Monks are getting smaller all the time."

"It keeps me warm," Garth said, his voice tight.

"It's kind of like a dress," Dyslan mocked. "If you had darker hair and acted kind of weird, I might have thought you were Merlin's sister."

"Leave Ganieda out of this," Merlin said, feeling his pulse speed up.

Rondroc pointed to the wheelbarrow. "What do you have a goat for? Taking your whole flock to pasture?" He and Dyslan laughed.

Merlin gripped the handles tighter. "We just had a look at the fortress."

"You?" Dyslan said. "Had a look? Ha!"

"Let's go, Garth." Merlin lifted the wheelbarrow, rolled it forward, and accidentally bumped into Rondroc's leg.

Rondroc grabbed the front edge of the barrow, stopping it. "You did that on purpose." His words were slow and dark. "No one uses *our road* without permission, so now you'll be paying our tax."

"Tax?" Merlin said. "My father pays every harvest."

"I've heard that your father's *behind* on his taxes."

"Liar. Our smithy does a good business, so the taxes are never late. And there's no tax for just walking."

"There is now." Rondroc rummaged through the barrow. His smirking voice made Merlin glad he couldn't clearly see Rondroc's face.

"None o' that is ours to give," Garth said.

"Hmm ... a tasty goat feast would pay your fee." The goat bleated as Rondroc picked it up.

"Stop ri—" Garth began, but there was a thump, and his voice choked as he fell to the dirt. Dyslan stood behind him laughing.

"We'll roast it on the fire tonight."

"Leave it alone," Merlin said as calmly as he could. He slipped his staff from the barrow, and the wood felt cold in his hands.

Rondroc set the goat down and swaggered over to Merlin. "Gonna make me?"

"Maybe," Merlin said, offering up a silent prayer. With his staff he tried to push Rondroc away, but the dark form disappeared. Someone kicked Merlin in the back, and he fell, banging his arm on the side of the wheelbarrow.

Rondroc laughed.

In the distance, a harp strummed faintly.

Merlin scrambled up and turned to face his mocker.

"Look out for Dysla—" Garth's voice rang out.

Too late. Rondroc shoved Merlin in the chest, and he fell back over Dyslan, who was crouching behind him.

A sharp pain shot through Merlin's skull as he bashed his head on a rock. Laughter swirled around him like thick fog, and for a moment Merlin lay still as his mind groped for its bearings.

"Stop it," Garth said. "Leave him alone!"

The voices intensified and faded as Merlin sat up. Time slowed. Someone yelled in pain at his left. Using the barrow, Merlin pulled himself up to a standing position and winced at the throbbing in his head. "Garth?"

The horses whinnied, and Merlin didn't hear the harp anymore.